> "The arc of the moral universe is long, but it bends towards justice."
>
> Martin Luther King, Jr.

BENDING THE ARC

BENDING THE ARC

NICHOLAS GRETENER

A *LawForce* NOVEL

qualitas
Qualitas Publishing

QUALITAS PUBLISHING

Copyright © 2025 by Nicholas Gretener

All rights reserved.

Part of the *LawForce* Series

Sales of this book without the front cover may be unauthorized. If this book is coverless, it may have been reported to the publisher as "unsold or destroyed" and neither the author nor the publisher may have received payment for it.

This is a work of fiction. Names, characters, places, and incidents either are the product of the author's imagination or are used fictitiously. Any resemblance to actual persons, living or dead, events, or locales is entirely coincidental.

The scanning, uploading, and distribution of this book without permission is a theft of the author's intellectual property. If you would like permission to use material from this book (other than for review purposes), please contact ngretener@shaw.ca. Thank you for your support of author's rights.

Qualitas Publishing
195 Cardiff Drive N.W.
Calgary, Alberta, Canada
T2K 1S1

First mass-market edition: January, 2025

Qualitas Publishing Mass-Market
ISBN 10: 1-897093-14-4
ISBN 13: 978-1-897093-14-6

www.nicholasgretener.com

Printed in the United States of America

TO PETER
for lessons on the harder side
of life and human nature

TO VRENI
for lessons on the softer side
of life and being a believer

BENDING THE ARC

1

TEXARCANA, TEXAS

Tuesday
March 6

"Call me Ishmael . . . Not."

Ernie Steubens couldn't believe his ears. He felt a cool breeze from the bench in response to his counsel's bizarre opening.

"And what, precisely, is this court and this jury to take from that, Mr. Shane?"

"All Ishmael had to do, your Honor, was battle a whale. A great white whale. That's a walk in the park compared to my job here. I need to convince these twelve fine citizens that my client may use his business name in the face of overwhelming odds. The plaintiff is a multinational concern with unlimited resources. I mean, just look at that army over there." Shane gestured at the counsel table where three lawyers from the One Stop Electronics team looked on, visibly amused.

Ernie's heart sank at the judge's scowl. "You knew all that before you took this case, Mr. Shane. Final argument isn't the time for a career crisis. Let's get on with it."

"Yes, your Honor. My apologies to the court."

Not an auspicious start. As Shane launched into legalese, Ernie stared at the swirls of oak on the counsel table drowned under a quarter inch of varnish. Straddling the state line between Texas and Arkansas, the old courthouse in Texarkana stood as a testament to time. The grandeur of the courtroom revealed itself in the stately oak-paneled walls, worn smooth by decades of whispered secrets. In the center of the room, the judge's bench towered over them, its leather-clad seat worn smooth over the years. The judge's gavel rested atop a polished block, waiting to dispense its measured justice.

Reclining in a soft leather chair, Ernie tried to see things through the jury's eyes. *Was his lawyer up to the job?* At 35, Steve Shane was young for a trial lawyer, but he made it into this year's exclusive *Top 40 under 40* of Texas litigators. And with Ernie's meager budget, he was lucky to get someone of that caliber.

Shane didn't fit your typical lawyer profile. The crisp, tailored black suit that fit his athletic frame with precision, maybe, but not the matching black cowboy hat with silver band, the bear-claw bolo tie featuring a large blue-green chunk of turquoise, and the polished black cowboy boots. A tanned face hinted at his ancestry and while shoulder-length, jet-black hair flowed out from under his hat, Shane never sported the ponytail favored by his Native brothers.

Ernie took a deep breath. It intrigued him to discover that Shane was born on the reservation in Kayenta, Arizona. With a Navajo mother and Swiss father, his split heritage helped form the world view Ernie found so appealing. Shane was intelligent and had a weakness for the underdog. Ernie tuned back to the proceedings as Shane's voice grew louder.

"One Stop Electronics is opening stores at an impressive clip, which some might say is good for Texas. But they should have searched for their name in Texas before they started. They would have discovered that my client has operated First Stop Electronics in this great state for over thirty years. Maybe my client doesn't have a national network, but over thirty years of loyal service should count for something. I know it does to First Stop customers.

"Now we have this megacorporation storming into town and its first order of business is to file a cease and desist action against my client to strip him of his corporate name. You might as well take his business too. The goodwill he's built up over the years is all captured in his brand."

The closing arguments droned on. After an hour, that felt much longer, Ernie sat watching Shane pack up his papers in the small breakout room that smelled of wood polish. "So what do you think, Steve? Are we going to win?"

"Honestly, I don't know. Juries are always a crapshoot and this case is complicated enough to go either way. Their federal trademark trumps your state mark. They obtained it first and it operates nationwide. Our case depends on the jury agreeing with us that the names aren't confusingly similar. So, you tell me. Would you mix up One Stop with First Stop?"

"Doesn't the fact that I'm a Texas company and this is a Texas jury help? Home field advantage, right?"

"Maybe. But again, juries are a crapshoot. Their verdicts have burned me too many times. Give me a judge any day. Juries are just a collection of people, and a lot of people are idiots."

As they stepped out of the room, an angry voice filled the hallway.

"You just don't get it. These charges are a sham. We should be able to short-circuit them right off the top if the system had *any* sanity!" The large man, with a short crewcut and dressed in a western suit, towered over a shorter, thinner man outside Courtroom 5.

"Just another satisfied client," Shane said.

"Do you know them?"

"I know the lawyer, Cal Stokes. He's been at this for thirty years but has never made a name for himself. Looks like he's got his hands full."

As they spoke, five dark-suited, serious types came out of Courtroom 5. Shane pointed at the leader of the group. "That's Drew Tillington from Todd Ives, along with his usual supporting cast. Tillington thinks he's hot stuff—a real legend of the Texas bar."

Ernie studied the dapper lawyer. He cut an imposing figure with his silver hair and well-groomed mustache.

Shane shook his head. "Cal is up against some significant firepower."

They watched as the lawyers huddled across from Stokes and his perturbed client. The group burst out laughing at a comment from Tillington.

This is such bullshit. Ernie turned to Shane. "It's all just a game to you guys. Hired guns. Win or lose, you're OK. It's all good work for you."

Shane's fingers tapped his briefcase as hectic red circles brightened his cheeks. "Some of us *do* care, and maybe you don't see it that way, but I like to count myself in that group. Do you think I'm making a killing on this file?"

"Sorry, I just feel for him." Ernie grinned sheepishly and pointed at the big guy.

Shane nodded. "Fair enough, and you have a point. I mean, look at that." Shane gestured at the group. "You want to tell me that having five Todd Ives lawyers up against Cal Stokes balances the scales of justice?"

Shane motioned for Ernie to follow him to the elevators. As they waited, Ernie noticed the Todd Ives group was still debriefing. They seemed awfully pleased with themselves as they slapped their client on the back. A rather shabby looking client at that. Sporting large sunglasses, he dressed like a homeless person. Maybe the great legal eagle was doing some pro bono work to round out his image?

"So, what are you saying?"

"I'm saying a lot of decisions in these courtrooms result from good lawyers beating bad lawyers. If we're really after truth and justice, the lawyer's ability shouldn't enter the equation, or at least it shouldn't be the deciding factor. Lady Justice is supposed to be blind."

Ernie nodded. "I never really thought about it that way. Everyone always assumes a good lawyer should beat a bad lawyer. But the case should be decided on its merits. Lawyers be damned."

"I wouldn't quite put it that way." Shane laughed. "But, yeah, I think you've got my drift."

As the elevator doors were closing, Stokes stuck his hand in and squeezed on board with his client. The big man's rugged frame was somewhat the worse for wear, likely the result of hard years in the oil fields. A generous belly reflected a more comfortable life since then, working the patch from an office instead of the rig floor.

"Looks like you guys were having quite a party," Ernie said.

"Some party," the big man replied. "A bunch of trumped-up environmental charges that keep me from making an honest living. Bullshit charges. But I tell you my company's bleeding anyway, goddamned green blood all over the place."

Ernie glanced at Shane. The old boy sure was hot under the collar.

They got off the elevator and strolled out into the plaza. Ernie noticed the big man walked with a limp.

Shane turned to Stokes. "Hey, Cal, you know I've got a pretty good environmental background. If there's anything I can do to help, let me know."

Ernie smiled inwardly at the shameless pitch. Stokes just scowled.

"Nice try, Steve, but I'm not in the habit of rainmaking for the competition. I can handle this."

"You bet. No offense." Shane winked. He turned to shake the big man's hand. "Steve Shane. I wish you all the best with your case."

The man offered his meaty paw. "BJ Whitter, son. Thanks. Looks like I'm gonna need it." He reached into his shirt pocket and pulled out a business card. "I'll give you mine for yours." The man smiled at Stokes. "Take it easy, Cal, you're not being fired. I just like to fill out my rolodex."

Shane strolled back to Ernie, waving the card and flashing him a lopsided grin. Ernie poked him in the ribs. "You're never gonna hear from him again. Why do you have to hustle business on my dime?"

Shane laughed. "Never say never, old buddy." He gestured at the hot dog stand near the fountain. "Since I'm on your dime, let me cover lunch. You can have your dog with chili, sauerkraut, refried beans, or just plain ol' American. Or if, like me, you're partial to Mexican, their tacos campechanos are killer."

Ernie licked the last of the sauce off his wax wrapper. Shane was right. Those street tacos were more than tasty. Watching the countryside roll by, he couldn't shake a nagging feeling that his counsel was on thin ice with this case.

"Hey, Steve, do you ever worry about losing?"

"Hell no, Ernie. I do my job well. The only way we can lose this case is if the jury screws up."

Leaning back in his seat, Ernie shut his eyes and tried to let the anxiety of the last few hours drain away. He felt himself dozing off. His counsel sure as hell was one confident son of a bitch. That confidence better be well placed or he, and First Stop, were in deep shit.

2

HOUSTON, TEXAS

Thursday
March 8

There must be something more. Shane wrapped his hands around the mug, relishing the warmth as the office's AC kicked into overdrive. His cases were becoming typical strip-mall stuff, no sizzle.

Stepping into Shane's office was like crossing the threshold into another era, where the spirit of the Old West met a modern-day law practice. The rich aroma of aged leather and polished wood evoked the sense of stepping into a frontier judge's chambers.

Historical memorabilia covered the walls, including framed sepia-toned photographs of lawmen and outlaws, replicas of antique wanted posters, and intricately tooled leather holsters hanging alongside rifles mounted in wooden racks.

The centerpiece of the office was the imposing mahogany desk, its surface polished to a deep sheen that reflected the flickering light from a wrought-iron chandelier above. Brass accents and a large, tooled leather blotter adorned the desk. Behind it sat a high-backed leather chair, its dark brown upholstery studded with brass tacks.

Leather-bound law books filled the shelves lining the walls, with gold-embossed spines displaying titles that spanned centuries of legal precedent. Interspersed among these tomes were artifacts that added to the western motif: a cowboy hat casually resting atop a stack of books, a pair of spurs glinting in the low light, and an old, weathered saddle perched on a wooden stand in the corner.

To the right of the desk, a large window overlooked a view that seemed to stretch into the frontier itself, although an urban frontier. Below the window, a worn leather couch and two matching armchairs created a cozy seating area, with a Navajo-patterned throw rug draped over the back of the couch adding a splash of color.

The coffee table was crafted from reclaimed barn wood and held law journals, a couple of old revolvers displayed under glass, and a crystal decanter filled with amber whiskey. A pair of matching glasses sat ready for clients who might need a drink to steady their nerves.

A sleek laptop rested inconspicuously on the desk and a state-of-the-art filing cabinet, disguised as an antique dresser, ensured that Shane's practice was conducted efficiently in this nostalgic setting.

He flinched at the shrill ring tone.

"Steve Shane."

"Steve, it's Dianne Marshall from Texas National."

"Hey, Dianne, what's up?" It was a rhetorical question. There was only one reason for Dianne to call.

"Your overdraft is in the red again. We need you to come in and show us a repayment plan or we're going to act on our security."

"Aw, Dianne, you know I'm good for it. Just need a little more time to get things humming. I'll pop by next week to go over the plan. Forget about any foreclosure for now. It's not as if Texas National needs another house in The Woodlands, am I right?"

"OK, Steve, but make sure it's within a week. Take care."

Shane sighed as he put down the phone and reached again for the mug. Ernie promised a fifty thousand dollar premium if they won. Not a game changer, but he could use the cash to buy more time. *What the heck was taking that jury so long?* They'd been out more than a day.

He kicked off his boots and dug his toes into the soft carpet. Leaning back from the desk, he enjoyed a long stretch as he gazed around the room. Numerous sandstone paintings hung on the walls, along with a large Navajo rug. He liked Native American art, in particular the clean designs of the Hopis. He wore two Hopi rings and had one of the largest collections of Native bolo ties in Texas. On a circular table in the corner was a large western bronze of a Navajo riding bareback chasing down a buffalo. Off topic were the three large cowbells hanging from a rod mounted to the ceiling. An echo of his Swiss heritage.

His father's last name had been Schanniger, but to blend into his adopted homeland, he changed it to Shane. Notwithstanding, being born to a Swiss National, his son had Swiss citizenship.

To please his mother, his father suggested giving Steve a Navajo first name, but she refused. To protect him from the bullying of an ignorant world, she insisted he have a conventional name, just as her husband had wanted for himself.

But his parents were adamant he know where he came from, so they spoke Swiss-German and Navajo at home. In later years, Shane was grateful for their efforts, as he was fluent in both languages. Learning a language as a child is more natural than in later years, when it comes burdened with an accent. Shane enjoyed being able to plop onto a bench in front of the tribal store in Tuba City or Kayenta and pass the time of day with the elders in their native tongue, just as he could in any neighborhood pub or "Beitz" in the German-speaking regions of Switzerland.

Shane wasn't unhappy with his lot in life. Graduating at the top of his class, editor of the law review, the top firms recruited him. But he was afraid if he joined Wall Street right out of the gate, he'd end up there for good.

So he bit the bullet and started his own firm along with a slight, but energetic, receptionist, Lee Chin. Lee was no nonsense and commanded the office with an air of quiet authority. Shane admired her organizational skills, likely because of his deficit in that regard. Legal briefs, case files, and client correspondence were always in their designated place at Lee's clutter-free desk. The wallpaper on her computer featured a serene image of a traditional Chinese landscape, a subtle nod to her heritage amidst the modern chaos.

Shane's only other employee was his first and only legal hire, Valentina Lopez. An inspired choice. Val was scary bright. Her practice also focused on commercial litigation. She graduated from Harvard in Shane's class, *summa cum laude*, and then topped things off with an MBA from Stanford. After practicing two years on Wall

Street, Shane lured her from the Big Apple—that her family were all from the Houston area didn't hurt. A real beauty, with cascading black hair framing a flawless face, he soon came to appreciate her Hispanic passion for all things in life, including the law. And her eyes! How could you not lose yourself in those deep, brown, almond-shaped pools? Within a year, they were romantically involved.

"Penny for your thoughts."

He turned to see Val peering over his shoulder at the mess on his desk.

"Just dreaming about our justice system and its habit of grinding us down."

She laughed. "You're such an idealist. That's why you started BLR and that's why we never make any money around here."

Shane winced. But he was proud of his Harvard initiative. Business Law Representation was based on the traditional student legal aid model, which assisted poor people in trouble with the criminal law. Shane saw the need for a similar service for small corporations that needed legal help in private litigation matters. BLR flourished in the Harvard environment, where the budding legal eagles were aiming for lucrative corporate, not criminal, careers.

"Too true, babe. Not sure if we can keep things going at this rate. May have to join one of those legal factories after all."

She rolled her eyes. "You? Not likely."

She was right. Despite the recent restlessness, he enjoyed his practice. With several high-profile successes, he was becoming sought after in technical, commercial matters. His dream was to grow the firm into a nice boutique, say fifteen practitioners, with the potential to service the blue-chip files. And yet, that first killer file eluded him.

He answered the phone on the first ring.

"Mr. Shane, this is Cynthia Wheeler at the courthouse. Judge Hillboro asked me to let you know your jury has reached a verdict. He would like you and your client in court at 4:00 p.m."

"Thanks, Ms. Wheeler. We'll be there." He bent over and pulled on his boots, savoring the soft leather and comfortable fit that had taken years to develop.

Val looked over quizzically.

"My jury's in. Gotta head up to Texarkana."

"That's the fight over the name of an electronics company, right?"

"Yup."

"I thought you said it was a Houston company?"

"You bet."

"So why the heck are you fighting in Texarkana?"

"The plaintiff's headquarters are in Little Rock, so they filed in Texas as close to their head-office as they could."

"Seems like a long way to nowhere."

She had a point. Texarkana lay halfway between Dallas and Little Rock.

"What's in Texarkana, anyway? I've never been up there."

"Well, maybe you should ride with me. It's a town of forty thousand. Land of pickups, chicken-fried steaks, and ice tea."

"Sounds wonderful. Maybe some other time."

"Don't knock it 'till you've tried it. It's kind of cool. The state line cuts right through the old federal courthouse. When you enter the courtroom, Texas is on your left, Arkansas on the right. And that court is becoming America's super bowl of billion-dollar lawsuits."

"Wow, who'd have thunk." Val appeared unconvinced.

"Babe, did you know Texarkana was home to that multibillion-dollar action filed by Texas against the tobacco industry?"

Val whistled. "*That* was heard in Texarkana? Why?"

"Number of reasons. The judge, for one. The experts were all predicting a drawn-out battle—at least five years in the courts. But this hotshot U.S. District Court Judge, Madeline Nabors, stickhandled the litigation to a fifteen-billion-dollar settlement in less than two years."

"Ah, see, it takes a woman to get things done."

Shane laughed. "You got me there. She's gained quite the reputation for handling complex cases. She's the one who pioneered the rocket docket, where both sides have to share evidence pre-trial to stop those fishing expeditions that go on for months, even years, before a case goes to trial."

"OK, so you got a woman who knows how to run a trial. You said there were several reasons for big-money litigation in Texarkana. What else?"

"The reputation Texas juries have of being generous doesn't hurt. Also helpful is that your chances of getting an untainted jury in a town light years away from the media mainstream are pretty good."

"Sounds reasonable. Not bad for the town either."

"You bet. Before the lawyers, the only things in Texarkana were a few paper mills, a tire manufacturer, some poultry operations, and an aluminum processing plant. The economic boost from the legal armies and their supporting casts that now flood the town for every big trial is a windfall for the community."

"So, Mr. Shane, when you go up there, why don't you see if you can't snag yourself some of that action?"

"You never know, babe." Shane winked at her.

Val wrinkled her nose and pointed at the cigar in his ashtray. "Come on, Steve."

He stubbed it out. After kicking his cigarette habit, Shane compensated by smoking more cigars.

"Hey, I'm trying." He'd promised Val to cut down on the cigars. He watched the dying plume of smoke as he punched a number.

"Is the jury in?" Ernie sounded nervous.

"You bet. They want us up there by four, so get your ass over here. It's a five-hour drive, but we'll cut an hour and a half off that."

"I look forward to driving, or should I say flying, in the Rocket. See you soon, Steve."

Shane chuckled as he cradled the receiver. The "Rocket" was his new, jet-black Porsche 911 Turbo. Shane was a sucker for fast cars, and his clients never missed a chance to kid him about it.

As he waited for Ernie, he wondered if he would ever graduate from chickenshit files like First Stop. That hollow feeling about the law was dragging him down. Ernie was a nice enough guy, but solving his problems would not make much of a difference in the universal scheme of things.

There must be something more.

3

TEXARCANA, TEXAS

Thursday
March 8

Shane felt the slight vibration on the stick as he eased into fourth and the Rocket surged forward. He loved the whine of the high-powered engine.

"Holy cow, this mother can move!"

Shane grinned at Ernie's reaction and shouted to be heard over the accelerating engine's high-pitched whine. "Gotta love that German engineering." He looked over at Ernie, who clearly needed a pep talk.

"Listen, Ernie. Despite what I said the other day, I think we have the better case. As long as that jury understands the evidence, this should all

BENDING THE ARC

be behind you in a few hours."

Ernie nodded. "What's the worst thing that's ever happened to you in a jury trial?"

Shane gazed at the fields rolling away in the distance, drumming his fingers on the soft leather of the steering wheel. "I lost a case when I was just two years out. A small environmental company, Green Badge, hired me to defend them against a small civil claim. They were being sued for a hundred and fifty thousand dollars. The complaint was failing to maintain a safe working environment."

"What did they do wrong?"

"Nothing. I said that was the *complaint*. A worker slipped on some plastic wrapping outside the lunchroom. It should have been covered by workers' comp but they denied the claim and the employee went after the company."

"Did the guy get hurt?"

"You bet. His leg suffered a severe break and never properly healed. We didn't deny the injury, but the way it happened had nothing to do with negligence. It was an accident, pure and simple. The board should have covered the cost."

A red light flashed on the console and a buzzer sounded. Shane winked at Ernie as he slowed down.

"So why didn't you win?"

"It was a jury trial. I was confident in our case. It was a slam dunk, so I didn't mount a positive defense. I let it go straight to the jury. The idiots brought back a guilty verdict. The company didn't have liability insurance. They were dead in the water."

"Bummer. Was your client pissed?"

"You could say that. The president wanted to take the stand. I advised against it. Looking back, I know the jury would have believed him if they had the chance. But they did what a lot of juries do. They drew a negative inference from his failure to face his accusers."

Shane pointed to the cruiser at the side of the road. "Won't be helping him reach his quota today."

"Bummer," Ernie repeated.

Well clear of the speed trap, Shane accelerated. "That jury killed the company. They didn't bother to think the case through. They took the easy way out."

"Yeah, well, you know what they say?"

"What's that?"

"Shit happens."

Shane looked at Ernie and nodded. "I suppose. OK, enough of the heavy crap." He turned on Sirius, tuned to the Sixties channel. An hour later, they were easing into a parking space next to the courthouse.

"Ernie, my man, it's game time."

As they sat down at the counsel table, Shane felt the familiar churning in his stomach. A major case of the butterflies.

He stood as the judge entered the courtroom.

"Has the jury reached a verdict?"

"We have, your Honor."

"How find you?"

"We find for the plaintiff."

Goddamn juries.

He turned to Ernie. "Easy, big guy. We can still appeal."

Ernie nodded, failing to keep the emotion from his voice. "I haven't got the money to chase this any further, Steve. I think I just have to let her go."

"I'll fund the appeal. You can't let it go, Ernie." Lee would give him shit, but it wouldn't be the first time he helped a client in trouble. But Lee was right. It was no way to build a firm. It sure as hell raised the pressure to land an anchor file that could support such a socialist practice.

4

HOUSTON, TEXAS

Friday
March 9

Kevin Flaig waited in a 2,500 square foot office in The Galleria. A small cubbyhole swallowed up by the 2.4 million square foot mall—Houston's largest. It even featured two swimming pools and a full-size ice rink, for Christ's sake. The swimming pools he understood, but why the hell do you need an ice rink in Houston? Maybe for the same reason that one of Dubai's over-the-top malls featured an indoor ski hill.

While Flaig's funding was open-ended, the office was utilitarian. *Can't portray a posh image.* They needed to be the underdog. Leave it to industry to flash the bling.

He stuffed his shirt tails in for the umpteenth time. Standing a meager five foot six, his slight frame seemed to almost disappear within the threadbare clothes he wore. His pants had a rumpled appearance, and his shirt, frequently missing a button or two, hung loosely over a body that looked like it hadn't seen the inside of a gym in years. A corduroy jacket, complete with leather elbows, hinted at his past. His most striking feature, however, was the constant presence of sunglasses. Day or night, indoors or out, Flaig always wore a pair of dark, oversized shades. His left eye was highly sensitive to light, a condition that had plagued him since a childhood chemical accident.

Once a promising academic, Flaig's descent into his current state was as murky as his clientele. He had been a brilliant mind in political science, his lectures at the university known for their depth and insight. But something shifted, a slow erosion of his ideals that led him down a darker path. The transition from academia to consulting for unsavory clients was a gradual one, marked by increasing disillusionment and the lure of big money.

Flaig's demeanor matched his disheveled appearance. He moved with a nervous energy, his gestures quick and erratic, like a man perpetually on edge. For those who could decipher his erratic speech, Flaig's insights were invaluable. He had a knack for strategy, his mind capable of untangling the most complex of problems, making him an asset to those willing to pay for his morally ambiguous services.

Flaig was proud of the lucrative contracting business he'd built, servicing deep-pocketed corporate clients. His newfound wealth provided the funds for a high-end cataract operation that restored the sight in his left eye. While the surgery was a success, doctors insisted he continue to wear the protective sunglasses. From behind those lenses, he surveyed the room.

The modest reception area comprised a simple desk and a stack of paperwork awaiting organization. The walls were plain, painted in neutral tones. Posters of Greenpeace campaigns adorned the walls.

The lighting was fluorescent, casting a sterile glow over the workspace. There were no outside windows, giving the office a claustrophobic feel. The lack of plants or greenery further added to the impersonal atmosphere. A few desks sat in the main room along with a copier and printer.

In the center of the room, an area had been walled-off with floor-to-ceiling glass dividers to contain a communications center. A large, enclosed cubicle at the back served as his control room. Through the window, he could see the main space and the communications center, the domain of his sole employee, other than the receptionist.

Information, or what some might characterize as misinformation, campaigns were what the GAC was all about. Matt Avery was a public relations specialist. Flaig also toyed with hiring a few students from Texas Southern but decided against it. Less is more for what he needed.

He took off his sunglasses, squinting in the glare. Taking out his cleaning cloth, he wiped the lenses as he recalled the instructions. They were brutally clear. Money was no object—it was results that counted.

Flaig dedicated considerable time to the game plan and received approval for his recommendation of aggressive litigation supported by some unfortunate *incidents*. The client liked the campaign's environmental focus. The public was increasingly sympathetic to the green movement, and any ability to tap into that was a definite plus.

To spearhead the litigation, Flaig created a new association—the *Green Action Coalition* or GAC, as it would come to be known. The name suggested diverse support. Several large contributions were made on behalf of the GAC to more established players, including Greenpeace and the Sierra Club. Their desired effect of generating endorsements provided credibility. *Money talks.*

Flaig folded his cloth and put the sunglasses back on, enjoying the instant relief. With the client stressing time was of the essence, Flaig had the GAC launch a couple of starter actions against the target oil company based on minor incidents. They would set the stage for the real catastrophes to come, courtesy of Scott Magruder. *Where was he, anyway?*

Flaig was confident in his choice of Magruder, who came highly recommended by a trusted, ex-military friend. Magruder's CV was impressive. His friend noted Magruder was not just hired muscle, but strategic. Flaig asked him to develop a plan of action. *Let's see if he's got the brains to match the brawn.*

The buzzer sounded. He got up and walked to the entrance. Through the glass door, he saw a large, powerfully built man. *Sure looks the part.* Flaig locked the door after Magruder, led him to the back office, closed the door, and gestured for him to take the chair across from his desk.

Jesus, this Magruder was a brute of a man. Standing six feet tall, his body bore testament to years of rigorous training and hard living. Muscles rippled beneath his weathered skin. The most prominent mark was a jagged scar running across his face, from his left eyebrow to the corner of his right jaw—stark white against his sun-kissed complexion. His hair, no longer the military buzz cut in the picture Flaig's friend had sent over, now grew in unruly waves of dark brown, streaked with premature silver and bundled in a pony tale. He kept his beard short, more out of practicality than vanity. His hands, calloused and strong, bore the marks of countless battles.

"So, why didn't you want to meet at my house?"

Magruder took a while to answer, measuring him up. "I don't mix the personal with business, man. You're not my friend. You're a job."

The gravelly voice was a surprise. Maybe a fallout from some battlefield injury. Flaig shrugged and adjusted his glasses. "I don't need a friend. I need a pro. Let's get down to business."

"Fine by me."

"You're ex-Navy, right? A SEAL?"

"You knew that before you called me."

"I want to hear it from you."

"Sure, whatever. I did four tours overseas."

"Is that where you got the tattoo?" Flaig pointed at the scar.

"Yeah, man. Some shrapnel from an IED that did in two brothers."

"And since then, you've been in this line of work?"

Magruder nodded. "My old insurance job didn't work for me after the Middle East. I used my new skills to cash in on the American dream. When people think of mercenaries, they picture operators fighting paramilitary campaigns in far-off lands. It turns out a solid market for my skills exists right here in the good old U. S. of A. The first few jobs were scarce, but lately the work finds me. I get results. But, again, you know all that or I wouldn't be here, man."

"OK, let's cut to the chase. You got my package and know what we want. Have you developed a plan?"

Magruder launched into a lengthy discourse. He described his campaign as a symphony, with a slow build to a climatic finale.

Flaig marveled at the detail, considering Magruder developed it in only two weeks. If he could pull it off, it was a bargain at the quoted fee of a million dollars, half up front and half on completion.

"I like it. Questions for me?"

"Yeah, do you need the oil to keep flowing after the accidents? I don't mind telling you I'm a card-carrying member, for chrissake." Magruder pointed at the Greenpeace poster.

Jesus, of all the hired guns in the world, I get the guy with a green conscience. "That's the job. We're paying good money. How you do the job is up to you. Loss of life is at your discretion."

Magruder snorted. "Needless killing is for amateurs, man. Increases the risk. An accident investigation is always less intense than a murder investigation."

That made sense. "Like I said, how you do it is up to you."

"You got the cash?"

Flaig reached for the duffel bag at his feet and slid it across the desk.

"OK, Mr. Magruder. You've done your homework. Execute this plan, and it will be my pleasure to deliver the other half. Don't contact me. I don't need updates."

"I don't do updates. You'll get all the updates you need through the media. You won't hear from me again until I'm ready for the other half. But I am curious. Who's behind all this?" Magruder waved around the office.

"The GAC is a—" Flaig recoiled as Magruder's fist hit the table.

"Don't tell me about your bullshit cover. This has nothing to do with the environment. Who are you working for? What's your end game?"

Flaig recovered his composure. *This prick was forgetting who was in charge.* "You don't need to know and you don't want to know."

Magruder glared at him for a minute. *Christ, what a face.*

Finally, Magruder shrugged. "You're right, man. I don't want to know. I'll let myself out."

5

HOUSTON, TEXAS

Monday
March 12

Brady James Whitter—BJ to his friends—kicked off his cowboy boots and collapsed on the sofa. He grimaced as he worked the flesh of his upper thigh. The familiar, dull pain was a constant reminder of an old rig accident. A piece of drill pipe mashed his leg like a train rolling over a strand of spaghetti. The leg was never the same.

His broad shoulders and barrel chest, softened by age and prosperity, hinted at a once powerful physique. His flushed cheeks acted as a reminder of the countless cigars and bourbon that had been his companions over the years. Beneath bushy, graying eyebrows, his eyes remained sharp and penetrating. Those eyes had seen the rise and fall of fortunes, the discovery of vast reserves, and the desolation of dry wells. They were eyes that had assessed risk, calculated reward, and never shied away from a challenge.

His thinning hair, once a robust chestnut, was now silver, cut in a sharp crewcut. The sides and back were closely clipped, while the top was slightly longer, hinting at a no-nonsense attitude. He wore a crisp white dress shirt, covered by a black blazer with subtle western details.

His laugh, a hearty, booming sound, could fill the room, revealing a man who, despite his stern exterior, knew the value of humor. He punctuated his speech with anecdotes from the field, sharing tales of wildcatters and boom towns, each story serving as a testament to his enduring love for the industry.

But it was his leg that drew the most attention, a constant reminder of the risks inherent in his line of work. BJ gave it another massage and then took a cigar from the box in front of him. He carefully cut the end off before reaching for a lighter. His office ventilation had been specially adapted to accommodate his politically incorrect habit. Running his hand through his bristly hair, BJ knew there wasn't much about him that was politically correct. A good 'ol boy from San Anton who believed in God and country, in reverse order. At the moment, he was worried about just where that country was going.

He looked up as his VP operations entered the office and placed his cowboy hat on the coffee table.

"Cutter, things didn't go well in Texarkana last week."

"Yeah, I guessed as much when I got your message." Bill Davis—aka Cutter—was vice president of operations for Wildcat Oil and Gas Ltd. The nickname was a holdover from his days as a driller. Cutter was an emaciated John Wayne, with a wiry frame and leathery face that reflected years of sun and wind burn. The type of man people look to in a crunch. He fit the tired cliché of the strong, silent type. His idea of formal wear was a pair of faded jeans and an open-neck shirt. A silver cross dangled from his neck. *Cutter's most prized possession.* It was a wedding present from his wife—Cutter put family ahead of God, country had to settle for third.

BJ went back to massaging his leg.

"Things are getting out of control. Those actions are bullshit, but they're picking up steam."

"Yup," Cutter said. "Sounds like it. What the heck are they suing for anyway, BJ? I haven't kept up with this stuff. And who are *they*?"

"An environmental group. They call themselves the Green Action Coalition or GAC. They've launched two suits. Say that we've been operating in an environmentally negligent manner. They're trying to shut us down."

"I still don't know what they're suing us for." BJ watched Cutter pick up his hat and tip it from side to side.

"They want us to do some kind of environmental assessment on emissions from our drilling engines."

"What the hell? Emissions? Don't all engines have emissions? What's the other action for?"

"One of our chartered tankers spilled five hundred barrels of oil. The idiots forgot to close an underwater valve while unloading, and the oil escaped before the ship's electronic controls signaled the loss of cargo. We're going after the tanker owners, but because we chartered it, we're the target. The leak was minor and we've already paid a fifty-thousand-dollar fine. The whole thing is bullshit."

Cutter frowned. "How can these guys sue us for the oil spill, BJ? I mean, isn't the ocean public property? If the public authorities don't see a lawsuit, where the heck do these guys get off suing?"

"They did what they always do. They recruited some people they say are directly affected. A bunch of their members are Gulf Coast oyster and shrimp fishermen, whose livelihoods have been *devastated* by the spill."

Cutter snorted. "Yeah, right. You know that British Petroleum runaway a few years back created all sorts of *fishermen* when it came time to line up for compensation. Guys that wouldn't know a crawfish from a turnup."

BJ sighed. "Damnit, Cutter, those assholes from Todd Ives are making a legal mountain out of a molehill, and my attorney, the esteemed Calvin Stokes, Esquire, can't seem to do anything about it."

BJ watched Cutter continue to twirl his hat. "Well, boss, I guess it boils down to the big green. We've blown our legal budget for this year. Stokes is all we can afford."

BJ nodded. Once again, Cutter was right. "What I'm trying to figure out is how the hell did this group, this GAC, get the money to come after us? I've never heard of them."

Cutter gave his hat one last spin and put it on his head. "Maybe they hooked up with one of the mainstream groups, Greenpeace or the Sierra Club. They have pretty sophisticated fund-raising arms."

BJ thought about it for a moment. "I doubt it. Those groups always carry their own actions. They don't like to share the limelight."

"I suppose. Hell, I'm all for the environment, but there's got to be some balance. This isn't fair."

"Fairness hasn't got a helluva lot to do with it. They're asking for fifty million dollars. It's a joke! I mean, they're comparing this case to the Exxon Valdez, for chrissake!"

Cutter stood up and ambled over to the window. He let out a slow whistle. "That's a pile of money. It could kill the company."

BJ suffered his share of tragedy in his lifetime. After his mother died of cancer when he was ten, his father went into a slide and never recovered. Just before his Vegas gambling debts caused the family ranch to be repossessed, he drove off a small cliff at the back of the property. The local authorities classified it as accidental, but BJ knew better. He was goddamned if he would lose his company now after fighting his way through all that.

The phone buzzed. He glanced at the Caller ID and looked over at Cutter. "ARI—what do they want?"

Cutter shrugged. "Go ahead, I've got stuff to do."

"Thanks. Shut the door, will you? I want to put her on speaker."

Anderson Resources Inc. was a huge, multinational energy company headquartered in Houston and run by Leona Anderson. Anderson was as much an easterner as BJ a westerner. Throughout the time BJ knew her, she always dressed impeccably and maintained a buttoned-down appearance—no casual Fridays in her playbook. BJ respected the driving ambition to prove herself, a result of a childhood spent in abject poverty and a career in oil, the ultimate old-boy's game.

Anderson's rise to the top of the oil industry had been anything but easy. As a woman in a male-dominated field, she had faced countless obstacles and prejudices. Yet these challenges only fueled her ambition. BJ sometimes wondered if that ambition wasn't too all-consuming. She possessed a relentless drive to prove herself, to not only match her male counterparts but surpass them. This determination had earned her a reputation as a real ballbuster who would do whatever it took to achieve her goals. She worked long hours, often burning the midnight oil.

Despite their differences, BJ considered Anderson a good friend. ARI was Wildcat's joint venture partner in an offshore Gulf Coast well. While they held equal interests, ARI was the operator. It meant that while not running the play, Wildcat monitored the job ARI was doing on its behalf.

ARI was interested in other mineral rights Wildcat held in adjoining offshore tracts. Anderson wanted to avoid a straight purchase, preferring a farm-in—a common risk-sharing mechanism in the patch where company A agrees to spend a certain amount of money, typically by drilling a well, to earn a portion of company B's mineral interests. It was a useful partnering technique for companies that held promising mineral interests but didn't have the money to develop them or simply wanted to share the development

BENDING THE ARC

risk. ARI was earning its interest in the Explorer 7 play through such a farm-in.

He punched the speaker button. "Hey, Leona. What's up?"

Anderson's soft voice came on the line. "Darn it, I hate being outed by Caller ID. I called to let you know Explorer Seven's mobilizing to the new site. Should start drilling in a few weeks. Just wanted to keep you posted."

Yeah, sure. BJ didn't need an update from Anderson. Wildcat's geologists were in constant contact with the boys at ARI. A Wildcat geologist left for Explorer 7 that very morning. He waited for Anderson to segue into the Wildcat leases.

"While I've got you on the line, BJ, I've done some more thinking about our latest offer to farm-in on your Block Twenty-Eight J leases. We're willing to raise the buy-in to twelve and a half million dollars, plus all costs to drill two wells. All for a fifty percent share."

BJ raised his eyebrows and stifled a whistle. ARI was putting a hell of a lot of value on those leases. *Had they gotten hold of some new seismic?* The offer was attractive. The last number was ten million. While BJ didn't want to joint venture on this play, at a certain price, it was plain bad business not to. He played it slow.

"Well, you're heading in the right direction, Leona, but I'm still not sure I'm interested. Why don't we wait and see what happens on Explorer Seven?"

"That's fine, but just so you know, this offer won't stay on the table forever, old friend. We have to get on with life, and if it's not with Wildcat, we'll look elsewhere."

Yeah, right, Leona darlin'.

"Say, BJ, I hear you're having some fun in court. You know, that's the new corporate tool?"

What the hell? She was up to speed on the court actions?

"What's the new tool?"

She laughed softly. "Litigation, my friend. It can be a powerful business tool when properly harnessed."

"Yeah, well, we're dealing with it."

"Let me know how things go. Maybe we can help if we start working together more closely."

"Bye, Leona." BJ chuckled. *Always looking for an angle.*

6

WASHINGTON, D.C.

Thursday
March 15

PHILIP MORRIS ORDERED TO PAY $28 BILLION TO SMOKER. The item was the lead in the *Los Angeles Times*. "Abominable!" Jonathan Hendrix threw the paper on the coffee table. He was following the case and expected an excessive damages award—it was a jury trial—but this was beyond his worst expectations. The plaintiff's attorneys crowed the verdict was the largest ever awarded to an individual plaintiff.

Hendrix knew the tobacco industry bore some responsibility for selling a dangerous product. But it was a *legal* product and the compensatory damages of $850,000 were more than adequate to address the matter. The astronomical increase of the award through punitive damages allowed a sharp legal team, with the ability to inflame a jury, to turn what should, at best, have been a modest personal injury award into potential corporate ruin.

He reached for the glass of single malt. His personnel collection was closing in on 300 bottles. Letting the golden liquid slide down his throat, he savored the slow burn. *Truly the nectar of the gods.*

With a tall, lean physique, Hendrix cut an imposing figure. His dark skin contrasted nicely with a tailored navy-blue suit. He reminded people of President Obama. Fighting his way up the ladder to the highest law enforcement post in his adopted country required something extra, especially when you were black.

Jonathan Hendrix had something extra. An imposing command of the English language coupled with a brilliant legal mind and keen understanding of human nature, created a deadly combination for his adversaries. At 46, Hendrix was a young man by the standards of those who had occupied the office of Attorney General before him, yet his gravitas belied his years.

Born to a British mother and American father, Hendrix's early life reflected diverse cultural threads. His mother, a professor of literature, filled their home in Birmingham, England, with the works of Shakespeare, Dickens, and Austen, while his father, an immigrant from New Orleans and a civil rights lawyer, infused Hendrix's upbringing with tales of the relentless pursuit of justice.

From a young age, Hendrix exhibited a keen mind and an insatiable curiosity. He excelled in his studies, often staying up late in the night with a flashlight under his bedsheets, devouring books on law, history, and philosophy. His father's well-worn copy of Winston Churchill's speeches became a favorite. The young Hendrix found inspiration in Churchill's words, drawn to the former prime minister's eloquence. While not a lawyer, Churchill mastered the English language and was awarded the Nobel Prize for Literature. By the time Hendrix reached adolescence, he could quote the British Bulldog with ease.

Hendrix's academic prowess earned him a scholarship to Oxford, where he studied literature. It was there, amidst the hallowed halls and centuries-old traditions, that he honed his passion for justice. He joined debate clubs, his oratory skills growing sharper with each spirited exchange.

After Oxford, Jonathan moved to the United States, enrolling at Yale Law School. His transition to American life was seamless, his British accent a charming anomaly that set him apart in the crowded lecture halls. He volunteered at legal aid clinics, fighting for the rights of marginalized communities.

Upon graduating from Yale, Hendrix's career trajectory was nothing short of meteoric. He clerked for Supreme Court Justice Clarence Thomas, worked at a prestigious law firm, and became a federal prosecutor. His pep talks to clients were peppered with Churchillian rhetoric. "We shall fight on the beaches, we shall fight on the landing grounds, we shall fight in the fields and in the streets, we shall fight in the hills; we shall never surrender," he would declare, drawing parallels between Churchill's wartime resolve and his own battles against injustice.

Hendrix's appointment as Attorney General was a historic moment. He felt honored to serve as one of the youngest-ever U.S. Attorneys General under President William Turner's administration. When he got the call from Bill, an old law school classmate and lifelong friend, he couldn't turn him down. Bill hadn't asked him to come on board as a lower-level bureaucrat. AG *was* the top job. Besides being an honor, serving as AG was an appropriate crowning of his legal career. He was famous for his speeches on the shortcomings of the American judicial system. Here was his chance to put up or shut up. Bill promised him a wide latitude in his new post.

He punched the speed dial to Oliver Weston, his bright young black assistant. Sporting wild dread locks, hiring Ollie was a calculated risk in the staid AG's office.

"Yes, sir?"

"Can you come in for a moment, Oliver?"

"Be right there, sir."

Hendrix leaned back in the overstuffed leather chair and took another sip of that heavenly nectar while studying the painting on the wall. It was a copy of *The Roaring Lion* that hung in the Canadian Parliament. He marveled at how Yousuf Karsh had captured the essence of Churchill. The kicker was how Karsh got that belligerent look from the Bulldog—just before taking the picture, Karsh had boldly plucked one of those ever-present cigars from Churchill's mouth.

On accepting his new appointment, the first thing Hendrix did was renovate his new quarters in the style of Churchill's cozy study at Chartwell Manor. To avoid a fight with the bean counters, he paid the extra cost above the more traditional office makeover every new AG was entitled to.

Because his corner office already had a fireplace and large picture windows, the makeover was feasible. The view onto Pennsylvania Avenue wasn't the same as looking out over the English countryside, but the whole of the surroundings provided Hendrix with a comfort hard to explain. The old Bulldog put it this way,

"We shape our dwellings, and afterward our dwellings shape us."

The floor to the office flew open as Ollie stumbled in. His gangly physique reminded Hendrix of that character Kramer from the *Seinfeld* TV series.

"Boss, I've looked into that case in Charlottesville. The Sons of Freedom claim that a confederate courthouse statue honors the region's history while the NAACP wants it torn down as a vestige from the Jim Crow era that promotes white supremacy. It's a real mess."

"You know, Oliver, Churchill once said, 'If we open a quarrel between the past and the present, we shall find we have lost the future.' He was urging his colleagues not to focus on past recriminations around appeasing Hitler, but to focus on future actions to defeat him. Similarly, Oliver, we as a nation cannot dwell on past inequities without losing sight of the path forward. We are the sum of our history, good and bad, and we must not try to reinvent ourselves by sanitizing the past. It is what it is."

"Understood, boss, but some of that history is very painful for a lot of folks. Perhaps we can keep the statue, but in a less provocative setting."

Hendrix gazed at the wall above the fireplace. Instead of the large painting of Blenheim Palace that had adorned Churchill's study, Hendrix's recreation contained a painting by American artist Eastman Johnson—*A Ride for Liberty-The Fugitive Slaves*—depicting a family of blacks fleeing enslavement in the south during the Civil War. Hendrix thought it fitting to be reminded of one of the great historical injustices of his young, adopted homeland.

"All right, son, go down there and see if you can broker a compromise. But that's not what I called you in here for. Have a seat and read this." He tossed over the copy of the *Los Angeles Times* article. Oliver made a grab for the paper, but it slipped through his hands and smacked him in the face.

Hendrix suppressed a smile. "Sorry."

"My fault, sir." Ollie collapsed on the couch and read the article. He looked up when he was done. "So? Another wild jury award. What's new about that?"

"Exactly. It's becoming an everyday occurrence. My concern is how an accomplished litigation team, one that can paint the picture of the helpless citizen overrun by the uncaring megacorporation, can all too often incite a jury to the point of extracting preposterous awards. You know, the U.S. Chamber of Commerce just released a study on the damaging effects of nuclear verdicts."

Ollie cocked his head. "Haven't heard that term before. What are nuclear verdicts?"

"Runaway verdicts that can have devastating impacts on businesses, entire industries, and society at large, even when they are later thrown out or reduced by appellate courts. These verdicts drive up the costs of goods and services, adversely affect the cost and availability of insurance, and undermine fundamental fairness and predictability in the rule of law."

Hendrix leaned back, studying the gnarled wood timbers adorning the ceiling. *So what are you, Jonathon Hendrix, going to do about it?*

"Oliver, do you know who said: 'The morale arc of the universe is long, but it bends towards justice'?"

"Yes, sir. That would be Martin Luther King, Jr."

Hendrix chuckled. Oliver was a bright bulb. "Yes, indeed. Although Mr. King borrowed it from an abolitionist, Unitarian minister named Theodore Parker. You know, that was one of Obama's favorite quotes. He loved it so much he had it woven into a rug in the Oval Office."

"No, sir. Didn't know that. Cool."

"But it was one of my predecessors, Eric Holder, that put the quote in the proper context when he cautioned that 'The arc only bends toward justice because people pull it towards justice. It doesn't happen on its own.' Justice is not preordained, Oliver. We need to help bend that arc. I want you to do some free-thinking for me. Come up with a few options for bringing these lopsided verdicts under control."

"I'll get right on it. I assume this is a priority."

"I know you're busy, but yes, it's a priority. I believe it is time I began doing something meaningful with this job."

"You said it, boss." Ollie winked.

"Dismissed!" Hendrix waved him out with a grin.

Ollie tripped on the carpet and ran into the door on his way out. *Cosmo Kramer was on the job!*

Hendrix had his own ideas, but wanted a fresh perspective.

It will be interesting to see what young Oliver comes up with.

7

HOUSTON, TEXAS

Thursday
March 22

Andrew Tillington III stared out the window, already looking forward to tonight's culinary creation. You could almost see the blue blood coursing through his veins. His family was considered one of the most prestigious in Boston. With a lineage that traced back to the Mayflower, the family crest proudly adorned the walls of the ancestral mansion in Beacon Hill. Upon inheriting a family fortune amassed in steel, his grandfather relocated the family to Houston at the onset of the oil boom and went on to build a second fortune in the energy industry. His father was a founding partner

BENDING THE ARC

of Todd Ives Tillington.

Standing a commanding six feet two inches, Tillington possessed an air of quiet authority. His tailored suits, always in shades of navy or charcoal, were custom made on Savile Row and complemented a distinguished mane of silver hair. Piercing blue eyes, framed by steel-rimmed glasses, seemed to look through people, assessing, weighing, and calculating with the precision of a legal mind trained at Harvard and perfected over years of battle in the court room.

Tillington's corner office reflected power. A massive oval slab of Italian marble dominated the center of the room. A smaller slab of matching marble made a nice corner table. The wall behind him contained a recessed wet bar, above which hung a plaque from Le Cordon Bleu. A comfortable black leather couch sat against the wall at right angles to the bar, facing a curved television screen mounted in the opposing wall.

He clicked his pen rapidly as he reviewed the e-mail from Kevin Flaig, president of the GAC. Beyond his slovenly appearance, Flaig was a general pain in the ass. Tillington and his team nicknamed him "Mr. Hollywood," after the ever-present sunglasses. Flaig was heavily involved in the file, both inside and outside the courtroom. Tillington had no problem taking instructions in the normal course, but objected to clients calling the legal shots. He suspected Flaig was trying to buy the blue-chip credentials of Todd Ives Tillington.

Todd Ives, as it was known on the street, was one of the nation's largest and most prestigious law firms. The reception area on the seventieth floor boasted a sweeping view of the Houston skyline. With its emphasis on billings and profitability per lawyer, it was fitting for the firm to be headquartered in the dollar-shaped First Interstate tower—a classy building in downtown Houston sheathed in rare blue-green reflective glass and sitting on a black emerald pearl Norwegian base. Its exterior banisters leading down to an outdoor cafe were resplendent in polished pink granite quarried in Spain and hand-sculpted in Italy. With seventy-one stories, the tower required diagonal cross-bracing between floors fifty-eight and fifty-nine for lateral stability. Todd Ives employees, who occupied the top floors and spent too much time changing elevators, joked about being only ten minutes from downtown.

The sum of it all oozed money and sophistication. The firm's clientele expected nothing less, believing they got what they paid for and expecting first-rate legal services to come with top-tier fees. Tillington smiled. This was an expectation that the partners at Todd Ives were all too willing to oblige.

While a full-service firm in the traditional sense, Todd Ives had a definite focus on corporate-securities and large-file commercial litigation. The firm had offices across the country, with a few international locations. In Houston, the corporate department was the largest, with two hundred and seventy lawyers, while the litigation department had a respectable contingent of one hundred and sixty. It was hardly surprising that the energy group occupied third place, considering Houston's status as the energy capital of the U.S. With fifty lawyers practicing in his department, Tillington headed one of the nation's largest collections of energy law experts, a group that enjoyed a worldwide reputation in natural resources and energy law.

The energy department spawned the firm's environmental practice group, which Tillington also headed. Todd Ives had always practiced some environmental law, although it took a while to develop into a distinct practice area. As heightened environmental consciousness swept the nation, environmental law departments took root. At Todd Ives, they estimated environmental billings would rival tax in the next decade.

Tillington punched his intercom.

"Yes, Mr. Tillington?" Judy Stinson was one of two assistants dedicated full time to Tillington's practice.

"Judy, can you have Cindy Webster drop down for a few minutes?"

"Yes, sir."

He stretched and placed both hands palm down on the desk, enjoying the cool granite. Cindy was the lead junior working the file with him. As he waited, his thoughts stayed with the GAC. They were an enigma. He'd never heard of them until Flaig approached him at a seminar he co-chaired on toxic real estate. A sophisticated environmental activist group, they were well-funded and appeared on the scene almost overnight.

A check on Flaig revealed he'd spent a few years as a professor teaching political science at the University of New Brunswick, in Fredericton, New Brunswick, Canada. While not quite the backwoods, it was close. Nobody on the local scene knew much about him. Somehow, the academic background seemed appropriate. After his stint in Canada twenty years ago, he'd dropped off the radar. Tillington's search picked up an arrest for forgery ten years back, but Flaig had served no time. He acted as president of the GAC, which he founded three months before Tillington was retained and the first actions were filed. The GAC claimed to have a broad following, although Tillington could not locate a membership roll. He'd asked Flaig for one, but never got a straight answer.

They *were* paying their bills—damn big bills. Monthly GAC accounts for the entire Todd Ives team were in the order of two hundred thousand, and Tillington, as lead counsel and the lawyer who made the kill—brought in the file—would get a good share of the credit for those billings.

Cindy stuck her head in the door. Two years out of law school, she was bright, and Tillington increasingly used her as a sounding board.

"You wanted to talk about the GAC?"

He waved for her to sit down. "I want to go over the causes of action for a minute. You never liked them, did you?"

Cindy fidgeted. "My research suggests the cases are weak, sir."

He understood her uneasiness. She was looking at the matter purely from a legal standpoint. He did the same in his early years. But he'd adapted to the practical, harder side of litigation. She would, too, or she wouldn't last. She would learn that litigation wasn't always about winning. A lawsuit could provide other strategic benefits to a well financed party.

The Wildcat actions were cheeky. They were borderline bogus. Normally, he would have been reluctant to sue, even at the client's insistence. Filing garbage suits can catch up with you. Tillington knew there was truth to the adage about a reputation being built over a lifetime but lost in an instant. But he wasn't beyond launching the odd aggressive action. This case promised plenty of publicity. Sharing a common trait with his litigation colleagues, Tillington could never get enough media exposure. In addition, the action was against a company that had paid a fine for the environmental infraction supporting one of the suits. That provided Tillington with enough cover to sue.

It also didn't hurt that the GAC was married to the cases, perhaps hoping to establish landmark legal precedents, and had an unlimited legal budget. Flaig's instructions were clear—deliver a successful result, and there was a large premium in it for Todd Ives.

"Cindy, when we took on the GAC, did you get the usual letter from the Conflicts Committee?"

"Of course, sir. It's on the file. No legal conflicts identified, although a strong sensitivity to business conflicts."

Tillington nodded. "Yes, yes, that's not surprising." The one bothersome aspect of moving forward with the GAC was that he would be taking a shot at the oil patch, and oil and gas companies firmly anchored Todd Ives's client base. Firms specializing in labor law faced this same conundrum. They acted either for management or labor, but rarely both.

The potential to antagonize other Todd Ives clients by going after Wildcat was real. But he could manage that. He'd have to make sure to spin Wildcat as an aberration, a fly-by-night operator in an otherwise responsible industry.

Judy's voice came over the intercom. "Mr. Tillington, Cal Stokes is calling. Are you in?"

BENDING THE ARC

Tillington never took or placed his own phone calls. He reasoned that at a thousand dollars an hour, his clients appreciated this efficient use of his time. He motioned to Cindy that they were finished.

"Yeah, I'll take it, Judy. Put him through."

He smiled. The added bonus to this file was that Cal Stokes represented the other side. While the lawsuits were a stretch, winning wasn't out of reach against a clown like Stokes.

"Cal, what can I do for you?"

"Mr. Tillington . . . Drew, I wanted to let you know that I'll be moving to dismiss the GAC actions. I want the motion heard before we get into discoveries. I've talked to Judge Nabors, and she'll hear it next Tuesday at ten a.m."

Tillington was expecting this. Stokes should have done it weeks ago. Any delay in moving to dismiss always hurts your chances. If the actions are without merit, you should raise the objection on day one, not six weeks after filing the actions and well into preliminaries.

"Sure, Cal. I understand. Naturally, we'll oppose. Make sure you copy me with the motion."

"Will do. Thanks, Drew." Stokes was *thanking* him—for what? Tillington chuckled to himself. It appeared Mr. Stokes was duly intimidated by the Silver Fox. He decided to have some fun.

"Before you go, Cal, you say you've already worked up the motion?"

"Yeah, I'll have it over to you in half an hour."

"For which case?" Tillington smiled at the pause.

"Ah, what do you mean?"

"Well, Cal, I just want to know which docket the motion is on. You know, we have two cases going here."

"Well, uh, the motion is actually for both dockets."

"Oh, great. So you've done two motions?"

"No, uh, no, I dealt with them together in the same motion, uh, that is . . . I . . . yeah, I am bringing two motions, one for each. They'll be heard consecutively."

"Great, and you say I'll have them in the half hour." Tillington smiled again as he anticipated the response.

"Uh, no. You'll get them in a few days. I'll just call Judge Nabors and try to get a new date. Her calendar's pretty full, so it may take a while. I'll let you know."

Tillington hung up the phone and burst out laughing. The dumb shit. He wanted to proceed as if the actions were consolidated, but they weren't. Although filed by the same plaintiff against the same defendant and being heard by the same judge, they were separate actions. Poor guy would have to trash his motion and work up two new ones. The bigger delay would be getting a new hearing date.

BENDING THE ARC

This wasn't a big deal in the scheme of things. The same arguments would arise. Tillington considered letting the issue lie and raising it once Cal put his motion to Nabors, thereby embarrassing him in court. But that was a low percentage play. It would only aggravate Nabors, who was very much a let's-get-on-with-it judge.

Nabors would likely have agreed to hear the motions as one, or at least heard the separate motions at the same sitting. As the presiding judge in both actions, she had the procedural power to do that. Apparently, friend Stokes wasn't too familiar with the rules of procedure. Tillington smiled to himself. *No, he wasn't dealing with a mental giant here.*

"Clint Farber holding for you, Mr. Tillington," Judy said.

What could he want? Clint was an old pal. They'd roomed together at Harvard and shared many a drunken stupor closing the local pubs. Clint entered university intent on a business major, with the unapologetically stated goal of raking in as much money in as short a time as possible. Somehow, he got sidetracked into journalism. Tillington knew that after Clint started his career in radio, he moved into digital media, landing his position as political reporter for the *The Texas Tribune* a few years back. They kept in touch, more through Tillington's efforts than

Clint's. Tillington knew that in his line of business you could never have enough media contacts.

"Clint, what's up?"

"Good day, Counselor. Have you heard about the Wildcat press conference at one-thirty tomorrow at the Hyatt?"

"No," Tillington said, surprised. Stokes hadn't mentioned any press conference. As far as Tillington knew, Wildcat hadn't held one since the litigation started. Perhaps Wildcat wasn't keeping Stokes in the loop.

"What's it about?" Tillington asked.

"Well, there's not a lot of detail, but it's about the lawsuits. I think Wildcat is finally pushing back. They're saying the media coverage has been too lopsided to date. I guess they want to try and balance the scales."

"Are you going?"

"It's not my beat, but it's a slow day, and I've been trying to make some headway with our cute new legal reporter, so, yeah, I'll float over there. Anything in particular I should be looking for?"

Tillington was waiting for that. He wanted to plant a question or two, without pushing too hard. Having Clint call fishing for ideas was perfect. The GAC had its own PR crew, but everyone in the press knew who they were. They couldn't ask questions at the conference without their motives being questioned.

"Clint, I think they may try to have the charges dismissed."

"Have they approached you?" Clint wasn't an idiot.

"No comment."

"Hmmm." Tillington smiled as Clint absorbed the noncommittal response. *Mission accomplished.*

Clint continued, "So what's their angle? What should we be looking for?"

"Well . . ." Tillington said. He had to be careful here. "I think they'll claim the actions are without merit. But if that's true, you have to wonder why they were so quick to pay the fine for that oil spill. As for the environmental audit we want done, it's high time the industry started taking a proactive stance."

"What do you mean?"

"It's like closing the barn door after the horse has bolted. If we only discover the harmful impacts of emissions after they've been emitted, we're left with a clean-up operation. If we know the potential damage going in, we can make a reasoned assessment whether it's worth allowing it in the first place."

"So, you're saying the industry is still in the Stone Age when it comes to environmental awareness?" Clint pressed.

Careful here. "Not the industry, Clint, but Wildcat. The oil patch as a whole doesn't have a bad record, but Wildcat sure as hell does. That's about all I can say. Got to go. Thanks for the heads up."

"Sure."

Tillington hit his intercom the minute Clint hung up. "Judy, get me Matt Avery." Matt was the GAC's PR point man. From his discussions with Flaig, Tillington knew the GAC understood that media coverage was the lifeblood of an action like this. The GAC's true audience was the public. The courts were just another medium to get the message through.

"Matt Avery's on the line."

"Matt, what's this about a Wildcat press conference?"

"Yeah, Drew, we just got the release. I'll email it over. It doesn't say much, just that the GAC has dominated media coverage to date and it's time for Wildcat's side of the story to be heard. You should be there. It's one-thirty tomorrow at the Hyatt."

"Yeah, I know. A source at the *Tribune* just tipped me off."

"Anything we need to do?" Matt asked. While Matt was the media point man, Tillington made it clear Matt took his instructions only from Tillington and Flaig.

"Nothing for now. Don't respond to their remarks at the conference. We should digest the stuff and then come out with a comprehensive rebuttal. If they ask you for any off-the-cuff comments, just note that the actions were launched two months ago and it's taken Wildcat a long time to decide they're baseless. You might also find some questions from the press gallery interesting."

"What do you mean?"

"You'll see. I'll be there. We can talk further then."

Tillington stood up and walked over to the floor-to-ceiling windows overlooking the Houston skyline. He thought about what he would conjure up for dinner. For all his legal prowess, Tillington's true passion came to life in his state-of-the-art kitchen—a sanctuary where the high-stakes tension of corporate law gave way to the therapeutic rhythm of chopping, stirring, and tasting. His love for cooking was no mere dalliance; it was an ingrained pursuit that led him to earn a diploma from the prestigious Le Cordon Bleu in Paris, proudly reflected in the certificate hanging in his office. His signature dish, a beurre blanc-draped poached lobster, reflected his New England roots and Parisian training.

So Wildcat was waking up. This would make the battle more interesting . . . and more lucrative. He had a harder time justifying huge legal fees on a file with little action. Perhaps a celebratory filet mignon, with riz pilaf, and a roasted vegetable medley? Having Wildcat kick back upped the stakes for the GAC. Yes, *Green Action Coalition versus Wildcat Oil and Gas Ltd.* was developing nicely.

8

HOUSTON, TEXAS

Friday
March 23

The Regency Ballroom at the Hyatt was filling up. In circulating the announcement on a slow news day, BJ emphasized this was Wildcat's first media conference. He wanted to highlight the contrast with the weekly events staged by the GAC. Obviously, the message got out.

He wiped his brow and gratefully accepted the glass of ice water offered by Tom Hannigan. A junior engineer at Wildcat, Tom had prepped him for the conference. BJ chugged the water without coming up for air. He chewed on a couple of ice cubes as he surveyed the thirty-odd media types and three TV video cams in attendance.

"Thanks, I needed that. This media stuff isn't my game."

"Why doesn't Wildcat have a corporate communications department, sir?"

"It seems a bit odd, doesn't it? We're a relatively small, privately held company, son. We don't have the sophisticated shareholder communications that are a given for widely held public companies."

Tom nodded. "Did you know, sir, the GAC put together a specialized PR team just to handle these lawsuits?"

"Yeah, sure. Form over substance. We don't have the payroll to play those games. When it comes to this"—he waved his hand at the TV cameras and assembled reporters—"the Wildcat media response team starts and ends with good 'ol BJ."

BJ did not invite Cal Stokes. Stokes called him when he got the press release to warn against the solo approach, suggesting Stokes had to be there since the conference was all about the lawsuits. But BJ wanted this to be Wildcat's story, from the heart. No legalese. Maybe that was naïve, but so be it.

Tom stood up. "I've reserved a seat in the front row. I'll watch your delivery from there to get the crowd's perspective. Keep your eye on me and I'll try and give you some useful feedback."

"Thanks, Tom. Appreciate that."

As Tom left the dais, BJ groaned. He spotted the sunglasses first, then the cheap suit.

"I came here to be educated. I trust you won't let me down." Kevin Flaig held out his hand. BJ ignored it.

"If you listen, you'll learn, Mr. Flaig. That's all I can promise you."

Flaig winked, unfazed. *Smug bastard.*

He reviewed his notes. Time to get this show on the road.

"Ladies and gentleman, if y'all would please take your seats. We'd like to get started."

He waited a few moments for everyone to get settled. "On February fourteenth of this year, the Green Action Coalition sued Wildcat Oil and Gas Limited to the tune of fifteen million dollars for adverse environmental impacts caused by emissions from Wildcat's fleet of drilling rigs. On February twenty-fifth, the GAC filed a second lawsuit against Wildcat, seeking damages of thirty-five million dollars for degradation of the environment from a five-hundred-barrel oil spill from the *Texas Star*, a Wildcat-leased tanker.

"Resolving these cases, as the plaintiff well knows, could take years. Essentially, they're trying to put us out of business.

"These actions are before the courts. Wildcat would be happy to leave them there. However, as y'all know, the GAC has been very active in presenting its case outside the courtroom. It's reached the stage where we have no choice but to speak to y'all as well. That said, we have to be careful to avoid acting in contempt of court, and so I'll keep my comments as generic as I can."

BJ saw Flaig in the front row, rolling his eyes. *Asshole*.

"Both actions constitute simple legal harassment. They are nuisance actions intended to provide a media platform for the GAC's wider agenda—an agenda aimed at freezing development of fossil fuels in the Gulf of Mexico." BJ took a sip of water, feeling more comfortable. He looked up from his prepared text.

"Let's look at the facts. The amount of oil spilled was negligible. Skimming operations recovered approximately sixty percent of that oil, and about thirty-five percent evaporated. The fuel is a light-end, refined product, not the heavy, gooey stuff you saw on the beaches from the Exxon Valdez.

"By the way, the Valdez spilled some two hundred and sixty *thousand* barrels that oiled fifteen hundred miles of shoreline. The Deepwater Horizon spilled almost five *million* barrels. That should help put the trickle lost from our tanker in perspective. I'd also like to point out that while Wildcat is pursuing compensation from the tanker operator, we promptly paid a fifty-thousand-dollar fine to the proper authorities."

He paused. They were listening and, more important, taking notes.

"Regarding the action relating to our diesel-fueled power plants, those emissions are legal and well within accepted norms. There's no basis for an environmental review. The composition of diesel emissions is well known. We can also readily quantify those emissions. We presented these numbers to the proper authorities when we got our drilling permits. To now ask us to stop everything to study nothing amounts to paralysis by analysis.

"Perhaps I can use an analogy. Most of y'all drove to work today using gasoline-fueled power plants. Adopting the GAC's logic, I could launch an action to stop you and every other car owner from operating your vehicles until you've presented me with an exhaustive report on the environmental impact of your vehicles' emissions. But that's ridiculous, you say. We all know that vehicle emissions are undesirable. But we, as a society, have decided the benefit of using our vehicles outweighs the harm to the environment, for now.

"The same is true for industrial pollution. No one likes pollution. But that doesn't mean we should eliminate all sources of pollution. If so, we'll all lead lives very different from the comfortable ones we enjoy today."

He spotted Tom, in the front row as promised, holding up a company brochure and pointing at it. Right.

"Let me digress briefly to give you an idea of what Wildcat has done on the environmental front. And I do this because the GAC claims Wildcat is an irresponsible operator. We were the first oil and gas company to adopt a set of company-wide environmental guidelines, our 'Green Code.' We won several awards, most recently, and this only some three months ago, from the Environmental Stewardship Foundation—ESF—a well-respected environmental lobby group whose members include most of the major established environmental associations. In fact, the ESF praised our emergency response to the tanker spill, citing it as a case study in state-of-the-art containment practices. They thought we did a terrific job. This isn't an industry agency talking but an independent, well-respected organization.

"So, back to the issue at heart. What you have is a situation where a responsible oil and gas company is being subjected to a concerted campaign of legal harassment under cover of so-called environmentalism. Wildcat is spilling green blood here." *Got to give them that sound-bite.*

"This isn't the way America is supposed to work. A legal system that allows opponents to drag a company into protracted litigation at their whim is fundamentally flawed."

He glanced at Tom again, and saw him drawing a finger across his neck.

BENDING THE ARC 71

"In closing, I'd like to note that y'all, the media, have some responsibility as well. Lawsuits provide natural media platforms. To prevent abuse, media coverage has to be balanced and fair. Environmental lawsuits involve technical matters that are difficult to evaluate without some homework. It's incumbent upon you to do that homework. If we allow junk science to go unchallenged, we exacerbate the problems I've been speaking of.

"Thank you for your attention. I'd be more than happy to take your questions."

Hands stretched out; some reporters shouted to be heard. BJ pointed at a tall man in the back. "Go ahead."

"Mr. Whitter, Bob Waldon, *Houston Chronicle*. If these actions are as baseless as you claim, why hasn't Wildcat petitioned the court to dismiss them? That's a routine response to nuisance actions."

BJ was ready for this one. "We have been slow on that front, I grant you. Wildcat is a virgin when it comes to lawsuits. And I'm proud of the fact that we have never been sued up to now. We took some time to retain outside counsel, who in turn needed time to digest these actions."

"Are you saying that you'll move to dismiss?

"That you'll have to follow in the courts. As I noted at the outset, I don't want to try this case in the media." Even as he said it, BJ knew that was exactly what was happening.

A thin man next to Flaig waved his arm and shouted out, "Mr. Whitter, Cliff Farber, *Texas Tribune*." BJ noticed Farber talking to Drew Tillington at the start of the conference, although he was seated well away from him now.

"You say these actions are groundless, yet in the same breath, you admit you paid a healthy fine for the oil spill. Isn't that an admission of guilt?"

"Absolutely not. The fine automatically applies to any spill of over three hundred barrels. It's what's referred to as a strict liability offense. My lawyers tell me that these are offenses for which there is no defense. If there is an oil spill, the fine applies, full stop. We never denied there was a spill. We could have tried to hide behind the company that owns and operates the tanker—remember, we were only leasing it. But we owned the oil, and we wanted to do the right thing. So we paid the fine. But we deny the spill had any significant environmental impact. That is a different issue from whether or not there was a spill. And if you look at the facts, they show there is no significant environmental impact."

Farber again out-shouted his colleagues. "Mr. Whitter, a follow-up if I may on the emissions case. You suggest Wildcat is being singled out. Rather than being an industry issue, doesn't this just boil down to the negligence of a particular industry participant?"

"Well, Mr. Farber, if you're saying that we're not being singled out, then you don't understand the lawsuit. Electrically powered drilling systems have not gained wide usage. The *entire industry* operates with diesel-fired units. There's nothing unique about the rigs Wildcat owns and, sometimes, leases.

"But *no one else* is being sued. In fact, if it's diesel emissions we're worried about, then a large part of industrial America should be our codefendants. It's that crazy. And that's what I mean about doing your homework. A superficial review of this action would make it apparent we're being targeted."

BJ couldn't resist the last bit. That arrogant jerk deserved it.

He spent another fifteen minutes fielding questions, after which he fought his way through the jostling mob. He caught up with Tom as he headed out the room into the hotel's airy thirty-story atrium. Reporters swarmed around the bank of telephones in the lobby; others milled about, talking into their cell phones.

"Well—too dogmatic?"

"A bit." Tom smiled to show it wasn't that bad. "You caught my eye just in time. You were taking off." BJ laughed, relieved to have the conference behind him.

"Yeah. I was kinda nervous. But I tried to get the good story across as well."

"You did fine, sir. Let me buy you a drink. The GAC will no doubt have a sharp rebuttal, but you've curbed their momentum."

9

BIG THICKET, TEXAS

Saturday
March 24

"*Damn!*" Magruder recoiled as a willow whipped across his face. He wore old army fatigues and had a large rucksack on his back, containing a collection of small branches, plants, and sticks that extended from the pack. The contraption kept getting hung up in the underbrush. Even though it was only a hundred yards from the gravel road to the banks of the creek, he'd carried the load about a mile and a half, having left his truck up the road in an open meadow. He'd taken particular care to park at the edge of the Thicket, well out of view of any road traffic.

The Big Thicket National Preserve, nestled in the heart of southeastern Texas, was a sprawling mosaic of ecosystems. While the Big Thicket area encompassed 3.5 million acres, the preserve covered just over 100,000 acres. Its establishment in 1974 aimed to protect the unique environment, often called a "biological crossroads" because of its extraordinary diversity of plant and animal species.

Towering pines, their trunks like columns of ancient cathedrals, rose high above. Gnarled hardwoods, draped with Spanish moss, were interspersed among them. The forest floor was a tangle of underbrush, where ferns and wildflowers, in hues of delicate white and vibrant yellow, peeked through the leafy detritus.

The air was thick with the earthy scent of damp soil and decaying leaves, mingling with the sweet fragrance of magnolias and azaleas. Waterways meandered through the preserve like veins of liquid silver, their surfaces covered with a shimmering layer of duckweed. Paddling through these waterways, you might glimpse a beaver dam or spot the sinuous movement of an alligator slipping into the water. It wasn't uncommon to catch sight of a white-tailed deer stepping through the underbrush or a wild boar rooting around in the soft ground. In the more remote areas, the elusive bobcat prowled, a shadowy figure glimpsed only by the most fortunate of visitors.

BENDING THE ARC

Magruder stumbled free of the brush into a small clearing next to the creek. *Looked like an appropriate spot.* He pulled off his pack and carefully removed the contraption, laying it down in the long grass. He enlarged the interior of the thatch of sticks and plants until it resembled a shallow bowl.

As he was reaching back into his pack, he heard the low rumble of a diesel engine. Headlights flashed through the woods. He crouched down, remaining still until the truck passed. The Thicket was illuminated by a full moon. Although he was below the road, he wanted to avoid unnecessary risks.

He pulled a plastic bag out of the pack, full of feathers, black and grey with white streaks. While some were full-sized, many were smaller and fuzzy. He spread them around the bottom of the bowl, weaving some of the larger feathers into the thatch of sticks and grass. After final adjustments, he pulled a pencil light out of the pack and studied his work.

Satisfied, he placed a sling around the bottom of the makeshift nest and attached it to the end of a rope. Wiping the sweat from his forehead, he cursed the ever-present mosquitoes. Hooking the other end of the rope to his belt, he climbed a large tree on the creek's bank, stopping about thirty feet above the ground in a notch formed by two limbs branching off the main trunk. He hoisted the nest from the creek bank and wedged it between the trunk and the off-splitting limbs. Reaching into his outside pocket, he pulled out a large metal canister. Carefully opening it, he removed two eggs, one at a time, placing them in the nest.

Goddamn. The humidity was a killer, even at night. The Thicket contained a lot of swampy real estate. Twenty minutes later, he took a last look. *Damn good, Magruder.* He slid down the tree and packed his gear. Retreating from the creek, he straightened the grass he'd bent during his approach. Even leaving only footprints wouldn't do. As he backtracked through the brush, he pulled out the odd twig that he'd bent or broken on the way in, stuffing it into his pack.

A quarter mile down the road, he ran into another truck. *They sure were hauling a lot of water!*

The operator of Texas Environment's anonymous hotline, established to encourage environmental whistleblowers, fielded a call late that evening.

"GreenLine, how may I help you?"

"Yeah, you should check out the access road to the Wildcat Oil and Gas Buffalo Thirty-Six well in Tyler County. Just off the Beaver Creek crossing, there's a big falcon nest. It's incubating season, man. That road should be closed."

"Sir, could you repeat . . ."

Magruder hung up. He knew all calls were taped. They had what they needed.

10

THE WOODLANDS, TEXAS

Sunday
March 25

A masterful blend of urban sophistication and natural beauty, the meticulously planned community of The Woodlands, located just north of Houston, offered an idyllic escape from the hustle of city life.

Manicured landscaping lined the roads winding through a picturesque setting of native plants and colorful flower beds. The homes ranged from charming, traditional residences to modern masterpieces, each nestled within the forested landscape.

Central to the charm of The Woodlands was its network of parks and green spaces. Over 200

BENDING THE ARC

miles of hiking and biking trails snaked through the community. On any given day, you'd find joggers, cyclists, and families enjoying the trails, which wound through dense forests, gentle streams, and serene lakes.

Lake Woodlands served as a hub for recreation and relaxation. Kayakers and paddle boarders glided across its still waters, while picnickers and sunbathers filled the lakeside parks. Hughes Landing, a vibrant mixed-use development on the lake's shores, featured upscale dining, shopping, and entertainment options, with outdoor patios offering sweeping views of the water.

Shane felt lucky to have afforded a home in The Woodlands last year. While it came with a hefty mortgage, he was OK taking on the debt for the lifestyle it offered. He watched Val standing at the picture window. "Here you go, babe." Passing her a chilled glass of sauvignon blanc, he hooked his arms around her waist and followed her gaze at the kids playing across the street. He knew she couldn't wait to have a few of her own. He whispered in her ear.

"That's one hassle we don't have." She struggled out of his grasp and turned to face him in mock anger.

"Steven Travis Shane. You're playing with fire!"

"Perfect. I need some warming up."

He motioned for her to join him on the couch. She curled up next to him and giggled as Gus sat down smack in front of the TV, blocking their view.

"He does that when he's feeling neglected." Shane reached for a pillow. "Hey, Gus." The little mutt turned to look at them and cocked his head as if to say, *Make my day!* When the pillow scored a direct hit, he yipped and scampered away.

Most people got a start when they first met the spirited cocker spaniel with the missing front leg. Val was as curious as the rest.

"You never did tell me how he lost his leg."

"A train ran over him when he was a pup. He was an abandoned street mutt in St. George, Utah, where I was going to school. When I saw his story on the local news, I adopted him."

"Why?"

"Not sure, but I think I saw him as a kindred spirit. The vet said he took the accident in stride. No whimpering, just a stoic acceptance of life's hard breaks."

Val nuzzled up to him. "You're such a badass in the courtroom. What if your opponents ever find out that you're just like Mexican fried ice cream, hard and crusty on the outside, soft and gooey inside?" She slid her fingers under his shirt and let them wander up and down his chest.

"Babe, I need to watch this." Shane turned up the volume. CNN was carrying a three-min-

BENDING THE ARC

ute clip of Wildcat's Friday news conference. *The big guy with the crewcut—what was his name again?—Whitter—came across well.*

Shane pointed at the screen. "What do you think of him?"

"He sounds sincere." She reached for a pack of cards on the table.

"You bet. I met him at the courthouse the other day. He's really pissed. Those actions against his company look pretty lame. And who the hell is the GAC? Ever heard of them?" Val shook her head.

"Pick a card, any card."

"Enough with the card tricks, Val. I want to watch this."

She massaged his upper thigh. He felt himself reacting. Val acted as if she didn't notice.

He continued. "Doesn't look like these GAC actions have any substance."

Shane stretched his leg. It concealed nothing. He was at full alert.

"Substance is in the eye of the beholder."

Val could be maddeningly tolerant. She continued to stroke his thigh, somewhat less gently.

He put his arm around her and kissed her neck. "Enough talk. Let's get some exercise."

"That's more like it," she murmured.

He woke up an hour later in the dark. Val lay curled next to him. *So beautiful and vulnerable.*

Shane gently lifted her arm to one side and got to his feet.

He walked over to his desk and took the phone out of its cradle. Shane was still in Jurassic Park on some things, including his refusal to give up his landline. He speed-dialed an old law school classmate that worked for Greenpeace.

"Hey, Tamara, it's Steve Shane. Long time no talk. How ya doing? Still saving whales?"

Her laughter filled the phone. "We do a heck of a lot more than that, Steve, you know."

"Yeah, I guess I do. Listen, I'm wondering if you can help me out. I'm trying to get some background on this group that calls itself the Green Action Coalition. Ever heard of them?"

"Just recently. They're behind a couple of lawsuits against an oil company. We never heard of them until a few months ago, when they made a big contribution to our *Save the Seas* campaign. I checked around when that money came in, but they haven't got any history. They seem to have come out of nowhere. And I'm not sure they're all that switched on."

Shane's ears perked up. "What do you mean?"

"Well, the actions they've filed aren't based on any solid science. I mean, there is so much to be done on the environmental front that I would think anyone committed to meaningful change could find some real problems to tackle."

BENDING THE ARC   85

"Yeah, I hear you. Thanks for that and maybe we'll do lunch one of these days."

"You know where to find me. Say hi to Val."

Shane poked around the desk for a cigar. *No. Better to work out on the loom.* He wandered into the guest room he'd converted into a weaving workshop. In the middle stood a large wooden loom containing a partially completed rug with a Navajo design.

He thought back to the countless hours spent at his mother's feet as she worked on her rugs. She would regale him with stories of his ancestors. His favorite was her sombre rendition of the Long Walk. The Navajo's forced march from their traditional homelands fueled his sense of injustice and spurred him to study the law.

He could still see her standing over the pozole simmering on the stove or hunched over the loom for hours, humming quietly. When he was sixteen, she was killed in a car accident, and in his grief, he'd taken up Navajo rug weaving. He had to believe she'd be proud to see him embrace his heritage. He continued the hobby when he started his law practice and found it a great way to unwind. The hours spent working the loom provided the best time to think through his cases.

Gus was blocking the foot pedals. Shane tapped him with his foot. "Come on, boy, get outta there." Gus yelped and retreated to the back of the room, glancing back to give Shane his best hurt-dog look.

Shane got into the rhythm of shooting the boat carrying the colored wool back and forth through the spanned twine. He didn't use a traditional Navajo loom, finding the pedal version more comfortable. While this was a departure from the ways of his ancestors, he knew they wouldn't hold it against him. And while he preferred modern designs, he stayed true to the past by only using wool with natural vegetable dyes.

He didn't notice Val creep up from behind, and jumped at the touch of her icy fingers on his neck. He felt his tense muscles melt under the slow, insistent probing of her talented fingers, and let out a grateful moan.

"Feels good." He turned to kiss her. She was wearing one of his dress shirts, nothing more, with the top buttons undone. "Babe, I'd love some more exercise, but I haven't got the energy right now."

"Honey, don't let the old man in," she chided. "What are you doing out here?"

"I just wanted to work on some things. That piece about Wildcat and the GAC got me thinking."

"About what?"

"A law school buddy once told me that Japan has seven engineers for every lawyer, while the numbers are reversed for the States. He said this reflected the fundamental difference in the way the two societies approach problems."

Val sat down on the bench next to him and toyed with the weaving boat. "What do you mean?"

"Well, when something goes wrong, the Japanese ask 'How can we fix it?' and the Americans ask 'Who can we blame?' I never checked his stats, but you have to agree we're a litigious society." He took the boat from Val and filled it with another bolt of yarn.

"I suppose. Come back to bed, Steve. We can solve the world's problems tomorrow."

"You go ahead, babe. I'll be there soon." He pointed at Gus, nuzzling her feet. "He'll keep you company until I get there."

"Great. Come on, Gus." She bent to scoop him up. Lifting one of his shaggy ears, she murmured in a stage whisper, "At least you don't snore."

11

BAR C RANCH, TEXAS

Sunday
March 25

"That's not fair!" Becky Davis screeched, struggling to escape her father's clutches. Cutter laughed. "OK, honey, I give up. Your old dad's had enough." He flopped down on the couch. Fifteen minutes of flat-out play with Becky was the same as an hour on the squash court.

Cutter lived on the Bar C—a ranch nestled in a beautiful valley west of Austin in Texas Hill Country. He loved the vast expanse of rolling plains, punctuated by patches of dense woodland and winding waterways.

BENDING THE ARC

Stretching across the landscape, the Bar C was a sprawling operation, with miles of barbed wire fences dividing pastures filled with cattle. The terrain varied from gently sloping hills to rocky outcrops, providing ample grazing land for livestock.

The vegetation consisted of native grasses—bluestem and buffalo grass—interspersed with mesquite trees, live oaks, and junipers. Along the waterways were stands of cypress trees and thick brush, providing habitat for wildlife such as deer, wild turkey, and various bird species. The climate was hot and humid in the summer, with mild winters, making it ideal for ranching year-round.

It was only on the Bar C that Cutter felt completely at home. He'd grown up on the ranch as had his forefathers. The ranching culture here ran deep, with many families tracing their heritage back generations to the early settlers and pioneers of Texas.

Cutter counted his blessings that he could share the Bar C with his wife of ten years, Sarah, and their two children, Becky, a bubbly blonde six-year-old, and Ben, two years younger, a real hellion.

Cutter's primary focus in life was his family, not work, despite his unwavering dedication to Wildcat and his commitment to giving an honest day's work for an honest day's pay. A tattoo on his forearm featured Sarah inside a Texas flag, with small yellow roses on either side sporting the names Becky and Ben.

Placing a pinch of Copenhagen in his cheek, he chewed the tobacco slowly, watching Sarah through the kitchen door as she prepared dinner. She was as lovely as the day he'd met her at Texas A&M. Sarah was an Aggies cheerleader while he played tight end. They knew they were meant for each other on their first date and never looked back.

When Becky was born, Sarah quit her job as a CPA for American Airlines to devote herself full time to motherhood. He loved watching her move. She had that simple, relaxed grace you are born with. The ringing phone interrupted his thoughts. Sarah poked her head out of the kitchen. "Honey, it's for you."

He groaned, pulled himself off the couch and walked back to the study in his trademark easy gait.

"Yeah, Davis here."

"Mr. Davis. It's Danny Pearson at Buffalo Thirty-Six." Cutter recognized the voice of his top roughneck on Wildcat's East Texas rig. "Sorry to bother you on a Sunday, but we've got a supply truck stopped on the access road, five miles from the lease site."

"It's stuck on the access road?"

"We thought that's all it was. I took a cat from the lease to pull it out. But the truck's not stuck.

Forestry shut down the Beaver Creek crossing. Seems there's some sort of environmental problem."

"What do you mean 'shut down,' Danny?"

"Forestry has a truck blocking the crossing. They're not letting anyone through either way. The supply truck's on the far side. I talked to the driver. He wants instructions. He's got perishables on board."

Cutter considered his options. "Danny, take your cell over there and get whoever's in charge from Forestry on it. I need to talk to them."

"Yes sir. I'll be a few minutes. I'll call you back."

Cutter waited by the phone, spitting out a stream of tobacco. He needed the details before he could call it in. As a true wildcat, Buffalo 36 sat in an unexplored area with only one access road. Wildcat had built the entire eight-mile stretch from an interconnect with the nearest state road.

The access road cost one and a half million dollars, even though it was little more than a dirt track. It traversed some severe terrain, with three water crossings, of which Beaver Creek was the largest. To create a makeshift bridge, they installed two culverts in parallel and piled dirt fill on top. For a wildcat like Buffalo 36, it made little sense to build a permanent structure. If the well was a strike and the area proved commercial, the company would upgrade the road.

From an environmental perspective, it also made sense to follow minimal impact engineering. They built the road as a temporary installation for easy reclamation if the region proved dry. Forestry approved the road and monitored its construction. On completion, Forestry issued a clearance certificate. Now, after all that, they apparently had a problem. The phone rang again. He got it on the first ring.

"Yeah, Danny."

"Sir, I have Cam Stearns from Forestry here to talk to you."

"Thanks, Danny. Mr. Stearns, my name is Cutter Davis. I'm the toolpush on this rig responsible for all operations. I understand we have some sort of situation at Beaver Creek. We have a certificate from you folks, so I'm at a loss as to what all the fuss is about. Perhaps you can explain it to me?"

"Yes, Mr. Davis. Above the bank of Beaver Creek, about a hundred yards from your access road, we've discovered the nest of a Northern Aplomado Falcon. This is a very exciting find. We recently had the first chick raised by a nesting pair of Aplomado Falcons in Texas since nineteen fifty. They're just starting to make a comeback in the area."

Cutter didn't share Stearn's enthusiasm. "What's the point of all this?"

BENDING THE ARC

"Well, Mr. Davis, they're an endangered species, subject to protection under Schedule Three C of the Texas Environmental Protection Act. Your certificate states that activities on the access road must comply with all applicable laws and regulations. According to the Texas EPA, it is prohibited to disturb Northern Aplomado Falcon nesting sites within a five-hundred-yard radius during their traditional incubating season from March first to June first. So we can't allow any further use of the Beaver Creek crossing for the next two months."

Cutter almost vented into the phone, but set it down and collected his thoughts. One bird nest would idle a thirty-thousand-dollar-a-day rig for two months. Where the heck was Forestry when the road was being built?

"Thanks for the explanation, Mr. Stearns. We understand the dilemma. But you realize we chose the Beaver Creek crossing on Forestry's recommendation. We're in the middle of operations here. Denying access to Beaver Creek will cause us severe hardship. There's got to be another way. Can we move the nest or even the crossing? We'd pay any costs."

"We cannot disturb the nest, Mr. Davis. As for an alternate crossing, that would violate our minimum impact guidelines."

"But it was under your direction that we chose the current site. We'd have chosen an alternate site had you informed us of the nest's location. I would think that in the circumstances, Forestry could show some flexibility and allow an alternate crossing. Again, we'll cover the costs."

"I don't have the authority to make that call, Mr. Davis. As I said, our minimum impact guidelines require that one and only one route be certificated when operating in a fragile ecozone such as the one your access road traverses."

"Let me get this straight, Stearns." Cutter's friendly tone was gone. He was dealing with a pencil-neck bureaucrat who wouldn't cut them any slack. "We constructed a crossing where you guys told us to. You've now discovered the site is inappropriate. Because of your 'one shot' rule, we're prevented from building an alternate crossing. And despite Forestry sanctioning this whole mess, Forestry isn't willing to show any flexibility. Does that pretty well sum things up?"

"Well, sir, I wouldn't say our recommendation for this crossing site was inappropriate. All we're saying is that it can't be used for the next two months."

"That we have an authorized crossing that is unusable may seem like a minor detail to you, Mr. Stearns, but to those of us in the real world, it's like saying, 'Other than that, how did you enjoy the play, Mrs. Lincoln?' We'll take this up with your superiors. Please put my man back on the line."

BENDING THE ARC

"Do what you have to, Mr. Davis. Just be clear that Beaver Crossing is out of commission for the next two months." Cutter heard Stearns talking as he handed the cell phone back to Danny. "Your boss seems a bit upset."

"Sir, it's Danny."

"Danny, I want you to stay there until we can sort this out. Tell the supply truck to hang tight as well. I'll call you back in a few minutes."

"Right," Danny acknowledged.

Cutter needed instructions. Whatever he did would be wrong, and he was damned if he'd leave his ass out there unprotected. Let the desk pilots at head office take some heat.

Damn! It couldn't have happened at a worse time. At the moment, Buffalo 36 was looking good. The well was on tight status, with maximum security. It was drilled to total depth and testing for oil. Initial production rates were promising. Trucks were using the access road to take away the oil produced during the production tests. If they shut down the road, they'd have to fill the holding tanks, which would limit the oil they could produce.

He dialed head office. "Wildcat Oil and Gas, how may I help you?"

"Yeah, it's Bill Davis. Can you patch me through to Phil Leeson?"

"Of course. One moment, sir."

"Leeson, Environmental Affairs."

"Phil, it's Cutter Davis. I've got a headache out at Buffalo Thirty-Six. Forestry blocked the Beaver Creek crossing. They've discovered a bird nest and say we can't use the crossing until the end of the incubating season, which is two months away."

"Jesus, we spent months scouting those water crossings. Forestry made us reroute three times. Now they discover we've invaded a protected site?"

"Yeah, I know. It's incredible. It seems we're not only responsible for our own screw-ups but for the rest of the world's as well. Anyway, I have to keep the supply train open, and we need to get our test oil out. They won't allow us to move the nest or build an alternate crossing. Any ideas?"

"Let me conference in BJ."

After a short pause, Cutter heard the familiar drawl. "Phil brought me up to speed. They startin' to get to you, Cutter?"

"Damn straight, BJ. I feel like a UN troubleshooter. We've got to keep the supplies coming, or we're going to be down in another twelve hours."

"Yeah, OK. We'll try and deal with Forestry, but that's going to take some time." A lengthy pause followed. Cutter could hear BJ's mind whirling. Then he was back on the line.

BENDING THE ARC

"Phil, are there any environmental restrictions on the airspace around Buffalo Thirty-Six?"

"I don't follow, sir."

"Well, you may remember how we saved Berlin when the Russkies set up their blockade following World War Two?"

"Of course," Cutter interjected. "We'll get an airlift going. We can borrow one of the choppers we use for ferry service on the offshore to keep Buffalo Thirty-Six supplied until we get the road up again. It's brilliant, BJ."

"Yeah, it solves our problem for the time being," BJ replied, "but it's not gonna be cheap. Phil, do you see any objections from Forestry or anyone else on this?"

"No, sir. We're licensed to use our helicopter fleet for land operations as well as the offshore. There is one restriction, we can't transport oil by air, that's against environmental codes. So any test oil has to be tanked on site until we get the trucks going again."

"OK. Cutter, I'll leave you to organize this. Borrow a big machine, a Two Twelve. We'll have to use it to haul water and equipment as well as food and men. And before y'all get to work, answer me one thing."

"Sir?" Cutter replied.

"Any indication from Forestry on how they discovered the nest at this time?"

"No, BJ. We didn't get into that."

"OK, get going and keep me posted."

Cutter reflected on the last question. *Just how the heck did Forestry find that nest way in the back country?*

12

HOUSTON, TEXAS

Tuesday
March 27

Shane stared out the window at the schoolyard. *Really should take an interior office.* He spent way too much time following the world outside. The kids were playing baseball. He chuckled, watching the little tykes chasing the ball around, running from first to third, second to home. It was total chaos and yet they were having a hell of a time. Soon enough they would learn about rules and winning, and slowly the natural exuberance of just *playing* the game would melt away. Made you wonder if it was worth growing up. He flinched as the phone buzzed.

"Steve Shane."

"Mr. Shane, my name is Monica Reed. I'm with *Turbo News Now*."

"Yeah." Shane was familiar with the weekly TV news magazine show.

"Mr. Shane, we're doing a segment on environmental litigation and wonder if you would be interested in appearing. We are a talk show with a panel format. The host, Peter McDermid, acts as moderator, with a panel of experts chosen to represent different sides of a particular issue. You'd be appearing with BJ Whitter of Wildcat Oil and Gas, a company embroiled in litigation with the Green Action Coalition, whose president, Mr. Kevin Flaig, will also be on the panel. You'd be our moderate voice between the extremes we expect we'll hear from Misters Whitter and Flaig. Are you interested?"

Shane resisted the urge to reject the invitation outright. He deplored most of the news talk show programs. The average quality of the discussions was abysmal. But Peter McDermid was one of the better hosts. He had intelligent guests, and his programs were known for their balanced discussions.

"I suppose Mr. Whitter's press conference triggered your interest in the Wildcat-GAC litigation?"

"Well, it certainly has advanced our timing, Mr. Shane, but we've been considering a show along these lines for some time. Mr. McDermid

BENDING THE ARC

is always looking for topical material, and we've noticed a substantial increase in environmental litigation in the last few years."

Reed pressed on in a softer tone. Clearly, she sensed his reluctance. "Mr. Shane, we'll be running the show in any event, and we really would value your input. You appear to be well-positioned to shed some light on the relevant issues for our viewers."

"Does your format allow for equal time amongst the guests?"

"Well, as I said earlier, Mr. Shane, you'll be the party in the middle, so to speak. Peter will want you to have at least as much time as Misters Whitter and Flaig, if not somewhat more, considering your role."

Shane warmed to the idea. *Let's see if she's done her homework.*

"You know, Ms. Reed, your assessment of my abilities and convictions may well be out to lunch."

"What do you mean?"

"What makes you so sure I'll be a moderating influence on this debate? I could be the greatest pro-development, damn the consequences lawyer you've ever met."

"I don't think so, Mr. Shane." Monica's voice regained its confidence. "I have an excellent support group here and they did their background work. I know that you've been out of law school for six-odd years. You rejected Wall Street and the big firms for your hole-in-the-wall practice. You typically defend smaller companies and environmental organizations. Your practice is unusual in its diversity. You act for both small business—read pro-development—and environmental groups—read anti-development. Your practice is not highly lucrative, but has been gaining recognition through some significant successes.

"In particular, your successful defense of Eagle Resources in what is rapidly becoming famous as the Cow Fart case, or Bovine Flatulence for the more sophisticated. Your tactic of presenting scientific evidence to demonstrate how the methane emissions from the farmer's manure pit dwarfed the emissions from Eagle's wells was inspired. The ultimate application of the offense-is-the-best-defense doctrine.

"And your recent success in shutting down Talbot Manufacturing's Pittsburgh mill for continued, egregious violations of its Clean Air Permits was a landmark case. It demonstrated the ability of grass root class-actions to achieve results on par with what the EPA can accomplish.

"No, Mr. Shane, I, for one, find your approach to the law and our environment refreshing. I think we have a good grasp of where you stand."

"OK, OK. Very impressive, I have to admit." Shane shook his head. "And of course you've maneuvered me into a corner with all those kind words. What the hell can I say now? I'm in. When do you shoot it?"

"Next week, Friday. We shoot live before a studio audience. We'll be in touch to confirm the details. Thank you ever so much. I'm looking forward to meeting you in the flesh."

"You bet," Shane replied. *Could be interesting.* And, as Lee never failed to remind him, it wouldn't hurt to raise his profile if he ever wanted a chance at roping in that killer file.

13

WASHINGTON, D.C.

Friday
April 6

Hendrix swirled his scotch as he watched the theatrics on the 65-inch flat screen TV. The energy segment made for entertaining television. Ollie suggested Hendrix catch the evening edition of *Turbo News Now*, something about a Texas case rapidly gaining national prominence. He chuckled at the huge sunglasses on the man speaking excitedly to the big fellow next to him. *Were those television lights really that bright?*

"You can't be serious." Kevin Flaig's voice cracked as he leaned forward, pointing a finger in BJ's face. "You run a company that spews toxins into the atmosphere, dumps oil into the oceans, and you sit there and tell me *you're* the victim? Anyone with a modicum of common sense would understand what your agenda is—money. The almighty buck at the expense of everything, including God's green earth, soon to be not so green, thanks to you!"

That oil executive, BJ Whitter, half rose out of his chair.

"Let's calm down and see if we can't keep this discussion civilized," Peter McDermid's rich bass voice interjected. "After all, it's the thrust and parry of differing points of view that makes life interesting, is it not?" McDermid waved a hand holding his mug to calm Flaig, but hit Shane, the coffee spilling onto Shane's leg. "I'm awfully sorry, Mr. Shane. Let's take a break while we sort things out."

After the commercial break, McDermid continued the questioning. "Prior to the break, I was about to ask Mr. Shane's opinion on the case. So, what do you think after having heard the positions of Wildcat and the GAC, so passionately presented by Misters Whitter and Flaig?"

Shane took a moment to respond. The man dressed in black, with his dark features and sharp eyes intrigued Hendrix. The longish hair peeking out from the back of the cowboy hat was a surprise.

"OK, Peter, let me tell you what I think. In a nutshell, the GAC actions are without merit. They don't deserve the court's attention, let alone that of the media. We shouldn't be wasting our time on them here this evening."

Flaig interjected, "That's absolutely ridiculous, you—"

"Mr. Flaig, we've heard from you. Mr. Shane has the floor, please." McDermid held his hand out, palm outward to silence Flaig.

"Mr. Shane, please continue."

"Our system doesn't provide a defendant with many options in the face of frivolous lawsuits. I could pay my filing fees and sue you tomorrow, Peter. I would allege that when you bumped into me, spilling your coffee on my leg, you assaulted me. I've suffered serious damage from that assault. I'll miss work because of the painful blistering. I'll suffer emotional distress. In short, my life's been turned upside down if not destroyed by this wanton assault."

"That's ridiculous, Mr. Shane. It was an accident. I mean, really, that's just ridiculous."

"You bet. It's ridiculous. That's the point. You should be able to shrug your shoulders, feel sorry for me, and walk away. But our legal system won't allow you to do that. Failing to respond will result in default judgment against you. And to respond meaningfully, you'll need to retain an attorney. The system's been engaged. It's like unleashing a wild animal—very hard to control."

BENDING THE ARC

Bloody hell, this kid was good. Hendrix watched as Shane continued, his passion hard to miss.

"What you have here is a thinly veiled attempt to bring down a company through the courts. It's an abuse of the legal system."

Hendrix punched his intercom. "Oliver."

"Yes, sir," came the instant reply from the outer office.

"Come in here for a minute, will you?"

"On my way."

He heard a crash as Ollie ran into something. Hendrix waved him to the couch opposite the TV. "It's that program you told me to watch. Take a look and tell me what you think."

Ollie watched the TV intently, listening to Shane's discourse on the ills of the system.

After a few minutes, Hendrix spoke up.

"What that young lawyer—Shane is it?—doesn't talk about is how an action like this can escalate from a mere annoyance to crippling a company that doesn't have the budget for a hot-shot legal team."

Ollie nodded. "It's like that guy who founded the Equal Justice Initiative, Bryan Stevenson, says. Our system of justice treats you better if you're rich and guilty than if you're poor and innocent. It's wealth, not culpability, that shapes outcomes."

"So, young man, have you come up with anything after our conversation three weeks ago? How are we going to bend the arc?"

"Yes, sir. I've given it a lot of thought. Meaningful tort reform is a challenge. To keep jury awards within reason, we could follow the example of other jurisdictions such as Canada and implement a cap on indirect damages like pain and suffering and emotional distress. We could also cap punitive damages."

"What do you think of that?"

"I don't like telling a jury what to do. The entire purpose of a jury trial is to serve as a check on the system. Large punitive damages are sometimes needed to get the attention of deep-pocketed corporations."

"So, what else?"

"In certain legal systems, punitive damages go to the state. If the policy behind these damages is to punish and correct misguided behavior, why should the plaintiff score a windfall in the process? The plaintiff is already kept whole through compensatory damages. If punitive damages go to the state, it might curb some of the more outrageous lawsuits filed in search of a pot of gold."

Hendrix nodded. "That makes sense, but that's a legislative change for the boys up there." He waved at the window behind him, framing a view of the capitol building. "Anything else?"

Ollie threw up his arms in mock disgust, nearly toppling a lamp on the side table.

"There is one other thing. I did an analysis of wonky awards over the past five years. By wonky, I mean an award that's out of proportion to the wrong committed. I found one strong common denominator in most of these cases—a difference in the sophistication of the legal representation. The successful parties inevitably retained high-powered legal teams while their opponents had more modest representation."

"So, where did that take you?"

Ollie frowned. "Ensuring equal representation is a tough one. In the criminal system, you can reverse a verdict if you can convince a court you had ineffective counsel that resulted in a miscarriage of justice. The Supreme Court said that's implicit in the Sixth Amendment's right to counsel. But there's no such constitutional protection in civil cases. There, your only remedy is an action for legal malpractice. Not a lot of help if the verdict has ruined your company."

Ollie caught his breath. Hendrix waited.

"You could put all the lawyers on a roll. You just pull a number and get the next one up. Like at a bakery."

"Are you saying that if a party wanted to sue, it would simply go to court and draw a number for a lawyer?"

"It sounds kind of wacky, but, yeah, that's the concept," Ollie agreed.

"So that's the only way to ensure a level playing field?"

Ollie shook his head. "No. It takes away the ability to buy better legal representation, but it still doesn't ensure counsel with *equal* skills, and it's not workable either. Who would pay for such socialized legal aid? And then you have simple cases and more complex cases. You want your senior people to deal with the serious stuff. So maybe you need a bunch of lists. But, again, that still doesn't ensure a level playing field. All it does is make it a little fairer because a fat wallet won't give you a built-in advantage."

Hendrix nodded. "Denying a choice of counsel is too extreme. You said it yourself, Oliver, the problem cases result from hotshot legal teams with unlimited resources going up against less-experienced, poorly funded counsel, correct?"

"Yeah."

"So what if someone put this hotshot team up against an equally sophisticated team?"

Ollie looked at Hendrix quizzically. "Yeah, I suppose that could work. But there's no way you could arrange that."

Hendrix stared at Ollie.

After a long silence, Ollie nodded his head, color draining from his face. "You don't mean . . . ?"

"Exactly, my dear boy."

BENDING THE ARC

"Christ!" Ollie exhaled with a low whistle.

Hendrix continued, thinking aloud.

"Other agencies can deal with special situations head-on. The navy has its SEALs. The AFT people have their 'hit' squads. The NTSB has its crack crash investigation teams. The army has its Green Berets and Rangers. The cops have their SWAT teams." He stopped to take a sip of his single malt.

"Yeah." Ollie took advantage of the pause. "Even the alien squad have their Men in Black," he said excitedly, Hendrix's passion rubbing off.

Hendrix continued, acknowledging the comment with a nod. "That's right. All highly specialized, focused, competent units trained to deal with exceptional situations. Tell me, Oliver, do you not think that the recent trend toward lopsided civil awards in U.S. litigation qualifies as an exceptional situation?"

Ollie furrowed his brow. "I suppose."

Hendrix got up from his chair and paced in front of the window.

"Why can't the Attorney General's office have its own elite SWAT team? A team that can step into landmark civil cases. A team of crackerjack lawyers, 'legal eagles' that could prevent targeted cases from being lost because of ineffective legal representation. Think about it, Oliver. Civil law precedents exert one of the most powerful influences on society. We can monitor major civil cases and, where appropriate, make the SWAT team available to a private litigant."

After a minute, Ollie asked, "Who would you use?"

"For a trial case, pardon the pun, I'd like to send in a team to take over the defense of Wildcat Oil and Gas." Hendrix pointed at the TV.

"Wow!" was all Ollie could manage. Then he nodded. "I've read that their lawyer is less than impressive, and he's up against a legal armada from Todd Ives."

Hendrix shut off the TV. He plunked himself back in his chair and stared at the ceiling timbers.

Ollie piped up. "What do you think of 'LawSquad' as a name for this outfit?"

Hendrix shook his head. "Too hokey. Right out of television. I would propose 'LawForce.' All we are trying to do here is engage a legal force to ensure the law is applied fairly."

Ollie nodded.

"LawForce it is. Oliver, I need you to put all your time on this from here on in. We need a point man for the legal team. I'm inclined not to pursue high profile, established litigators—they would have too much baggage. We need someone young and sharp, but with an ego that is still manageable. Get me all the information you can on this fellow, Steven Shane. He's a Houston attorney, runs his own practice. You can get his details from the *Turbo News* people. Time is of the essence. The trial is moving along as we speak."

Ollie headed to the door, but turned before exiting. "You know, sir, Shane sounds like a lone wolf. Is that really who we want for this kind of operation?"

Hendrix smiled. "Yes, Oliver, I think that's exactly who we want. This project needs someone with an independent bent. Remember what Churchill said, 'Solitary trees, if they grow at all, grow strong.'"

14

HOUSTON, TEXAS

Thursday
April 19

"Mr. Hendrix, sir, it's a pleasure to meet you. I'm Steve Shane."

The imposing figure that approached with an open hand confirmed Hendrix's first impression from the *Turbo News* segment. Shane's steady eyes held his gaze, and his grip was firm. Hendrix noted the western theme. Not your typical legal layout, but then there didn't seem much typical about Steven Shane.

Ollie's check on Shane revealed a formidable legal talent. Shane lost a case early on involving a company called Green Badge, which Ollie's research suggested was winnable. But every rook-

BENDING THE ARC 115

ie is allowed one mistake. Since then, Shane's record was impressive. He'd won a few sizable awards for his clients in corporate/commercial cases, including several environmental matters, and he'd successfully defended a similar amount. He had no difficulty in acting for both plaintiffs and defendants.

Hendrix knew that when Ollie called Shane, he introduced himself as being with the Attorney General's office but volunteered little information other than to say the AG wanted to talk about a job. When Shane pressed for details, Ollie said simply that his country was calling. He'd requested a meeting at Shane's office, but with none of his staff in attendance.

"I'm sure this is all very mysterious for you, Mr. Shane. Do you have somewhere we can talk?"

"It's Steve, and if you'll follow me to the boardroom, it's not up to Grade A Washington standards, but it should do the trick."

They sat around the oval wooden table with turquoise inlays. Hendrix and Ollie on one side, Shane on the other. Hendrix admired the southwestern motif. Dominating one wall of the room was a large painting of Monument Valley, with the iconic "mittens" butte formations conjuring up countless classic westerns shot in the area. The opposing wall featured a large, worn Navajo rug. Shane clearly had no appetite for the bland art found in law offices across the land.

"It's your dime, gentlemen. What brings the AG himself down from Washington to meet with a small-time practitioner? I trust my professional dues and liability insurance are up to date."

"Of course, Mr. Shane—Steven. There is no sinister motive for our visit. In fact, we have a unique proposal for you."

Hendrix settled back into his comfortable leather chair and pulled out a cigar. "Do you mind?"

"No, go for it. This office is politically incorrect in most ways, including allowing our clients to smoke if they're so inclined. I had a tough time negotiating a special provision in our lease to accommodate that. I myself indulge from time to time."

"Then please join me." Hendrix handed over a cigar and lit both before leaning back. "Have you ever had any misgivings about our legal system, Steven?"

"You bet. Any lawyer who thinks has."

"What in particular?"

"Well, we could be here all day."

Hendrix blew a stream of smoke at the ceiling, admiring the painted thunderbird that stared back at him.

"Just provide me with a few highlights."

"Well, for one thing, I've had some bad experiences with juries that aren't all too smart."

Hendrix was taken aback. *Was this their guy?*

BENDING THE ARC

"Steven, remember what Winston Churchill said, 'The jury system has come to stand for all we mean by English justice. The scrutiny of twelve honest jurors provides defendants and plaintiffs alike a safeguard from arbitrary perversion of the law.'"

Shane nodded. "That may be true, but he also said, 'The best argument against democracy is a five-minute conversation with the average voter.' That applies to jurors too."

Hendrix was impressed with the quick retort, but also surprised. "Steven, I have to tell you I'm a bit disappointed. It is a poor lawyer that blames his losses on juries." Hendrix saw Shane's troubled look.

"Well, yeah, I didn't mean to say that. What really gets my goat is that the lawyers who get guilty clients off by playing fast and loose with the rules end up media darlings, seen as brilliant legal tacticians by juries and the public. That whole O.J. thing made me sick to my stomach. Bugliosi got it right with his book *Outrage*."

Hendrix leaned forward. "What exactly was it about the Simpson trial that bothered you?"

Shane raised his hands. "Other than everything, I think it was that two things influenced the scales of justice, things that should never have come into play. One was the celebrity aura around Simpson. Juries go stupid when dealing with celebrities. There's not much you can do about that."

"What's the second factor?"

"The idea of the defense assembling a 'dream team.' The amount of money Simpson threw at the trial was obscene. Jury selection experts, a who's who of trial lawyers, an appeals expert, an armada of detectives and investigators. All of this against the people's counsel. Prosecutors are civil servants, and civil service doesn't attract the best and brightest. I mean, Marcia and Chris did the best they could, but they were no match for the dream team. And the sad thing is, I think the dream team was more of a nightmare. Yet they still outmatched Marcia and her team."

Hendrix nodded. "So what was the problem?"

"Well, I just told you about idiot juries. There's a prime example."

"But, Steven, it was also a jury that convicted Mr. Simpson of wrongful death in the civil trial, right?"

"You bet, but in the civil trial Simpson was up against a first-rate litigation team. In the criminal trial, you had the Cowboys playing some college squad. It wasn't a level playing field. I see that all the time in my civ-lit practice."

Hendrix saw Shane catch his glance at Ollie. "That's what this is all about? You guys have come up with a way to address inequities in legal representation?"

"Bingo. I thought that if you are the man for the job, you could get to this point on your own. 'Great minds think alike,' as they say."

"But they also say 'fools seldom differ.' Pop psychology will give you a line for whatever you want. I take it you have a few more details to share with me?" Hendrix sensed Shane's impatience.

"OK, Steven, no more mystery. We agree with you that a tilted playing field in terms of legal representation is a leading cause of distorted jury decisions. Decisions that exert a chill on American business. They harm the economy by passing costs through to consumers. Ultimately, they create a vicious spiral, encouraging more actions for ever more excessive awards. They represent a clear and present danger to the national interest. We need to regain control."

"And?" Shane was leaning forward.

Hendrix blew another stream of smoke at the ceiling and looked Shane in the eye. "Steven, what I am going to tell you next, I want you to keep in strictest confidence. If you decide you do not want to work with us, this meeting never happened. That is why we needed to meet with you alone this afternoon."

Shane nodded. "You bet. Mum's the word."

"We want to set up an elite unit, a legal SWAT team if you will—LawForce. This team will have access to government support across the board. It can tap into the investigative power of the FBI as required, access the Department of Treasury, and so on."

Hendrix explained the LawForce concept, including further details he and Ollie had worked out since first coming up with the idea. On finishing, he sat back and waited.

After a few minutes, Shane asked, "Is it workable?"

"What do you think, Counselor?"

"It sort of amounts to high-powered legal aid. But it isn't legal aid if it's not universally applied." Shane continued, thinking out loud. "The government supporting actions against private litigants? It has a bit of a *Brave New World* feel to it. Big brother and all that . . . I don't know."

"It is definitely a novel concept and you are going to need some time to consider it. I assume you have deduced that we would like you to be part of LawForce. You'd be on salary, with decent pay, close to the Tier I, big law level. You'd also get a percentage of any fees we recover or cases we take on contingency. But this is about much more than money. It would be your chance to make a difference, to do something for your country. As Churchill reminded us, 'We make a living by what we get, but we make a life by what we give.'

"We would like to get up and running ASAP as there is already a case we are interested in. Think it over. If you do not think you can do it, let us know within a week, and this meeting never happened. If you would like to take it on, we will talk further. In either event, contact Oliver."

Ollie flipped a card across the table as Hendrix stood up. The card caught an edge and sailed through the air, landing back at Ollie's feet. Ollie stooped to pick it up and there was a loud crack as his head met the boardroom table. He sheepishly handed Shane the card, muttering.

Hendrix winked at Shane, who was trying unsuccessfully to suppress a smile. After sizing him up in person, Hendrix knew Shane was right for Lawforce. *Let's hope the young man agrees.*

15

HOUSTON, TEXAS

Thursday
April 26

The Spindletop in Houston was a dining experience that transcended the ordinary, blending culinary excellence with breathtaking panoramic views of the city's skyline. Named after the famed Texas discovery that ushered in the modern petroleum industry, it was perched atop the Hyatt Regency. Completing a full revolution every 45 minutes, the iconic rotating restaurant offered patrons an ever-changing perspective.

Stepping out of the elevator, the sense of elevation—both literal and figurative—was impressive. With floor-to-ceiling windows, the circular dining area offered unobstructed, 360-degree views of Houston. By day, you could see for miles, watching the hustle and bustle from a serene vantage point. As night fell, the cityscape transformed into a sea of twinkling lights, with the glow of skyscrapers and streets creating a mesmerizing, almost magical ambiance.

Shane marveled at the view from their secluded table. Hendrix had acted immediately on receiving Shane's call, flying down to meet Shane the same day.

"Good to have you aboard, Steven. I was not sure you would sign on."

"You and me both. Let's be clear. I'm not in yet." Shane knew from experience not to reveal his eagerness, it would only dilute his leverage. "It all depends on how this talk goes. I have several concerns and, frankly, a number of preconditions."

Hendrix put a hand up to stop him. "First things first, my boy. Care to share a Chateaubriand?"

"Well, since I'm not likely to get a decent burrito up here, you bet, a steak sounds great."

It was nice to talk about matters other than the law. Hendrix was an enigma. He'd come a long way. Attorney General was top of the heap for a lawyer, with the possible exception of Chief Justice of the Supreme Court. Renegades rarely make it to these lofty heights. That breed isn't attracted to such positions, and the system doesn't reward nonconformity, making it so much more remarkable that LawForce was conceived by Hendrix.

But Shane liked the man, despite the residual stiffness from a strict British upbringing. Hendrix appeared sincere in his efforts to reform the system. Shane was still concerned with possible interference from the AG's office, but he took Hendrix at his word.

They continued to talk about anything but work while they enjoyed their meal. After the plates were cleared, Hendrix motioned to the waiter. "Oban, neat, please." He looked over at Shane with raised eyebrows.

"Another beer will do me just fine, thanks."

When the drinks arrived, Hendrix cradled his in the palm of his hand. As he stared into the amber liquid, slowly swirling it, Shane could sense he was ready to talk business.

"You know, Steven, this is as new for me as it is for you. We will have to work through it together. So, what are your concerns?"

"First, I have a problem with working within the AG's office. I'll need to maintain my independence. I understand we have to work as a team, but I need to know my decisions will count."

"All right, I expected that. What specific assurances are you looking for?"

"Number one, I'm the head of the legal team. All courtroom decisions are mine. Naturally, we'll consult, and I'll consider your input, but when push comes to shove, it's my call."

Hendrix sipped his scotch. "Go on, get it all out. I will give you my thoughts when you're finished."

Shane nodded. "Number two, I'll be in control of hiring the legal team, primarily my co-counsel and lead investigator. Number three, I have a veto on what cases LawForce takes on."

He leaned back from the table, taking a long sip of his beer. "I think those are the highlights. I've tried to keep my demands to the deal breakers. I have a few other items on my wish list, but nothing I can't live without."

Hendrix sat in silence for a few seconds. "My lord. What's left for us, Mr. Shane?" He looked around the room, then back at Shane. "I must confess, I am not surprised. I would have been disappointed if you didn't want to ensure you had considerable hands-on control. Let me address condition two first, the composition of your legal team. I believe we can live with you choosing your inner circle. Naturally, you may want to entertain our recommendations from time to time."

Shane nodded. "I suppose the AG's office may come up with some suitable candidates, but

I think I'll be tapping the power of the office primarily in a support role."

Hendrix continued. "Condition one is acceptable with a slight modification. Your consultations with me and my team will be full and complete. You will not hold back anything—no surprises. You may have the deciding vote, but we will always know the trial strategy and be apprised of any changes as they take place."

Shane grunted. "Not a problem. When I'm in trial, you'll need your liaisons on site. It'll be difficult to provide detailed debriefings while conducting the litigation."

Hendrix nodded. "Finally, condition three, your veto over LawForce cases. Again, I can agree with that." He paused, looked at Shane for a minute, then continued. "You know, Steven, I like you. And I want to start this relationship on the right foot. Accordingly, I am going to be completely candid with you. If we have a real breakdown regarding conditions one or three, our ultimate remedy will be to disband LawForce."

Shane looked up sharply. "You mean leave me high and dry?"

Hendrix nodded.

Damn. Shane bit his lip. He hadn't thought about LawForce abandoning him mid-trial.

"That's not going to be in anybody's best interests, is it?"

"It is preferable to a situation where we have to back you if you go off on a tangent we cannot support," Hendrix replied.

"Aren't we forgetting something here?" Shane asked. "I mean, we're talking as if we're the defendants or plaintiffs. We're still just legal counsel. The ultimate decisions in the case belong to the named party."

Looking out the window at the Houston skyline, Hendrix drained the last of his Oban. "Please, Mr. Shane, you know as well as I that if we are taking over cases of poorly funded parties, they are going to defer to the advice of their lawyers on trial strategy. At least if those lawyers are sharp enough to gain their confidence."

"OK," Shane acknowledged. "Let's see if this works. If we're in synch on taking the case, we're going to be on the same page regarding the desired outcome, so there really shouldn't be any hardcore disagreements. If there are, you won't pull LawForce but will see the trial through. However, you won't be obligated to continue to any appeal stage. As for my right to veto cases, you'll have your own veto in that you won't even make LawForce available for actions you don't believe in."

Hendrix signaled the waiter for a refill. He kept his head down, pondering Shane's demands.

Shane pressed on. "Jonathan, I think that's a fair way to split control."

After a few minutes, Hendrix looked up and chuckled. "You are a decent negotiator, Mr. Shane. I hope your courtroom skills are as refined. I think we have an understanding."

"Should I write it up?" asked Shane.

"Definitely not, Counselor. Remember, this is a covert operation. Nothing illegal here, but nothing to be gained by creating a paper trail, either."

"Right." Shane kicked himself. He had to think. LawForce was a tricky assignment. While there was still a lot to work through, it made sense to keep things low profile, at least for the time being. Hendrix's refill arrived with a tray of smoked almonds. Goddamn things were addictive. Shane felt his side and grimaced at the slight love handle.

"Now that we have the formalities out of the way, let us get down to brass tacks. It is best that you keep your present office. We will have a Washington office staffed with support personnel. The core legal team will work out of your office in Houston. You should staff-up immediately. At a minimum, as you indicated, you will need a co-counsel and investigator. They will coordinate with Washington. Again, I can pledge government assistance across the board. For example, your investigator will have full access to FBI agents, the FBI lab, and so on."

Shane shucked back some almonds. "Quite the supersonic pace. You said in our first meeting that you've already got the first test-case scoped. Is that right?"

"Yes, indeed. In fact, it is a case you have some familiarity with—GAC versus Wildcat."

"Hot damn!"

"Yes, we thought that would attract your attention. So, Mr. Shane, do you think you will exercise your veto in this instance?"

"Hell, no. This is *exactly* the kind of case where LawForce can make a difference. I mean, I don't know why, but that company has some real enemies."

Hendrix nodded. "That's not necessarily a bad thing, son. Remember what Churchill said, 'You have enemies? Good. That means you've stood up for something, sometime in your life.'"

"That may be true. They have definitely targeted Wildcat. Cal Stokes is hopelessly outlawyered. If the GAC is successful, it's going to have a big impact on the oil and gas industry. Nobody will know what the rules are anymore."

"Down, boy, down," Hendrix chuckled. "I like to see that kind of fire, Mr. Shane. I do believe we have chosen well. I trust Wildcat will agree."

16

HOUSTON, TEXAS

Monday
April 30

Shane looked around the table with satisfaction. The team was a good one. He'd worked with each member before and knew their capabilities on a personal level. It was the only way he could recruit with confidence.

Val was on his left, sporting a sharp black dress accented by the silver Navajo squash blossom necklace he'd given her last Christmas. He knew her well enough to see she could barely wait for things to get going.

Next to Val sat an older, red-headed woman, attractive in a mature way. Jennifer Nelson was an ex-FBI agent—tough, savvy and full of sass.

Her trademark fiery red hair cascaded in thick, unruly waves to her shoulders. It stood in stark contrast to her sharp, chiseled features—high cheekbones, a strong jawline, and piercing green eyes that seem to see through any facade. Her skin was fair, with a smattering of freckles she long ago stopped trying to conceal. There was a ruggedness to her appearance, with a few faint scars from past encounters. She wore minimal makeup, just enough to highlight her features without masking them. Her lips, often set in a determined line, softened only occasionally into a rare, genuine smile.

Exuding such a tough exterior, Shane was surprised to discover she was into yoga. While she had a sense of humor, Jenn hated to waste words or actions. She took no bullshit from anyone, male or female. Shane had used her several times on particularly tough cases and found she was the equivalent of a full team of run-of-the mill PIs.

She maintained good contacts at the Bureau and was an exceptional judge of human character. But what appealed to Shane was her integrity. He knew that when he got her reports, he was getting the real goods, with no ego-induced embellishments or bias. She stuck to the cold, hard facts. And in her line of work, the facts often were cold and hard.

Dealing with the underbelly of society, Jenn had become hardened, but Shane admired how she still kept a sense of compassion and humanity. While it was probably sexist to say so, Shane believed women were the more sensitive sex. Jenn was proof this trait survived, even in the harsh world of law enforcement.

Speaking of sexist, Shane realized he was surrounded by women. Val, Jenn, and Lee. It wasn't intentional. They were simply the best people he knew for the positions he had to fill.

While Lee was his executive assistant and not part of the legal team per se, he intended to include her as much as possible. The more she knew about what was going on, the more valuable she would be. Ultimately, the success of LawForce depended on the commitment of all members of the team.

His offer intrigued them. He laid out the LawForce concept for them in as much detail as he himself understood it. Hendrix agreed that he could fully brief all prospective members of the team to give them the opportunity to make an informed decision on whether to sign up. To Shane's relief, they all did.

"So, Steve, you going to get this show on the road or what?" Count on Jenn to keep the meeting on track.

"Well, as you all know, you're the founding members of LawForce—an exciting new concept in American justice. Make no mistake, the work we'll be doing is important."

BENDING THE ARC 133

"We've heard the speech, Steve, and we're all here, so I think you can safely assume you're preaching to the choir."

"OK, OK, cut me some slack."

Shane passed around a handout. It was simply labeled *GAC*.

"I want all of you to review the information in this file. Our first case is GAC versus Wildcat Oil and Gas, a case I'm sure you've been reading about and following on the local news. The actions amount to legal grandstanding and have the potential to result in a dangerous jury award given the lopsided legal representation. We're interested in representing the defendant, Wildcat Oil and Gas."

"Have you met with Wildcat yet?" Val looked up from the cards spread out before her.

"No," he said. "That's going to be my first order of business. Their CEO called me the other day to set up a meeting but in the meantime, I wanted to get you working on this without delay. Time is going to be tight. I'll let you know when we get the formal green light. I don't expect any problems on that front."

"What about Washington? A pile of people I've never heard of have been calling the office and sending all sorts of equipment."

"Yeah, Lee, I know," Shane replied. "You're going to have to go up to Washington to meet with their people and sort out logistics. We need to set up direct communication links, video feeds, et cetera, between the two offices. They'll also provide you with any back-up staff you want for this office."

Shane looked around the table. "Let's be clear, folks. Money is no object here. Our job is to get the right verdict. We'll have awesome support. That's the strength behind LawForce. We'll be going up against the best in the business. It will be critical that we delegate well and make the most of the resources we have.

"If we need research, analysis, manpower to sort through evidence—anything to advance the case—we have access to the help we need. What we'll have to get used to is tapping that support. For example, Jenn, you've often used your contacts at the Bureau to provide you with some off-the-record help, haven't you?"

"Yeah, my old friends have been helpful at times. But they aren't free to release a lot of government secrets."

"Well, now you'll be able to pick up the phone and, rather than getting the odd sliver of information as a favor, you can have those people working *for* you. Again, we have no limitations on resources or money."

They nodded their understanding.

"Of course, you know what that means?" Shane continued. He grinned at their puzzled expressions. "If we blow a case and want to know why, we'll only be able to look in the mirror. OK, that's it. I need to make some calls."

"Cal, it's Steve Shane."

"Hey, Steve, what's up?"

"I'm calling about that GAC lawsuit against Wildcat."

"Yeah, what about it?"

"I think I can be of real assistance to Wildcat. It's an area of law I've been practicing for some time. I'm going to be talking to BJ about it."

"You son of a bitch! I told you to stay away from him."

"Actually, it was BJ who called me." Shane had to admit Hendrix engineered an elegant solution to the frowned upon practice of poaching clients. He'd arranged for an old war buddy, now in the management ranks of a midsized oil and gas company, to call BJ. His buddy was a golfing partner of BJ's. He told BJ he'd caught the *Turbo News* segment and was concerned with the potential for the GAC actions to hurt the industry. He suggested BJ upgrade his legal representation and noted the guy on the show with BJ sounded like someone BJ could use.

The next day, Shane got the call from BJ's office asking for a meeting. Shane didn't feel great about knocking Stokes off the case and was making this call partly out of professional courtesy and partly out of a personal need to do the right thing. He didn't expect Stokes to understand.

"Well, the case is going south in a hurry," Stokes said after a long pause. "I guess I can't do anything if BJ asks you to take over the file. If you do get it, you're gonna have your hands full with those bastards from Todd Ives. I don't know why, but they're throwing everything at these cases. I'd almost be happy to get rid of Wildcat. At least I'd be able to concentrate on the rest of my practice again."

"I understand. Thanks."

"Oh, one more thing, Steve. I have a couple of motions to dismiss that I need to argue first. With any luck, BJ won't ever need your services."

"Yeah, sure, Cal, you bet." Shane tried not to grin. Cal just didn't get it. His blind faith in his own abilities defied reality. And that was a big part of the problem.

17

HOUSTON, TEXAS

Tuesday
May 1

Wildcat occupied the thirty-fifth and thirty-sixth floors of a nondescript downtown Houston skyscraper. A receptionist looked up as he exited the elevator. "Welcome to Wildcat. How can I help y'all?"

"Steve Shane to see BJ Whitter."

"Yes, sir. Please have a seat. Mr. Whitter will be with you shortly."

Shane settled into a soft leather couch. The circular coffee table displayed several bronzes of cowboys roping steers and taming broncs and some promotional material on Wildcat. Shane flipped through a leaflet, noting the emphasis on the company's Green Code.

"Mr. Shane?" A stern, matronly woman held out her hand. "I'm Marge Bessemer, Mr. Whitter's assistant. If you'll come with me."

Shane followed her down the hall to a corner office. "Can I bring you a beverage?"

"No, thanks." Shane turned to face BJ as he walked out from behind his desk to grab Shane's hand in that meaty paw of his.

"Good to see you again, son," he greeted Shane enthusiastically in his warm Texas drawl. "I meant to tell y'all how much I appreciated your analysis of things on that *Turbo News* show. Christ, Flaig and those Todd Ives people are assholes." He shook his head. "Actually, pardon my lack of etiquette, but in my experience, most lawyers are." He gave Shane a direct, challenging look. "Say, son, what do you have when a lawyer is buried up to his neck in sand?"

Shane had heard it before. Like most attorneys, he knew all the lawyer jokes. He humored the big guy. "What?"

"Not enough sand!" The deep laugh resonated through the office.

"Have a seat, son. Have a seat."

"Thanks." Shane settled into a padded armchair BJ pointed at next to the side table in the corner of the office. BJ sat down across from him. Sitting at the table put them on equal foot-

BENDING THE ARC

ing. Most men in BJ's position would just as soon have sat behind their desks.

The modesty of the office surprised Shane. He'd expected something more lavish for a president of a company the size of Wildcat. A large mural dominated the far wall. The vivid colors depicted the final moments of the siege at the Alamo, with Davy Crockett and the boys heroically holding back Santa Anna's army.

"Call me BJ. Everyone else does."

"Fine. And Steve will do for me."

"OK, Steve. I'll cut to the chase. You're familiar with our case against the GAC. Those bastards are coming after Wildcat, and for the love of me, I don't know why. You also know Cal Stokes, my lawyer."

Shane nodded.

"Well, Cal's a nice enough guy, and I'm sure he's a pretty decent corporate lawyer. But he's out of his depth on this one. Those slick suits from Todd Ives are chewing us up and just about ready to spit us out if I don't do something fast. Hell, Steve, you know what I'm talking about. I need help."

"Are you asking me if I'll take the case?"

"Well, I sure as hell didn't ask you over for tea. Hell, yes, son, that's what I'm asking. The cases have developed a pretty good profile. It couldn't hurt for you to be associated with them, now could it?" Shane watched BJ massaging his leg.

"Except for setting myself up for a big fall," Shane answered noncommittally. It was important to make BJ push a little.

"Aw, come on, Steve. You think the GAC's full of shit. You said so yourself on *Turbo News*. Don't tell me you're afraid to fight the good fight. For chrissakes, son, think of where we'd be if Davy Crockett, Bill Travis, and Jim Bowie thought like that. You're a goddamn Texan, aren't you?"

Shane grinned inwardly at BJ's analogy. He kind of liked this good 'ol boy. "Well, I didn't say I wouldn't take the case, but I need to know that I'm going to be in control of the legal strategy."

"Sure, son. All I care about is making these goddamn actions go away. I've got a company to run. I'm not going to second-guess y'all on legal strategy as long as you're not doing anything to damage Wildcat. The only problem is, I'll be honest with you, we have a pretty tight legal budget."

"Fair enough, BJ. As for the budget, don't worry about that. I can promise you my team will be available to you for no more than what Mr. Stokes was charging."

BJ looked surprised. "How can y'all offer that?"

"Let's just say we have alternate forms of support. The important thing right now is that you got yourself a new lawyer."

"That's good, son, because we have to be in court this afternoon, and it's a bit of a drive."

18

TEXARKANA, TEXAS

Tuesday
May 1

Madeline Nabors surveyed her courtroom. Designed to elicit awe and respect, the walls were paneled in a rich, dark mahogany with a ceiling that soared thirty feet. At the front, her podium hovered above the room. Dressed in a full-length robe, she peered down at the mere mortals appearing before her.

She watched Cal Stokes fumble at the counsel table. Drowning in a sea of paper, he had no supporting associates, not even a law student. She shifted her gaze to the table across from him, which barely contained the Todd Ives contingent. Drew Tillington sat in the lead chair, flanked on one side by a fellow partner seconding the file, and on the other by two associates. Amongst the four, they had three laptops and half a dozen litigators' briefcases—those wide leather cases with wraparound straps that prevented them from falling apart under their weighty loads. The cases were nicknamed brainbags, although Nabors knew this wasn't always an accurate description of their owners.

She looked up as Stokes launched into his submissions on the first pretrial motion.

"Your Honor, I'm asking you to dismiss the GAC's action for damages as a result of Wildcat's past drilling rig emissions and the ancillary request for a cessation of drilling activities pending an environmental impact study on rig emissions. Wildcat's drilling activities are generally conducted in accordance with applicable environmental laws and regulations. There is simply no legitimate basis on which this court can rule in the plaintiff's favor."

Stokes took another few minutes to make his case. He pitched all the obvious points, banging the podium to make his points. But the legal arguments were uninspired, despite the theatrics. Nabors sighed. She was reminded of the old trial lawyer's saying. *If you have the facts, pound the facts. If you have the law, pound the law. If you have neither, pound the table.* She tried to suppress her annoyance. Stokes was outgunned. While she could try

BENDING THE ARC 143

to balance the scales, there were limits to what she could do. A judge can't call crucial evidence, present convincing witnesses, or test the credibility of witnesses through tough cross-examination.

God help Wildcat Oil and Gas. They clearly needed more than the mediocre, albeit well-intentioned, efforts of Mr. Stokes. Not having questions for Stokes, she looked over at the Todd Ives table.

"Your argument, Mr. Tillington."

"Yes, your Honor. Our position is simple. The test to dismiss an action is a high test indeed. The law does not lightly deny a party its day in court, nor should it. All we need to do here this morning is persuade you that our client has at least an arguable case at law. At least an arguable case."

"I heard you the first time, Counsel." Nabors expected experienced litigators to cut back on the dramatics when arguing before her as opposed to a jury. Apparently, Tillington's flowery style was a second skin he found hard to shed.

"Yes, your Honor." Tillington continued, unfazed.

"Our action is for damage to the environment, or, as we have described it in our petition, *environmental negligence*. The emissions are merely supporting evidence thereof. We submit that the magnitude of the emissions, which will be supported by the evidence you will hear at trial, clearly meets the low threshold test of an arguable case at law. Mr. Stokes carefully argued that the emissions *generally* meet legal requirements. Generally isn't good enough, your Honor. As you know, a case should be dismissed at this early stage only if there is no possibility of the plaintiff receiving a positive decision. It is *impossible* for you to reach that conclusion here."

Nabors was frustrated. She wanted to throw this one out despite the possibility of being overturned on appeal. Unfortunately, she could not do so now.

"Mr. Stokes, any reply?"

"No, your Honor. I don't think Mr. Tillington has said anything that detracts from my original submissions."

Some snickering was heard from the Todd Ives table. Nabors sighed. The last word is worth its weight in gold to a good lawyer, not something to be so cavalierly dismissed as Mr. Stokes just had. Tillington's direct attack on Stokes' main argument regarding *general* compliance with the law made Stokes' silence on reply that much more baffling.

"Thank you, Mr. Stokes. I don't need to reserve on this. Your application for dismissal is denied."

A loud thump rang through the courtroom as BJ, seated beside Stokes, slammed his fist on the

BENDING THE ARC

table. His question to Stokes was loud enough for Nabors to hear, "Goddamn it, Cal. We're going to trial?"

"Mr. Stokes, please control your client. And yes, Mr. Whitter, this action is going to trial. Mr. Stokes, you have a second motion?"

Cal got to his feet.

Nabors listened, unimpressed. Tillington made another convincing rebuttal. He had a sharp delivery, even injecting some humor. Similar to the first motion, he presented the second action as a general one for environmental negligence, with the oil spill merely providing supportive evidence thereof.

When she dismissed the second motion as perfunctorily as the first, the pained expression on Mr. Whitter's face did not escape her.

"Unless there's anything else, we stand . . . "

"One moment, your Honor." Heads turned as a deep voice resonated through the courtroom. Shane strode up to the defendant's table. Tillington stared in confusion.

Shane and BJ huddled with Stokes, who then turned to address the court.

"Your Honor, my client is exercising its right to replace counsel. I hereby request that my name be struck from the record. My colleague, Mr. Steven Shane, will take it from here."

Shane addressed Nabors. "Good morning, your Honor. I respectfully request to be instated as counsel of record for Wildcat Oil and Gas. I'd also like to request a brief continuance on the present applications so that I might familiarize myself with the relevant facts and issues."

Nabors breathed a sigh of relief. She knew Shane as a first-rate litigator.

"I accept your recusal from the proceedings, Mr. Stokes. Welcome aboard, Mr. Shane. Mr. Tillington, any comments on the requested continuance?"

"A moment, please, your Honor." Tillington huddled with his small army.

Too many cooks. Tillington said something that caused the group to snicker.

"You want to share the hilarity, Mr. Tillington?"

"Nothing of note, your Honor. We have no objection to a continuance, though we trust it will be brief."

"Thank you."

Nabors looked over at Shane. "Six days enough?"

"Yes, thank you, your Honor."

"Fine. We'll reconvene on Monday, 9:00 a.m. Court is adjourned."

19

HOUSTON, TEXAS

Friday
May 4

BJ entered his office to see an attractive woman with distinctive red hair gazing at the sign from the state's latest anti-litter campaign, *Don't Mess With Texas!* For BJ, it was a slogan to live by. Marge must have escorted her from reception. She often did that to save him the trip.

"Ms. Nelson, BJ Whitter. Pleasure to meet you. Hope you haven't been waiting too long."

"Not at all, Mr. Whitter. I was just admiring the artwork." She gestured at the Alamo mural.

BJ nodded. "Those were the days, Ms. Nelson. People knew right from wrong. Men stood up and were counted when the chips were down."

"And men were men, women were women?" Jenn asked with a smile.

"No offense. I suppose I'm right out of Jurassic Park. At least that's what my wife used to say."

"She must have been a wise woman."

"Yeah." BJ's eyes misted slightly. "Charlene was a helluva gal. Didn't deserve to get cut down by cancer the way she was. Hell, I'm the guy smokin' all the stogies. Just goes to show you life's one hell of a crazy ride. Doesn't make a whole lot of sense sometimes."

Jenn's tone softened at the display of vulnerability. "Just know this, Mr. Whitter. I was head of my class at Quantico and a top agent at the Bureau, *not* through affirmative action but through merit. I put in my time, paid my dues, and caught my share of bad guys. So, let's get over this boy/girl stuff and see if we can't deal with business, OK?"

BJ looked straight into her eyes and saw the steely resolve. *What a firebrand!*

"Touché, Ms. Nelson. My apologies. Let's start over. I'm really not that bad. Call me BJ, by the way. Everyone else does."

Jenn appeared to relax. "OK, BJ, and I'm Jenn. Ms. Nelson is my mother." She gave him a warm smile.

BENDING THE ARC 149

"So, why did you want to talk to me?"

"Steve tells me you run the investigative side of his practice."

"Yes, sir."

BJ walked over to his desk and pulled out a map. He motioned for Jenn to join him. "This is the land surrounding one of our oil wildcats. A wildcat is . . ."

"An exploratory well drilled in virgin territory," Jenn ended his sentence for him. "I'm a Texas gal, BJ. My dad worked the rigs. I'm familiar with oil patch jargon."

He was starting to like this lady. "Good. It'll make things that much easier. Nice to hear you're grounded. I thought all FBI agents were easterners." He gave her a good-natured smile before continuing.

"So we just finished drilling this wildcat—Buffalo Thirty-Six—and got the well on test, when Forestry calls the other day to tell us they're shutting down our access road."

"Why? I assume you have all your permits?"

"Yeah, sure, of course. This is a multi-million dollar well. We don't take any risks when that kind of money's on the line. Forestry found a falcon nest during incubating season within one hundred yards of one of our creek crossings."

"Nobody noticed it when the road was surveyed?"

"Well, that's just it. Forestry didn't notice it, and they do their own surveys. We didn't notice it, and we're pretty careful about these things. We always have crews running detailed environmental surveys before we finalize the route. And this damn nest isn't like a robin's. I mean, the thing's two *feet* in diameter. And it's in a tree right on the goddamn bank of the creek."

"Well, isn't it still possible they just missed it? People do make mistakes."

"I'd say possible, but highly improbable. Mistakes, sure, but not like that. And the kicker is the way Forestry found out about it. They got an anonymous call on one of their hotlines."

He saw her raise an eyebrow at the last bit. "That is strange."

"Tell me about it. Look, my men have secured the site. Do you think y'all could get out there and have a look?"

"Sure," Jenn agreed.

"We need to get that road opened up. For now, we're using a chopper to supply the site, but we can't airlift the test oil. We'll have to shut down soon if we can't get to the bottom of this."

Jenn stood up. "I know what's at stake, BJ. I'll get on it right away."

20

BIG THICKET, TEXAS

Sunday
May 6

Magruder gazed at the rugged terrain of the Big Thicket. They were flying uncomfortably close to the ground. Despite the darkness, he could make out the occasional well sites and pumpjack pads that interrupted nature's raw beauty. During the first decade of the twentieth century, thousands of wildcatters poured into the Thicket, searching for petroleum deposits. When oil was discovered, boom towns sprang up overnight. The crude early drilling methods, combined with the neglect of the operators, left telltale scars that took decades to heal.

But Buffalo 36 was located in undisturbed terrain, far from past discoveries, where the Wildcat Oil and Gas team obviously thought there was undiscovered potential.

The Bell 206B JetRanger eased its way into a small clearing. The pilot waited a scant fifteen feet above the ground before turning on his landing light. He touched down lightly. Magruder hopped out, squatting as the chopper lifted off, killing its light when it cleared the site.

He waited for the noise to fade into the cool Texas night. After a few minutes, his night vision returned. The omnipresent crickets chirped their nighttime concert. He wore a black jumpsuit and carried a small black rucksack. After tightening his boots, he started off. His watch read 1:15 a.m.

Within half an hour he'd reached the edge of the lease site, lit with powerful floodlights. He spied two lookouts patrolling the perimeter. Security was tight. Espionage in the oil patch was not uncommon. Magruder knew that scouts watching a drill site could glean a lot of information.

When wells were being drilled, scouts could count the drill stem lengths as the bit was being changed and estimate the well's depth. During testing, scouts could count and time the trucks leaving the site to get a rough estimate of the flow rate of the well being tested. To address such industrial spy tactics, companies took several countermeasures, including hiring security companies to patrol their sites.

Magruder's boots squished in the swampy ground as he crouched behind a tree, studying the rig with his binoculars. He shivered in the cool breeze. *Texas nights can still be damn cold in the spring.* All the drill pipe was racked. The engines that powered the turntable were idle. Hoses were hooked up to the wellhead, with several trucks parked close to the rig. *Of course!* All those trucks he'd seen the other night on the access road weren't hauling water. They were hauling *oil*. The goddamn well was on test! It was at total depth. That made the job so much sweeter. While his original target was one of the mud tanks, an oil tank would be much better.

With the drilling engines idled, he was thankful for the cover provided by the roar of the diesel engines from the light plant. Studying the guards, he calculated they were on a regular schedule, looping the site every quarter hour. Two large holding tanks stood on the far side of the lease. Each tank had a capacity of three thousand barrels of oil.

He skirted the rig, taking care to stay clear of the geologist's trailer. Waiting for a guard to pass, he crept up to the first tank and circled it, searching for the outlet flange. On older models, the tank level was still determined using a measuring gauge from the top—essentially a giant dipstick.

These tanks, however, were state-of-the-art. Next to the outlet flange was a digital gauge displaying the tank's liquid level. The tank was almost empty. He crawled to the second tank and located the gauge and outlet flange quickly this time. *Yesss.* The tank was full.

He removed his rucksack, took out a pair of latex gloves and slipped them on. Then he reached into the pack and carefully pulled out a plastique charge. The preset timer had a fifteen-day delay, which was not a problem in this environment. Without being able to be everywhere at once, he relied on timers to ensure the movements of his symphony of destruction played out in their proper sequence. He placed the charge under the lip of the outlet valve, well out of sight of probing eyes.

Damn! He felt a sharp pain in his finger and grabbed the pipe running from the outlet valve to keep from falling backward. His hand had caught on a bolt on the underside of the valve. He saw it ripped his glove and left a slight flesh wound. *No matter.* He always carried a spare pair. Peeling off the glove, he replaced it and finished securing the timer.

The charge was assembled to ensure it left no trace. Only one tank was rigged. Having both tanks fail would be a dead giveaway. He'd been careful to place the charge, which was as small as he could make it while still large enough to do the job, flush against the weld connecting the outlet flange to the tank. The failure needed to be bad enough to drain the tank before it could be fixed. A slow leak would be detected and repaired without serious damage. As per environmental code, the tanks were in a bermed area, ensuring minor leaks were contained.

He cocked his head, picking up a faint sound over the rumble of the light plant. *Whump . . . whump . . . whump.* He trained his binoculars toward the noise. In a few minutes, he saw the outline of a Bell 212. *Why the hell were they using a machine the size of a 212?*

Damn! He almost dropped the binoculars in the bright flash of the helo's landing light. While momentarily blinded, he knew being outside the main perimeter he was safe from detection.

The cone of light grew focused as the chopper approached the landing pad. He watched five men hop out and unload crates of supplies. They connected hoses to tanks Magruder hadn't noticed before. Each tank was mounted to one of the chopper's skids. *Of course.* Magruder kicked himself for not factoring the possibility of chopper traffic into his plans. Wildcat was airlifting supplies and water to keep the test going. *Smart bastards.* Figured they could get around the access road blockade. Well, the blockade was still useful. Without it, the holding tank wouldn't have been full.

He waited for things to settle down. After twenty minutes, they disconnected the hoses from the chopper's skid tanks. Four rig hands climbed in as the pilot cranked the rotors for takeoff.

After the helo was clear, Magruder backed off into the night and retraced his steps. With his satellite-based GPS system, he could navigate to within a few feet. About a mile from the lease site, he pulled out his radio and tuned into the preset frequency. "Fox One to Skybird, Fox One to Skybird."

The response was immediate. "This is Skybird. What is your ETA, Fox One?"

"Ten minutes."

"Roger."

The entire conversation took less than six seconds. The chopper had flown back to a holding spot twenty miles from the lease site. It would return to the clearing in precisely ten minutes. Magruder would be waiting.

It had been a productive evening. Something his client would surely agree with in a few weeks' time, when he received another "update" on Magruder's progress through the press.

21

TEXARKANA, TEXAS

Monday
May 7

Shane watched Nabors peering down at him. "Mr. Shane. I see from your motion that you are now up to speed on these actions. I'll hear you on that motion now."

"Yes, your Honor. I won't repeat the points raised in my brief. We believe the case to consolidate the two GAC actions, one for unlawful emissions and one for an oil spill, is made most compellingly by Mr. Tillington himself."

Tillington looked up quizzically.

"You may recall, your Honor, that in arguing against the motions for dismissal made by my predecessor, Mr. Stokes, the plaintiff changed direction. No longer did we have one action based on emissions and another based on an oil spill. No, suddenly we had two actions for environmental negligence, with the emissions and oil spill being merely supportive evidence of this principal claim. So, Mr. Tillington himself has told you he has two actions for the *same* claim."

Nabors tapped her pencil. Shane was aware of the old judge's dictum - *be clear, be brief, be gone*.

"Those are my submissions, your Honor, subject to any questions you may have."

"Thank you, Mr. Shane. No questions. Mr. Tillington?"

Tillington caucused with his team. Another Todd Ives group discussion.

"Mr. Tillington, I'm waiting."

"Yes, your Honor. We have no objection to streamlining this litigation and indeed would like to do what we can to further that objective. We support Mr. Shane's motion."

Nabors nodded curtly. "I agree, Mr. Tillington. Your cases are against the same defendant and your principal claim in both cases, as you pointed out, is similar, if not the same. Cases consolidated."

"Anything more before we wrap up here today?"

Shane rose. "Your Honor, I kept this for last because it depended somewhat on the outcome of the motion. I'm now filing in this consolidated action a counterclaim against the GAC for damages in the amount of fifty million dollars for libel, defamation, and legal harassment."

Excited murmurs rippled through the courtroom. Nabors banged her gavel.

Tillington was on his feet. "Your Honor, this is trial by ambush. We had no notice of this counterclaim. This is highly inappropriate."

Shane noticed the pen in Tillington's hand clicking furiously in unison with his submissions. Nabors was looking at him to see if he had any reply.

"Your Honor, we are still within the required time limits. We could have filed a counterclaim a few days ago, once in each action, but we awaited the outcome of the consolidation motion because we thought it would be more efficient to file once."

Nabors nodded at Tillington. "That's true, Mr. Tillington. The defendants are within their rights." She glanced at Shane. "I want to warn *both* of you I expect this action to be conducted in strict accordance with the rules of court and with due expedition. I urge you to proceed with your discoveries in a timely manner. And let's make a serious attempt not to try this case in the media. We stand adjourned."

BJ jumped from the table. "Hot damn, son. I like your style." Shane felt his lungs compress as BJ wrapped him in a bear hug.

"Take it easy, BJ. This is just the start. Remember, we're playing the long game."

"Yeah, but for the first time I feel like we have a chance."

Shane silently thanked Hendrix. He called a few days before to stress the need to shift the momentum. It was his idea to apply counter pressure to take away the 'no downside' aspect for the GAC.

Tillington stopped at their table. "Congratulations, Mr. Shane. Enjoy the moment. I assure you when this trial is over, today will have been your high-water mark." He turned and strode away, followed dutifully by the rest of team Todd Ives.

BJ chuckled. "I don't think our friend Tillington likes you."

"Yeah, well, the feeling's mutual." Shane felt energized. He recognized the sensation that always signaled the waiting was over and the battle engaged.

22

WASHINGTON, D.C.

Tuesday
May 8

Hendrix was proud of what they had achieved in short order. He wasted no time or expense in setting up the LawForce Washington control center. While Shane maintained his small-time law firm image in Houston, for LawForce to achieve its true potential, Shane would need support off-site. LawForce was set up on two floors of downtown Washington office space. The lease was in the name of Hendley Enterprises Inc., an import-export cover company.

The main communications center comprised multiple high-definition displays and an interactive whiteboard. It also featured a sophisticated telephony system that supported both traditional phone lines and Voice over Internet Protocol (VoiP) technology.

Video conferencing capabilities enabled virtual meetings with participants from across the globe. High-definition cameras, noise-canceling microphones, and dedicated video conferencing software ensured a smooth and immersive communication experience.

Security was paramount. Biometric access controls, surveillance cameras, and encrypted communication safeguarded sensitive information. Firewalls, antivirus software, and regular security audits further enhanced the center's resilience against cyber threats.

The installation of a direct communications link to Shane's Houston office included dedicated fax machines, phone lines, and a secure e-mail connection. Several offices occupied the lower floor. The nerve center on the second floor was like a large newsroom with no interior walls. The layout comprised a wide-open war room surrounded by tables and computers. In the middle was an oval conference table with a large video screen looming over one end.

With a dozen people working the computers and phones, the room hummed with activity. The team included several lawyers seconded

BENDING THE ARC

from Justice, a few FBI special agents, and some senior staffers from the EPA. The lawyers and FBI agents would form part of LawForce's core personnel, while the EPA staffers were on loan specifically for the GAC litigation.

Jenn's face filled the video feed, with Shane's law library visible in the background.

"Mr. Hendrix, I need some help."

"What can we do for you, Ms. Nelson?"

"Jenn—please, it's Jenn. What I need is a first-rate biologist. Someone who's good in the field."

"Any other qualifications, *Jennifer*?"

Jenn chuckled at Hendrix's emphasis. "Jennifer, I can live with. You'll learn that I'm not the formal type, Mr. Hendrix. What we're looking for is an ornithologist, familiar with species found in Texas, specifically the Big Thicket. Can you help us?"

"Of course. That's what LawForce is all about. We have a few people from the EPA assisting us. Just a moment, please." Hendrix beckoned for one of the EPA staffers to join him in front of the video feed.

"Jennifer, this is Michael O'Day. He's with the EPA."

Hendrix turned to the young man next to him. He'd chosen Michael on the strong recommendation of his old college roommate, now head of the EPA, emphasizing Michael's intelligence and passion for his work. With a lean physique and very fit, Hendrix guessed Michael spent most of his time in the field. That would excuse the beard and jeans. Hendrix pulled him over and whispered, "Just give her some background so she knows you know what you are talking about."

Mike turned to face Jenn. "Ms. Nelson, er, Jenn, I have a PhD in biology and did my thesis on bald eagles. I've done my share of field work. I was in charge of an extensive six-year field study on the bald eagle in Alaska before I copped out and got a desk job back here in DC. So how can I help you?"

Jenn appeared impressed.

"You guys don't waste any time. Just a coincidence that you were recruited for LawForce, Mr. O'Day?"

"Well, let's face it. This is an environmental lawsuit. You're on my turf. When Mr. Hendrix went ahead with the GAC, he knew he needed to involve us. We've got a team back at the EPA taking apart the GAC allegations, and, frankly, we've been waiting for you to call. By the way, it's Mike to you and the rest of the world save for our formal friend, Mr. Hendrix."

"All right, Mike, I need you to fly down and bring a field team with you. I'll brief you on the specifics when you get here. Meanwhile, keep your team working on those actions. We'll be going into discoveries soon, and would greatly appreciate any ammunition you can get for us to use against their experts."

"Sure, can do."

23

BIG THICKET, TEXAS

Friday
May 11

Amazed at how quickly the trip to the Buffalo 36 nest site was arranged, Jenn hung on as their Jeep flew down the gravel road, trailing a swirling dust tunnel that hung in the sultry air. Mike geared down for the next curve.

"What the hell's wrong with the people who put in these roads? We're miles from anywhere, on land as flat as a pancake, and the damn road curves around like a wounded snake. *Jesus!*"

Jenn laughed. She was starting to like this mad scientist.

BENDING THE ARC

"Actually, Mike, the oil companies put these curves in on purpose. The well operators who drive these roads every day love to push their pickups to the max. The companies got tired of the high accident rates and disability benefits they were paying out because of all the rollovers. Putting in a curve every couple of miles keeps the operators honest."

"No kidding." Mike shook his head.

Jenn glanced at the backseat. Two kids from the EPA sat stiffly, clutching their armrests. "Almost there," she said reassuringly. To keep them engaged, she turned to the young lady with the large, circular lenses who was the expert on falcons.

"Leslie, can you tell me a bit more about this species that might help me figure out what is going on here?"

"Absolutely, Ms. Lopez." Leslie was only too happy to concentrate on something other than the road. She spoke at a machine-gun pace, with an undeniable passion for her subject.

"It is a bit of a puzzle. You have to understand that Northern Aplomado Falcons are raptors. They're known for their slender build and striking plumage. The thing is, they look for open landscapes for their nests. This"—she waved her arm in an arc at the window—"vegetation is quite dense, not where you would expect to find them.

"Their nests are typically located high in the canopies of sturdy trees like pines or oaks, with a good vantage point that is both strategic for hunting and safe from ground predators. Often, you'll find their nests near the edge of the forest, where the trees thin out and give way to open fields. This allows them to swiftly launch into the open air in pursuit of prey, taking advantage of the clear sightlines and minimal obstructions. The nest itself is a sizable structure of twigs and branches, lined with softer materials like grass, leaves, and feathers, ensuring a comfortable and insulated environment for the falcon's eggs and chicks."

Clearly warming to her subject, Jenn was happy to see Leslie had all but forgotten the rough ride as she continued to gush, finally finding an audience for what folks all too often considered a mundane topic.

"During the breeding season, like now, the falcon's nest is a busy place. The male and female share responsibilities, with the male hunting and bringing food, while the female tends to the eggs and, later, the chicks."

The Jeep careened around another corner and entered the thin forest at the edge of the Big Thicket National Preserve.

"Thanks, Leslie, that is helpful." Jenn turned to face the front and looked over at Matt.

"OK, Mario Andretti, slow it down. We'll get to the roadblock in another couple of miles."

They parked in a small glade just in front of the barrier across the road with the sign:

> **ROAD CLOSED BY ORDER OF TEXAS DEPARTMENT OF FORESTRY**
>
> **NO VEHICLES BEYOND THIS POINT**
>
> **TRESPASSERS WILL BE PROSECUTED**

Mike pulled a large pack from the Jeep.

"Lead on, fearless leader, lead on."

Jenn led them up the road to the Beaver Creek crossing, then a short distance through the brush to the creek at the base of the tree holding the nest.

Mike motioned to the others. "Give me some room here, people. Whose tracks are these?" he asked, pointing at the hodgepodge of footprints in the soft, muddy creek bank.

Jenn shrugged. "I imagine they're from Forestry's visit. They checked out the nest after getting the anonymous call. They didn't shut down the road until after they made their own assessment."

Mike looked up at the nest and frowned. "This isn't where a Northern Aplomado Falcon would nest. Not so near to water. Leslie is right. They prefer grasslands, and they don't build their own nests. They're too lazy for that. They inhabit stick nests built by other birds, usually hawks. I need to get a better look."

He shinnied up and wedged himself in the tree's fork, next to the nest. After a few minutes, he shouted down to Jenn. "This is interesting. What the hell are eagle feathers doing in an Aplomado Falcon's nest?"

He poked around at the edge of the nest and dropped a line to one of his assistants below. "Hook my pack to the line, would you, please?"

He hauled up the pack and pulled out a test kit. Placing a small feather in a vial, he added some liquid from a flask and shook it violently for a minute.

"Human hands have touched this feather."

"How can you tell?" Jenn shouted.

"Acid test. The human body secretes all sorts of acids. While feathers are water repellent, they will show micro traces of these acids if they're touched by human hands."

"So what?" Jenn was puzzled. "The Forestry folks were probably poking around up there. What's that prove?"

"I took this feather from *inside* the side of the nest. I pulled it out by its tip. The part I tested was buried in the wall."

Jenn frowned, looking up at him. "I'll be damned. This case is getting more interesting by the minute."

24

GULF OF MEXICO

Wednesday
May 16

"Wow!" Standing in the wheelhouse, Phil Desmond stared in awe at the silhouette looming in the distance. "I didn't know these things were so big."

The cabin cruiser rocked from side to side in the rough chop of the Gulf as it approached the large drilling rig. Seemingly invincible, the soaring structure was an impressive sight in the black of night. With marine safety lights running to the top of the derrick tower, it resembled a massive, well-adorned Christmas tree. The luminescent watch dial glowed 2:30

a.m., near the middle of the graveyard shift. The day shift wouldn't provide relief for another five and a half hours. Magruder chose the time carefully. Although the rig was well lit, anyone on the rig floor would struggle to see anything gazing into the dark sea below. And at midshift, the number of active personnel was minimal.

"Yeah, well, there's a lot you don't know, boy." Magruder questioned for a moment his choice of Desmond for this assignment. Stretching full length, Magruder's powerful muscles flexed as he reached around to pull a black wetsuit out of a gear bag. He grunted as he wrestled into it. *Added a few pounds since the last time.*

Magruder was a lone wolf. When he needed help on a mission, he chose fresh blood. The trick was to find someone intelligent enough to do the job, but not overly bright.

He watched Desmond continuing to stare at the rig as it grew larger. "I still don't understand how these things can float out here in this kind of weather."

Magruder shrugged. This gap-toothed kid fit the not overly bright criteria. They were dealing with a jack-up rig, with its four support columns seated firmly on the ocean floor. The only thing floating was Desmond's brain.

He felt the shock of the cold water as a large wave washed over the side of the cruiser, sloshing around the black dry bags at the bottom of the boat.

"Goddamn it, boy! I said keep her turned into the wind."

"Sorry."

Magruder shook his head as he opened the first dry bag and checked its contents. Satisfied, he walked into the wheelhouse, squinting in the brightness of the approaching lights. In a few minutes, he gestured at the throttle. "Ease it up, boy, we're getting close."

Within half a mile of the rig, Magruder tapped Desmond on the shoulder. "Kill the engine and lights." Desmond pulled back the throttle and the cruiser settled in the water.

"Give me your watch." Magruder held it up to his own. He adjusted Desmond's and handed it back.

"OK. Two forty-five. Don't leave this spot until I'm back no matter what happens, understand?"

"Yeah, sure." Desmond shrugged.

Didn't look like the kid appreciated how serious he was. "If you're not here when I get back, you are a dead man. Is that clear?"

"Chill. I'll be here."

Magruder stepped off the diving ramp. He puckered at the salt water as he adjusted his snorkel. About five hundred yards from the rig, he exchanged the snorkel for a regulator and slipped beneath the surface. He could only see a few yards in the murky water, zeroing in on the glow from the rig lights.

Flaig told him the rig was staffed twenty-four hours a day. Magruder recalled his blunt declaration that loss of life was at Magruder's discretion. *A real cold fish.*

He checked the timed charges, set at ten days. As part of his due diligence, Magruder learned of plans to increase security for the rig through an electronic alert system that would include motion sensors and laser security. That made it necessary to get in now.

The extended lead time increased the risks of detection and degradation of the charges from the environment. Magruder weighed those risks against the need to coordinate the blowout as part of a larger program. He smiled to himself. And what a program! *He was a fucking genius.* At the end of this, if everything went off without a hitch—and Magruder had no doubts on that count—he'd apply a premium.

This wasn't your run-of-the-mill op, this was a goddamn symphony of environmental sabotage—a sequence of seemingly random events, jigsaw pieces that would achieve their goal with no one, beyond Magruder and Flaig, knowing how they all fit together.

Arriving at the first platform leg, he moved to the inside of the column. While it was doubtful anyone could see him from the deck fifty feet above, he preferred to play it safe. Rising to the surface, he pulled himself up on a barnacle-encrusted support girder and caught his breath. His watch read three-ten. Right on schedule.

Dragging four dry bags behind him in the water, he hauled up the first one. Carefully pulling out one of three small blocks of plastic explosive, he wedged it between a cross brace on one girder of the triangular support leg. He repeated the procedure with the other two blocks of C-4, attaching one to each girder. Next, he wired them together and connected the timer.

As he lowered himself back into the water, he heard a splash from the other side of the rig. A beam pierced the darkness, fanning the far-side support legs. He froze, listening to muted voices from above. He waited five minutes, but there was no further activity.

While he could bring the platform down by only taking out one support leg if he used a massive charge, the real trick was making it look like a mechanical failure. That meant using the explosives sparingly and shaping them so the supports wouldn't appear blown off. The initial charge would be just large enough to break the first support and strain the surviving three. He set the charge on the second support, the one that would bring the platform down, to go off fifteen minutes later. Not only would this give nonessential personnel time to abandon the rig, it would also create a more realistic scenario of structural failure. The primary partial failure would be blamed on metal fatigue, while the secondary full failure would be attributed to the resultant overloading of the remaining supports.

He swam to the second support and repeated the procedure. After finishing, he reached around and clipped the empty dry bag to his belt. *This wasn't that hard.*

The last piece was the trickiest. He had to set a small charge to take out the hydraulic controls operating the rig's emergency blowout preventers—BOPs. He hauled himself out of the water onto a narrow deck and took off his fins. A ladder led to the platform surrounding the drill string. He winced as the cold steel rungs dug into his bare feet. Safely reaching the platform, he followed the gangway to the BOP control panel.

Holding the remaining dry bags in one hand, he pulled out the last charge. As he did so, the bags squirted from his grasp. He watched them fall out of sight, hearing them splash lightly as they hit the sea. *Damn!* He took a few minutes to assess the situation and seriously considered going after them, but it wasn't worth it. He'd been careful to use standard-issue detonators that were routinely used in the oilfield industry. Still, losing the spare detonators irritated him. He hated deviations from the plan, no matter how trivial. *Plan the dive and dive the plan.* But he still had what he needed. He carefully placed the last charge.

The piercing siren almost knocked him into the water. *What the hell?* He was relieved to hear the announcement.

"All hands, all hands, we are on Condition Heavy Weather One, Condition Heavy Weather One. Activate HW1 protocols immediately."

Looking down, Magruder saw the ocean chop had developed into a nasty swell. He checked his watch—five after four. *Getting tight.* That delay with the dropped bags encroached on the comfort zone and now this developing storm. He took two deep breaths. *Not to worry.* There was still time to get back to the cabin cruiser and well out of the area by daybreak.

Submerging into the heavy waves, he swam toward the cruiser, propelling himself with strong, even kicks of his fins. After five minutes, he surfaced, searching for the cruiser's lights. By four fifteen, he was concerned. *This is a damn big ocean.* He held up his waterproof flashlight, signaling in a wide sweep away from the rig. Nothing. Then, off to the left, a flash. *All right!*

In another five minutes, he was pulling himself up the steps at the back of the cruiser, bucking like a bronc in the storm. "Let's get the hell out of Dodge." Desmond put the cruiser in gear and turned for the coast.

Magruder smiled. This crew would soon have a new appreciation for the expression *crack of dawn*.

25

HOUSTON, TEXAS

Thursday
May 17

Shane popped the last bite of sincronizada into his mouth and grimaced. It was a corn tortilla, not flour as he preferred. Lee must have ordered quesadillas by mistake. He sat back from the table and stretched. Files and stacks of law books surrounded Val. The boardroom served as the war room for the GAC litigation. He waved his arm around the room. "What a mess."

They'd taken over the rest of the top floor of the three-story office building. Shane wanted plenty of room, including several vacant offices for their Washington visitors. He was winding down his practice, referring his clients to reputable colleagues. LawForce was a full-time job.

"Hey, you!" Val laughed as Gus gallumped down the hall toward her. With his trademark lack of coordination, his three legs became entangled, and he did two somersaults before rolling to a stop at her feet.

She stared down at the furry bundle. "You OK, Gus?"

He peeked up at her and gave a yip.

She pulled him onto her lap. "You're such a klutz, aren't you?"

Shane often brought Gus into the office. He was good company. But they had work to do. He looked up from the Texas Code he was reviewing.

"Val, it looks to me like the rig emissions are within allowable tolerances and the oil spill was too small to qualify as an Actionable Discharge under the Texas Natural Resources Code. I don't think the GAC can scientifically support its claims."

Stroking Gus's silky coat, Val looked at him. "I just sent you an email from a guy named Mike O'Day. He's with the EPA. Jenn asked him to look into this for us. You want to have a look. It's pretty impressive."

Shane opened his laptop and reviewed the email with its attached report. "Wow, lots of detail here." As he skimmed the Excel spreadsheet, he saw it contained comprehensive statistics of Wildcat's rig emissions and the oil spill. The EPA was expert at analyzing such releases. It confirmed Shane's suspicions they were free and clear of the legislative limits. In the normal course, they would never get an expert report in such short order.

He heard a sharp yelp and looked up to see Gus squirming in Val's lap. She set him down and they watched him wobble off. He picked up speed, failed to negotiate the turn at the end of the hall, and thumped into the wall. They couldn't help laughing out loud. Gus turned to give them a dirty look, yelped once more, and turned the corner.

Shane grinned at Val. "Lucky for that mutt he's got rubber bones."

Shane returned his attention to the computer screen, reviewing Mike's data. This LawForce concept was something else—like being a small-time country with the ability to draw on that pinnacle of military might, an aircraft carrier. LawForce was the ultimate legal aircraft carrier, at his beck and call.

After finishing his review, Shane reached for the video console. "Let's try out this newfangled setup and see if we can get this guy O'Day on the line. I'd like to ask him a few questions."

In a minute they were looking over the boardroom table in Washington, also piled high with papers and books. Shane noted a blinking light and heard the buzzer announcing the incoming call in Washington. He saw a man sitting at the boardroom table look up at the screen.

"Hi. My name's Mike O'Day."

"Mike, I'm Steve Shane, this is my partner, Val Lopez. You sent us those stats this morning. Thanks for that."

Mike grinned. "No sweat. You gotta like this technology, don't you? Instantly puts a face to a name."

"That's not always so great," Val noted.

"Yeah, well, in your case I'd say it's pretty darn great."

Shane's tone was cool. "Hey, let's stick to business, shall we? Mike, we just wanted to touch base and get your input on something."

"Shoot."

"In your experience, would it be abnormal for a company to discharge the kind of emissions Wildcat is releasing from its drilling operations?"

Mike was unequivocal. "No."

"And the spill from that barge. Is that unusual in the scheme of things?"

A little more equivocal this time, Mike looked up at the screen. "What you have to understand is that these types of ships do leak from time to time. It's not good, but it happens more often than people think. The amounts involved here are not out of the norm. The legislative fine acts as a deterrent in addition to recovering the cost of the clean-up. But at the end of the day, I'd say most operators in the Gulf routinely experience these kinds of low-level incidents."

Shane looked at Val to see if she had anything. She shook her head.

"OK, thanks Mike. We're on the same page. Just wanted to hear it from an expert."

Just as they got off the call, Lee poked her head in the door. "Steve, I have a Drew Tillington on Line Two for you."

Val got up, but Shane signaled her to stay.

"Hello, Drew. You're on speakerphone with my partner, Val Lopez. What can we do for you?"

"Nice to meet you, Ms. Lopez. Steve, my client has instructed me to table a settlement offer."

Shane looked at Val with raised eyebrows. To talk settlement before discovery was unusual. Any smoking guns usually turned up in the discovery process. But a good litigator had to know when to when to fold 'em just as much as when to hold 'em. Apparently, the weakness of the GAC's case had become clear to Tillington.

"Drew, you realize we have a counterclaim. I doubt whether my client is interested in a settlement. What did you have in mind?"

"A five-million-dollar payment from Wildcat to the GAC, with no admission of guilt. The GAC abandons the action. Wildcat drops the counterclaim. Both parties execute full and final reciprocal releases."

Shane's response was swift. "That's unacceptable, and you know it. I'll take it to my client, but I have to tell you that I'm going to strongly advise against it."

"Do what you have to do, Counselor. The offer stands for one week. The paperwork is being FedExed to you as we speak."

26

BIG THICKET, TEXAS

Monday
May 21

The plastique went off at 2:00 a.m. The charge was weak, just enough to blow out the intake valve at the weld, with the valve still dangling from the tank. The explosion wasn't loud enough to be heard over the engines of the light plant. Oil gushed through the opening. Within minutes, it breached the bermed holding area, seeping onto the lease and into the Thicket. In fifteen minutes, the tank was empty.

Danny Pearson was the first to see it. "Mr. Davis?" He tapped Cutter on the shoulder, pointing to the oil.

Jesus, Lord Almighty! "Danny, we're on our Emergency Response Plan as of now! Go cut the engines at the light plant." Cutter knew those engines weren't bermed and could be in contact with the spilled oil. Thank god he'd decided to work the graveyard shift.

He rushed to the service hands running the production test. "We've gotta shut this baby in *now*! If that oil catches, we've had it."

They nodded. "You can shut her in. Our instruments aren't in the way."

Cutter ran back to the control room and hit the kill switch operating the hydraulic wellhead valve. The flow meter bled off to zero. *Good.* At least no more oil was flowing into the tanks.

Cutter couldn't figure it out. Clearly a tank failed, but with such a rapid discharge? It didn't compute. These tanks were solid and checked regularly. And the two tanks at Buffalo 36 were virtually new. He glanced out the control room window just as the lease site went black. Danny was at the light plant.

There was an emergency generator located off the main lease site, behind bermed walls. Once Cutter got the backup generator going and some lights back on the site, he called the service crew and Danny into the trailer.

"Listen up, people. We have to contain this fast. Danny, I want you to use the cat and put up some holding walls at the side of the lease. We

BENDING THE ARC

can't do anything about the stuff that's already escaped, but let's make sure that we hold it from here on in."

He turned to the service crew. "I know it's not in your contract, but I need your help. We're into our ERP now. I need you guys to hook up a couple of hoses to the vacuum truck and start sucking up the oil. When you fill the truck, you can transfer the oil to the second tank."

"Will it hold any more oil?" Danny asked.

Cutter nodded. "As luck would have it, the full tank failed. The second tank is only a third full." He motioned the men out of the trailer. "OK, let's get going!"

When they'd cleared out, Cutter reached for the Houston hotline.

"Wildcat Oil and Gas." The nighttime answering service took the call.

"Yeah, this is Bill Davis at the Buffalo Thirty-Six lease site. We have an emergency oil spill. I want you to activate the ERP for a code three response. It's in your red emergency manual. After that, I need you to call Phil Leeson, wake him up, and get him to call me back."

"Yes, sir. What's your number there, sir?"

"Just tell him to call Cutter out at Buffalo Thirty-Six. He's got the number."

"Very well, sir. I'll call him right away."

"Make sure you activate the ERP first."

"Yes, sir."

While waiting for the call back, Cutter checked his watch: two-twelve. The chopper ferrying supplies would be about halfway to the site. "Buffalo Base to Eagle One, Buffalo Base to Eagle One, come in. Over."

"This is Eagle One. Go ahead. Over."

"Eagle One, we need you to head over to the main supply depot. We've had a spill out here, and we're going to need you to ferry in some containment equipment. We're operating under our ERP. Call me from the depot, and I'll confirm what we need. You'll have to bring in some of Leeson's environmental response people as well. Over."

"Roger that, Buffalo Base. We're only ten minutes out. Do you have any casualties? Over."

"Negative, Eagle One. We don't need you to land here. We need you to get the ERP supplies. Over."

"Ten-four, Buffalo Base. We're heading to the depot. We'll call you on the landline from there. Over and out."

Cutter felt sick. He was proud of his operation. Before the spill, his lease site was pristine, exceeding all environmental codes. The industry had come a long way in the last few decades. When Cutter started in the oil fields, it was common for rigs to flow their spent drilling fluids into unlined sump pits that were simply bulldozed over. Today,

BENDING THE ARC

great care was taken to contain all fluids and reclaim sites to pre-drilling condition. *Yeah. They'd come a long way, baby.* But now this.

He watched the crew hook up the hoses. They were knee-deep in crude. *What a mess!* He saw the blinking red light a second before the buzzer.

"Yeah, Phil, is that you?"

"Naw, Cutter, it's just me."

Cutter grinned at the familiar drawl.

"BJ. How the hell did you hear so soon? I haven't even heard from Phil yet."

"Well, you activated the ERP. Now you know I always have to be in the loop, so I built myself into the ERP. I'm at the top of the notification list right after the regulators. What are we dealing with here?"

"One of our tanks failed in a big way. It was topped up and has discharged. The berm's been compromised. We've got oil all over the lease, and it's been seeping offsite."

"So no hope for a full containment at this point?"

"'Fraid not, BJ. Sorry. I can't figure out how the tank could fail the way it did, but . . . it did. We've got to deal with it."

"Yeah, right. I'm sure Phil will be in touch soon. This is gonna be another PR disaster. I'll work on damage control from here. Do your best, Cutter."

"Yes, sir. You know I'll do my damndest. We're going to try and clean up the lease site before the media arrives. I'm sure they'll have choppers out here for aerial shots at daybreak."

"Well, old buddy, y'all have your work cut out for you. I'll get out of your hair. Naturally, you've got my full support. If you get any flak from anyone, you have them call me, ya hear?"

"Yeah, BJ, thanks. There is one thing. Do you think you can do a press conference this morning in Houston . . . I'll get Phil to give you the details?"

"Sure, Cutter. Not a fan of those things but whatever I can do to help. Make sure Phil gets back to me soon, though, not much time to prep for that."

"Will do. Thanks BJ."

A few minutes later, Leeson was on the line. Lots of talk of keeping a detailed log about what they were doing to contain the spill. Cutter shook his head. Like he had time to keep a diary at the moment. At least he could get Leeson to help on one front.

"Phil, with the ERP activated, the word is out. We're going to have the press crawling all over us at sunup. You're going to have to coordinate the media response. What we need to work on right now is making this place look half decent by the time the cameras are on it. If you could buy me some time, it would sure help."

BENDING THE ARC

"What do you have in mind, Cutter?"

"Arrange for an early morning press conference in Houston. I told BJ you'd help him set it up. With any luck, that'll divert the newsbirds for an extra couple of hours."

"Will do, Cutter. Good luck."

The landline from the chopper base was the next to ring.

"Cutter here."

"Yeah, Cutter, it's Tim." Tim was Wildcat's head pilot in charge of the Buffalo 36 airlift operation.

"Hey, kid. I need you to start a massive airlift out here. We need all the standard oil spill response materials—get another Bell Two Twelve. But we also need hay."

"Hay?" Cutter heard the question in his tone.

"Yeah. Hay bales, Tim, lots of them. You can get some from the Bar C, and I'll email you a list of local ranchers and farmers I know. We can find some stockpiles pretty close to the Buffalo Thirty-Six site. Pay whatever you need to, this is an emergency. You can sling them in with the big hauling nets.

"The point is, we've got quite a spill, and we haven't contained it all to the lease site. We need to surround the lease with bales. By the time the media gets out here, I don't want them to see a rig in the middle of a pool of oil. I want them to see a rig surrounded by hay bales. It's gotta look pretty as a post card, know what I mean?"

"I hear you. That's pretty slick, Cutter. You sure you haven't taken any of those high-powered management courses?"

"Yeah, right. My mind hasn't been polluted yet with all that mumbo jumbo behind those degrees the boys in Houston have on their walls."

"Hey, Cutter. I've got an MBA."

"See what I mean?" Cutter chuckled at the momentary silence and shot a stream of chew at his feet, careful to miss his boots. It felt good to relax, even for an instant.

"So, get that hay lift happening, Tim. We'll have a makeshift landing pad, clear of oil, ready in thirty minutes."

"You got it, chief. See ya soon."

27

HOUSTON, TEXAS

Monday
May 21

Matt Avery was in full swing by 6:00 a.m. Kevin Flaig had alerted him to the spill at Buffalo 36. Flaig told him he got the scoop from an anonymous phone tip. Avery felt thrilled that his GAC spin team was way ahead of the curve on this one.

The office space had a minimalist design, but Avery had to admit it was more than functional considering the short time in which it was put together. Located in the heart of the Galleria gave it the ability to get the GAC name out there through the steady foot traffic. Floor to ceiling environmental shots and slogans covered the windows facing the interior of the mall.

Avery was relieved that his communications center had been spared the spartan approach. Flaig met all his requests for state-of-the-art computer and com equipment, but made it clear he expected proportionate results. Flaig understood the importance of shaping the news.

In the middle of the center, a series of ultra-high-definition screens displayed a shifting array of data streams, news broadcasts, and social media feeds. The nerve center was a semi-circular console, bristling with state-of-the-art equipment. Touchscreen interfaces allowed Avery to manipulate data in real-time, crafting compelling yet deceptive narratives that would be disseminated through various channels. High-speed servers hummed quietly beneath the console, ensuring rapid access to vast reservoirs of information and analytics. A sophisticated AI system scanned for trends and suggested optimal times to release particular pieces of misinformation to achieve maximum impact.

Not having the details of the spill didn't concern Avery. He knew that timing was everything in shaping a story. The media would be hungry for any reactions once the story was out. They would quote whoever had something to say, particularly in the early hours, when solid information was scarce. While early statements would

BENDING THE ARC

contain more speculation than fact, that was not the driving concern. Someone would fill the information vacuum. Better the GAC than Wildcat. He asked AI to develop a brief statement, tying the recent spill into the ongoing litigation, but making no libelous allegations.

The statement was simple, yet effective.

Houston, 6:30 a.m., C.D.T. - The Green Action Coalition has learned of a major oil spill at a wellsite in eastern Texas 100% owned and operated by Wildcat Oil and Gas Ltd. The GAC is in litigation with Wildcat, attempting to stop Wildcat from operating in an environmentally negligent manner. This most recent spill is of serious concern to the GAC, as it should be to all Texans and people who value our natural heritage.

The statement did not directly claim that Wildcat's negligence caused the oil spill, but simply referred to the existing litigation. While not containing any libelous statements, anyone reading the release would view the Buffalo 36 spill as further evidence of negligence. *This will work just fine.* He emailed the release to all major news outlets in Texas and a select list of national media contacts.

28

WASHINGTON, D.C.

Monday
May 21

The video conference was much too early for Shane. He'd flown up to DC the night before to visit with Hendrix in the new LawForce offices. A morning person, Hendrix called the meeting for 7:00 a.m. Apparently, this was the norm for Washington, as the streets were far from empty when he made his way over from the hotel. He shrugged. Could have been worse. For the folks dialing in from back home, it was 6:00 a.m.

He entered the LawForce boardroom where Val's face filled the wall-sized screen. She looked tense. "BJ says there's no way Wildcat will en-

BENDING THE ARC

tertain a five-million-dollar settlement. Insurance wouldn't cover it, so they'd have to sell significant holdings. He's also dead against the idea of *any* settlement. He says it's like negotiating with terrorists and would set a dangerous precedent for the industry."

Val's brow furrowed the way it always did when she was trying to make an important point.

"Steve, he's right. A settlement wouldn't only cripple Wildcat, it would send a terrible signal. Just dust off a law book, look up a cause of action, pick a target with deep pockets, file your suit, retain your hired guns, and wait for the check to be cut."

"Whoa, slow down there, Counselor, slow it down." Shane glanced at Hendrix, who was chuckling but had the good sense to turn his back to the camera.

Shane stood up and faced the screen. "I know the offer is a nonstarter, but I had a duty to pass it on to BJ. I told him it was B.S. Don't sweat it, Val. Nobody ever seriously considered it."

"Good, because this suit isn't about five million dollars or fifty million or a hundred million. It's about an important principle."

"We understand your position, Valentina," Hendrix answered. "Let's use some of that passion to put the GAC in its place. You know, if we do our job right, this case *will* set a precedent. A good precedent. If we can expose this action for what it is and extract punitive damages, it should have a substantial chilling effect on future, similarly ill-founded actions."

"Yes, sir," Val replied. Shane sensed Hendrix intimidated her. It wasn't every day you had the U.S. AG as co-counsel.

Val stood and waved. "I'd better get back to trial prep." The screen flickered out.

Hendrix leaned back in his chair. "She is a handful. Nice to see there are still young attorneys in America with fire in their bellies to do right by the law. What do you think? It's an unrealistic offer, but it shows they're getting nervous. Does it not?"

Shane shrugged. "I don't know. The only thing I can figure is they don't think I'm any better than Cal Stokes. But Tillington knows his case is weak. In the circumstances, maybe they think BJ might go for a quick settlement. If they believe that, they know him even less than they know me."

"Well, my boy, arrogance has an amazing ability to dull the senses."

"That could be it. They still have no idea what they're up against," Shane agreed, thinking out loud. "That's good. The element of surprise is invaluable in war, and a trial is war."

"Of course, my boy, of course. The confidentiality surrounding LawForce is designed to preserve that advantage. You can wager Tilling-

BENDING THE ARC

ton and Company would behave differently if they knew who was supporting you."

The buzzer sounded with the flashing of the red light, announcing another video link. Val's face again filled the screen, looking more perturbed than last time.

"Have you heard?" she asked breathlessly.

"Heard what?" Shane asked.

"The offer's been withdrawn. Tillington called a few minutes ago."

"Why?"

"There's been an oil spill at one of Wildcat's east Texas wells. It's all over the media. And BJ just called to say he needs me at a press conference in an hour."

"Holy shit . . . give us a minute." Shane caucused with Hendrix, then turned back to Val.

"OK, Val. Get over there and help BJ with that conference. Lord knows he can use some pointers. Let's make sure we avoid saying anything that could make things worse. I'll fly back this morning. See you soon."

As Val raced out of the conference room and the screen went blank, Hendrix turned to Shane. His voice was grim. "Looks like Mr. Whitter doesn't have to make a settlement decision after all. I just bloody well hope there's a good explanation for this. We chose this lawsuit based on Wildcat's reputation. The last thing we need is for that to start falling apart."

"Easy, Jonathan. I'm a reasonable judge of character. I'm pretty confident that BJ Whitter's a straight shooter. If they have a problem at one of his wells, it's an accident, pure and simple. There's no way that man is running a bad outfit. And there may be something funny going on at Buffalo Thirty-Six. Jenn was out there with Mike O'Day a few days ago. It looks like the falcon nest that closed the access road was a plant."

Hendrix looked puzzled. "What do you mean, *a plant*, Steven?"

"I don't have solid info yet, but all may not be what it seems. I'm just asking you not to give up on BJ just yet."

"Very well, but I hope you're right, my boy. I do hope you're right. For the moment, we have to keep our shoulders to the wheel. Remember what Churchill said, 'If you're going through hell, keep going.'"

29

GULF OF MEXICO

Monday
May 21

From the towering heights of the offshore drill rig, the Gulf of Mexico spread out like a vast expanse of liquid gold, its surface shimmering under the relentless gaze of the early morning sun. A warm breeze danced across the platform. The horizon, where the sky met the sea, was a perfect, unbroken line. The offshore platforms and boats, many mere specks in the distance, added to the sense of majesty.

From his vantage point high above the waves, Herky Cantrell observed seabirds soaring on the thermals, their cries echoing across the water as they hunted for fish. The sun boomeranged off the waves, shattering into thousands of tiny diamonds that sparkled against the deep blue waters. He leaned on the railing, watching a school of dolphins playing in the distance, their sleek bodies slicing through the water with effortless grace.

Explorer 7 was a hive of activity, a mishmash of clanging metal and whirring machinery that echoed across the open water. The deck beneath his feet vibrated with the steady rhythm of the drill, sending reverberations through his bones. The air was thick with the smell of oil and diesel, mingling with the briny scent of the ocean to create a heady aroma that was, for an old oilhand like Herky, intoxicating. He breathed deeply and turned to Duane Follet, the other roughneck on his shift. "Not your ordinary office, is it?"

"Sure ain't." Duane sounded like he meant it. "This job isn't as bad as I thought it might be."

Herky nodded. While the work was tough, it had its rewards. Moments like this made it all worthwhile. He stood on the lower platform of Explorer 7, fifty feet above the sea.

As one of the most advanced units operating offshore in the Gulf, the Explorer 7 platform was the pride of ARI's drilling fleet. AllOceans Group, the owner of the two-hundred-million-dollar rig, contracted it to ARI for one hundred and fifty thousand dollars per day. The rig was built in Singapore. It had been towed from the Port of Houston to its present location in just over two hundred feet of water on the Texas-Louisiana Shelf, one hundred miles southeast of Galveston, Texas.

The rig sported all the creature comforts. It featured a comfortable crew lounge complete with satellite entertainment system, gymnasium, sauna, film, training rooms, and desalination equipment. With its touch-screen controls, Explorer 7's drilling panel was state-of-the-art.

Four massive legs standing on the ocean floor supported the rig. Measuring six hundred feet long, they were used to support year-round drilling operations in up to four hundred feet of water. The platform was rated to withstand eighty-foot waves, 130-mile-per-hour winds, and currents of up to two knots.

Herky watched as the rig's overhead crane lifted a few company officials onto the drilling platform in a yellow and black nylon rope cage. The basket was used to ferry personnel from the rig to transfer vessels. Most crew changes were made via helo, but occasionally people were transferred to or from ships.

Herky leaned back from the railing, massaging a sore arm. The drill string had banged into it while they were making a connection—tripping back into the hole on the last shift.

Duane pointed at his arm. "Can be shitty work at times, huh?"

"At times. But on the whole, I wouldn't trade it for anything in the world."

Duane nodded. "Hey, Herky, I've heard the guys talking about ARI's reputation as a wildcatter. What's that all about?"

"ARI built its rep wildcatting. In the early days of the Gulf, ARI was one of the most successful, or some would say luckiest, wildcatters. They put together an impressive string of strikes."

"But Explorer Seven isn't a wildcat, is it?"

Herky snorted. "You are green, my boy. Hell, no, this isn't a wildcat. This here's a development well, bud. An infill well. Explorer Seven's going to help drain an existing field."

"So that's why it wasn't a big surprise when we struck oil on the last shift," Duane said, almost to himself. "I wondered why everyone was so matter-of-fact about it."

"Hell, Duane, if we hadn't established production pretty damn soon, we might all have been out of a job. Old Ms. Anderson gets pretty impatient with dusters in the middle of an established play."

Herky continued his lecture, happy to have an audience. Too many of the young bucks in the industry today showed little curiosity beyond the size of their next paycheck.

"These days, activity is mostly focused on development. The Gulf is what's known as a mature producing basin. At least the stuff on the

BENDING THE ARC

inner shelf. They drilled the world's first offshore well, out of sight of the coastline, in the Gulf. We've punched down seven hundred thousand wells in this basin. Current estimates are that the Gulf holds about ten percent of the world's oil and gas reserves."

"Wow!" Duane looked impressed. "Is there much left?"

"Yeah, sure, we're still draining fields. And lately there's been a lot of interest in the deep water. Places we couldn't get to in the past. New technology has opened up another frontier beyond the continental shelf. There's lots of wildcatting going on out there."

"So how much longer are we going to be on site?"

Herky rolled up his sleeve, revealing a mean-looking bruise on his well-muscled upper arm. "I figure another few weeks. Once we finish the production tests, we'll be moving the rig to a new location. They'll tie this well into a central production platform. But don't worry, son, there's plenty of work. Explorer Seven's contracted for the next three years. If you're willing to put your shoulder to the wheel, the sky's the limit."

"Yeah, right. If I'm still around. I'm not sure I want to make a career out of the patch, but it's nice to know there's work to be had."

Herky nodded. He and Duane were at the bottom of the rig hierarchy. The crew comprised two roughnecks, a derrickman, a motorman, and a driller. Every rig also had a foreman or toolpush, who oversaw general rig operations. Herky had been a roughneck for too long. Recently, he'd started taking drilling courses at a local community college. He wanted to make push on Explorer 7 in five years. He enjoyed working the offshore, with its long, twelve-hour shifts and two weeks on, one week off rotations. Having a whole week off allowed him to spend meaningful time with his wife, Karen, and their three-year-old twin daughters, Jessica-Ann and Brittany.

The downside was being away for two weeks at a time, but the money made up for it. He couldn't imagine another job coming close to the pay he was pulling down with ARI. Serious coin. With his salary, he could sock away ten thousand dollars a month after covering expenses. A few more years of that and he'd be able to burn his mortgage. Karen put up with rig life in anticipation of the ultimate rewards.

Herky and Duane had come off the graveyard shift and were looking forward to breakfast, which would be a substantial affair. Most guys had a good feed, then hit the sack until about four in the afternoon. They'd get up, shoot a little pool and play cards or watch a video before eating a hearty dinner and going back on shift at eight.

BENDING THE ARC

The food was first-rate, much better than he ate at home, although he'd never admit that to Karen. When a bunch of men were cooped up in close quarters with a lot of time on their hands, they attached special importance to food. Good food meant a productive, happy crew, and the oil companies knew it. Budgets were generous. The menu included steak two or three times a week, lots of fresh fruits and vegetables and plenty of seafood, including live lobster—Texas size—flown in from Maine on Sundays.

"Hey, what's that?" Duane asked, pointing at the water.

Herky looked down and could just make out what looked like a bag tangled in one of the support columns. "Just some Gulf junk. You'd be amazed at how much stuff is floating around in this ocean."

He squinted. *Wonder where it came from?* "Better go have a look." He walked to the end of the deck and descended the ladder to the lower level.

Once he got the bag free, he looked closely. It was an ordinary, black dry bag. He opened it and reached inside. It appeared to be empty, but then he felt something. He pulled out two small cylindrical devices, holding them up to the sun for a better look. From his construction days, he recognized them as blasting caps. *Strange.* Nobody was doing any demolition work around the rig that he knew of.

"You go ahead, Duane. Save me some pancakes. I'm gonna go see Rick for a minute." Rick Santos was the rig's toolpush. He might know what this was about.

But Santos knew no more than Herky. He looked at the caps closely. "We haven't done any blasting around here for months. Thanks, Herky, you've got sharp eyes."

"Not me. It was the new guy, Duane Follet. I'll pass on the thanks."

Santos nodded, still studying the caps. "Come on, I think we should let Anderson know."

Herky had never met or talked with the boss. "You sure you need me on the call?"

"Yeah. She may have questions."

Herky followed Santos into the doghouse—the driller's control room on the rig floor. Santos punched in a number on the console. Within a minute, Anderson's voice came over the speaker phone. "Hello, Rick, how are things on the water? Are you fellows making good time?"

"Yes, ma'am, everything's fine. We're calling to tell you we found something peculiar wrapped around one of the rig legs. A small dry bag with a few blasting caps in it. We haven't been doing any blasting. Thought you should know."

There was a brief pause before Anderson came back on the line. "Thank you, Rick, but I don't think it's anything to get excited about. With all the junk floating around the Gulf and all of those rigs out there, it's not surprising some blasting caps went overboard somewhere, even if they're not ours. But thanks for calling and keep your petal to the metal. We need this project to stay on schedule."

"Yes, ma'am, we'll do our best. Thanks."

Santos looked at Herky. "I guess that's that."

Herky shrugged. "If the big gal's OK with it, then so am I." That said, he pulled out his cell phone. Couldn't hurt to pass it along to his buddy at Wildcat.

30

HOUSTON, TEXAS

Monday
May 21

The Hyatt Regency Ballroom was humming with a lively crowd considering the time of day. Under Wildcat's Emergency Response Plan, relevant regulatory authorities were notified after Cutter activated the plan at 2:20 a.m. The GAC surprised them with how quickly they reacted, issuing their news release at 6:30 a.m. They were obviously well connected.

Seated at the podium with Val at his side, BJ studied his notes. He knew they had to hold the press conference. Falling behind in the battle for hearts and minds would hurt the company on all

BENDING THE ARC 211

fronts. He even put on one of his best bolo ties for the occasion.

Cutter's plea for an early conference to divert the press from flying out to the site immediately worked. The media prepared for the 8:00 a.m. conference in Houston, buying Cutter the time he needed. BJ was glad when Val showed up. This time around, he was happy to have a lawyer with him. He had much more confidence in his new legal team.

He glanced at Val. "So what do I focus on here? We don't know squat yet other than the oil leaked."

"Let's put the emphasis on our ERP and containment practices. Cutter's doing a hell of a job. They won't have the type of sensational pictures that really get to people. So, we need to play it down. Mention it's contained and say we're going to do a complete investigation."

BJ shook his head. "I don't know. I hate stalling people."

"And I'm not asking you to. Look, compare it to when a jetliner goes down with a lot of casualties. The NTSB makes a statement immediately. They don't want to, and they end up saying they don't know anything yet. But they *do* face the media. They understand that a press conference with little hard information still beats an information vacuum, hands down. And if you're still not convinced, remember, not knowing anything didn't stop our friends the GAC from getting a statement out in hours."

"OK, OK, I get it. I just have to get up there and talk. Even if I've got nothing to say, they just need to hear from Wildcat at this point."

"That's it." She gave BJ a supportive smile.

BJ grabbed the mike. "Ladies and gentlemen, please take your seats. My name is BJ Whitter. I'm president and CEO of Wildcat Oil and Gas Limited. On my right is Ms. Valentina Lopez, part of our new legal team.

"As you may have heard, there was a minor oil spill at our Buffalo Thirty-Six facility in east Texas. As far as we can tell, one of the holding tanks developed a leak, and it released some oil. We have now fully contained the spill, and are pleased to report that we captured most of the oil on the lease site. Some oil migrated into the surrounding environment, but it has been contained and is being removed."

He went on for another fifteen minutes, explaining Wildcat's ERP and the steps taken to mitigate the spill. When he opened it up for questions, the reporter in the front row wildly waving his arm came as no surprise.

"Yes, Mr. Farber?"

"Can you tell us why you stored so much oil in the holding tanks on the lease site? Isn't that unusual?"

BENDING THE ARC   213

"The oil was being stored in the tanks, since the wells are currently being tested for their production potential. Nothing unusual about that. In fact, that's why the tanks are there."

Farber followed up. "But isn't produced oil trucked out rather than stored on site to prevent precisely the incident you've just experienced?"

"Generally, that's true. However, our service road is temporarily closed. Until the road is reopened, we're storing the oil in tanks."

While he tried to get to another reporter, Farber shouted out his third question.

"Isn't it true that the Department of Forestry shut your road down because Wildcat breached an environmental condition in siting the road?"

Where the Christ was he getting his information?

He felt Val tug his arm as she stood up to field the question.

"Mr. Farber, the road was *not* closed because of any breach of condition by Wildcat. Forestry discovered a nest from a rare falcon species near the road and closed it down for the rest of the incubating season, which will end in a week. Forestry provided a full site approval for the road and issued a license for its use. The discovery of the nest after that approval was as much a surprise to Forestry as to Wildcat. By the way, we are investigating the incident, and while I can't go into specifics at this time, we don't believe the nest is legitimate."

The last comment sparked a minor uproar. BJ had given Val his blessing to release their suspicions. She convinced him that the disclosure was needed to stir things up and divert heat from Wildcat. While BJ didn't like going public until all the facts were known, in the end he deferred to Val.

"Ms. Lopez, what do you mean the nest is not *legitimate*?"

"I'm sorry, that'll be all for this morning. We'll keep you posted on events as they develop. For those of you who would like to view the Buffalo Thirty-Six site, we have arranged tours. Please see the Wildcat reps at the door on your way out."

The last point was Val's idea. She was quickly earning his respect with her practical advice. A far cry from Mr. Stokes. If the media would be flying over the site anyway, they might as well do it accompanied by Wildcat personnel, who could provide the proper context.

BJ was surprised to see that the conference lasted well over an hour. He pulled Val aside as she gathered her things. "Got time to join me in a breakout room next door."

"Sure, why?"

"I need to discuss the case with you and then I'm going to watch the coverage from the wellsite.

The first crews should get out there pretty soon. This conference only bought Cutter a few hours."

After a lengthy discussion on the status of the case and how Shane's team intended to handle the upcoming trial, they gathered around the large, flat-screen TV set up in the side room and stared at the aerial shot of Buffalo 36. As he massaged his leg, BJ noted with satisfaction that Cutter had done well.

Patches of oil surrounded the lease site, but the surrounding area was a golden sea of hay. How the hell Cutter had gotten those on site within hours was beyond him. A large circle of bales spread out to meet untouched brush at their outer edge. The reporter provided an audio feed.

"This is Channel Five's Eye in the Sky reporting to you live from the scene out here in the Big Thicket, about one hundred miles northeast of Houston. In the early morning hours, one of two large tanks holding oil produced from this well sprang a leak, and we understand over two thousand barrels of oil escaped. The well belongs to Wildcat Oil and Gas, a company headquartered in Houston, which is embroiled in litigation with an environmental public interest group, the Green Action Coalition. The lawsuit claims that Wildcat operates in an environmentally negligent manner. The GAC issued a statement this morning that this development fits the pattern of Wildcat's negligent operations. Wildcat officials deny any negligence, although they have no explanation yet for the cause of the spill. This is Rick Panetti for Five's Eye in the Sky."

Val turned to BJ. "Looks like your guys have done as well on the containment and cleanup as they could, under the circumstances."

BJ nodded. "Cutter's first rate. I'm lucky to have such people working for me, I will say that. Let's just hope there's no more surprises before y'all have time to put this lawsuit to bed. Christ knows, the GAC doesn't need any more ammo."

BJ felt his cell vibrating and saw it was Cutter. He put the phone on speaker. "What's up, Cutter, I'm here with Val Lopez. We just watched the coverage from Buffalo Thirty-Six. Great job on the containment."

"Thanks, boss, but that's not why I'm calling. I just got a call from a friend of mine, Herky Cantrell, who's part of ARI's crew on Explorer Seven. Herky may just be a roughneck, but he's been around the block. He said they found a dry bag with some blasting caps floating around one of the rig supports. Not ours. He and the push, Rick Santos, took it to Leona Anderson, but she told them to stand

BENDING THE ARC

down. She didn't think it was a big deal. I'm kind of thinking it might be. I mean, what the hell would a bag of detonators be doing anywhere near one of our rigs?"

BJ nodded. "OK, take it easy. First off, it's Anderson's play. We're not the operator. But I take your point. It does seem strange. Let me talk to her and see what's up."

"OK, BJ, but sooner rather than later. This could be important. Take care."

BJ turned to Val. "You're going to have to excuse me."

"I understand. I've got to get back to the office, anyway. Good luck."

As Val closed the door, BJ punched a number on his cell and soon heard the familiar east coast accent. "BJ, what can I do for you?"

"Leona, I just heard they found a dry bag out at Explorer Seven floating around one of the support legs with blasting caps in it and they aren't ours. Do you know anything about that?"

"Sure, the boys called earlier today. With all that garbage floating around out there, I didn't think much of it. Probably came from another rig or a supply barge."

"If it was chocolate bar wrappers or soda cans, I wouldn't be calling. But blasting caps? I think we need to do something, maybe call law enforcement to have a look."

"I think that's an over-reaction, BJ, but I'll get the security team to send someone out to follow-up."

"OK, Leona. Keep in touch and let me know what y'all find. Maybe it's worth a quick check-dive to ensure everything is A-OK."

"Leave it to me, you've got your hands full with the GAC."

"Don't I know it. Thanks, Leona, talk soon."

31

GULF OF MEXICO

Saturday
May 26

Herky wolfed down a mouthful of pancakes. He was a big man with a big appetite. This was simply an appetizer, to be followed by a full farmer's breakfast of steak and eggs, biscuits, gravy, and a flood of coffee.

"Hey, Herky, what's the rush? The chopper won't get here any earlier just because you've inhaled your breaky."

Herky interrupted his attack on the three-stack to look up with a grin. "Relax, son. It's an old habit. My parents didn't have a lot of money. I grew up with three brothers. You learn to pack it away pretty fast when you have to."

"But you don't have to anymore. There's plenty to go around here."

Herky shrugged. "I guess it's that thing about old dogs and new tricks."

Duane laughed and reached for the maple syrup, just as they heard a faint thump. Duane held the syrup in mid-air. "Did you feel that?"

Herky nodded. "Probably just the pumps being charged up. Nothing to get excited about." Maybe, but he hadn't felt those pumps before. He shrugged it off and returned his attention to the three-stack.

Fifteen minutes later, Herky stretched back from the table, holding his stomach. "That should last for a while."

Duane rolled his eyes. "I can't believe the way you pack that stuff away. I . . ." The room tilted abruptly, sending everything on the table crashing to the floor. They felt a strong shudder and heard a muffled *whump*. The platform continued leaning, then stopped at ten-degrees off vertical.

Herky leapt out of his chair and scrambled for the door. It didn't budge, jammed by the tilted wall. Herky and Duane charged the door together, and it gave with a loud crack. Herky headed for the rig floor. He heard Duane screaming at him.

"We've got to get to the evac stations. This baby's gonna blow."

BENDING THE ARC

Herky ignored the warning, operating on instinct. They might need help on the rig floor, and Herky was damned if he would hightail it before he knew the active crew was OK.

On the floor, Herky saw Rick Santos lean out of the doghouse and scream at the roughnecks. "Dawson, Wright—check it out. We've got a Level Two alarm on the lower level. It feels bad." Santos stabbed at his control panel, engaging the BOPs. A jarring buzzer sounded, and red lights flashed. The BOPs were jammed. Herky ran up the stairs to Santos. "Thank Christ you're here, Cantrell. Get to the manual override and set the Blow Out Preventers *now*!"

BOPs are massive hydraulic valves used to shut-in a well and prevent any backflow up the drillstem, which can lead to oil spewing unchecked from the wellbore. Explorer 7's BOPs featured combination blind-shear rams that would close off the wellbore once the drill pipe and tools were extracted from the hole. In an emergency, when it wasn't feasible to remove the drill pipe, the rams could be closed on the pipe, severing it. The BOPs were on a subsea stack, operated hydraulically from the rig. Herky knew there was a primary hydraulic switch in the doghouse and a back-up switch on the lower deck.

The rig groaned as metal surrendered to the immense forces being exerted. Herky saw the crew on shift change come tumbling out of the sleeping quarters and head for the evac stations. Confusion reigned. Herky heard Santos give the general evacuation order over the intercom, which somehow was still functioning. *This rig is going down!*

The evac stations were below the rig floor, just above ocean level. The crew scrambled for the boats. Launching into the roiling sea was no easy feat. Herky had practiced evac procedures, but it sure as hell was a different story when the platform was falling apart around them.

He watched in horror as a cook attempted to board a small repair boat by straddling the gunwale. The man shrieked when the boat crashed into the rig, mashing his leg against the platform. Hands reached for him, but he was gone, swept away by the turbulent waters.

Herky knew that the repair boat wasn't intended to be an evacuation vessel. Explorer 7 had the latest in offshore safety, including modern evacuation capsules. These well-insulated, self-contained pods could hold up to a dozen men strapped in with seatbelts. Herky was skeptical when they were told in the safety meetings that the enclosed and sealed pods could withstand any storm. *Please, dear lord, let them be right on this one.*

He knew the design of the pods was a fallout from one of the worst rig disasters in history. In the eighties, an offshore rig, the Ocean

Ranger, went down in rough seas in the North Atlantic, off the coast of Canada. All eighty-four men aboard died. In the wake of this tragedy, researchers developed the new pods. The trick was to load them properly. To prevent the jamming that caught the cook, the designers on Explorer 7 created pods that allowed the crew to enter from above, by essentially dropping into them.

Herky reached the BOP control switch on the lower deck and activated it. He was on his way back to the rig floor when he saw Dawson and Wright racing down the stairs, waving him back. Apparently, they had secured everything on the floor. As he watched them descend, he heard another *whump*, and the rig teetered.

Dawson and Wright flew off the stairs and crashed onto the deck thirty feet below. Santos found himself stranded at the top. It didn't matter. Shuddering continuously now, the rig tilted dangerously. Herky knew he wouldn't make it to the evac stations. Only one thing to do. He ran to the railing, scrambled over, and flung himself into the greatest high dive of his life.

The cold water was a shock, and he felt himself sinking ever deeper. His work boots and coveralls were dragging him down. He struggled to untie his boots, finally kicking free. Breaking the surface, he sucked in a chestful of air. He'd expected to be some distance from the rig, but found he was under the rig floor. The current must have pulled him back.

Jesus! The rig was disintegrating above him. *At least the well was shut in.* But then he felt another tremendous *whump*, and all hell broke loose. He knew instantly what the deep rumbling underneath him meant. *The BOPs had failed!* Fighting for air, he disappeared in the bubbling sea as the oil, under enormous pressure, spewed out of the wellbore and up through the remaining pieces of the rig.

Damn! He sure would have liked seeing Karen and the girls one last time.

In a few seconds, the sparks from the rending metal lit Satan's fuse.

32

BIG THICKET, TEXAS

Saturday
May 26

The noise was deafening as the choppers circled the site. BJ watched the oil-stained hay being gathered and bunched in piles. They were flying it out using large haul nets, lined with plastic tarps to prevent the gooey sludge from raining on the countryside. Cutter had organized the troops well. In the space of twenty-four hours, the situation went from a potential disaster to a controlled, minor spill.

From the air, the site resembled a dartboard, with the lease surrounded by a golden circle of hay bales. The scene had its own kind of beauty. Val Lopez was using the action to showcase Wildcat's environmental response team. Some reporters displayed a genuine interest in understanding what was going on and would file balanced reports. BJ knew it was still imperative to determine what caused the leak. All the reports shared a common conclusion on this point. Without knowing the cause of the spill, the jury was out regarding Wildcat's role in the whole affair.

Landing next to the rig, BJ breathed in the earthy scent of the Thicket, with the bog's rich aroma of damp soil and decaying leaves fighting to counteract the smell of condensate.

He saw Cutter signaling him from the engineer's trailer.

"What's up?"

"You gotta see this, BJ. It's not pretty."

He followed Cutter into the trailer. The coverage of Explorer 7 was on. BJ dropped onto the couch. "*Jesus H. Christ!* What next?"

He watched the telecast in silence. It was hard to absorb. Explorer 7 was a huge play for Wildcat. Their fifty percent interest represented the company's largest investment. He focused his attention on the screen. Fifteen crew missing, more than were lost on Deepwater Horizon, an uncontained blowout spewing thousands of barrels of oil a day into the fragile Gulf ecosystem. Brutal.

"Cutter, you know how serious this is. You need to get in touch with ARI's folks, stat. Find out how they're handling things."

Cutter nodded, twirling his hat on his knees. "I'll meet with their ops guys tomorrow, once I stabilize things here."

"Today, Cutter, today. Things here are under control—thanks to you, old buddy. I need you on Explorer Seven from here on in. We have to make sure those ARI people get that sucker under control yesterday. I don't want to see images of birds mired in a gooey seashore and dolphins fighting to breathe in an oilslicked ocean . . . *Goddamn it*, Cutter. What the hell is going on?"

Cutter patted BJ on the shoulder. "I sure as heck don't know. But something's fishy here. Before I go, I want you to see something."

Cutter led him across the lease site and around the cats, busy piling up the mixture of hay, oil, and mud into piles for transfer to the hauling nets. They reached Tank 1 at the edge of the site. Cutter knelt beside the remains of the outlet flange. A large hole was visible where the valve had separated from the tank and was still hanging to one side.

Cutter pointed to the ragged edge of the opening. "This doesn't look right, BJ. I've seen lots of failed welds, and the edge of the break is a lot smoother."

BJ examined the hole. It looked as though the valve had popped out to him. But Cutter was right. The edges were ragged.

Cutter stood up. "You wouldn't have any connections with a good investigative agency, would you, BJ?"

"I'll see what I can do, Cutter. You just concentrate on Explorer Seven for now."

Flying back to Houston in the JetRanger, BJ tried to digest the news from Explorer 7. Losing life was tragic. Combined with the unfolding environmental disaster, it made him sick to his stomach. The consequences for Wildcat could be severe. While ARI operated the rig, the Joint Operating Agreement between ARI and Wildcat put Wildcat on the hook for its share of damages.

BJ watched the Texas grasslands roll past below them. The potential damages would be big-league. The property damage was incidental. It would pale compared to the environmental fallout, not to mention actions from the families of the deceased crew members. While impossible to quantify the exposure, BJ knew it had the potential to kill the company. The buzzing of his cell phone interrupted his thoughts.

"Whitter here."

"BJ, glad I finally caught up to you. You've heard the news?" Anderson sounded shaken.

"Yeah. What the hell happened out there?"

"I don't know. A million safeguards had to fail."

"Well, we don't have time to sit around navel-gazing. Have you lined up a well-control team? We've got to stop this thing *now*."

"I know that, BJ. For god's sake, it's my well and my people that perished out there."

"OK, relax. I'm just dealing with a lot of my own crap right now. So what's the well control status?"

"I have a team lined up. They're getting their equipment together. We need to see what's left of the rig before they can figure out what to do. They'll be on site in a few hours. Meanwhile, I've hired Drew Tillington over at Todd Ives."

"That bastard!" BJ couldn't contain himself. "You know he's acting for the GAC against us, right?"

Anderson remained calm. "Yes, he told me. But BJ, you have to understand, he's our go-to litigator. Explorer Seven is the biggest disaster in our companies' history and I'll be darned if I'm going to defend myself with my hands tied."

"Not asking you to do that, Leona. But there are plenty of sharp litigators in this town."

"Drew's our man, that's final." BJ knew there was no changing Anderson's mind.

"Well, good luck with that. I'll be using the counsel that's acting for us on the GAC actions, a guy by the name of Steve Shane."

"Yes, I've heard of him. You should also know that I've hired Seabright and Company to start an investigation. They've promised a preliminary report in a week."

Seabright and Company? BJ knew of them as a smaller outfit, not one of the patch's better-known engineering outfits.

"Shouldn't we use someone with a higher profile?"

"BJ, I can't be second-guessed on every decision at this stage. You said it yourself. We've got to act fast. I know some people over there." She moved on. "Look, the main reason I called is to ask you to come over for a meeting on Monday. We need to circle the wagons and talk damage control."

BJ paused. He knew it wasn't fair to dump on Anderson. She obviously knew little more than anyone else at this stage.

"Yeah, sure, that makes sense. I'll be there."

"Oh, and BJ?"

"Yeah?"

"Bring your lawyers."

"Yeah, right." BJ knew from here on in, lawyers would be omnipresent. Like one of his international oil patch buddies used to email back to the home office when things got hot, "Fertilizer has hit the fan. Send guns, money, and lawyers!" BJ grimaced. *And not necessarily in that order.*

33

HOUSTON, TEXAS

Saturday
May 26

Shane grudgingly admired the GAC's website. It was state-of-the-art, with its spinning green globe set against a deep blue universe. A banner screamed *Wildcat Wildness— Scorched Earth Policy Continues.* The article was full of inflammatory language on the Explorer 7 fiasco, with plenty of colorful graphics. A window provided live feeds from the Gulf. The images showed a barge heaving offside the mangled, flaming remains of the rig.

Damn, but the GAC was good at PR. What pissed him off was the connection to Wildcat. Wildcat was a half-owner in the oil lease, but, significantly, Wildcat was not the operator. The rig operations were run by ARI—a fact that seemed to escape the GAC.

Shane grabbed the phone on the first ring, continuing to scroll through the website. "Steve Shane."

"Why won't sharks attack lawyers?"

Shane recognized the drawl. Shane let the air out of his tires on this one. "Professional courtesy."

"Damn straight."

Shane held the receiver back from his ear as the laughter boomed through the phone. "How you doing, BJ?" Shane knew the big man was under a lot of stress.

"Well, son, I have been better. Sorry to bother you on the weekend, but there have been some developments and we need to act fast."

"No worries, I'm in the office anyway. No rest for the wicked and all that. And BJ, that spill at Buffalo Thirty-Six is no big deal. In fact, I think your team has made a believer out of some of the media. I was reading a report in the *Houston Chronicle*. It said the containment effort was first class."

"Yeah, great, Steve. But have you heard about the well in the Gulf?"

"Heck, yeah, the 'Crisis in the Gulf'? Who hasn't? Hell of a mess for ARI."

"Steve, we're a fifty percent partner in that well."

BENDING THE ARC 233

"I know, BJ. I've been following the GAC's website and they're making sure everyone is aware of the connection. Not good." He found it hard to do anything but state the obvious.

"Not good at all, Counselor. Listen, Steve, I know that you and Val just started working for us and aren't our regular attorneys, but I need your help. I got a call from ARI, and they want to meet. They're a valuable industry partner and their president, gal by the name of Leona Anderson, is a good friend. We want to work with them as much as we can. I want you at that meeting."

Shane foresaw this complication. He'd discussed it with Hendrix. While LawForce was deployed for the specific GAC action, the team would inevitably build relationships with their clients, who would have legal needs beyond the actions LawForce was targeted to deal with. Hendrix and Shane agreed to deal with this on a case-by-case basis, with Shane using his discretion. He couldn't take on cases that would compromise the main LawForce effort, but he had to manage the client as well as the case.

As soon as he heard of Wildcat's involvement in Explorer 7, Shane prepared himself for just such a request from BJ. What clinched his decision was the GAC playing up the Wildcat connection. That was enough of a tie to the main litigation to warrant LawForce's involvement.

"I appreciate the vote of confidence, BJ. It would be my privilege to act for Wildcat on Explorer Seven."

"Thanks, Steve. One more thing you should know." BJ sounded subdued. "Leona has hired Drew Tillington."

The silence was palpable. *Jesus.* This could complicate matters.

"Did you tell Ms. Anderson that Tillington is acting against you on the GAC actions?"

"Yeah. Didn't make a difference. They use him for all their high-stakes litigation, and Explorer Seven is as high stakes as it gets. There was no way I could convince her to change horses."

"OK, BJ, we'll deal with it. I'll take that meeting with you. And I should tell you that Val and Jenn really enjoy working with you and your team."

"You mean that hard case Jenn actually likes me?" BJ chuckled.

"Let's just say you're one of the few guys she has some good things to say about."

"Son of a bitch. She sure as hell didn't say any of those things to me."

"Aw, come on, BJ. You're an old fox. You know that's not how the game's played. It's a lot subtler than that."

"What about Val? I think she's kind of sweet on you, son."

"You bet. She's a class act."

"Are you dipping your pen in company ink? You know that kind of thing can come back and bite you in the ass."

"We're seeing each other, but we know how to separate personal from professional. And besides, Shane and Company isn't really a company. I think you're applying the rules a little too strictly, my friend."

"I didn't mean to say there's anything wrong there, son. I think she's great."

"Yeah, well, we both have more important things to concentrate on. We need to get ready for the GAC. Now that they've withdrawn their settlement offer, bad as it was, you can bet they will use Buffalo Thirty-Six in their lawsuit. And with their media campaign linking you to Explorer Seven, I think we'll have the same problem there. We need to develop a strategy. More important, we need to know *now* what the hell is behind these incidents."

"Yeah. Speaking of which, I wanted to ask you a favor. Cutter Davis, my VP operations, thinks something funny went down at Buffalo Thirty-Six. Could you ask Jenn if she has any good connections with investigative agencies? What we need is a forensic investigation unit, people with some solid experience in industrial sabotage and explosives. Know anybody like that, Counselor?"

Shane grinned. *Yeah, just a little outfit with the initials FBI.* "You bet. Jenn does. She's already working with some of those people. I'll make sure she touches base."

34

HOUSTON, TEXAS

Sunday
May 27

The global headquarters of Anderson Resources Inc. occupied the top fifteen floors of a gleaming glass and steel skyscraper in Houston's downtown. In a huge corner office, Leona Anderson stood motionless in front of the TV, her jaw set in a grim line. Flames engulfed the rig, with black smoke billowing high into the sky, twisting and curling like a monstrous serpent. The screen flickered as the camera zoomed in on the epicenter of the inferno where the blowout had occurred. The heat was palpable through the screen, shimmering waves distorting the air. Anderson could almost smell the acrid scent of burning oil and molten metal.

The camera cut to a wider shot, revealing the chaos unfolding around the rig. Emergency vessels circled the site like frantic ants, spraying jets of water towards the blaze. The sound of sirens and the urgent, clipped voices of the responders crackled through the TV speakers, adding to the sense of urgency.

Anderson's eyes, usually so sharp and cold, now betrayed a flicker of emotion. Her company logo, a stylized *ARI* emblazoned on the side of the rig, was barely visible through the thick smoke and flames.

She watched as a helicopter hovered above the mangled remains of the rig, silhouetted against the fiery backdrop, lowering a rescue basket towards the platform. The grainy footage showed tiny figures scrambling, their movements frantic and disjointed. Anderson's grip on the remote tightened, her knuckles white.

The media was relentless. Explorer 7 caught the imagination not only of Texas but of the nation. The story had all the ingredients—major disaster, fatalities, ongoing catastrophe with the out-of-control well. The nighttime shots of the gigantic cigarette lighter were riveting. People could see the glow from Galveston. One escape pod containing three crew members was far enough away to escape disaster. Among the

BENDING THE ARC

twenty-man crew, they were the sole survivors, along with two crew members who had been airlifted off the wreckage. It was the biggest story out of the Gulf since Deepwater Horizon.

The news anchor's voice cut through the cacophony of the scene, providing updates in a tone that balanced professional detachment with an undercurrent of shock.

"The blowout off Galveston is that much more distressing as it occurred in an environmentally sensitive region. Congress has been deliberating for some time on whether to impose a drilling moratorium in the area. This unfolding natural disaster will no doubt impact that debate. For further details on our coverage, 'Crisis in the Gulf,' look us up on our website, www dot kifc dot com. Shelly Thomas, KIFC News at Six."

With a final, resolute nod, Anderson muted the feed and turned away from the TV. Thoughts whirling in her head, she returned to her desk. There were calls to make, plans to execute, and lives to save. The fire might be out of control, but Leona Anderson was not. She would tackle this disaster head-on, with the same relentless drive that had built her empire. This was her rig, her company, her responsibility—and she would see it through to the end. That said, she knew where her priorities lay. The company had to be saved at all costs, even if it meant losses along the way. This was a tough business—even tougher for a woman. She'd learned from her parents long ago that in business, ethics are excess baggage.

As lead operator of the well, ARI had a lot to answer for. Early reports shed little light on what happened. The survivors mentioned hearing various sounds, such as muffled snaps, cracks, thuds, or pops. From first accounts, leg three was the first to fail, followed by the rest of the rig minutes later.

Anderson was assembling a damage control team. The first order of business was to tame the blowout. She'd sent for a team of ARI specialists. Joe Copithorne headed the group. His rugged, six-five frame filled the chair opposite Anderson. It looked like he hadn't slept.

"I'm glad you finally muted that thing. We were out yesterday for an initial assessment. It's a hell of a mess. We've got a good unit, Ms. Anderson. Don't get me wrong. But for this job we should be going outside. We're not set up to handle something this complex. I mean, we're talking about a total runaway in two hundred feet of water. Our group was set up as a general troubleshooting unit to deal with problem wells where bits get stuck in the hole, deviated holes cave in, and so on. We've never handled a large blowout."

"Come on, Joe, you're too modest. Your boys have done some pretty amazing things. I know your team can handle this."

BENDING THE ARC 241

"That's nice, ma'am, and I appreciate the vote of confidence. But, with respect, it's not a matter of modesty. We've always contracted out blowouts to the specialists—people like Red Adair or Boots and Coots. Explorer Seven is ARI's worst blowout ever, by far."

"We don't have time to call in outside help, Joe. Get your crew together and go cap that well for me. If you don't think you can handle it, I'll find someone else in ARI that can." She knew there was no way Joe would let his guys go in under someone else's command.

Joe nodded. "I'll do it. But, Ms. Anderson, I hope you remember this conversation."

Anderson waved him away. Joe was covering his butt. In the circumstances, that was understandable.

The next order of business was to get an investigation going. People would expect that from the company. As she'd told BJ, she intended to commission Seabright and Company, a petroleum engineering consulting firm, to prepare a report. Normally, her lawyer, Drew Tillington, would commission a sensitive report like this. That way, if the report contained any damning conclusions, ARI could sit on it, sheltering under the blanket of attorney-client privilege. No need to call Tillington on this one. With her brother-in-law being a VP at Seabright, Anderson was confident the report would reach its conclusions in their proper context.

35

GULF OF MEXICO

Tuesday
May 29

From the chopper, Cutter could see the general-purpose barge chartered by ARI, *Langley II*, positioned close to the flaming inferno that was once Explorer 7. The intensity of the heat was palpable, even from half a mile away. The oil around the well site burned in patches, with wisps of flame licking at the barge.

"How the hell are you, you snake dog son of a bitch?" Joe Copithorne's voice boomed over the roar of the waves crashing against the offshore barge.

"Goddamned, am I glad to see your sorry-ass face. Welcome to hell."

Cutter winced at the crushing handshake. "Yeah, you've got your hands full on this one, Joe. Not much left to work with." He motioned at the ragged skeleton of metal in the middle of the burning swirl of oil.

Cutter wiped the oil spray off his face. "What's the game plan, kid?"

"We've got to kill the fire first, then we're going to put on a new Christmas Tree."

Cutter couldn't believe his ears. He was familiar with the two methods of bringing a blowout like Explorer 7 under control. If the casing was still solid up to the remaining rig structure, then the crew could place a new wellhead assembly—a Christmas Tree—over the wellbore and bolt it onto the well casing. The fire had to be extinguished first. That was the easy part. They detonated dynamite at the point where the oil exited the wellbore to starve the fire of oxygen and snuff out the flame.

Then they moved the assembly into position with the valve open, allowing the oil to keep shooting out through the opening. Once bolted in place, the valve was closed and the well brought under control. The tricky part was swinging the assembly over the gushing oil. They had to deal with the pressure of the oil column, that worked to shove the assembly out of the way.

The second option was to drill a relief well. They used directional drilling to intercept the blowout well subsurface. Once contact was made with the wellbore, they pumped mud down the relief well and into the blowout well to counteract the pressure of the oil column and force it back downhole, thus taming the well.

What shocked Cutter was that Joe thought he could use the first method on Explorer 7. Looking at the tangled wreckage, he knew the surviving infrastructure could never support a wellhead capping program. There was nothing to attach a Christmas Tree to.

"Joe, you can't be serious. There isn't a snowflake's chance you've got enough to work with to cap this sucker. Have you thought of what's going to happen if you kill the fire and can't cap the well? You're going to have thousands of barrels a day spewing into the Gulf. Christ, Joe, you're just going to lose time fooling around with a cap attempt."

Cutter saw the concern in Joe's eyes. "My team really doesn't have the equipment or training for this. I talked to Anderson about it, but she just wanted us out here fast."

Cutter shook his head. "I understand, Joe. It's a lousy situation. You guys are doing the best you can. But forget about a cap. Let's concentrate on a relief well."

"It may get to that, Cutter, but I'm gonna try the cap first. If it works, we can get this baby under control in a matter of days. A relief well's gonna take weeks. Hell, you know that. Sometimes you have to throw the dice. This is damn well one of those times."

Cutter pulled a tin of chew out of his pocket. Placing a pinch under his lower lip, he looked at the roaring flame. "Not when you're playing with dice as loaded as these," he murmured to himself, realizing he wouldn't get any further with Joe. One thing was certain. Joe was scared shitless. Hell, Cutter was scared shitless. Who wouldn't be? Maybe Joe was right. Try a cap first and then go for the relief well if necessary. But why wait to get the relief well started?

"Joe, let's start a relief well now. If we don't need it, fine. But if the cap doesn't work, we'll have saved a lot of time."

Joe shook his head. "I'm not authorized to spend money on parallel control options. A relief well's gonna cost a pile of dough."

"Aw, come on, Joe. We've got a potential Deepwater Horizon unfolding here. Cost can't be a factor in fighting this son of a bitch."

Joe looked at Cutter. "I appreciate your coming out and offering a hand, but it's my show, and I'm gonna do the best I can with what I've got. I'm not gonna start a relief well while I think a cap is possible. You can help or you can get out of the way."

Cutter shrugged and launched a stream of chew over the railing, watching it arc through the air. Joe wasn't thinking straight. For the moment, all Cutter could do was assist the capping effort.

Yeah, right! We're going to put out Dante's inferno with a candlesnuffer.

36

HOUSTON, TEXAS - BIG THICKET, TEXAS

Tuesday
June 5

The alarm shrilled to life at 4:45 a.m. Jenn slammed the snooze button and rolled over. When it went off again fifteen minutes later, she groaned and reluctantly kicked off the covers. The sun was already peeking around the corner of her blackout curtains. She stumbled out of bed and groped her way into the shower. At Shane's request, she'd asked Mike O'Day to set up a meeting with an FBI pal who was one of the Bureau's top explosives experts. *Of course he had to follow Bureau practice, and set the meeting for the crack of dawn!*

Entering the hotel cafe, she spied Mike at a back booth in animated conversation. As she approached, she smiled inwardly at his friend's considerable paunch squeezed against the table. Looking over Mike's shoulder, she saw the paper open to the latest from the *Houston Chronicle* on the "Crisis in the Gulf." The reports were disturbing.

"It's a real mess, ain't it?" She slid into the booth.

Mike smiled. "Dave Bannion, Jenn Nelson. Jenn's an investigator with Wildcat's legal team. Former FBI, so really part of the family."

He handed Jenn a menu. "And Dave here is with the Bureau's Explosives Unit."

"Nice to meet you, Dave."

"Same here. Can't say I understand what all the fuss is about, though." He gestured at the paper. "Isn't this just another oil spill? I mean it's not the first and it won't be the last, right?"

Jenn accepted the mug of coffee from the waitress and shook her head. "This is different, Dave. An oil spill like the Valdez in some godforsaken corner of the far north is bad enough, but this one is unfolding on our doorstep. It's definitely caught everyone's attention. Just look around." They could hear snippets of conversation from the other tables. Most were talking about the Gulf. How would they cap it? How long would it take? Would the oil reach the

BENDING THE ARC 249

beaches? Was it going to be BP and the Deepwater Horizon all over again?

"OK, Jenn. I hear you. Are you going to tell me why I was invited down to Houston on half-a-day's notice? Who the heck do you know in the Bureau, anyway?"

"Let's just say I have an inside channel and Mike couldn't say enough nice things about you." She looked at Mike. "How do you two know each other?"

"Dave and I go way back. We spent five years as special agents operating out of the FBI's Seattle field office. I moved on to the EPA, but we maintained contact through the years. Now he's became one of the Bureau's top explosives experts, although he won't tell you that. He heads up training at the Bureau's Hazardous Devices School in Huntsville, Alabama, and was instrumental in the Oklahoma City investigation, helping pull together the physical evidence that led to the successful prosecution of Timothy McVeigh. He was also part of the Unabomber task force that brought Ted Kaczynski to justice."

Jenn nodded and smiled at Dave. "Very impressive. Looks like we've got the right guy for the job." She described LawForce, the GAC litigation, and Wildcat's problems at Buffalo 36. "We need to inspect that holding tank. The outlet valve failed at the point where it was welded to the tank. Wildcat suspects foul play. You're the guy to tell us if there's anything to that. We've got a bird waiting at the hangar."

"Sounds good."

As they approached the lease site, the scene was noticeably different from a few days ago. No oil-stained hay was visible. The lease was covered with a fresh layer of gravel and newly graded.

Jenn loved the Thicket. Looking beyond the edge of the lease, she admired the old cypress trees with roots arching above the water in surreal, twisted shapes. Their knobby knees rose like sentinels from the murky depths, creating a labyrinthine network of passages and pools. The water was still, a mirror reflecting the green canopy above, broken only by the occasional ripple of a frog or, as she'd been told, the gliding form of an alligator or two.

Cutter Davis, who was taking a break from Explorer 7, waited at the pad to welcome them.

"Hey, kids. Nice to see some friendly faces. It's been a bit of a zoo around here the last few days."

Following introductions, Cutter led them to the trailer.

"Have a seat. I just brewed a fresh batch." He passed around mugs and filled them from the steaming pot he grabbed off the hotplate.

"Mr. Bannion, I assume that Mike and Jenn

have updated you on the sabotage of our access road?"

"Yeah. Pretty creative. A lot subtler than just blowin' the damn thing up."

"Sorry I don't share your admiration for those bastards," Cutter said without humor. "This is costing us a ton of money. I don't think our tank out there just sprang a leak for the sake of it. And there's nothing very subtle about that."

"Hey, man, chill. I didn't mean any offense." Bannion stood and patted Cutter on the back. "I don't like these guys any more than you do."

"OK." Cutter accepted the oblique apology. "I'm a bit on edge these days. The timing of this whole thing stinks. Our well is on test, flowing oil, so we've been filling up the tanks. Any other time, they would have been empty. We normally truck the oil out."

Herding the group back outside, Cutter grabbed some hardhats out of the back of a pickup, threw one over to Bannion, and passed a couple over to Mike and Jenn. "White hardhats, kids, that means you're top dogs on the lease site." He grinned.

Jenn chuckled. Despite his rough edge, Cutter Davis was a nice guy. She noticed the two guards walking the perimeter. *These guys are serious about security.* Fluorescent flagging tape cordoned off the area around the tank.

Cutter motioned Bannion to the side of the tank, where the valve still hung from a connecting shard of metal. Bannion looked over the scene carefully. Then he knelt on one knee next to the feeder pipe leading to the tank.

"Interesting," he said, reaching for his smart phone. Holding it close to the pipe, he took several pictures. Then he reached for his backpack and pulled out a small kit with what looked like tape. He applied it to the pipe, then carefully peeled it off and sealed it with another piece of tape. Finally, he took out a metal spatula and scraped something off the pipe, smeared it on a small pad and sealed it in a plastic evidence bag.

Jenn couldn't contain her curiosity. "What is it, Dave?"

"Don't know yet. Maybe nothing, but worth checking out. Now let's have a look at that valve."

He pulled out a magnifying glass and flashlight. Poking his head through the opening, he examined the tank from the inside. After carefully withdrawing his head, he stood up and looked at Cutter.

"I can cut the valve off and take it to the lab for testing, but I know what we're gonna find. Residue of some pliant, shapeable explosive. Likely plastique. You were right, Cutter. There's no doubt about it. This wasn't a weld failure. This was sabotage."

"How can you be so sure so quickly?" Jenn asked.

"Here." He handed her the magnifying glass. "Have a good look at the ragged edge of the opening." Jenn knelt and studied the damage. Bannion pointed at the sharp edges. "See how those small shards are bent *inwards*? Any weld failure would have left the surrounding edges in a neutral position or even facing out slightly, following the outward pressure of the liquid head behind the valve. The only way you could have these shards bent inwards is in reaction to a force being exerted from *outside* the tank. It's as simple as that."

"Son of a bitch," Cutter swore. "*Son of a bitch*. Along with that damned fake nest, this is starting to look like somebody really has it in for us. Jenn, I'm counting on your team to help us get these bastards before they do some real damage and kill people."

Jenn nodded. "We've got the best in the world on it, Cutter. Just give us some more time."

Cutter shook his head. "We may not have more time."

Feeling tense when she got home., Jenn opted for some exercise before bed. After putting out a saucer of milk for her cat, Oscar, she retired to the den that did double duty as a workout room. She stretched, then settled into Mountain

Pose as she mulled over the day's events. Easing into Warrior II, she concentrated on the planted falcon nest. *Why?* To block the access road? But, again, why? As she transitioned into Triangle Pose, she thought back to what Cutter had said about the only reason for storing so much oil on site was the closure of the road.

She sat down and moved into Seated Forward Fold. The planted nest was all about disrupting rig operations. While the saboteur may have planned the added consequence of loading the tanks ahead of the spill, or it may just have been a lucky break, the events had to be connected, part of the same program. Too much of a coincidence for any other conclusion. She rolled over into Corpse Pose, staring at the ceiling.

What the hell was going on?

37

HOUSTON, TEXAS

Friday
June 8

Shane watched BJ survey the lavish surroundings in the Todd Ives reception area. He turned to Shane.

"So this is where those legal fees go. Just think of it, Steve, my boy. All this paid for by the clients."

"Maybe you appreciate my operation a little more now. No one can criticize us for having a high overhead."

"They can't at that. Hell, those cubicles y'all work in remind me of a rabbit warren." He laughed at Shane's hurt look.

"Don't worry, son. Your team gets me out of this GAC mess and I promise there'll be a healthy premium to pay for whatever upgrades you need." He slapped Shane on the back as they both stood watching the hazy skyline.

Shane had to admit, the reception area was a class act. Stepping out of the elevator and onto the polished marble floor, the atmosphere conveyed an aura of sophistication. The space was vast and open. The reception desk, a sleek monolith of black granite, anchored the room. Its surface was devoid of clutter, save for a state-of-the-art touchscreen monitor and a single orchid in a minimalist vase. The receptionist, dressed in a tailored suit, had offered a warm, yet professional greeting.

Bold, brushed steel letters displayed the firm's name on the wall behind the desk. The backdrop of rich wood paneling added a touch of warmth. To the left of the reception desk, a wall of glass offered a stunning panoramic view of downtown Houston.

Plush leather chairs and sofas in shades of charcoal and cream were positioned around low, glass-topped tables. Neatly fanned out on the tables, current issues of prestigious law journals and business magazines showed the firm's engagement with the latest industry trends.

Large, striking pieces of art adorned the walls. Not in the western motif Shane preferred, but abstract paintings in bold colors and intricate patterns. Along one wall, black-and-white images of the founding partners, candid shots of landmark cases, and photos of high-profile events offered a glimpse into the firm's illustrious past.

Shane stiffened as BJ wrapped a beefy arm around his shoulder. "Santa Claus, the tooth fairy, an honest lawyer, and an old drunk are walking down the street together when they all spot a hundred-dollar bill at the same time. Who gets it?"

Shane rolled his eyes. "I don't know, the honest lawyer?"

"Naw, the old drunk, of course. The other three are mythical creatures." The receptionist frowned as his deep laughter rolled through the room.

Shane smiled. "You're a riot, BJ, a veritable riot." He plopped onto one of the oversized leather couches.

"Listen, I need a little background for this meeting. Who is this woman Anderson, and what kind of company is ARI, anyway?"

"Anderson is good people, Steve. She may be an easterner, but she's been around the patch for two decades now. Smart as a whip. Founded ARI fifteen years ago, made a ton of money on a couple of sweet oil strikes and hasn't looked back since. ARI is a senior oil and gas company compared to Wildcat. ARI's capitalization is twenty times ours."

"And what about Tillington acting for ARI? Have you given that any more thought?"

"Hell, Steve, I don't like Tillington. I don't like that he's acting for the GAC. But I understand he's a sharp lawyer. He's got a helluva reputation. I can't tell Anderson what lawyers she can hire." He shrugged. "It's business."

"Yeah, I guess. Do you do a lot of business with ARI?"

"Not really. Explorer Seven is our only joint play. ARI would like to farm-in on the balance of our Gulf offshore blocks, but we're not interested. That acreage is what's going to transform Wildcat into an energy dynamo."

"Why is ARI the operator on Explorer Seven?"

"They've got the manpower and a heck of a lot more offshore experience than we do. That's why we let them farm-in on the Explorer Seven play. We originally held a one hundred percent interest, but allowed them to earn fifty percent by drilling several wells for us. We want to go to school on these guys. Our plan is to learn as much as we can from our joint operations and use it to develop the rest of our acreage."

"So you've got a good relationship with them?"

"Better than good, Steve. We're competitors, sure, but I would never have farmed out to an outfit I didn't think was solid."

BENDING THE ARC

They rose as Judy Stinson came out to greet them. "Thank y'all for waiting. They're ready for you now. If you'll follow me."

She led them to the boardroom. On entering, Shane noticed that they were badly outnumbered. Tillington was with Cindy Webster and two other Todd Ives associates, as well as Anderson and another ARI executive. After the obligatory handshakes and exchange of business cards, they seated themselves, following the unwritten law that attorneys sit next to their clients on opposite sides of the table.

Tillington cleared his throat. "I want to get one thing out in the open right at the start. I trust my representation of the GAC against Wildcat won't affect your ability to work with us as we stickhandle through this Explorer Seven situation?"

BJ smiled. "Shucks, Mr. Tillington, if I wanted to hold that against you and ARI, I wouldn't be here. I do question your judgment in representing outfits like the GAC, but that's got nothing to do with Explorer Seven, so let's get on with it, shall we?"

Tillington nodded. "I believe Leona mentioned to you that Seabright and Company were engaged to do an initial analysis of events at Explorer Seven. We needed some fast information to formulate our damage control plan. They provided us with their initial report in less than two weeks, something of a record for an event of this magnitude. I want to stress that these findings are by no means conclusive, nor indeed should they be considered meaningful in any real sense."

With all the weasel words, Shane knew what was coming. He tapped BJ's arm and pointed to his legal pad, where he'd scratched *ARI screwed up!* BJ grunted in quiet acknowledgment.

Tillington droned on. After ten minutes of caveats and cautions regarding how little they should rely on the report, he nodded to his associate. She pulled several copies from a brainbag behind her and distributed them. The report was twelve and a half pages, one of which was an executive summary.

"You can read the report at your leisure. The preliminary conclusion is that the Explorer Seven failure is the result of negligent maintenance. Specifically, a failure to have the rig's support structure, the legs, inspected at the required interval."

Anderson sat stone faced. BJ let out a low whistle.

"Goddamn, Leona. Y'all missed your mandatory inspection?"

"It looks that way, BJ. I can't explain it at this point. Naturally, we're doing an internal investigation as we speak."

Tillington spoke up to shift the focus off his

client. "While this report was not, strictly speaking, produced under attorney-client privilege, we are obviously treating it as confidential. We shared its contents with you since the report was commissioned on behalf of the Explorer Seven partners, not on behalf of ARI in its individual capacity. We ask that you keep the report at a need-to-know level within your organization, as indeed ARI will be doing."

BJ snorted. "I sure as hell don't want this floating around out there. It's just an initial guesstimate. We need a hell of a lot more information and definition here."

"Yes, of course, BJ," Anderson said. "Seabright and Company have a big team on it."

Shane interjected. "May I have a minute with my client?"

"Sure." Tillington stood up. "You can talk in there." He gestured to one of two doors at the end of the boardroom leading to breakout rooms.

BJ closed the door behind them. "What's up, Steve?"

"Seabright and Company may be well and good for a follow-up report, but you have to put up the money for another consultant. Call it a second opinion. With this initial report, you can bet that Seabright and Company have already formed opinions that will influence their final report. For something as significant as Explorer

Seven, you need to invest in at least a second, fully independent investigation."

"Yeah, that makes sense. You know, Seabright and Company isn't a mainstream engineering firm. I'd like to get one of the blue-chip outfits involved."

They stepped back into the boardroom.

Shane took the lead. "We'd like to have a second engineering firm retained to conduct an independent investigation. The stakes here are enormous."

Anderson nodded at BJ. "I think that makes sense. I appreciate your willingness to look at this objectively—to search for some real answers."

BJ grinned painfully. "Yeah, well, our neck's on the line too."

Anderson stood up and hugged BJ. "Thanks, old friend. It's tough enough going through this as it is, but it'd be a heck of a lot tougher with partners that weren't onside."

They stood in the elevator, lost in their thoughts. Shane broke the silence.

"What do you think?"

BJ frowned. "Something's rotten in the state of Denmark, ol' buddy. I don't know or trust these damn Seabright and Company people. How the hell can anybody be concluding negligence knowing as little as they do? I tell you, Steve, someone's got an axe to grind with ARI."

38

WASHINGTON, D.C.

Saturday
June 9

With Hendrix insisting on a face-to-face, Shane hopped a red-eye to DC. He headed straight from the airport to the LawForce center. Two boxes of doughnuts sat on the boardroom table. Hendrix washed down the last of a Boston Cream with a swig of coffee.

"You know why you're here, Steven. What in the bloody hell is going on down there? You have a case to run. Why is it we only hear from Ms. Lopez these days?"

"Come on, Jonathan. You read the papers. Wildcat's in a lot of trouble. I can't ignore that."

"That is not your problem. LawForce cannot solve all the world's problems. We have a specific goal here. Let us not lose sight of that. If we cannot take care of that blasted GAC lawsuit and prevail with our counterclaim, I perceive significant difficulty in keeping this unit together. This is LawForce's debut, and if it fails to pay dividends, well . . ."

"I know that, Jonathan. And I understand how important it is to stay focused on the GAC, but we can't try this case in a vacuum. Life is messy. If our point is that the GAC lawsuit is a bunch of crap, then it seems to me we can't ignore these new accusations. Public opinion is being influenced by these developments. We're going to pick a jury soon and that jury will have read about Wildcat's latest troubles, even if those incidents aren't part of the lawsuit."

"Yes. I hear you, Steven. And be clear, I am not saying that you should ignore these breaking developments. All I ask is that you remember what LawForce's objective is . . ."

The door burst open. Mike O'Day couldn't contain his excitement. "We got a match on a print from Buffalo Thirty-Six. You guys won't believe it."

Shane looked at Mike. "What print? What are you talking about?"

"When Dave Bannion, an FBI explosives expert working the case with us, was out at the

Buffalo Thirty-Six site with Jenn the other day, he picked up a print on the pipe next to the failed valve. And we hit the jackpot. We have an ID."

Hendrix got up from the table. "If you have something we need to know, Michael, let's have it."

Mike moved over to the console, pushed some buttons, and the image of a rugged, well-tanned man in uniform filled the screen. A mean scar ran across his face, from the left eyebrow to the right lower jaw.

"Gentlemen, allow me to introduce Mr. Scott Magruder, ex-Navy SEAL with a slew of commendations and awards earned on multiple missions in the Middle East."

Hendrix was intrigued. "Can you be more exact, Michael? Exactly what kind of action did this man, Magruder, see?"

"Several tours. In Iraq, his first major deployment was during the Second Battle of Fallujah, codenamed Operation Phantom Fury. That was one of the bloodiest battles of the Iraq War, sir, and Magruder's role was pivotal. Leading a SEAL platoon, he cleared insurgent strongholds in the city's urban landscape. In one mission, he lead his team through a maze of tunnels, neutralizing enemy combatants and recovering critical intelligence. His actions earned him the Silver Star, awarded for gallantry in action.

"In Afghanistan, during Operation Red Wings, Magruder's unit received orders to capture or kill a high-ranking Taliban leader. The mission took place in the mountains of Kunar Province. Under the cover of darkness, Magruder and his team were inserted via helicopter to navigate the rugged terrain and establish an overwatch position. The mission went to shit, pardon my French, when a larger-than-expected enemy force ambushed the team. Magruder coordinated an effective counter-attack, personally taking out multiple enemy fighters while calling in close air support. His actions not only saved the lives of his team members, but also inflicted heavy casualties on the enemy. They awarded him the Navy Cross for that one.

"In Pakistan, he was involved in a support role in Operation Neptune Spear, the mission that took out Osama bin Laden. Magruder played a crucial role in the intelligence gathering and planning phases of the operation. His experience in urban warfare and close-quarters combat was key in training the SEALs for the raid.

"Finally, in Helmand Province, Afghanistan, Magruder was involved in a series of counter-insurgency operations aimed at destabilizing Taliban supply lines and safe havens. He led his team on numerous direct-action missions, often deep behind enemy lines. One mission required insertion via fast-roping from helicopters into a heav-

BENDING THE ARC

ily fortified village. His team breached the enemy defenses and engaged in a fierce firefight. His coolness under pressure turned the tide of battle, resulting in the capture of several high-value targets and the seizure of a significant weapons cache. For this one, he earned multiple commendations, including the Bronze Star with Valor."

Mike stopped, looking at the grim faces around the room.

"Is that all?" Hendrix sighed. "Clearly, we have one accomplished individual who, unfortunately, has flipped to the dark side. After all that, it's a wonder the man is still functioning, so to speak."

Hendrix studied the image a moment longer, then glanced at Shane with a questioning look before turning back to the screen. "Are you absolutely sure of your identification? It is a lot to believe that such a highly decorated American soldier would be involved in this tawdry business."

"Yes, sir. Sorry. No doubt on this one. We also got a DNA match. Did I mention Bannion also picked up a blood sample at the Buffalo Thirty-Six site? The DNA was in the military's special forces database. I've never gotten a faster response to a DNA request—would have never been possible without LawForce. But, yes, this is our guy, no doubt."

Hendrix nodded. "Thank you, Michael. Steven, I think your course of action is clear."

Shane walked up to the screen for a closer look. "You bet. We'll put a full court press on finding this bastard."

Hendrix paused at the door. "Work with the FBI. This is when LawForce will demonstrate its true power."

39

GULF OF MEXICO

Sunday
June 10

Cutter watched the Bell 205A-1++ *Skylift* hover above the flaming wreckage, the explosives swinging wildly below it. *Christ, what an operation.* The bundle had to be positioned precisely over the mangled wellhead. At the right time, electronic ignition would detonate the dynamite and *Skylift* would have to withstand the upward pressure wave. They figured two thousand feet provided the necessary clearance.

Skylift was on loan from Lone Star Construction. The president sat on ARI's board. While the four-man crew specialized in high-angle construction lifts, it never faced an assignment like this.

There was little choice. For a land operation, they would have wheeled the dynamite into position using a jury-rigged boom extending from a caterpillar. The cat, modified with a large metal heat shield, would approach close enough to suspend the dynamite above the wellhead. The crew would then retreat to a safe distance before detonation.

But on the water, Cutter knew things were trickier. They originally planned to use the *Langley II* as an aquatic caterpillar. But no matter how they worked the problem, they couldn't overcome two hurdles. First, there was no way to construct a boom that provided the *Langley* with enough clearance from the explosion. Second, the Langley was not stable enough to place the explosives with the required accuracy. The heaving seas would have the package flying around like a cork in a whirlpool.

Cutter knew Joe was at his wit's end when he came up with the idea for an airborne placement. He had to know it was an extreme-risk operation.

Cutter squinted at *Skylift*, barely making it out in the smoky haze. He was against the dynamiting operation and tried to talk Joe out of it. Even if they killed the fire, there was no way to cap the well in a conventional sense with the loss

BENDING THE ARC

of most of the platform and the twisted wreckage surrounding the wellbore.

When he realized Joe would not listen to reason, Cutter called BJ and asked him to fly out to the *Langley*. Meanwhile, he could only watch and wait.

Holding the electronic detonation device in his hands, Joe guided the helicopter crew by radio. He had a better view of the wellhead from the *Langley*.

"Skylift, are we go for detonation?"

"Roger that, Langley. Tell us where you need the package and when you're happy, let 'er rip."

"OK. Your line is good. Ease it down another twenty feet. That's it—easy, easy . . ." Waving one hand in the air, Joe hit the switch.

The roar was deafening. As a tremendous geyser of water shot skyward, *Skylift* shook before regaining control. They watched in fascination as the fire suffocated before their eyes. A curtain of water descended, drenching everyone on deck. After a few seconds, a cheer went up from the *Langley*'s crew.

Skylift spiraled down for a closer look at the flame-free plume of oil gushing from the mangled wellhead.

"Langley, this is Skylift. Congratulations. We're coming in for a fly-over."

Oh, God! Cutter raced over to Joe.

"Joe, call them off," he screamed. "They've got to stay clear for at least fifteen minutes. This baby could catch . . ."

An enormous roar drowned out the rest of his warning.

He watched in horror as the flaming column of oil, reignited by a lit pocket of oil surrounding the well, spiraled skyward. In seconds, *Skylift* was consumed by the flames. A bloodcurdling scream came through the open radio link seconds before a spectacular explosion. The big bird disintegrated before their eyes, glowing shards of metal showering down, with random pieces landing on the *Langley*'s deck.

"Oh, Christ! Jesus H. Christ!" Joe sobbed uncontrollably. Cutter put an arm around him.

"Joe, they should have known better. They were crazy not to stand back until the situation stabilized. You couldn't help what happened."

"That's bullshit, Cutter. I should have briefed those boys. They weren't an oil patch crew."

Cutter knew he was right, but this wasn't the time for brutal honesty.

"Listen, Joe, we need to get that relief well going now."

"I can't do that, Cutter. It would mean these guys just bit it for nothing. You saw the helo placement. It worked. We just have to control the surrounding fire. I've got some pumper units coming in from Galveston. They'll be here in a few hours. By then, we'll have another helo and charge lined up."

"Goddamn it, Joe. You are one stubborn son of a bitch. You're wasting time, money, and now lives on this hopeless capping attempt."

The last comment hit too close to home. "Fuck you, Cutter! I told you before it's my play. If you have a problem with it, you can take off anytime."

Three hours later, Cutter walked out to greet the Bell JetRanger as it landed on the *Langley*'s aft helicopter pad.

"Hey, Cutter. Why do y'all need me out here? I've got a lot on my plate at the office."

Cutter knew he was stressed, but BJ still took the time to listen carefully to Cutter's briefing. Cutter emphasized his concern with ARI using an in-house crew to tackle what was one of the most complicated blowouts in oilfield history.

They looked up as another chopper positioned itself over the wellhead, lowering its bundle of dynamite. This time four pumper barges surrounded the site. The operation unfolded much like the first, but with two significant differences. The chopper shot skyward on detonation, and the pumpers immediately unleashed a shower of chemical foam on the surrounding ocean. There was a deathly calm for many minutes before they allowed themselves to believe the fire was out for good this time.

BJ turned away from the unfolding drama. "Cutter?"

"Yeah."

"I want you to contact some specialists *now*. We need help along the lines of Red Adair, some outfit of that caliber. I'll leave it to you. I want you in charge out here. I'll call you as soon as I talk to Leona."

"OK, BJ, will do."

Tears welled in BJ's eyes as he watched the oil spewing into the Gulf. His look of despair scared the hell out of Cutter.

"This is everything I've worked against all my life." He waved at the black pool surrounding the ship. "It doesn't matter how it happened. The bottom line is we're responsible for this nightmare."

40

HOUSTON, TEXAS

Wednesday
June 20

The Hyatt Imperial Ballroom was humming. Despite the upgrade from the Regency Ballroom, the larger venue, five times the size, was full. Explorer Seven had sparked the interest of a nation.

Thankfully, BJ was getting used to this press conference thing. Shane grinned. If everything went south at Wildcat, BJ might earn his living as one of those smooth-ass media consultants. Shane used to think they were useless as tits on a bull, but he'd come to appreciate the impact the media had on a business. Spin doctors were in.

He watched Val lean over and whisper into BJ's ear. Hopefully, she was warning him to concentrate on Buffalo 36 and not get dragged into Explorer 7. That was ARI's mess.

BJ nodded and tapped the mike to get everyone's attention.

"Nice to see y'all again, although I hope we don't start making this a habit."

The members of the media chuckled politely.

"I wanted to give y'all an update on what's happening with our operations at Buffalo Thirty-Six, probably the best-known well in Texas these days . . . er, maybe the second best."

They laughed.

"As y'all have seen, the cleanup operation was an unqualified success. We recovered virtually one hundred percent of the spilled oil and have reclaimed the area. We got a clean bill of health from Texas Environment yesterday and . . ."

Shane flipped off the office TV and returned his attention to the thin binder in front of him.

Something didn't feel right about the report. It was one of the briefest, most direct expert reports he'd ever read. But what made it stand out was the definitive conclusion. The report's lack of weasel words, of those "conditionals on" and "subjects to," was disturbing. The assertive conclusion of negligence was curious, considering the report was based on preliminary investigations spanning a scant few weeks. In reaching its conclusions, Seabright and Company relied heavily on the failure of the rig to undergo its mandatory structural integrity examination. The rig was overdue for that inspection by over a hundred days.

The eyewitness reports followed a structural failure scenario. Leg three failed first, followed by leg two and the BOPs. With no physical evidence, the report coupled the eyewitness reports with the rig's failure to undergo its mandatory inspection and concluded that the disaster could reasonably be attributed to negligent maintenance.

Shane had confidence that Kenton Engineering, the highly respected firm BJ engaged for an independent study, would offer an alternative perspective. But it came down to physical evidence, no matter who was conducting the investigation. And that evidence was lying at the bottom of the Gulf.

He wandered into Jenn's office. Typing away on her laptop, she looked up excitedly as he entered.

"We got some dynamite evidence on Buffalo Thirty-Six, pun intended. I'm just writing it up. That leak was no accident, unless you call sabotage an accident."

"That's interesting, Jenn, but Explorer Seven is the focus now. We just got a prelim report that points the finger at ARI for negligence. I think something's wrong with that picture, but unfortunately, all the clues of what really happened are lying on the ocean floor."

Jenn looked up. "So? Dive it."

Shane sounded as incredulous as he looked.

"Dive it? Geez, I never thought . . . Could you do that? I mean, the site's a goddamn inferno for miles around."

"Steve, we're talking about the ocean *floor*. It's a different world down there. There's nothing to stop a dive team from checking out the wreckage. The water cover's deep enough."

"Right. Use whoever and whatever you need from LawForce. I want a team on this right away. If we're going to get any answers about what really happened to that rig, the wreckage is the key."

"Roger that. Stick around for a minute." Jenn typed a link into her computer and waited for the LawForce Washington office to flicker onto the monitor. The technical wizards at LawForce had made the video system securely accessible online. Shane saw Mike O'Day sitting at the boardroom table.

"Mike, it's Jenn. I've got Steve with me. How's it going?"

"Good. The lab confirmed that they used C-Four on that tank. No doubt about it. A pretty standard type, easily accessible on the global terrorist-paramilitary market. I don't think we're going to be able to trace it."

"Just knowing it was a bomb and not material failure is a lot of help, Mike. Would this evidence hold up in court?"

"No doubt about it. Dave's the best there is. His testimony, along with the lab results, make for as high a confidence level as you're gonna get."

"That is good news. Thanks Mike."

"*De Nada*. We'll send you the certified lab results by Fed-Ex. Let us know if you want to use Dave as an expert witness. Catch ya later."

"No, wait, Mike. That's not why we called. Is Dave still available to work for LawForce?"

"Listen, Jenn, our instructions are that *anyone* is available to work for LawForce. You guys have a standing priority order from the AG himself. Why do you still need Dave?"

"You've heard about Explorer Seven?"

"Who hasn't?"

"We need to investigate the wreckage on the ocean floor."

Mike let out a low whistle. He glanced up at the camera.

"Now that's gonna be some fun. I'll call Dave right away. We'll get a team from the military's Deep Sea Rescue Unit. Those guys have all the deep-water experience and equipment. And

I know Dave has some good SEAL connections on the underwater demolition side."

"Thanks, Mike. As usual, we need to get on this yesterday. Let me know if you need anything from us to help with the staging area, dive ship, or whatever."

"You just concentrate on getting that evidence in shape for the GAC action. We'll take care of Explorer Seven."

"Right. But keep it tight, Mike. Need-to-know."

"Hey, guys, that's my middle name. Talk to ya soon."

Fifteen minutes later, Jenn entered Shane's office and threw the emailed lab results on his desk.

"Like Mike said, C-Four, someone blew up that tank. The evidence is solid."

"Great work, Jenn. But I got to tell you, this case is getting too complicated for my liking. The GAC litigation was one thing, but this Explorer Seven mess. I don't know. I keep wondering, what's next? I'm a lawyer, Jenn, not Double O Seven."

"That's why you got me. And now the rest of the LawForce team. You and Val just concentrate on the petitions, briefs, depositions, and all the rest of that stuff. Leave the gumshoeing to us."

Shane laughed. "You got it."

Jenn turned to leave, but stopped at the door. "I almost forgot. We now have the FBI engaged in the search for Magruder. They've put a guy named Ted Kratz on it. He's their senior domestic terrorism agent in DC. They are clearly taking this seriously."

Shane punched BJ's number on the speed dial. "BJ, I've read that Seabright report. I have to agree with you. It looks like someone's trying to put the screws to ARI. We're going to investigate the Explorer Seven wreck." Shane explained the plans for the dive.

"That's good stuff, Steve, but I've got to concentrate my efforts on bringing Explorer Seven under control."

"Sure, you bet. I'll need some help preparing for the GAC litigation, but I can get most of my info from the rest of your staff. You take care of that well."

41

GALVESTON, TEXAS

Friday
June 22

Clint Farber stood looking out the window. The view from his eighth-floor room at the Hilton Galveston Island Resort was spectacular. The outdoor tropical pool sprawled below him, complete with waterfall and swim-up bar. Across the road was the beach and beyond that, the vast expanse of the Gulf. Staring at the ocean, he could watch the waves roll in forever.

But business called. The envelope, which the bellman had delivered, was stamped URGENT and had no return address. Whoever delivered it to the Galveston Hilton knew his itinerary. The muffled message on his voice-mail simply said,

"Brown envelope at the front desk. You want to read it *immediately*."

His curiosity piqued, Farber opened the envelope and pulled out thirteen stapled pages. The cover read: EXPLORER 7–PRELIMINARY ANALYSIS, SEABRIGHT AND COMPANY. Thumbing through the pages, he let out a low whistle. He fought his rising excitement. Must think it through. Hoax? Not likely. No apparent motive, and the report looked legitimate. He grabbed the white pages and looked up Seabright and Company. A structural engineering consulting firm. That fit. The name Ray Cramont appeared at the end of the report with Cramont's contact details. He dialed.

"Good morning, Seabright and Company."

"Yes, Mr. Cramont, please."

"I'm afraid he's not in at the moment. Could I take a message?"

"Yeah, I think he may have left something here in Galveston. There've been so many people through our office lately. Would you know if he was down here in the last couple of days?"

"Mr. Cramont was on a Gulf offshore job last week. He may have stopped off in Galveston. What did you say your company is?"

"That's fine, thank you. We'll forward his papers right away."

Farber dropped the phone in the cradle. *Yessss!*

He wasted little time grabbing the phone again.

"Leona Anderson's office, may I help you?"

"Yes, is she in, please?"

"I'm afraid she's in a meeting. Can I take a message?"

"It's Cliff Farber with *The Texas Tribune*. I need to talk with Ms. Anderson. It's urgent, and I will hold."

"Well, I'm afraid Ms. Anderson will have to call you back."

"You don't understand. I said urgent. I have information which involves some serious allegations against ARI. This information will form the basis of a story we are going to run with online in tomorrow's edition. I'm calling to provide Ms. Anderson with the courtesy of a comment before we go live. Does that explain things?"

"I'm sorry, Mr. Farber. If you'll hold, I'll get Ms. Anderson for you."

After a few minutes, Anderson was on the line.

"What is it, Mr. Farber?"

"Sorry to trouble you, ma'am, but this is important and time sensitive. I've just received a copy of a report by Seabright and Company which alleges negligence on behalf of ARI in the Explorer Seven blowout. Care to provide me with any comments for our coverage?"

Farber enjoyed the long pause. It confirmed

BENDING THE ARC

the report's authenticity. If Anderson knew nothing about any report, she wouldn't take a minute to collect her thoughts. Her voice had an icy detachment when she replied.

"Mr. Farber, I'm not in a position to discuss any report with you now. Our investigation is evolving and it would be premature to reach any conclusions at this time. Might I ask you to refrain from running your story until all the facts are in?"

"That's not how my business works, Ms. Anderson. Today it's a scoop. Who knows how many people might be on it tomorrow. We've got a little more background work to do, but I'm afraid we'll be running with this Monday morning."

"Will there be any pictures running with the story?"

"Yeah. Our editors wanted to run the piece with some video of the mess out at Explorer Seven. You know, a picture is worth a thousand words. We've got some spectacular shots of the oil gushing out like a deep-sea Old Faithful. The guys thought the video footage would bracket the story nicely."

"It just might at that," Anderson acknowledged coolly. "Just know that we are pulling out all the stops to bring that well under control. Good day, Mr. Farber."

42

GULF OF MEXICO

Monday
June 25

"Hey, boss, why do we need to dive with the Michelin Man? Can't we just report what we find?"

"Back off," Tom Jackson growled. *Sometimes Carter could be an ass.* Jackson had been leading SEAL Team Six for over two years. The guys were used to saying what they thought, unfiltered. They were also used to operating as a closed unit and trained together so often they knew each other better than blood brothers. Through that training, a bond developed that outsiders found hard to penetrate. Sure, this guy Bannion wasn't as fit as a SEAL, but that wasn't his job. He was an explosives expert and knew a hell of a lot more on that front than Carter. They needed Bannion to see the evidence first hand. It was that simple. Pictures or video feeds couldn't replace a real, on-site examination. Time to make sure everyone was on the same page.

"Dave Bannion is an ace demolitions expert. There's no one that can read an explosives record like he can. Yeah, he may be overweight, but that doesn't mean he can't do his job. So let's go through this one more time." He led the crew through the pre-dive briefing.

The dive ship pulled up a half a mile from the gushing well. They were upwind but still surrounded by a gooey, oily sea.

He checked out his team. Each diver was using lightweight commercial gear. A hose supplied the helmet with air from the surface. The helmet incorporated a communications system. They wore standard neoprene wet suits. Their diving depth of two hundred feet was at the outer limit of their equipment because of nitrogen narcosis, a degradation in thinking and reaction time caused by excessive nitrogen inhalation. While the air hoses allowed an unlimited air supply compared to scuba tanks, they limited movement and required extra attention from the four-man dive team.

Jackson asked the men to huddle up. "OK, Carter, you'll dive with Cooper. I'll go with Mr. Bannion. Mr. Bannion, you can communicate with the surface at any time through your helmet. You don't need to push any buttons, just talk. You're on an open feed to the surface. You can't talk to us directly. Keep an eye on us and we'll signal you if needed. In an emergency, you can relay a message to any of our team through the surface crew. Carter, make sure you have a high-beam strobe. I'll take one as well. It's dark enough at two hundred feet under normal conditions. With all this oil, there's going to be precious little light on the ocean floor."

He saw Bannion fumbling with his mask. "You OK, sir?"

Bannion smiled. "Don't worry about me. You guys just get me down to that wreckage. I'll be all right."

Jackson examined each diver one last time. Satisfied, he pulled on his helmet and signaled for the others to do the same. With a final thumbs up, he eased himself off the diving platform and into the oily water.

They descended at an angle toward the wellbore, taking care to stay on parallel tracks to avoid tangling their lines. As they swam closer to the well, the oil canopy blocked much of the light. Their strobes emitted defined tubes of light, slicing through the murky darkness.

Descending from the sunlit shallows into the mesophotic zone, the water darkened to a deep azure, and the sea floor began to reveal its secrets. Colorful fish darted amongst them and in the distance, Jackson could make out the graceful glide of a sea turtle.

Further down, the landscape transformed as they entered the twilight zone, a realm of dim light and muted colors. The temperature dropped and the pressure increased, creating a more challenging environment for life. A fine layer of silt and mud covered the sea floor, a testament to the slow but constant rain of organic material—marine snow—from the waters above. Venturing even deeper into the abyssal plain, the sea floor became a vast, desolate expanse stretching endlessly in all directions.

Jackson strained to get a better view as the strobes picked up hazy outlines of what appeared to be very large structures. Sure enough, four platform legs were standing intact on the ocean floor. Not surprising, since the point of failure was near the surface. That also was not unexpected. Strong winds and pounding waves exerted severe shear forces on the structure near the surface.

He swam to the ocean floor, keeping Bannion, his dive buddy, in view. The legs were tilted. Again, this was consistent with the platform's failure, reflecting the forces at play when the upper section toppled. He swam around the base of one leg and let out an involuntary shout. Floating listlessly near the platform leg was the body of Herky Cantrell. A blank expression revealed none of the horror that must have consumed his final moments.

His com system crackled to life. "Are you OK, Jackson?"

"Yeah, sorry, just spooked for a second. All is good."

He saw Bannion swim past the body and examine the platform leg. He was studying the base of the steel structure and appeared to pull something out of a bag pinned under the leg on the ocean floor.

Jackson did a 360. His eyes widened as he observed the subtle movement of one of the giant legs. He gestured frantically at Bannion to clear the area, but Bannion was still studying the ocean floor. Jackson heard the groaning steel as Bannion finally looked up. The platform leg listed back. For a split second, Jackson thought Bannion would clear the area, but then he jerked to a stop as his airline snagged on the platform leg.

Even fifteen feet away, Jackson heard Bannion's agonizing scream as the weight of the steel settled on his lower right leg. As soon as the structure stopped moving, Jackson swam over. He saw the bones in Bannion's shin snapped like popsicle sticks. The leg below the knee was bent back at a sickening right angle. A piece of jagged bone cut through the wetsuit. Blood gushed out, forming a red cloud around them. *Jesus Christ!* Thankfully, the snagged airline was now clear of the shifting platform leg and still functional.

Jackson grabbed a sling from the emergency pack strapped to his waist. He placed it around Bannion's lower thigh and tightened the tourniquet using his diving knife as a lever. With the bleeding stopped, Jackson looked into Bannion's helmet, checking his eyes. They were out of focus.

Carter and Cooper were now by their side. Through his com system, Jackson barked instructions to the surface. "We have an emergency. Bannion broke his leg and is pinned. He's unconscious. Tell Cooper to surface with me. Tell Carter we'll be back asap. He can't let the tourniquet slip. Tell him not to worry about circulating blood through the fractured leg—we won't be able to save it. The priority is keeping him breathing. And call in an emergency medivac team from Houston stat."

The response was immediate. "Roger that. We will be ready for you topside. Don't shortchange your decom stops."

Despite the need for speed, Jackson knew he had to respect the laws of physics. Ascending too rapidly, they would develop the bends and be incapable of continuing the rescue effort. He tapped Cooper on the shoulder and pointed at his depth gauge to remind him of the decompression stops.

The odds of Bannion surviving a rescue attempt were slim, but the SEALS never leave a man behind, not even a civilian. *Damned if I'm gonna break that code.*

43

HOUSTON, TEXAS

Monday
June 25

Tillington looked up in surprise. "What the hell, Kevin. How'd you get past Judy? You can't just barge in here whenever you feel like it. I have other clients."

"Not clients like me, Drew. I need you to look at this." He grabbed the remote off Tillington's desk and turned on the TV.

". . . story broke in *The Texas Tribune* this morning. KIFC News has obtained a copy of the report, which contains claims of negligence by ARI in the Gulf disaster. According to the report's authors, a Houston engineering firm, ARI failed to have its rig undergo a mandatory maintenance inspection. A full copy of the report is available on our website. For an update on the Crisis in the Gulf, here's Rick Dattonio with a live report."

"Thanks, Shelly. We've been flying over the site for the last hour. It's absolutely stunning to see the oil shooting into the Gulf. As you know, the fire was extinguished a few weeks ago, but not before a spectacular and tragic accident. An explosion blew a helicopter out of the sky. With the fire now out, a massive slick has developed. An armada of vessels is maneuvering containment booms in place, but it's clear from this aerial shot that it's a losing battle. The Galveston coastline is now in serious jeopardy. Some footage shot this morning shows the impact of the spill on marine life."

The piece cut to a clip of two dolphins frolicking in the ocean, blissfully unaware of what was to come. Upon entering the slick, they sensed something was wrong. They dove and circled back, but the slick, pushed by the wind, was spreading fast. As they surfaced, their skins became coated in oil. Having difficulty breathing, they cried out. The plaintiff chirps were heartrending. Confused, they swam further into the slick.

The smaller one slipped beneath the surface while the larger one attempted to suck in some air before its cries died away as it, too, sank from

BENDING THE ARC 295

sight. The camera caught the dolphin in a full frontal shot before it disappeared. They played that piece back in slow motion. That trademark built-in smile that all dolphins share was twisted into a painful grimace, stained with oil. The haunting eyes stared straight into the camera as the picture froze.

"This may be the start of one of the world's greatest environmental catastrophes. Certainly, one of the worst the Gulf has seen. Rick Dattonio, KIFC News."

Flaig switched off the TV. "If you go on the KIFC website, you'll find a copy of that Seabright and Company report. Besides concluding negligence, the report notes that while ARI operates the well, it only owns fifty percent. I'm sure you know who owns the rest?"

Tillington's answer was curt, "Wildcat. I've known since the well blew. It doesn't affect your lawsuit, Kevin."

"That's about to change. I want you to add Explorer Seven and Buffalo Thirty-Six to that lawsuit as supporting evidence of environmental negligence. And I think we have to up the claim for punitive damages to one billion dollars. Explorer Seven is a game changer."

Tillington kept his expression neutral. After a brief pause, it was time to put his cards on the table. "I have to tell you, Kevin, I'm already acting for ARI on Explorer Seven. I can't act against one of ARI's joint-play partners on that file. It would be a serious conflict of interest."

Flaig jumped to his feet. "You were acting for me long before Explorer Seven became an issue. Get someone else to act for ARI. Take it to Leona Anderson, she's the CEO over there."

"I sure as hell know who Leona Anderson is. I just told you she's my client. No way will she agree to stand down."

"Doesn't hurt to ask."

What was Flaig smoking? "Do you know something I don't?"

"Just ask, Drew, and let me know what she says."

Once he'd learned of Wildcat's connection to Explorer 7, Tillington knew Explorer 7 would be dragged into the GAC lawsuit and he would have to face the conflict presented by his acting for both the GAC and ARI. But stand down on Explorer 7? Would Anderson go for that? Judy interrupted his thoughts. "I have Ms. Anderson on the line."

Tillington grabbed the phone. "Leona, we need to talk. With that mess out at Explorer Seven, it's quite possible the GAC will be dragging ARI into the lawsuit against Wildcat."

The response was predictably cool. "You think?"

BENDING THE ARC

"Leona, you have to understand our position. The GAC retained us over a year ago. There was no way of knowing the lawsuit against Wildcat would expand to its present state. You know we wouldn't act against ARI. You're one of my best clients, for chrissake. I'm not into professional suicide."

"I'm not convinced, Drew. You've made a wonderful career off ARI and the oil and gas industry. To take on that GAC action was a betrayal of your client base."

While Tillington expected a tough talk, it was drifting into dangerous territory. Anderson needed some love.

"OK, Leona, I hear you. I meant it when I said that ARI means a lot to me and Todd Ives. Hell, we go back a long way. If you can see your way clear to us staying on the GAC file, I can recommend competent counsel to act for you. But if you want us off the GAC file, we're gone. Just say the word. We'll tell the GAC we can't act for them if they want to litigate Explorer Seven. No hard feelings."

Tillington's pen clicked madly during the long pause.

"I never did like you acting against my good friend, BJ Whitter, but I suppose it is what it is at this stage. What about the information you and Todd Ives have about Explorer Seven? Can you use that against us in the GAC litigation?"

"With the Seabright and Company report now public, we're not privy to anything confidential pertaining to Explorer Seven. I checked with our team and we've never represented you on any matters in the past related to Explorer Seven. Not surprising as it's a recent play."

"Yes, I suppose that's right." Another long pause. "Who would you have in mind to act for us in the GAC lawsuit?"

"A first-rate litigator, old law school classmate of mine, Charlie Hillerman. He's over at Cheney Cox."

Anderson's response took an enormous weight off his shoulders. "Set up a meeting, Drew."

44

GULF OF MEXICO - GALVESTON, TEXAS

Monday
June 25

"There's only two options—cut the leg or cut the steel. And we haven't got the equipment or time to cut the steel. He's in severe shock. If we don't get him medivaced within the hour, he's had it."

Jackson gave one of the ship's crew a curt order and checked his helmet and airline, gesturing to Cooper to do the same.

Within minutes, the crew member returned and handed Jackson a saw and Cooper a long-range spear gun. Jackson clipped the saw to his weight belt. Cooper looked at the spear gun.

"You really think we'll need this, boss?"

"I saw a few big ones in the distance. If we spill a lot more blood down there, they may get anxious. I want you to backstop us. Safety first."

Cooper nodded. "Sure."

Jackson finished adjusting his gear. "All set?"

"Let's do it." Cooper flashed the thumbs-up.

They reached Bannion and Carter in double time. The next twenty minutes were the worst of Jackson's life. He pulled out a large plastic bag and wrapped it around his sawing arm and Bannion's leg.

Grateful to see Bannion still passed out, he began to saw through the bone below the knee. It was all he could do to maintain his composure. The bag filled with blood, which gushed out and then slowed to a trickle as the tourniquet held. But the blood prevented him from seeing what he was doing. He slipped the bag off once the worst bleeding was over and sealed it, but not before enough blood escaped to surround them in a reddish cloud.

He heard the muffled shout before he felt the tap on his shoulder. Carter was pointing at a big shark heading straight for them. Jackson looked over at Cooper, who'd also spotted their guest. Cooper grabbed the spear gun and after a moment calmly lining up the shark, he shot him under the gills. A slight puff signaled the detonation of the explosive within the head of the spear.

Where they last saw the shark, hundreds of pieces of shark meat filled the water. Other sharks circled in for the feeding frenzy.

Jackson finished the surgery, surprised and thankful at how quickly it went. Bannion remained oblivious to it all.

When he was done, Jackson dropped the saw and allowed it to settle on the sea floor. He checked his watch. *Damn!* Been on the bottom close to thirty minutes. With the decompression stops, it would take over two hours to resurface. Carter and Bannion would need even more time. They'd been down at two hundred feet for almost an hour now. There was no choice but to grind it out.

All four ascended together to the first stop fifty feet below the surface. Jackson could see Bannion fading fast. His face turned an alarming shade of blue. Knowing they couldn't continue at the required pace and still get Bannion to the surface alive, he made an executive decision.

He scratched a message on his chalk tablet and held it in front of Cooper's mask.

> **going up fast w/ ban'n**
> **decomp @ utex**
> **c u up top**

Cooper's eyes widened. He shook his head violently. Jackson grabbed his shoulders and looked him in the eyes. He signaled an X with his arms—final decision, no debate. Cooper nodded and helped secure the dragline from Bannion to Jackson's dive belt. He gave Jackson a thumbs-up.

Jackson kicked his fins with all his strength, making a beeline for the surface. That decompression chamber at the University of Texas was now their only hope.

As they ascended rapidly, the inert nitrogen that diffused in their tissues on the way down reverted to its gaseous state, bubbling out of the blood. The pain became excruciating, but Jackson had no choice. His goal was to get to the surface before he blacked out. There was no time to worry about Bannion. They could provide him with emergency medical care on the flight out.

Within fifteen minutes of surfacing, Jackson and Bannion were in the Boeing MD Explorer *Sky Angel* air ambulance, skimming the Gulf waters en route to the University of Texas Medical Branch at Galveston. The chopper flew as low as it could to avoid aggravating the divers' decompression symptoms.

Sky Angel carried a crack trauma team from Houston Methodist Hospital. They'd flown in as soon as the dive ship raised the alarm. With Jackson and Bannion displaying severe decompression symptoms, the team rerouted the chopper to Galveston, the location of the closest decompression facilities. They stabilized Bannion, but

BENDING THE ARC

the real trauma work would have to be carried out in the decompression chamber.

A doctor examined the wound as he sterilized it. He turned to Jackson.

"Pretty good work, considering the conditions."

Jackson, barely conscious, whispered, "Thanks, Doc. I hope that was my first and last operation. How you guys do that for a living is beyond me."

"Yeah, well, I suppose I could say that about your job, sailor. You boys don't exactly lead a sedate lifestyle."

Jackson tried to laugh. "Touché!"

Jackson watched the nurse checking on Bannion. She was prying Bannion's fingers from an object in his right hand. He must have been clutching it in a virtual death grip.

Galveston had been alerted to their incoming emergency flight. The University of Texas Medical Branch (UTMB) hyperbaric facility was a great resource for the Gulf community in treating victims of diving accidents and other medical emergencies requiring hyperbaric oxygen therapy.

From previous adventures, Jackson knew that the facility had two treatment chambers. One of them, a twenty-six-foot cylindrical chamber that could accommodate up to eight people, was prepped for them. It had a double lock, allowing personnel to enter or leave the chamber while it was in use.

Jackson was conscious enough to overhear the surgeon briefing the trauma team. "Both victims are experiencing Type Two decompression sickness. In addition, one victim has suffered a field amputation. He's unconscious and has lost a large amount of blood. They transfused three units on the flight in. We're going to monitor his fluids first. Second priority is to clean up the amputation. They were working under pretty rough conditions. We've got all the basics of an operating theater set up in the chamber. You guys will have to do what you can in there. They're going to be there for a long time. We can't wait to operate until they get out. And don't forget, if you need to leave the chamber or need us to send anything in through the lock, we can do that. Questions?"

Apparently, there were none. The team's composure calmed Jackson. For them, this was just another trauma treatment, although it was being carried out in unique surroundings.

The voices faded.

45

TEXARKANA, TEXAS

Wednesday
June 27

Shane watched the big man rubbing his leg under the counsel table. "BJ, I need to bring you up to speed on the latest developments."

Shane explained the recent GAC motion to add the Buffalo 36 and Explorer 7 incidents to the lawsuit.

BJ scowled as he continued to massage his leg. "How can they do that? If they keep piling shit into this lawsuit, it's never gonna get to trial."

Shane shook his head. "This is much more serious. The stuff on the tanker spill and emissions amounted to a nuisance suit at best. Even this Buffalo Thirty-Six thing is a joke. But Explorer Seven, that's in a different league. I'm going to fight to keep it out. But if we win, they can simply launch a separate suit."

"Jesus Christ. I've got my hands full trying to get that damn well under control. And these guys can sue my butt off at every turn."

"Calm down. What's this about getting the well under control? I thought ARI was the operator." BJ started to answer, but Shane motioned him silent as Nabors entered the courtroom. "We'll talk later," he whispered.

Nabors nodded at them and Tillington, Flaig, and company across the way.

"Good morning, all. I've read your motion, Mr. Tillington. I have a few questions. Am I to understand that you are now amending your claim in the consolidated action to one billion dollars in punitive damages?"

Tillington rose from the Todd Ives counsel table. "That is correct, your Honor. The added incidents, in particular Explorer Seven, warrant that increase."

"Very well. And are you ready to proceed on the current schedule if these new incidents are added to the consolidated action?"

"Absolutely, your Honor. We have some work to do, but we will not be the reason for any delay in the schedule."

Nabors turned to Shane. "I'm ready for your submissions, Mr. Shane." Shane's heart sank. She didn't need to ask Tillington anything further as she was ready to decide in his favor.

"Your Honor, these incidents have no connection to the main action."

"But, Mr. Shane, the consolidated action is for environmental negligence. The GAC alleges the new incidents provide further evidence of environmental negligence. How is that unrelated?"

"Well, your Honor, these incidents occurred in different areas, and in the case of Explorer Seven, the operations in question were not conducted by my client's company but by its partner."

"Fine distinctions, Mr. Shane. Too fine. I listened to your arguments about legal efficiency when you made your submissions to consolidate the GAC actions some weeks back. It seems to me we're singing a different tune today. It reminds me of what my law professor used to say—'arguments are like socks, you change them every day.' Allowing the amended petition would be in the interests of an efficient proceeding. I will allow the amendment. Do you still want to bring your motion to dismiss?"

"No, thank you, your Honor."

Shane had briefed BJ on the legal team's proposal to bring a renewed application to dismiss the GAC action based on Mike O'Day's advice that the emissions were well within legislated limits. That Stokes had gummed up the initial motion didn't prevent Shane from trying again. But that was before the Buffalo 36 and Explorer 7 incidents. The ruling from Nabors allowing an expanded action killed any chance of a successful dismissal motion. The level of the spill on Explorer 7 already far exceeded an Actionable Discharge under the Texas Natural Resources Code.

BJ and Val were visibly upset. Val turned to him. "Don't you think we should at least have tried with the motion to dismiss? I mean, Mike's work is solid."

"Sure, Val, it is. But you have to read the judge. Nabors was brutally clear when she allowed the amended petition. After that, the dismissal motion didn't have a snowflake's chance. Sometimes in court, less is more. I think it was Robert Benchley who said, 'Drawing on my fine command of the English language, I said nothing.'"

BJ sounded tired. "When the hell are we going to get to trial?"

"I hear you, BJ. The judicial process can be a long and winding road. But we're almost there. This should be the last pre-trial dustup."

BJ snorted. "Why did god make snakes before he made lawyers?"

Shane shrugged.

"He needed the practice."

As they descended the courthouse steps, Shane turned to BJ.

"Hey, BJ, what was that you said about Wildcat working on Explorer Seven? Isn't that an ARI responsibility?"

"ARI's the operator, but they haven't had much success to date. I have more faith in Cutter and ARI agreed to let him take over."

"You realize you just significantly increased your legal exposure for anything that happens out there?"

"Well, hell, maybe I did. But the focus now is to get that son of a bitch under control. Covering my ass isn't a priority."

Shane sympathized with BJ. What scared Shane was that in the last fifteen minutes, the complexion of the lawsuit had changed dramatically. A fact not lost on BJ, who clearly sensed the turning tide.

46

GULF OF MEXICO

Saturday
June 30

Cutter spit a line of chew overboard and grimaced. After the *Skylift* well-capping catastrophe, BJ held a heart-to-heart with Anderson and after two weeks of failed capping attempts, he persuaded her Joe had to go. He recommended Cutter as the right man for the job. *So, this unholy mess is now squarely on my plate. Great!* But Cutter knew his limits, and his first action was to reach out for help.

The drill ship *Ocean Scout*'s dimensions were impressive. Fitted with a derrick standing two hundred feet above the waterline, the ship was three hundred feet long and fifty-five feet wide.

During drilling operations, ten computer-controlled thrusters, besides the primary propulsion system, kept *Ocean Scout* in position over the drill site. The rig could suspend fifteen thousand feet of drill pipe to an ocean depth of ten thousand feet.

The moon pool, a twenty-foot-wide hole through which the drill string was lowered, was located near the center of the ship. The water within the pool was a dark, swirling abyss, churning with the motion of the ship and the turbulent current. Staring down into it, Cutter had a sense of both awe and trepidation, as if peering into the heart of the ocean.

Overhead, the massive derrick rose like a sentinel, its lattice structure supporting the weight and movement of the drilling apparatus. Cables and hoses snaked their way from the derrick to the moon pool, connecting to the complex system of pipes and drills that plunged through the water. The drill string descended through the moon pool, disappearing into the depths. Each pipe joint was ninety feet long and weighed two thousand pounds. The drill crew used the drawworks to thread each joint to the drill string. Lowering the drill bit affixed to the end of the drill string—tripping in—took six hours in nine thousand feet of water. To drill through the sea floor, the entire drill string was rotated. The thrusters mounted underneath and facing perpendicular to the long axis of the ship kept the massive vessel from rotating.

At night, the scene took on a surreal quality. Powerful floodlights illuminated the moon pool, casting a stark, almost otherworldly glow on the water's surface. The contrast between the bright ship lights and the inky blackness of the ocean was striking.

Cutter was lucky to catch *Ocean Scout* between jobs in the Port of Houston. They were able to get the ship on site much quicker than another jack-up rig. Although *Ocean Scout* was not designed to drill in the shallower waters of the continental shelf, the captain recognized the emergency and reluctantly agreed to help.

They positioned the ship a mile away from Explorer 7 on the upwind side. The plan was childlike in its simplicity and devilishly difficult in its execution. Using the latest in directional drilling technology, *Ocean Scout* would drill diagonally to intersect the Explorer 7 wellbore—a target of only twelve inches.

When drilling, fluids flowed down the inside of the drill string and through the bit, cooling the three interlocking heads. On the way back up, the fluids carried drill cuttings to the surface in the annulus—the space between the drill string and the outside wall. Once the team intercepted the Explorer 7 wellbore, they would pump weighted muds downhole to counterbalance the escaping

BENDING THE ARC 313

oil column. Steel casing would then be set and the well sealed with a cement plug. The hardest part of the operation was hitting the target.

Once Anderson called off Joe and BJ gave him the green light, Cutter wasted no time engaging a crew from Wild Well Control. WWC was one of the world's premier blowout control outfits. The lead driller on the WWC team, Federico—Fed—Romero, was an old friend of Cutter's.

"It's a bitch, isn't it, Fed?"

Fed frowned. "I think you're right, Cutter. A cap is out of the question. Hell, there's nothing *to* cap."

"Yeah, that's where I was at from the beginning. On the environmental side, Explorer Seven's a high-volume well, and there's just no way containment is effective. How long do you think it will take for a relief well, Fed?"

"At least two weeks, quite possibly longer."

Cutter shook his head. "We've already lost a ton of oil over the last few weeks. We can't afford to lose any more. I'd rather take my chances with some black clouds from a flaming well. It's a damn site better for the environment. I'm going to reignite."

Fed gave him a long look. "Just don't blow us up, boss."

Cutter chuckled. "Not a chance. We're far enough from the well site. That stuff floating to the surface is a mile off and we're upwind of the slick."

Fed studied the oil slick, visible under the powerful spotlights fanning the ocean. "Do you know what grade this oil is?"

"What do you mean?"

"I just came off a job in Oregon. There was a beached cargo ship leaking bunker oil from her fuel tanks that held about four hundred thousand gallons. The pounding surf was breakin' her apart, with the oil staining miles of coastline. Three tanks ruptured and a storm was threatening to tear apart the rest of the ship.

"Couldn't pull her free with the tugs, so with the storm coming in, the best option was to torch the oil. We used grenades and gasoline, but the crude was too heavy, like tar. It flamed out. After a brief flash and a plume of oily smoke, a smoldering glow in two cargo holds was all we had to show for the effort.

"We brought in a team of Navy demolition experts. They blew the fuel tanks first to allow the oil to fill the cargo hold. Then they covered the oil with a twenty-barrel layer of napalm gel and ignited it by remote control with C-Four. That did the trick, although it still took three days to complete the controlled burn."

Cutter shook his head and shot a stream of chew into the ocean. "Shouldn't have that prob-

BENDING THE ARC

lem here. This stuff is light, high-end oil. She'll burn, no problem. I'm gonna reignite."

Fed reached for a cigarette. "Some folks may try and turn that around on you, but it's the right thing to do, Cutter."

WWC had the capability to mobilize anywhere in the world on a moment's notice. Often the most complicated and overlooked aspects of implementing emergency projects were service and equipment logistics. For offshore capping operations, large multi-service vessels—MSVs—were required, most of which were stationed in the North Sea. The MSVs could support surface blowout control operations on offshore structures with cranes, fire pumps, monitors, and living quarters. Within four days of hearing from Cutter, WWC had one MSV and *Ocean Scout* stocked with all the specialized equipment and personnel for the job. Within a further three days, both vessels were on site.

Once *Ocean Scout* was in place, its computer-directed thrusters ensured it didn't drift off target. Angus Stewart, *Ocean Scout*'s Scottish captain, monitored the console. While relatively young at forty-one, Stewart had more oil patch experience than most captains twice his age. Cutter stood at his side, watching the dizzying array of instruments.

"Looks more like a damn computer room than the bridge of an oceangoing vessel."

Angus chuckled. "And I feel more like a computer analyst than a captain of the high seas. This won't be easy."

"What do you mean?"

Angus pointed to an instrument displaying the ship's exact position within a circular display centered on the well's ocean floor location. "This ship is designed for drilling in deep water. Two hundred feet is going to be a real challenge."

Cutter nodded. "I know, Angus. I wouldn't have called on you if I thought there were any other options. How much harder is it?"

"Well, the deeper the water, the easier my job. The accuracy of our dynamic positioning system is measured as a percentage of the water depth. We have a five percent accuracy requirement. In one hundred feet of water, that means we can't drift off target by more than five feet, which is impossible. But in ten thousand feet of water, the allowable radius of surface movement is a generous five hundred feet."

Cutter nodded. "Yeah, I guess it's pretty logical when you think about it." He frowned as he did a quick calculation. "So, I guess we can't drift off site by more than ten feet."

Angus nodded. Cutter forced a grin and slapped him on the back. "Well, kid, I just hope you know your stuff."

BENDING THE ARC

"Thanks," Angus replied. "I know we'll be exceeding ten feet from time to time, but we'll do our damndest to keep her locked in." He stared down at the front of the ship. "We have a more immediate problem."

"What's that?"

"We're having issues with the automatic activation of one of our thrusters. The thing kicks in and out. It was supposed to be fixed in Houston during our maintenance stopover but we figured it was more important to get out here fast, so it's still an issue. It's out right now. We need to send a diver overboard to activate the thruster manually. Do any of your men have diver training?"

Cutter thought for a minute. "Yeah, a roughneck who came out with me, kid by the name of Danny Pearson, has a master diving ticket."

Cutter leaned on the ship's railing and watched the thick black clouds boiling off in the distance. The fireworks from the reignited well were spectacular in the black of the night. He shared BJ's emotional response. Cutter loved the Gulf and hated what was happening. He'd grown up a few miles from the coast. This was his backyard—not some disaster unfolding on the other side of the globe.

Fed joined him at the rail.

"Got its own kind of beauty, don't it?"

"Yeah," Cutter acknowledged. "How does

this compare to Kuwait?" Cutter knew Fed was the lead on the WWC team that bagged the most well kills in Kuwait after Saddam Hussein's troops torched seven hundred wells during their retreat. Compared to the worldwide average of twenty blowouts per year before the Gulf War, Kuwait was the mother of all blowouts. During the peak of the disaster, six million barrels of oil were lost each day. The thick smoke filled the skies over the Middle East. What appeared to be a full moon on a dark night was actually the sun.

At the outset, experts feared the wells would burn for a decade and cause inestimable damage to the earth's ecosystem. The international firefighting community rose to the occasion and successfully extinguished the blowouts in nine months.

"Kuwait was a helluva lot different, Cutter. One of our biggest problems was access to water. We pumped about one and a half billion gallons before those fires were snuffed."

Cutter snorted. "No problem with water here."

Fed didn't respond, but stared at the billowing black clouds. "Kuwait was one son of a bitch, all right. It was like a goddamn international firefighting convention. There were teams from the U.S., Canada, Britain, France, China, Iran, Romania, Hungary, the Soviet Union, and Kuwait. Supported by thousands of people from over forty countries and more than a hundred thousand tons of equipment, it was the largest mobilization in peacetime history. And those Hungarians and Romanians," Fed laughed at the memories.

"The bastards used ex-MIG jet engines, reversed them and mounted the suckers on T Fifty-Four tanks. Then they injected water into the jet stream, and goddamned if that monkey rig didn't work. Those boys surprised us all. We could use a little of that lateral thinking here, don't you think?"

"Whatever works, Fed. It doesn't have to be pretty. Just kill the sucker."

Taming Explorer 7 would require all of Fed's and WWC's skill. Fed sounded confident, but Cutter knew what they were facing was a far cry from a well in the desert. Offshore operations were inherently difficult, and Cutter couldn't recall a previous job where the entire offshore platform was gone. He rubbed the cross hanging from his neck. Lord knows, they would need all the help they could get.

47

GALVESTON, TEXAS

Saturday
June 30

That distinctive, sterile hospital smell was universal. Hospitals always gave her the creeps. She was thankful she'd spent precious little of her life in them. Jenn had flown to Galveston on getting the call from Tom Jackson. Bannion was out of surgery.

Towering palm trees flanked the main entrance to the sprawling campus of UTMB Galveston, welcoming visitors to a place where the wonders of the ocean and state-of-the-art medical innovation came together. As Jenn approached the reception desk, a friendly attendant greeted her. "Good morning. How can I help you today?"

BENDING THE ARC

"I'm looking for my friend's room in the hyperbaric medicine ward. He would have been brought in on an emergency helicopter evacuation from the Gulf a few days ago."

"Yes, of course. His arrival caused quite a stir. Let me find his exact coordinates for you." The attendant tapped on the keyboard. "Mr. Bannion is in room 412, on the fourth floor. You'll take the elevators down this hall to your left."

Jenn started down the corridor, her footsteps echoing in the quiet hallway. *How the hell do you deal with losing a leg like that?* While the hospital did its best to mask the sterile smell with a subtle, calming scent of lavender and eucalyptus, it didn't work. *God, I hate these places.*

She found the bank of elevators easily enough. Pressing the button, she waited, her mind racing. *One day you're whole, the next . . .* Exiting on the fourth floor, she followed the signs to the hyperbaric ward. A frosted door slid open as she approached. Inside, the air was crisp, with a gentle hum of medical equipment blending into the background.

A nurse at the ward's reception desk looked up and smiled.

"Hi, I'm here to see Mr. Bannion in room 412."

"And your name, please?"

"Jennifer Nelson."

The nurse looked down at a list on her desk and checked off a name. "Of course, Ms. Nelson. Let me just tell you, he's been through a lot. He had two extensive surgeries over the last few days. The first operation was a rough procedure in one of our hyperbaric chambers. That's why they needed the second operation, to tidy things up."

"What about family?"

"Apparently, he hasn't any. You, along with some of his colleagues, are the only visitors he's had. We got a list of approved visitors from the FBI. Your timing is good. He hasn't been conscious for more than a few minutes at a time, but we expect him to come out of it today. You may need to wait a while, though. He's in a private room, just down this hallway, second door on your left." She pointed the way. "He's still sleeping. You're welcome to wait in the visitor's lounge, or his room, if you prefer."

Jenn found room 412. It was large and comfortable. Bannion, the sole occupant, was sleeping peacefully. She saw the depression under the sheet where the rest of his right leg should have been. *Jesus.*

She settled into the bedside chair. It was about four hours later that she heard him stirring. She rushed into the hallway and summoned the nurse. They returned in time to see him open his eyes and look questioningly around the room.

BENDING THE ARC

Jenn tried to keep it light. "You gave us a bit of a scare, Mr. G Man. Quite the heroics playing big fish out in the Gulf."

He smiled weakly. "What the heck happened, anyway? The last thing I remember is the rig coming down on me. Is my leg OK?"

Jenn didn't meet his eyes. She looked at the nurse, who shook her head. *God, no one had told him yet!*

She sat down on the side of the bed. "You've been out for almost a week, Dave. You survived pretty well, all things considered." She squeezed his hand, and her voice lowered to a whisper. "The full weight of the support leg fell on you. Your lower leg was shattered."

She held his hand tightly. A tear escaped despite her attempt to keep it together. "They couldn't save it."

Bannion stared at her in disbelief.

"What do you mean? I can *feel* it. It hurts like hell, it's throbbing, but I can feel it."

Jenn knew amputees often experienced phantom pain after losing a limb.

Bannion pulled himself up and looked down at his leg. He let out a low moan, "Oh, God, noooo." Jenn felt the warmth of tears now flowing freely down her cheeks.

Bannion punched the bed below his knee, trying to understand. Jenn hugged him.

"It was the only way, Dave, the only way."

"No, goddamned it, no! He started flailing at the space below the leg. The nurse brushed Jenn aside and administered a strong sedative, returning Bannion to blissful unconsciousness.

It was twelve hours later that Jenn heard the moaning, signaling his return to reality. The look on his face ripped through her. The old Bannion spirit was nowhere to be seen. Instead, just a hollow, resigned stare.

He whispered something. She leaned over, as she saw his eyes flicker back and forth.

"Did you get the detonator?"

"Yeah, Dave, we got it. Hell, you were holding on so tight we almost had to operate to get it out of your fist." She chuckled at the image.

"I found it in a dry bag next to one of the rig supports. There were a couple of them in there. Did anyone find anything else?"

"No, that was it."

"And did we get anything from forensics?"

"Nothing conclusive. The detonator is a type commonly used in the industry. Your people in Washington are still analyzing it, but . . ."

Bannion slouched back in disappointment. "You mean I lost my leg for nothing? Geez, Jenn, I thought we might have something there."

"Did you notice anything down there, anything out of the ordinary?"

"We didn't have time for a good look. What I saw was compatible with material failure. It looks like it toppled over and sank. No evidence of the separation you'd expect to find from an explosion."

"What do you mean, 'separation'?"

"Well, any explosion powerful enough to take down that rig would throw off a lot of shrapnel that would have settled on the ocean floor randomly. You'd expect some pieces to land a considerable distance from the wellbore. Everything we saw was located tight-in, mostly attached to the structure."

Jenn nodded. "That engineering report we got may be right. Simple material failure. Although it's hard to believe a rig like that could just fall over."

Bannion groaned. "Jesus, how can a leg that's supposed to be gone hurt so much?" He massaged the knee joint above the stump.

"What engineering report?"

Jenn described the Seabright and Company report, complete with its conclusions.

Bannion frowned. "You know, we looked into the operational history of that rig. It's relatively new and state-of-the-art. New things sometimes have bugs that need to be worked out. The missed inspection would have been the first scheduled since the rig went into service. That makes it a lot more significant."

"Yeah," Jenn said. While hard to accept, the evidence was piling up against their client. She felt conflicting emotions. BJ was a likeable guy, and it seemed unfair for him and Wildcat to be in such a mess because of their partner's mistake. And yet, Wildcat was a 50 percent owner and stood to make a lot of money from its investment. Why shouldn't it share responsibility for drilling operations on its lands? It was hard not to want to blame someone for the ecological disaster unfolding in the Gulf. And if *she* felt that way, God help them before a jury.

48

BAR C RANCH, TEXAS

Sunday
July 1

Shane stared into the embers of the campfire, enjoying the end of a fine day at the Bar C. While mostly an urban cowboy, he loved the free-range country. It was a welcome contrast to the urban sprawl of Houston. Shane, Val, and Jenn received an invitation from BJ and Cutter to join their families for a quiet weekend ahead of the July 4th craziness. Cutter was on a brief leave from the relief well operation in the Gulf. They spent the afternoon horseback riding. Gus must have chased down every prairie dog within five square miles.

After feasting on the finest Texas barbecue Shane could remember, they retired to the fire pit. He looked forward to spending the balance of the evening lounging around the fire with a cold longneck or two.

At the heart of the ranch, a weathered wooden barn stood as a silent sentinel against the fading light. Its weathered exterior spoke of generations past. Inside, the soft glow of string lights cast a warm ambiance. Shane could see the outline of some farmhands tending to their end-of-the-day chores.

Hay bales lay scattered about the fire pit. The scent of mesquite smoke wafted through the air, mingling with the sweet aroma of freshly baked cornbread and savory barbecue. Flames from the crackling fire danced in the cool evening breeze. Shane relaxed, looking at the circle of friends swapping stories and sharing laughs as they roasted marshmallows and sipped their drinks.

As darkness descended, the stars emerged, dotting the night sky like diamonds scattered across a velvet blanket. The Milky Way unfolded overhead, seeming to stretch on for eternity. Away from the glare of city lights, the ranch offered a front-row seat to the wonders of the cosmos.

As the evening wore on, the ranch settled into a peaceful rhythm. Amidst the rolling hills and whispering trees, there was a sense of connection—to the land, to each other, and to the simple joys that make life worth living. Shane had to admit, it was a perfect evening on a ranch in the heart of Texas Hill Country.

Cutter shot another stream of tobacco into the dark behind the pit. Shane stifled a laugh as he saw Jenn recoil. "That is so gross, Cutter."

Cutter grinned. He pulled out a guitar and starting singing old cowboy ballads, the ones Marty Robbins made famous. His rendition of "El Paso" had everyone spellbound.

Shane noted with an inward smile that BJ seated himself next to Jenn. He wasn't close enough to be too obvious, or so he thought. During the day, his interest in Jenn became apparent to all—an interest that appeared to be mutual.

BJ looked over at Shane. "Hey, Counselor, I've got one for you."

Jenn gave Shane a wink. She'd become fond of the lawyer jokes.

"A woman diagnosed with a brain tumor is told by her doctor she needs a transplant of her one-pound brain. The doctor asks 'What type of brain do you want?' She asks, 'What type?' The doc explains, 'Yeah, there's a real difference in price. For example, a one-pound surgeon's brain costs sixty thousand dollars, while you can get a one-pound brain of a nuclear scientist for fifty thousand and so on.' The woman thinks for a minute, then asks, 'Can you give me a one-pound lawyer's brain? Ever since I was a little girl I've dreamed of being a trial attorney.' 'That'll be two hundred and fifty thousand dollars,' the doc says.' 'Why so much?' she asks. 'That's over four times what a surgeon's brain costs.' The doctor replies, 'Do you have any idea how many lawyers it takes to produce a pound of brain?'" An exaggerated groan from Shane accompanied BJ's booming laughter.

"BJ, you've got to get some new writers."

Val and Sarah still had energy to burn and were playing badminton under the outdoor lights. Val looked every bit the vibrant, free-spirited, natural beauty Texas was famous for. Gus ran between the two, bumping into their legs, flopping around, and generally creating havoc. Their laughter echoed across the field.

BJ offered a Havana. Shane accepted and grabbed a twig out of the fire to light it.

"As your counsel, I won't ask you where this came from." He winked at BJ.

"And I won't tell you." BJ laughed.

BJ grabbed one himself. Lighting it, he looked at Shane. "We need to talk about that lawsuit. How important are these latest motions?"

Shane took a minute to make sure the cigar was lit.

"It's serious, BJ. The Buffalo Thirty-Six claim is no big deal. There wasn't much oil spilled and the emergency response was excellent. Explorer Seven is another story. It's a disaster."

"Can they be suing us now, before we know anything about what caused the blowout?"

"You bet. There are no rules on when you can sue as long as you establish a cause of action. Here, the blowout's occurred. Just because it's continuing doesn't prevent someone from suing. Normally, people will wait until the case is more defined, but amongst us girls, we know what the GAC's real agenda is. They're desperate to make a name for themselves. Facts aren't at the top of their list."

"But ARI was the operator. Why sue us?"

"Yeah, I wondered about that myself." Shane scratched his chin. "I figure that since they've already got the suit going against you, it was probably just easiest to focus on Wildcat, particularly with the basket of other claims. Don't kid yourself. If they're successful against you, they'll go after ARI later. But that brings up a point we have to discuss. We need to third-party ARI ourselves."

"What do you mean, *third party*?" BJ asked.

"That's when you add another party to an existing lawsuit. In this case, we can add ARI to the GAC lawsuit ourselves."

"Now why in hell would I want to drag Leona into this mess? It's bad enough we're being targeted."

"You have no choice, BJ. If Wildcat is found liable, it will want to cross-claim against ARI. At the least, ARI would be responsible for fifty percent of any damages as a fifty-percent partner. With any luck, we'll get more than that, since ARI is the actual operator. While you could sue ARI after the fact, it saves you the time and money of a separate lawsuit if you bring them in now. Of course, it'll also allow the GAC to bring any separate claims against ARI."

"Jesus, Steve, I sure don't like the feel of that. How the hell is Leona going to take this?"

"She'll understand. I'm sure her lawyers have already warned her about this. It's business, BJ, plain and simple. Nothing personal. And don't forget, as the actual operator of the well, it's ARI that holds the insurance policy that's going to be tapped."

"Yeah, I guess so. But, goddamn, what a way to do business. I'll call her next week and let her know."

"Actually, if it's OK with you, I'd like to call Tillington. This should be lawyer to lawyer. I'm inclined to get it over with now, before we head back to town."

"OK. Go ahead. Wish him a happy fourth and lay that turd on him."

"Yeah, well, it's a turd for us, too, BJ. And don't feel too bad for them. Remember, this happened on ARI's watch. Before I forget, speaking

BENDING THE ARC

of insurance, have you guys looked into that? It's quite possible the damages here are going to overwhelm any insurance ARI has in place on behalf of the partners. Does Wildcat have a self-standing policy?"

"I'll have a look, Steve. I know we carry standard liability insurance, but I'm not sure what the limits are or what kind of pollution coverage there is."

"You'd better find out fast."

Shane pulled out his cell and sauntered away from the fire. He stared up at the clear, star-filled night as the phone rang.

"Drew Tillington."

"Good evening, Drew, it's Steve Shane calling. Sorry to bother you on a Sunday."

"No problem, Steve. Spending a quiet evening cooking for the missus. She just got to savor some of the finest coq au vin this side of the Atlantic. What's up?"

"Drew, with Explorer Seven now forming the core of the GAC lawsuit against Wildcat, we need to third-party ARI into the suit. As operator and joint partner, Wildcat may well have a claim over to ARI for any of its damages."

Tillington spoke in a measured voice. "I was expecting this call, Steve. I understand where you're coming from. You should know that I am no longer acting for ARI on Explorer 7 matters. I told Leona Anderson that ARI would likely be dragged into the GAC lawsuit. She was surprisingly understanding. I've referred her to Charlie Hillerman over at Cheney Cox. You know Charlie, don't you? You'll have to take this up with him."

Shane wasn't surprised. The conflict was evident. The good news was Hillerman wasn't the sharpest knife in the drawer.

"Yeah, I know Charlie. We've crossed swords before. Get back to your fancy chicken dinner. I'll follow up with him."

Shane strolled back to the fire and took BJ aside. BJ was relieved to hear Anderson took the news in stride. "See, Counselor. I told you Leona's a stand-up gal."

Becky and Ben Davis came running out of the house in their PJs to say goodnight. *Cute kids.* Shane caught Val's eye as she and Sarah joined them. Her cheeks were flushed. Perhaps not all because of the exercise. She sure was looking forward to her own family one day.

"Daddy, Daddy, goodnight kiss." Becky jumped into Cutter's lap. He brushed her hair back and gave her a peck on each cheek. "OK, pumpkin, now sleep tight."

Little Ben Davis stood at attention in front of Shane in full salute. "Good-nye, sir," he said with all the dignity of a southern gentleman.

"And goodnight to you, sir," Shane responded equally seriously. Val poked him in the ribs.

BENDING THE ARC

"You're terrible," she whispered. She pulled five cards from her pocket. "Before you hit the sack, little man, let's see if you can pull an Ace. Ace of Spades, of course, is the cat's meow."

Shane grinned at the look of utter concentration on Ben's face. After some hesitation, he tapped the center card. Val pulled it out and, after a dramatic pause, turned it over.

"Yaay, yaaaaay, Ace of Pades, Ace of Pades." The little piker's joy broke them up. Shane didn't know how Val did it. "Pure magic," she'd say when he asked. "Giving secrets away kills it."

They waved goodbye as the children skipped back to the house with their mother. "How the heck did a guy like you ever produce such nice kids?" BJ asked with an impish smile on his face.

"Beats the hell out of me," Cutter said. "I love those rug-rats, but I thank the good lord they got their mother's looks."

They all laughed as Cutter shrugged at the miracles of nature. Shane had to admit, these Wildcat guys were a good bunch. He was damned if he would let the likes of Tillington railroad them. But Explorer 7 was a whole new ballgame and Shane knew he'd have to up his game to keep things on track. That nagging feeling he was missing something wouldn't go away. They needed a break. And soon.

49

HOUSTON, TEXAS

Thursday
July 5

Shane wrote it all out on the whiteboard in the boardroom. It helped him think things through. When he sat back down next to Val, there was a list of five items on the board: (1) Original GAC nuisance actions; (2) Buffalo 36 access road closure; (3) Buffalo 36 tank spill; (4) Explorer 7 blowout; (5) Addition of Buffalo 36 spill and Explorer 7 blowout to GAC lawsuit.

"What do you think, Val?"

"A lot of bad luck in an awfully short period."

"Yeah. That's what it looks like to me, too, and I don't believe in a lot of luck at any time, good or bad."

Val studied the board. "We're missing something. We know Buffalo Thirty-Six, both the road closure and spill, were sabotage. Unless you look at it as bad luck to be the target of someone's sabotage campaign, luck had nothing to do with those incidents."

"Right. So what can we conclude from all this? Any evidence of what happened at Explorer Seven?"

"Nothing helpful. The SEAL team that dived the site didn't report any evidence of an explosion, although one agent spotted a bag with some detonators and recovered one of them. By the way, the guy lost his leg during the mission." She filled him in on Bannion's disastrous dive.

"Isn't that the guy who got us the print and DNA at Buffalo Thirty-Six? Jesus, poor S.O.B." Shane pondered the whiteboard.

"You're right Val, we're missing something here. I can *feel* it." He reached for a fresh churro from the bowl on the conference table. Lee always kept it well stocked, bless her soul.

"I don't want to go to trial with what we have right now. The other allegations are easy, but we haven't got squat on Explorer Seven."

Val stood and walked over to the whiteboard. Grabbing the marker, she wrote, "Explorer 7—Missed Inspection—Simple Negligence?"

Shane frowned as he brushed some cinnamon sugar off his pants. "No way. If that's the case, we're cooked. We might as well just try to settle—and you know there's no way the GAC will settle now."

He looked hard at her. "Val, I've got to go for broke in the deposition on Anderson. I hope you did the same with Flaig. We need as much as we can get. There's something out there that's going to shed some light on this case. I don't know what. But I'll know it when I see it."

Val sighed. "The old needle in a haystack assignment. I sure hope you're right about this. I don't want my legacy to be defined as being on the legal team that unsuccessfully defended one of the worst environmental disasters ever."

Shane didn't respond. He was concentrating on the whiteboard. He heard the phone ringing in the background. A minute later, Lee poked her head in the door. "You'll want to take this. It's Mr. Hendrix."

Shane popped the last of the churro in his mouth and motioned Val to sit next to him. He punched the console and the Washington LawForce control room appeared on the screen. Hendrix was standing, frowning into the camera.

"Hello, Steven, Valentina."

"Hey, Jonathan, Ollie, how are things in DC?"

"Not optimal, Steven. This Explorer Seven situation has me and Oliver concerned. It is not what we set out to do with LawForce." Shane could see Hendrix was worked up, scowling and chomping down on his cigar.

Hendrix continued, "Things have gotten very complicated. We wanted to take this case to put a damper on spurious environmental litigation motivated by bad faith and premised on junk science. Explorer Seven frightens me. This Gulf mess is a full-blown, apparently legitimate environmental disaster. The operative word being *legitimate*."

Shane shook his head. "Jonathan, don't forget that I signed on for the same reasons. Goddamn it, we can't run this thing based on knee-jerk reactions. The GAC's original actions are bullshit. I think we all agree on that. Ergo, the GAC isn't motivated by good faith. That hasn't changed. What has changed is that Wildcat has experienced an unbelievable run of bad luck."

"Bad luck or negligence?" Ollie interjected.

"It's not negligence. I'd stake my career on that. Look, we know Buffalo Thirty-Six was sabotage. Why we don't know yet, but certainly not negligence."

Hendrix puffed out a thick cloud of smoke. "That is not the action that counts. Explorer Seven is now what this lawsuit is all about."

"Sure, I agree with that," Shane replied. "But something is wrong here. I can feel it. I've told you before, BJ Whitter is a straight shooter. He runs a good outfit. When you guys hired me for

LawForce, you pledged your faith in my judgement. Yes, things have gotten complicated. No doubt about it. But we need to finish what we started."

Hendrix grunted. "All right, Steven. I did hear from Michael O'Day that the nest and spill at Buffalo Thirty-Six were not accidents. I am just very concerned about this Explorer Seven development and I needed to test your commitment. But I agree that now is not the time to pull out. But this has become an uphill battle. You are going to need to rely on LawForce more than ever."

"You bet." Shane grinned a lopsided grin, the tension broken. "Hey, I'm no cowboy. You guys take care. We'll be in touch." Shane killed the call and looked at Val.

"Well, the pressure is on. How *did* you make out in your deposition of our friend Mr. Flaig?"

"Nothing earth-shattering."

"Yeah, well thanks, babe. I didn't expect much. There's no history to the GAC."

"Hey!" Val flinched as a furry ball fell into her lap. Gus tried to jump on the table behind the couch. He succeeded, which seemed to surprise him. But he miscalculated the time required to stop. He hurtled across the table, legs skidding in front of him, and catapulted through the air to a soft landing courtesy of Val.

"You're unbelievable." Val laughed as Gus looked up at her sheepishly.

Shane had to admit, Gus was one of a kind. He sure made life around the office more bearable. He saw Val looking at him. "What?"

"So what about your deposition with Anderson? She's on our side, right?"

"You bet. She's a good friend of BJ's, but it's still important for us to conduct a thorough deposition for Wildcat. They share any exposure that might come out of the Explorer Seven action, and it's my job to make sure ARI takes on their fair share if it comes to that."

"Sounds like a bit of a balancing act," Val noted.

"Maybe. But I have one advantage. Anderson's retained Charlie Hillerman."

"I've heard of him. Cheney Cox, right?"

"Yeah. He's a decent-enough lawyer. I've crossed paths with him a few times on other files. Not a bad litigator, but not great either. A mechanic with no flair. The deposition should be fun."

50

GALVESTON, TEXAS

Thursday
July 12

Stepping into the Strand Historic District of Galveston was like taking a journey back in time. Victorian-era buildings lined the cobblestone streets, their ornate facades adorned with intricate ironwork, colorful awnings, and towering arches. Storefronts beckoned with charming displays, offering everything from artisanal crafts and antique treasures to savory seafood and sweet treats. The scent of fresh baked bread mingled with the salty tang of the sea, enticing passersby to linger a little longer.

As evening fell, the Strand took on a magical quality, bathed in the soft glow of gas lamps and twinkling lights. The district came alive with the soulful strains of jazz, blues, and classical melodies drifting from open-air cafes and historic theaters. Couples strolled hand in hand along the waterfront, their silhouettes cast against the backdrop of a fiery sunset.

Phil Desmond's eyes widened in awe as he watched the red Mercedes AMG GT R Coupe turn onto Avenue B. *Man, that is one sweet ride.* He cradled the Baby Glock inside his jacket and waited for the approaching car. As it rolled to a stop at the red light, he knocked on the tinted glass. The female driver lowered the window—her first mistake. She asked, "How can I help you?"

Desmond stuck his hand in the window, gun pointed at her, and said, "Open the door, now."

Too stunned to understand what was happening, she opened the door—her second mistake. Desmond grabbed her by the arm, ripping her out of the seat. He jumped in and felt a sharp blow to his head from the passenger side. He hadn't noticed the slight man slouched down in the passenger seat.

Acting on instinct, Desmond fired, hitting the man in the face. The victim jerked towards him. Desmond fired another shot square in his chest. The body slumped over and Desmond got his first good look at him. *Christ, it's just a kid!* He wrestled with the body, reaching across and shoving it out the passenger door onto the pavement.

As he sat back, he felt a slap on his arm and heard an ungodly scream. The driver, probably the kid's mother, was flailing away at him in a frenzy. Being well past the point of no return, Desmond grabbed the Glock off the passenger seat and shot the woman twice in the torso. She fell to the ground as he slammed the car into gear and stepped on the gas.

A quick getaway wasn't in the cards. On a late Friday afternoon, tourists and their cars crowded the streets of the historic district. Desmond heard sirens approaching from two directions. *Shit!*

To get around the cars blocking his path, he pulled up on the sidewalk and made his way towards Harborside Drive. As he drove past the Texas Seaport Museum and the cruise terminal, he saw a roadblock in front of him. Pulling a desperate U-Turn, he thought he might clear downtown, when he spied another roadblock in the distance. Hitting the brakes, he was turning onto 25th Street when, at the last second, he saw the cruiser closing fast. Then his world went black.

"I'm not sure if he'll regain consciousness anytime soon, officers."

Desmond felt his head throb. After a minute, he saw the fuzzy outline of a nurse talking to two uniformed police officers. He groaned. "Where am I?"

The nurse looked into his eyes, searching for signs of trauma. "You're at The University of Texas Medical Branch emergency room. You've been involved in an accident and have a mild concussion."

"That's enough, thank-you, we'll take it from here." Desmond saw one of the officers wave the nurse away.

"But we haven't cleared him. He still needs to rest."

The officer didn't hide his impatience. "We've cleared his release with the doctor, nurse. Thank you again, but he's our responsibility now."

Desmond looked around at the familiar surroundings. He'd been in and out of interrogation rooms like this his entire life. Police station architecture was uniformly dull, if pragmatic. With its simple steel table and chairs and the ubiquitous one-way window, the room could have been in any police station in America.

The primary interrogating officer, the one Desmond figured was playing bad cop, sat across from him. "We know who you are. Phillip J. Desmond of no fixed address with a rap sheet a mile long. Well, Mr. Desmond, this is the end of the road. In the course of your botched carjacking, you murdered a mother and her son in cold blood. And in full view of half of Galveston. Son, a criminal genius you are not. I'm just here to see if you have anything you want to say before we send you away for the rest of your life, which is likely to be shortened considerably by the great state of Texas. We still like to kill our killers in this state."

Desmond knew it was over. "I want to make a deal."

The officer laughed. "You got nothing to work with, son. I told you, we have half of Galveston as eye-witnesses."

Desmond shook his head. "Not talking about that. Have you heard of that Explorer Seven disaster out in the Gulf?"

Desmond could see a flicker of doubt in the officer's eyes. "Of course, who the hell hasn't?"

"Well, someone blew up that rig and I know who did it."

There was a long pause. "I'll be back." The officer left the room.

Desmond looked at the other officer, the one playing good cop. "What do I have to do to get something to drink around here?"

The officer shook his head. "Can't leave you in here alone. When my partner gets back, I'll get you a coffee."

Desmond stared at the wall. He thought back to that dark night in the Gulf, with the scary guy laying charges on the rig. He needed to remember every detail. He knew he was bound for a life in prison, but he needed to make sure it was still *life*.

The door opened and bad cop marched back in. "OK, tell us what you got, and we'll see if it warrants any concessions."

"I need more than that. I need it in writing."

The officer grunted and sat down with a pad of paper and a pen. "I'm writing it out now. It says that if you provide us with information leading to the arrest of the person responsible for blowing up Explorer Seven, we will recommend the State not pursue the death penalty. That's as good as I can do, and the deal is only on the table for the next five minutes."

The officer finished writing, signed the pad, and turned it over to Desmond.

"OK." Desmond signed the paper. "Get me a copy of that and I'll tell you what I know." Desmond turned to face the other officer. "Now would be a good time for that coffee."

When he had his copy, Desmond recited the events of that night in the Gulf. The officer playing bad cop did not seem impressed.

"So, you don't have a name. No address. No way of finding this guy and no picture. Is that about it?"

"Maybe no picture, but I could ID this guy out of any lineup. He's got a wicked slash across his face, so that won't be hard to do. That's got to be worth a lot, seeing as how you guys aren't getting anywhere with your investigation."

Desmond smirked at the officer. Didn't look like the sharpest knife in the drawer. Probably didn't believe a word he'd said. He doubted the report would get into the system.

Desmond felt conflicted. His story might get him off death row, but he wasn't keen for that brute to be picked up. Might not bode well for him. Maybe just as well if the dumb shit sits on the report.

51

HOUSTON, TEXAS

Thursday, Monday
July 12, July 16

When Shane entered the boardroom at Cheney Cox, he was introduced to three of Hillerman's juniors. *Talk about gang tackling a file.* He shook hands with Anderson.

"Go easy on me, will you, Steve?" Anderson grinned. "After all, we're in this together."

Shane smiled. "Don't sweat it. I've just got a few run-of-the-mill questions. Standard stuff."

They seated themselves and went on the record.

"Ms. Anderson, you are the chief executive officer of Anderson Resources Inc., is that correct?"

"Yes."

"Are you responsible for ARI's day-to-day operations?"

"Yes, along with my company's senior officers and management."

"And was ARI the operator of the Explorer Seven well at the time of its blowout?"

"That's correct."

"So would it be fair to say that ARI records pertaining to Explorer Seven operations would be relevant to this lawsuit?"

"Yes." Anderson answered without hesitation, giving Hillerman little opportunity to object. Shane turned to Hillerman, glad to see he was asleep at the switch.

"I'm requesting that ARI provide for examination all company documents, in electronic or paper form, relating to Explorer Seven."

Hillerman paused. He pulled one of his associates aside. After a brief huddle, he turned back to Shane.

"We'll have to determine what is subject to attorney-client privilege. We'll release the balance."

Shane nodded. "That is acceptable, provided we expect very little to be subject to attorney-client privilege. Privileged information relates to items prepared by ARI in contemplation of litigation—that is after the blowout, just a few days ago. And, of course, the Seabright and Company document is now in the public domain."

BENDING THE ARC

Hillerman appeared flustered. "We'll provide whatever we determine isn't covered by attorney-client privilege, full stop."

Shane gathered his papers.

"Thank you, Mr. Hillerman. That's the second time you've reminded me of your right to withhold documents subject to attorney-client privilege, few though they may be. I did understand your caveat the first time."

Turning to Anderson. "Thank you, Ms. Anderson. I have no further questions."

Walking back to the office, Shane reflected on the deposition. It took less than half an hour. He'd expected having to fight much harder for an undertaking to cough up the Explorer 7 records. But Anderson was cut from the same cloth as BJ. A no-bullshit oil executive who gave a straight answer to a straight question, despite her lawyer.

Four days later, on the first day of the trial, Shane couldn't believe the mess in his boardroom. Val threw her arms up in mock resignation. "Not much to go through," she said with a laugh.

Surrounding her were stacks of boxes, floor to ceiling, and piled three high on the large table, filling every bit of space in the modest-sized boardroom.

"How many boxes?" Shane asked.

"Only one hundred and fifty-three. They obviously worked through the weekend. But that's not the best of it." She pointed at a smaller metal box. Rows of external hard drives filled the box.

"Twenty-odd high-capacity drives. I can't believe they'd release these. They appear to be backups of ARI's mainframe." That Hillerman released backup disks of ARI's computer files was surprising. But then he may not have known about it. He probably instructed ARI to provide its corporate records relating to Explorer 7 without checking what was released. Sloppy lawyering.

Shane shook his head at the mass of information. Trust Hillerman to use a standard tactic of big-file commercial litigation—if required to disclose anything, bury the other side in a paper blizzard or, more recently, an electronic avalanche. Finding anything incriminating would be difficult.

Val shook her head. "We haven't got time to digest this. It would take multiple woman years to comb through it all."

Shane grinned at her inverse sexism. "That's what the other side is banking on."

"What you're forgetting, Ms. Lopez, and what Mr. Hillerman has no way of knowing, is that we have LawForce on the case. This is where LawForce's resources can make a difference. Let's

BENDING THE ARC

get this stuff up to Washington ASAP. We have to get going. The trial starts at two and we've still got a bit of a drive."

As they were heading for the door, the LawForce direct line flashed on the console. *What now?* He punched the console and the screen came to life. Shane saw a tall, grey-haired man peering into the screen. "Hello, I'm Steve Shane, lead attorney. Can I help you?"

"Hi Steve. My name's Ted Kratz, and I have been assigned to your case by the FBI."

"Right, nice to meet you. Jenn told me you'd joined the team. Glad to have you on board. So, what's up?"

"You won't believe this. A few days ago, local cops in Galveston arrested some kid on a carjacking that ended in murder. The kid is fishing for a deal and says he was in the Gulf on a job a couple of months back, about ten days before Explorer Seven blew. He said the guy he was with set explosive charges on the rig, with timers. Not sure this isn't just a tall tale from a desperate perp, but I thought you should know."

Shane sat back in his chair, absorbing the news. "Ted, I've had my suspicions lately about Explorer Seven. If there is *any* chance this could lead to evidence that someone sabotaged Explorer Seven, we need to investigate it."

"I thought you might say that. Unfortunately, the kid doesn't have a name, address, or picture for us. The best he could do was promise to ID the guy if he saw him in a lineup. The cops got him to review all the local databases and federal most-wanted lists. So far, no luck."

Shane nodded. "Well, keep at it, Ted, and thanks for the heads up."

As he was about to punch the console, Kratz spoke up. "There is one thing, don't know if it means much. He said the guy had a wicked scar across his face."

Shane felt a chill run up his spine.

"Hot damn, Ted. That may mean everything. Check with Mike O'Day for the background on the guy we ID'd for the Buffalo Thirty-Six sabotage. He's ex-military and has a nasty scar. Send his pic down to the cops in Galveston for the kid to look at. But make sure they do a photo array that has similar types, also in uniform and also with scars. I need any ID that kid makes to hold up in court."

As he punched out of the call, Shane felt the table vibrating. Looking down, he saw his leg trembling against the table leg.

52

TEXARKANA, TEXAS

Monday
July 16

Shane and Val sorted through their trial notes one last time. Making good time in the Rocket, they had an hour to spare before showtime. They were in the field office LawForce set up a few blocks from the Texarkana courthouse. There was a direct video and data link to the Houston and Washington offices.

The thought of last week's pre-trial procedures still weighed on Shane's mind. Val questioned whether they should have moved for a change of venue—a common tactic in high-profile trials. But to where?

A Texarkana jury might feel more emotional about a disaster in the Gulf, unfolding in their backyard, but so would any town in Texas. And Shane knew that a Texas jury was more likely to sympathize with the oil and gas industry, which provided a lot of high-paying jobs in the state. A change out of state was practically impossible. And Shane felt comfortable that Nabors would run a fair trial. That left jury selection.

The modern game of jury selection was just that—a game. The aim of trying a case before a balanced selection of peers was long forgotten in the stampede to choose a jury that would deliver the right result. Modern trial science, per Dr. Bull of television fame, held that jury selection was more important than the trial itself. *Crazy.*

Today, however, was all about opening statements. A chance to frame the case for the jury. Shane considered that a critical part of the trial, coloring how the jury perceived the evidence to follow. A good opening statement had you starting at the 20-yard line, while a bad one set you behind your goal line.

He closed his briefcase and headed for the door, motioning Val to join him. "Come on. We can't be late on the first day."

Reaching the entrance to Courtroom 5, Shane gave her a wink. "Into the forum."

BENDING THE ARC

Nabors tapped her gavel and faced the jury. "Ladies and gentlemen, today begins our trial. Thank you all for your service. I estimate this trial will take in the order of three weeks."

She turned to face the courtroom, glancing at Tillington and Shane. "Before we start, I have a procedural matter. Last night, a juror asked to see me about a potential conflict of interest. She found out she is related to one of the crew members who died in the Explorer Seven explosion. Due to their distant relationship as second cousins, she was not aware of this during jury selection. She became aware of the connection when a family member reached out after tracking her down on an ancestry website. The juror believed that the connection compromised her ability to render a verdict in an unbiased manner. I agreed and released her from jury duty. You will see we have seated an alternate juror in her place. I presume that is acceptable to all parties?"

Shane was the first to speak. "Not a problem for us, your Honor. And we appreciate the retiring juror's conscientious approach to her duties."

Tillington rose. "In the circumstances, we have no objections, your Honor."

"Very good, thank you, gentlemen. Mr. Tillington, the floor is yours."

"Ladies and gentlemen of the jury. We are not happy to be here today. We are not happy to be across the table, in part, from that industry which has done so much to build this great state of ours. But we have no choice. We have to be here today. We have to challenge an oil and gas company. Why? Because we love this state with all its natural beauty. We feel an obligation to preserve that beauty for yourselves. We feel an obligation to preserve that beauty for your *children* and *their children*."

Tillington paused. Shane saw he had the jury's attention and grudgingly admired the way he expressed empathy for that industry which has done so much to build this "great state of ours." Tillington was alive to litigating in the industry's backyard. He was neutralizing the issue right off the top and was at his commanding best.

"Now counsel for Wildcat, Mr. Shane, will suggest my client's motives are less than genuine. He might suggest my client has some alternate or hidden agenda, aimed perhaps at destroying his client's company and tarnishing the reputation of the oil and gas industry. He might suggest my client is seeking to enhance its status through high-profile litigation. What you won't hear Mr. Shane suggest, much as he might like to, is that my client is a gold-digger. That it is seeking financial enrichment by suing.

"Why won't he attack the GAC on this front? Quite simple. My client will not make *one red cent* out of this lawsuit. The GAC has agreed to donate any punitive damages recovered in this case to the Environmental Protection Agency. In fact, my client is incurring significant costs in pursuing this litigation, costs which it may not recover."

Tillington stopped and swiveled to face the jury head-on.

"That's right, folks. You heard correctly. *Not one red cent.* As you are likely aware, this is highly unorthodox for a civil trial. In fact, in all my years of practice, I've never experienced it. My client understands the right thing to do is to flow any damages back to the people, the true victims of Wildcat's cavalier approach to the environment. These monies will go to environmental programs for *your* benefit. For the benefit of your children and grandchildren."

Christ. Things were getting syrupy. But Tillington was scoring points. How better to present the bona fides of his client than to point out they didn't stand to gain financially from the lawsuit? Shane sighed. *It was a bitch.*

The revelation that any award would go back to the public through EPA programs helped align the GAC with the public. And as Tillington pointed out, the jury was part of that public. An extreme extrapolation of that line of reasoning could consider the jury to have a conflict of interest. To decide for the GAC would cause funds to flow to the EPA and thereby the public and thereby the jury. Shane shook his head. *Must stay focused.* He had the advantage of making his opening statement after Tillington. It would allow him to take the edge off Tillington's best points.

"What exactly has Wildcat done, is Wildcat still doing, that has brought us all here today? Wildcat has shown a reckless disregard for the environment in conducting its operations. Wildcat has been grossly negligent. In this trial, we will show you a course of conduct that has produced excessive atmospheric discharges, a major oil tanker spill, a major onshore oil spill, and, most disturbing of all, an offshore environmental disaster of monumental proportions that continues as we speak."

Tillerman stopped again, for dramatic effect. Shane guessed, correctly, that he was nearing the end, as his voice was rising. He walked over to a tripod facing the jury that held a large poster covered by a blanket. After whipping off the blanket, he spoke in such a subdued voice that the jury strained to hear it, "*Monumental* proportions." Some gasps could be heard, followed by a hushed silence during which Tillington quietly strode back to the counsel table and sat down.

Too late to object, Shane saw the poster was the classic shot of the oil-covered dolphin with the pained grimace. Even the coldest-hearted juror had to feel some pity for the suffering of that innocent animal. For crying out loud, most of the jury grew up watching *Flipper*.

BENDING THE ARC 361

A goddamn brilliant move. Shane's fingers dug into his armrests as he saw several jurors fighting back tears.

He remained riveted to his seat, aware of Val's troubled look. Finally rising from his chair, he walked over to the tripod. Slowly, deliberately, he picked up the blanket and draped it back over the poster.

"Nobody likes an oil spill. Nobody likes an earthquake. Nobody likes a flood. Nobody likes a plane crash. Nobody likes war. But, ladies and gentlemen, in life we all know these things happen despite our best efforts to avoid them." He spoke calmly and concentrated on making eye contact with each juror.

"And when these things happen, it's natural for us to want someone to blame. Lash out at someone on whom we can vent our anger. A scapegoat. It's very hard sometimes to accept that there may be no deserving scapegoat. But that's the case with the frivolous claims relating to diesel emissions and the tanker spill. Minor incidents in the stream of industrial life. Like that drip onto your driveway from your oil pan, or the smoky emissions from your campfire. Pollution? Sure. But at an acceptable level? You bet.

"Now that addresses the minor infractions on which this lawsuit was originally based. But the much more significant incidents, those relating to the spill at Buffalo Thirty-Six and, in particular, the blowout at Explorer Seven, those claims are a different matter.

"Is Wildcat responsible for these incidents? Emphatically, it is not. We will show you what kind of company Wildcat Oil and Gas is. We will show you what kind of man BJ Whitter, CEO of Wildcat, is. We will not hide BJ behind the corporate veil. We will not shelter him from the witness stand. We don't want to do that. We know that once you get a chance to hear from BJ first-hand and get to see him respond to the tough questioning he will get from Mr. Tillington, you will understand he is not one to shirk from responsibility. You will see he spent considerable time, effort, and money in establishing Wildcat's reputation as a good corporate citizen and, in particular, as a champion of the environment."

Shane debated whether to make BJ an integral part of the trial. He decided he had no choice. With the in-built bias the jury would have against corporate America in an environmental lawsuit, he had to crack that corporate facade. He needed to put a human face on Wildcat, a face and personality the jury could relate to.

"We will demonstrate that Wildcat is in no way responsible for the incidents Mr. Tillington referred to. Now Mr. Tillington took great pains to point out that the GAC will not be receiving any punitive damages recovered in this case. So what?" He looked at each member of the jury.

"So what? That's supposed to imply their case has some credibility? Mr. Tillington glossed over the fact that this is, indeed, a high-profile lawsuit. The type of lawsuit that can launch or bury legal careers. Here I'm talking about Mr. Tillington and myself, of course." The jury chuckled at the last remark. OK, they were loosening up.

"But this type of suit can also do amazing things for a professed public-interest group such as the GAC. A victory in this lawsuit would make the GAC a household name in America. In fact, in launching this action, the GAC has already raised its media profile. This is publicity money can't buy. Don't forget the old adage that the only thing worse than bad publicity is no publicity at all. So for Mr. Tillington to stand up here and tell you, with the utmost gravity, that there is nothing in this for his client is, I would suggest to you . . ." He paused, turning to face the jury.

"No, I don't have to suggest anything to you. I trust you to reach your own conclusions." A few jurors nodded. *Good.*

"Ladies and gentlemen, at the end of this trial you will know what kind of company Wildcat is, you will know what kind of man BJ Whitter is, and you will also know the GAC's allegations are without merit. It is for this reason that we are asking you to consider our counterclaim against the GAC for libel, defamation, and legal harassment. We are confident that as the case unfolds, so will the evidence supporting our counter-claim. The evidence that will deliberately, layer by layer, reveal the GAC allegations for the fraud and abuse of process they are."

It was time to close before he lost their attention. He walked back to the blanketed dolphin poster.

"Ladies and gentlemen, I told you that at the end of this trial you will know what kind of man BJ Whitter is. Well, maybe you won't have to wait so long. He pulled the blanket off the poster. A murmur rippled through the courtroom. Out of the corner of his eye, he saw Val frowning.

"It's not a pretty sight, is it? Would it interest you to know that BJ Whitter has contributed, in a personal capacity, over three million dollars to the Greenpeace campaign against harvesting tuna with nets, the type of nets that trap and kill dolphins. He is the largest single contributor to that campaign. And he was instrumental in pushing through federal legislation stipulating minimum requirements for tuna cans to be labeled 'dolphin safe.'"

Tillington was on his feet. "Objection, your Honor. Mr. Shane is introducing evidence in his opening statement."

Nabors was quick to sustain the objection.

"Sorry, your Honor. In terms of evidence, Mr. Tillington had no problem showing his poster to the jury. But in my case, I should have said

BENDING THE ARC 365

we will show that Mr. Whitter was the single largest contributor to the dolphin campaign and *we will show* that Mr. Whitter was instrumental in efforts to legislate dolphin-safe tuna."

Shane turned to face the jury. "Folks, in closing, let me simply say my faith in my client is complete. It is total. It is absolute." He looked briefly at each juror. "At the end of this trial, you will know why."

He returned to the counsel table and took his seat. While the opening statement went reasonably well, he was nervous. He'd made a lot of promises about what they would prove. Val's words echoed in his mind. *I don't want my legacy to be defined as being on the legal team that unsuccessfully defended one of the worst environmental disasters ever.* He shook his head. They were in *trial*, goddamn it. This was no time for doubts.

Nabors addressed the courtroom. "We'll start with the GAC's direct evidence tomorrow morning. Before we rise, I'd like to . . ."

Tillington interjected, "If I may, your Honor, I have one motion to put to the court before we recess for the day."

Shane looked at Val. *What now?*

"Your Honor, the GAC requests the court arrange, as soon as practical, a physical visit to the Explorer Seven wellsite. The parties would include yourself, of course, a court reporter to record any events you rule should go on the record, the full jury, including alternates, and counsel for Wildcat and the GAC. We believe that in the circumstances, it would be invaluable for the jury to see for themselves the environmental impact of the Explorer Seven blowout, which lies at the heart of this litigation."

Shane was stunned. *An inspired move.* Jury visits are rare, but such a tactic could prove pivotal to the case. It was one thing for the jury to hear court testimony on Explorer 7, but if the jury could see that hell on earth live, it would be devastating to Wildcat's case.

Nabors was looking at him for a reaction.

"Your Honor, we oppose the motion. Such a visit would be highly prejudicial to my client and provides no information beyond that which can be obtained through conventional evidence, such as pictures, and video. In fact, Mr. Tillington has already availed himself of that sort of demonstrative evidence in the poster he made use of in his opening statement."

"I'm sorry, Mr. Shane, but I have always been a firm believer that a picture, or better yet a live view, is worth a thousand words. I have to agree with Mr. Tillington. A visit to the Explorer Seven site would help the jury understand this case. Indeed, both you and Mr. Tillington seem in agreement on one issue, that the Explorer Seven blowout is central to this case. I am ruling in favor of a site visit. Mr. Tillington requested a visit as soon as practicable. Any submissions on timing, Mr. Shane?"

"Your Honor, we request that the visit not be scheduled until the start of our case in chief." At this stage, Shane was simply trying to buy time. If they brought the well under control and completed the cleanup before the visit, it would be a nonevent. It might even work to Wildcat's advantage if there was only a clean ocean to view.

Tillington leapt to his feet. "Your Honor, the blowout is what this action is all about. It's imperative that we get out there as soon as possible. I mean, the real point is . . ."

"Mr. Tillington, I've heard enough. Time is of the essence here. I see no valid reason for delaying the visit. I'll schedule it for one week from today, that being next Monday. We will work with your people, Mr. Shane, on trip logistics."

Shane sank into his chair. He could sense Val's distress, although it didn't show. She was enough of a courtroom veteran to avoid showing the jury how she, and their case, were hurting. Nabors was still talking.

"Members of the jury, I want to remind you to refrain from discussing the case amongst yourselves. You are to save your deliberations for when all the evidence has been presented. And I want to remind you that we have sequestered you to prevent your exposure to any media coverage of this case. We stand adjourned until nine tomorrow morning."

BJ approached the counsel table as the courtroom emptied.

"Jesus, Steve, is it always like that? What a roller-coaster. After Tillington's speech, I felt we were screwed. After your speech, I figured not so much. And now, with this goddamn site visit, I don't know what to think."

Shane knew what BJ meant. He noted it often in court himself. When two competent counsel argued their cases, you could feel the momentum swing back and forth and back again.

"What you should think right now, BJ, is very clear and very simple. If that well isn't under control by next Monday, we're in deep shit."

53

GULF OF MEXICO

Wednesday
July 18

The operating console of *Ocean Scout* was a marvel of modern engineering—a maze of screens and displays, each pulsating with vital information. High-resolution monitors provided real-time data on everything from drilling depth and pressure to temperature and mud flow rates. Color-coded charts and graphs illustrated the complex interplay of forces at work beneath the ocean floor, guiding the crew in their decision-making and troubleshooting efforts.

At the heart of the console sat the control panel, a gleaming expanse of polished metal adorned with an array of buttons, dials, and levers. The control panel was labeled and positioned to enable operators to adjust parameters and fine-tune the drilling process with the flick of a switch or the twist of a knob.

Cutter and Fed Romero studied the plot of the relief well's progress. Explorer 7 was producing from the prolific Miocene sandstone out of the Lagarto formation at a depth of eight thousand feet. The planned intercept point was near Explorer 7's total depth, at seven thousand feet subsurface. At an average rate of penetration—ROP—of thirty-five feet per hour, Cutter estimated the job would take about two weeks. In directional drilling, the drill path was always longer than for a conventional, vertical well. They were already below five thousand feet subsurface.

The actual drill path spiraled down because of the drill bit's rotation. With refined measurement while drilling—MWD—technology, gauges in the drillstem behind the bit provided a real-time feed of its location to the surface.

By utilizing the force of the drilling fluid flowing through the interior of the drill string, a downhole steerable mud motor rotated the bit while keeping the drill string stationery. The driller made the required adjustments to keep the bit tracking the plotted intercept course. Drilling progressed rapidly until an hour ago, when they encountered hard rock in the lower portion of the Goliad formation. The drilling rate slowed to ten feet per hour.

"This is going to be tight," Fed mumbled.

BJ called Cutter that afternoon to update him on the trial. With the jury visit less than a week away, they had three days to reach target. They needed at least two days beyond that to kill the well and carry out a rough cleanup program.

"Too tight. Even if we get back to a rate of thirty-five feet per hour, we're not going to make it. Do your geologists have any idea how thick this formation is?"

Cutter had consulted Tom Richards, ARI's chief geologist, who'd flown out to *Ocean Scout*. "Yeah, about five hundred feet. I think we may be drilling through the Corsair Fault Zone. With our projected diagonal track, we're going to be cutting through this hard rock for a distance of about nine hundred feet."

Fed pulled out his pocket calculator and did some quick number crunching. "Not good enough, Cutter. We don't have that kind of time if you want to meet your trial deadline." He looked back at the plotted drill path. "We'll straighten the path. That'll shorten the distance through this formation. If we can limit that distance to six hundred feet, we'll gain more than a day."

"Won't that screw up the drill path—make it a lot harder to work with?" Cutter asked.

"It will make things trickier, but with a six-hundred-foot path, we'll still be angling through the formation. It won't mean going to straight vertical. I think we can manage that. Bottom line is I'll do what I can to meet your deadline, but I won't jeopardize the operation."

"OK, Fed. BJ's on board with that. It would be nice to have this sucker cleaned up by the time that jury comes out here, but we can't risk having to start all over again."

"*Damn!*" Cutter heard the shout from the driller at the console. "We're slowing down again." Cutter stepped over to the console and watched as the ROP fell off again.

"What the hell is it now?" he asked Richards, who was standing next to the driller, watching the dials.

"We're into a super hard rock formation, harder than the Goliad. Explorer Seven didn't hit this member until seven thousand feet downhole. On this hole, we hit it at five thousand, one hundred. We're updip. The goddamn formation must angle up steeply from the Explorer Seven site."

"What's that going to do to our target time?" Cutter asked Fed, who was charting the latest information on the downhole plot.

"It won't help, that's for sure . . . *Aw shit.* We've stopped making hole." An alarm sounded, and a red light flashed above the drilling console.

BENDING THE ARC

The ROP slowed to zero. The motors were overheating. They had the best drilling motors money could buy from The Motor Company, a premier supplier around the world. But even TMC's famed *GeoDrive®* motors were no match for this formation. Fed lunged for the kill switch.

Cutter knew instantly they were stuck in the hole. It happened in tough formations. The drill bit would bind and threaten to blow the engines. There were several techniques to free the bit. They could alternately push and pull on the drill string. They could vary the viscosities and velocities of the drilling muds circulated through the hole. They could circulate solutions to dissolve the binding rock outside the drill string. Sometimes, they were able to free the bit within minutes. Sometimes it never got jarred loose and they had to sidetrack or abandon the hole.

Cutter pulled Fed aside. "I know you're doing your best to keep our schedule, but I'm going to call BJ and tell him to prepare for the worst."

Fed nodded. "We'll do our damndest, but you know what it's like out here in the water. It's a helluva lot harder to control that drill string."

Cutter walked back to the ship's communications room. "Patch me through to head office."

54

GULF OF MEXICO – BIG THICKET, TEXAS

Monday
July 23

Shane had to admit, it was a unique setup. Judge Nabors, Tillington, and Shane held a separate conference to agree on the logistics of the jury visit. Everyone agreed that they would rather have an aerial view instead of trying to do it by ship. They agreed to use the European Helicopters EH101 Heliliner that ARI offered. Shane knew this was the chopper used for ARI's longer offshore shift transfers. It could hold up to thirty passengers in airline comfort and had a range of over six hundred nautical miles.

BENDING THE ARC

From the vantage point of the EH101, the world unfolded beneath them—a mosaic of colors, textures, and patterns stretching as far as the eye could see. They gazed out through the panoramic windows as the rotor blades sliced through the air with a rhythmic hum, feeling a sense of wonder at the vastness of the landscape below.

The helicopter would circle the Explorer 7 site for ten minutes. Tillington insisted they follow any prevailing oil slicks for up to ten miles from the site. Shane asked that they also circle *Ocean Scout* for five minutes to show the jury the mitigation efforts under way. Nabors ordered that a court reporter accompany them to keep an official record of any comments counsel might want on the record for context.

The upbeat atmosphere in the chopper surprised Shane. The jurors were excited to escape the confines of the courtroom. Flying in a helicopter was a first for many. As the morning haze burned off, the unfolding ocean view on the beautiful Gulf morning was impressive. They flew at one thousand feet, low enough to get a good view of the numerous rigs they passed. The shallow continental shelf was a busy area.

One juror gave a shout as he spotted Explorer 7's distinguishing black plume. The rest of the jurors craned their necks for a better view. Nabors signaled Tillington and Shane closer.

"I'm going to ask the pilot to hover sideways to the well for a minute on each side when we're ten miles out and two miles out. The pilots won't go any closer. I want each juror to get the same view. Any objections?"

Shane thought two approach views might be excessive, but Nabors was determined to do it her way. Both he and Tillington nodded.

One juror pulled out a camera. Out of earshot of the juror, Shane asked Nabors to confiscate it. She did so promptly. The jurors were to form their impressions from the visit alone. No supplementary photographic or videotape evidence was to be entered into the record or otherwise considered by the jurors.

The sight from the air was spectacular. The raging fire in the oil-slicked ocean captivated the jurors. Shane smelled the burning oil despite the advanced climate control system of the EH101. As they circled the site, he bit his lip. At least the fire was effective in burning up a lot of the oil. To Tillington's chagrin, there were only a few patches around the well site and not the prominent, heavy slick that was there before the well reignited and which Tillington hoped they could follow.

One juror couldn't help himself. "What a damn mess!" Nabors was on it in an instant. "Please, keep your thoughts to yourselves. We're only here to observe. I remind you, you are not

BENDING THE ARC

to reach any conclusions or discuss the case amongst yourselves until you've heard all the evidence."

They hovered over *Ocean Scout*. Shane was glad he'd insisted on this view. The ship was impressive, and the jury saw the actions being taken to deal with the blowout.

On the way back, Shane had a sudden inspiration. He pulled Nabors and Tillington aside.

"Your Honor, we'll be putting down at Port Arthur for a rest and refueling. From there, it's not much of a detour to fly north over the Buffalo Thirty-Six site on the way back to Houston. Since we're here, and Buffalo Thirty-Six is one element of this action, I'd ask that you allow the jury to view the Buffalo Thirty-Six site from the air."

"No way. That is not what this view was for. We object, your Honor." Tillington's knee-jerk response was predictable.

Nabors thought for a moment. "Mr. Tillington, I've got to admit I'm surprised. I would have thought that you'd be thrilled to have the jury view the site of one of your client's other concerns. In fairness, I see no reason why we shouldn't view Buffalo Thirty-Six, since we're practically flying over it, anyway. I'm going to allow it."

The helicopter hovered over Buffalo 36. The lease site was pristine. It had been cleaned and resurfaced with bright, white gravel—a textbook example of responsible operatorship. Just off the lease, a few deer could be seen grazing next to the tanks that displayed the Wildcat logo on their roofs. Shane noticed jurors nodding.

Flying back to Houston, Shane stared at the setting sun. He'd done the best he could with the hand he'd been dealt. But the Explorer 7 view made a powerful impression on the jury. From now on, whenever they were dealing with evidence relating to the blowout, they would have vivid visual images to draw upon—sights and sounds, and even smells, with which to put the abstract and often dry courtroom testimony in context. He groaned inwardly. Despite his best efforts, the case was slipping away from him.

55

GULF OF MEXICO

Wednesday
July 25

On the deck of *Ocean Scout*, the scene was controlled chaos. Crew members scrambled to secure loose equipment and batten down the hatches. Despite the danger and uncertainty, there was a strange beauty to an offshore storm—a primal, elemental force that reminded everyone of the awesome power of nature.

Cutter woke to Danny Pearson's insistent shaking. He immediately noticed the rolling of the big ship.

"What's up, kid? Feels like we got ourselves a bit of a storm."

"Yes, sir, it blew in about two hours ago."

"No reason to get a man out of bed. *Ocean Scout* should be able to handle this sort of thing."

"Yes, sir. That's not why I woke you. Mr. Romero asked me to get you. We're about half an hour away from projected intercept. He wants you with him in the control room."

"Right. Tell Fed I'll be there in five minutes."

As he washed up, Cutter reflected on the operation. With any luck, they'd kill Explorer 7 in another few hours. He put on his slicker and headed out the door.

Cutter felt the excitement the minute he stepped into the control room. An uneasy stillness filled the room. Monitors flickered with real-time data, displaying wind speeds, wave heights, and barometric pressure readings that provided vital information about the storm's intensity and trajectory. Engineers and meteorologists conferred quietly, their voices drowned out by the cacophony of the storm outside.

Hunched over the drilling panel, Fed and his team worked feverishly. He glanced up. "Cutter, I'm glad you're here. We should intercept in the next fifteen minutes. It looks like we're right on target." He pointed to the plot of the drill bit, now almost on top of the Explorer 7 wellbore.

"Have you started circulating heavy mud?"

BENDING THE ARC

"Yeah, we started circulating a heavier weight half an hour ago. We're all set. There may be a bit of a kick when we intercept, but nothing we can't handle."

The wait was excruciating. Ten minutes elapsed. Fifteen . . . eighteen.

"Have we overshot?" Danny Pearson couldn't help himself.

"Quiet, dammit!" Fed was concentrating on the drilling instruments. Another three minutes passed. Cutter's shoulders sagged. An overshoot would mean a long delay as they either backed up the hole to drill a step-out—a well that would kick out of the existing wellbore at an angle to try once again for an intercept—or tried to intercept at a lower depth.

"That's it!" Fed shouted, pointing at the pressure needle, which kicked noticeably. "We're in."

The next few minutes were total chaos.

"She's still kicking, pressure's climbing." Fed pointed at the panel. "Damn, she should've stabilized by now. We need to pump more mud and crank up the weight."

With no foolproof way of measuring the pressure in the blowout well, the WWC crew made an educated guess of the pressure they would encounter at the intercept point. They underestimated. Cutter knew Fed was trying to counterbalance the greater than expected pressure by increasing the weight of the mud column in the intercept well and pumping at increased pressure.

"What the hell is that?" Fed shouted at the crew above the ship's moonhole. "We've got pressure on the drill string!"

The last comment sent a chill down Cutter's spine. Pressure on the string could mean only one thing—the ship was drifting out of position. If it drifted far enough, the drill string would snap. In the present circumstances, where they were fighting a pressure kick in the well, losing the intercept well would be disastrous.

"What the hell's going on? People, I need some answers fast. The drill string is getting torqued. We gotta get this boat under control. Get the captain down here, stat!"

Captain Stewart was already on his way. He burst through the door moments later. "We've lost that thruster again. We can't hold the ship without it. You guys are going to have to try to shut in the hole. I estimate we have minutes."

"That's great. We can't shut in the well. We're fighting a pressure kick. Your timing stinks, Angus."

Cutter remembered something from a few days back. "Is that the same thruster that quit on us when we were first getting into position?"

"Yeah, that's right."

"So, we sent a diver over to start it on a manual override then. Why can't we do that now?"

BENDING THE ARC

"Not enough time. To rig up a diver with a safety line will take at least ten minutes. And I don't think it can be done in this weather, anyway."

Everyone sat frozen for a few seconds, absorbing the last remark. In a few minutes, they might face blowout number two. And who knew how long after that it would take to bring the two wells under control?

Danny Pearson grabbed a small flask off the rack behind the drill panel and ran out the door.

Cutter turned to Angus. "What the hell did he take?"

"One of the scuba breather packs. Divers carry them in case their main tanks fail. It gives them enough emergency air for a quick escape to the surface."

Cutter was stunned. Without thinking, he grabbed another pack from the rack and ran out onto the open deck. He could see Danny running along the ship's rail to a point above the malfunctioning thruster. *Jesus H. Christ*, he was going after it.

"Danny, stop! You can't do anything. The goddamned thing will suck you in like a twig if you get it started. For chrissakes, kid, don't do it!"

Danny turned and held out his hand, signaling Cutter to keep his distance. "So, we just sit here and let this one blow too? I can't do that. I can stop this, sir, and I'm going to."

He was over the edge before Cutter could respond. Cutter's next reaction was pure reflex. Sarah, Becky, and Ben flashed before his eyes. He didn't want to hurt them, but he knew if Danny was on his own, he was dead. A second man would double the odds of resisting the suction of that thruster if they got it started. There was no way of knowing whether he could make a difference, but it was not a question he wanted to live with for the rest of his life. *Forgive me, Sarah.* He kissed his pendant cross, jammed the breather in his mouth, and jumped the rail.

The cold water stunned him. He tumbled over backwards and took a few seconds to get his bearings. The ship's hull banged into his knee, and the pain focused him. Danny was ten feet below, against the ship's side. *Can't drift off track.* The ship's other thrusters were still operational and capable of sucking them in if they got too close. The salt water stung his eyes.

He swam down to Danny and tapped him on the shoulder. Danny's face registered surprise. He motioned for Cutter to return to the surface. Cutter shook his head. Danny shrugged and pointed to the thruster override handle. Cutter nodded and took off his belt, motioning for Danny to do the same. He tied both belts together and gave one end to Danny. Danny understood the plan and grabbed his end of the makeshift safety line. Cutter wrapped his end around one arm and

BENDING THE ARC

with the other took hold of a ladder rung welded to the side of the hull, positioning himself as far away from Danny as the belts would allow. He braced himself and gave Danny the thumbs-up.

As Danny reached for the lever, Cutter thought again of his family. *Lord, forgive me if . . .* He felt the incredible pull on the belts, and in his last living moment came the realization he would need that forgiveness.

In the control room, Fed saw the pressure come off the drill string. "Goddamn, they did it!"

The thruster was again doing its job as the ship's position stabilized. The mud in the relief well started winning the battle, overcoming the pressure in the Explorer 7 wellbore. A cheer went up as spirits rose. But not for long. Two operators who'd left with Cutter re-entered the control room. In response to the enquiring looks, they simply shook their heads.

Tears rolled down Fed's cheeks. He ran out of the room. Leaning over the ship's rail, he heaved his dinner into the black water.

During the blowout, the Coast Guard assigned the cutter *Dallas* to stand by Explorer 7. On the deck, the crew stood in awe. The ear-piercing roar and billowing black clouds that were constants in their world over the past weeks disappeared in an instant. Replaced by silence—an all-encompassing, glorious silence. After removing their ear guards, they listened to the screeching of seagulls for the first time since arriving on site. It was the most beautiful sound they'd ever heard.

56

BAR C RANCH, TEXAS

Thursday
July 26

The wheels of the old Jeep ascended the winding road cutting through the rugged terrain of the Bar C. The landscape stretched out before BJ, a patchwork of sun-dappled fields and rolling hills cloaked in shades of green and gold. The sun hung low in the sky, casting long shadows that stretched across the road like fingers grasping at the fading light.

The road twisted and turned with each bend, leading ever higher. The engine hummed softly, a steady rhythm that provided a comforting backdrop to the turbulent thoughts swirling through his head.

He reached the crest of the hill, where the road leveled out and the world seemed to hold its breath in anticipation. As he took in the sweeping views, he gently massaged his leg, thinking of the good times. How often had they driven up here together, laughing and bullshitting after a long day of catching their quota on the Trinity? Cutter sure loved the Bar C. He used to say that if he hadn't got roped into the oil business, he could have spent a happy life working the ranch. But BJ convinced Cutter to join him in taking high-paying rig jobs when they graduated high school. Cutter took to the oil patch like a duck to water. He had the right temperament and was a natural leader to the rugged individuals the industry attracted.

Damn! The cold water spraying up through the floorboards jolted him back to reality. The Jeep rounded the last curve before the road straightened into the narrow valley, at the end of which stood the ranch house. He choked back a sob. *Why the hell did you have to go after Danny?* Even as he asked the question, he knew the answer. That was Cutter.

And now what the hell was he going to tell Sarah? *Jesus H. Christ.* He stopped the Jeep. Staring across the green fields, watching the cattle grazing in the background, tears streamed down his cheeks. He sobbed uncontrollably, allowing the full rush of emotion to wash over him.

BENDING THE ARC

After ten minutes, he felt completely drained. Leaning back on the seat, he continued thinking of the good times with Cutter. A sudden knock on the door jolted him out of his reverie. He rolled down the window and stared into the curious little face of Ben Davis.

"What wong, Onka Beejay? What wong?"

Sitting on his bike, Ben was looking at BJ with that concerned look kids have when they sense something is wrong.

BJ wiped his face and pulled himself up by the steering wheel. "Aw, just a bit tired, Benny. Is your mom home?"

"Yeah, mommee home, mommee at house. Follow me?"

"OK, captain, lead the way."

BJ sucked in a lungful of air as he put the Jeep in gear and followed the little tyke on the wobbling bike down the last hundred yards to the ranch house. Sarah stood in the doorway, having heard Ben's shouts of "Mommee, mommeee, Onka Beejay heeer."

BJ pecked Sarah on the cheek and led her inside. "Benny, can you go and play for a bit? I need to talk to Mommy."

"OK, bye-bye, Onka Beejay."

BJ smiled despite himself as Ben toddled out the door.

"Coffee?" Sarah looked puzzled, not sure what to make of this midafternoon visit.

He couldn't string it out. She didn't deserve that. He knew there was no right way to do it. Just do it.

"Sarah, there's been a bad accident on Explorer Seven."

Her look tore into him like a jagged knife. Her eyes full of terror. They searched his, seeking the smallest shred of reassurance. They found none.

She let out a gurgling scream and collapsed against him. "Nooooo, ooh noooo. Not Cutter, not now."

He held her tightly, knowing that was all he could do at the moment. An hour later, after two cups of tea and an ocean of tears, she got out a few sentences without breaking down.

"I need to know how it happened."

He went through the details, emphasizing that Cutter went after Danny. She needed to know it wasn't a thoughtless act of heroism. Cutter loved her and the kids more than the world. He wouldn't have gone for that thruster himself. He would have let the blowout rage. But when young Danny Pearson, with the reckless sense of immortality common to youth, selflessly leapt overboard, Cutter had to go after him. It was in his nature, part of his DNA, part of why Sarah loved him.

She nodded, starting to process the loss. "You know, BJ, Cutter was on edge the last little while. He talked about things happening at that

BENDING THE ARC

Buffalo well site he was on, things out of the ordinary. Oil tanks blowing up and stuff like that. And then Explorer Seven. He didn't like how things were being handled there. And he didn't care for Anderson either."

That surprised BJ. "What was his problem with her, Sarah?"

She shook her head. "I don't know, exactly. He thought the initial Explorer 7 response was a gong show. I think he thought she was in over her head."

BJ held her hand. "Leona may have made some mistakes, but she's just trying her best to deal with this mess, as are the rest of us."

Sarah sat quietly, looking out the window at the kids playing in the yard. "How am I going to tell Becky and Ben? Becky's old enough to understand. I don't know about Ben. How am I going to tell them, BJ?"

He had no answer. He considered volunteering, but he knew Sarah needed to do this herself.

"I'm here for you. Anything you need, Sarah. We'll discuss finances later, just know that you and the kids are set for life." He hugged her and walked slowly back to the Jeep.

As he started down the road, he heard her calling from the verandah, "Rebecca, Benjamin! Mommy needs to talk to you . . ."

57

TEXARKANA, TEXAS

Friday
July 27

Shane sat at the counsel table, reviewing his notes. Try as he might, he couldn't stop thinking about that call from BJ. The well was killed, but so was Cutter and a twenty-year-old kid. The news of Cutter's death hit the Law-Force team hard.

Shane, Val, and Jenn all came to like the quiet oilman, seeing through his tough outer shell to the soft core beneath. BJ felt devastated. Cutter was with him from the start. He was in some ways the son BJ never had and was being groomed to take over the reins at Wildcat. All that came to an abrupt halt in the cold, dark waters of the Gulf.

Shane shook his head, trying to focus. He stared at the ceiling rafters. With the fingerprint and DNA, Magruder was linked to Buffalo 36. Now, with Phil Desmond's positive ID, they could also connect him to Explorer 7. He was the key to the puzzle. They needed to buy some time to locate him. Shane wanted an adjournment, but feared Judge Nabors wouldn't give him much leeway.

He watched Tillington approach his counsel table. "What's up, Steve? Wasn't that jury view impressive? Sets the stage, don't you think? Dragging this out won't help your client."

"Take a Valium, Drew. I haven't heard the fat lady sing."

Tillington chuckled and returned to his table as Nabors entered the courtroom. "Mr. Shane, what is it this time? I'm getting motion sickness. I trust this isn't going to be a waste of the court's time."

"Your Honor, I assure you that will not be the case. The entire world knows by now of the tragic accident on Explorer Seven that took two lives just days after our jury visit. We have no interest in wasting the court's time. What we want is a chance to get to the truth in what is becoming a complex case. We have received new information that could have a significant impact on the trial. We require an adjournment of three weeks to follow up. I give you my undertaking that if you grant us this adjournment, we will demonstrate the legitimacy of our request."

"It seems to me that this is one of those requests where the court has no way of knowing its legitimacy in advance. Essentially, it's a *trust me* request."

"That is true, your Honor. The exercise of the court's wide discretion involves an element of trust from time to time. It's not that different from when you provide counsel leeway in cross-examination based on counsel's assurance that relevance will be established."

"Quite true, Mr. Shane. Mr. Tillington, any submissions?"

"Yes, your Honor. We've heard a lot from Mr. Shane about the need for legal efficiency and a streamlined courtroom process. He passionately makes the case we need to administer justice expeditiously. Well, that cuts both ways. My client deserves to have this case prosecuted promptly. Mr. Shane is watching his case evaporate in front of him and is now grasping at straws to delay the inevitable. We urge you to reject the request for an adjournment and allow us to get on with it."

"OK, gentlemen, thank you. I'm going to give you two weeks, Mr. Shane. And I expect you to have something noteworthy for us when we reconvene. This court stands adjourned until Monday, August 13th, nine a.m."

58

HOUSTON, TEXAS

Wednesday
August 1

It was Swiss National Day, but Shane begged off the usual celebrations hosted by Houston ex-pats. He was in no mood to celebrate. All he wanted to do today was honor a man who had rapidly become a very good friend.

Houston National Cemetery stood as a solemn tribute to the valor and sacrifices of the United States' servicemen and women. An imposing gate marked the entrance, adorned with intricate wrought ironwork. Just beyond, a long, tree-lined avenue stretched forward, flanked by beautifully manicured lawns.

A vast expanse of emerald green unfolded, with row upon row of uniform white headstones, stretching as far as the eye could see. Perfectly aligned, the headstones, carved from pristine marble, gleamed under the Texas sun.

A week after Cutter's death, Shane listened to the bugle's plaintive tones float over the sea of somber faces assembled in a corner of the cemetery, near the hemicycle, a semi-circular colonnade that served as the cemetery's focal point. "Taps" always gave him the chills. As an ex-Marine and Medal of Honor Vietnam veteran, Cutter warranted a full military funeral.

After a private ceremony at the Bar C two days earlier, Sarah agreed to the public service. Shane knew she felt duty-bound to allow the nation to honor her husband. The geometric rows of tombstones, stretching away in the distance on the bright green lawn, were hauntingly beautiful. As the bugler finished, Shane felt the warmth of tears on his cheeks. He wasn't alone.

The roar of approaching Air Force jets drowned out Sarah's sobbing. Shane held Val's hand tightly as he watched the five jets streak toward them. Overhead, silhouetted against the brilliant blue sky, one jet broke from the pack and entered a steep vertical climb. The "Missing Man" formation hit him hard. Cutter recounted the history behind the maneuver at the Bar C barbecue when he showed them pictures from

BENDING THE ARC

his Vietnam days. The term originated in missions flown during World War II. Each pilot in a formation was assigned a position. When a pilot was shot down, the other pilots maintained their original positions, creating a gap where the missing pilot had been.

Shane felt Val's arm slip around his waist. They flinched at the twenty-one-gun salute. Jenn, BJ, and Anderson stood next to them, BJ's face a mask of anger. He'd graduated from grief to rage.

The hardest part was watching Ben. His face filled with the curiosity and wonder of any boy his age surrounded by all this commotion. Saddened by his mother's tears, he looked lost and forlorn. The image of little John Kennedy saluting his father's coffin came to mind. Gus licked Benny's hand, understanding on some animal level the need to comfort the boy.

He was just four years old, but today, in his neatly pressed navy suit and polished black shoes, he seemed far older. The suit was a size too big, the jacket sleeves brushing his knuckles, and the pants bunched awkwardly around his ankles, as if time had thrust him into adulthood too quickly. A black tie, knotted under the collar of a crisp white shirt, hung slightly askew, a testament to the careful yet shaky hands of an adult who dressed him that morning. Likely Sarah, whose own heart was breaking.

Tears welled up in Ben's large, expressive eyes, a striking blue that mirrored the cloudless sky above, as he tried to blink them away. He clutched a small American flag in his left hand, the fabric crumpled from the tightness of his grip, and stood close to Sarah. Her hand rested gently on his shoulder.

Around them, the ceremonial guard performed their duties with precision and respect. As the rifle volley rang out, Ben flinched. The sharp cracks startled him and his small body recoiled instinctively towards his mother. She bent down, whispering soft words of comfort, but Ben's gaze remained fixed on the casket, the finality of the moment sinking in. He did not yet understand the full scope of his father's bravery, but he felt the void left behind.

The assembled thousands heard the priest's address relayed over a sound system. "William Ronald Davis was a true son of Texas. 'Cutter' to his friends—which included pretty well everyone he'd ever met—died trying to save one of those younger friends, Daniel Pearson. But he also died for Texas . . . for America. Danny Pearson was bravely trying to end one of the greatest environmental catastrophes to hit Texas. Cutter couldn't let his friend go it alone . . ."

Shane tuned out and stared into the sky. He hadn't spent a lot of time with Cutter, but enough

BENDING THE ARC

to gain a healthy respect for the man—one of Texas's finest, no doubt. He embodied the same spirit as those heroes of the Alamo depicted in BJ's huge mural.

As he watched the young marines fold the flag with military precision and hand the triangular bundle to Sarah, his thoughts turned to Magruder. His stomach tightened. When Jefferson said all men were created equal, did he really mean it?

As the ceremony drew to a close, Shane saw the crumpled flag fall from Ben's hand. A minor act of defiance against the unfairness of it all.

Shane felt the familiar vibration of his phone. Call display showed it was Lee. He grabbed it, stepping away from the graveside group. "This better be good. You got me at Cutter's funeral."

Lee's voice was all business. "Yes, as a matter of fact. Val and Jenn are in the boardroom. They've been waiting for you to call in. The folks in Washington arrived ten minutes ago. Something big is going down. I'll patch you through."

"Steven," Hendrix's voice came on line. "I'm here with Valentina, Jennifer, and some of my crew. Sorry to disturb you, but there's been a big development. As Churchill once said, 'This is not the end. It is not even the beginning of the end.

But it is, perhaps, the end of the beginning.' Or as you people in Houston might say, we have ignition."

Shane felt the blood rush to his head.

"You've found Magruder."

59

LAUGHLIN, NEVADA

Saturday
August 4

Nestled along the western bank of the Colorado River, Laughlin, Nevada emerged as a dazzling oasis in the Mojave Desert. This small resort town, an hour and a half south of Las Vegas, beckoned visitors with a blend of vibrant nightlife, scenic beauty, and old-world charm.

Approaching Laughlin, the vast desert landscape seemed almost barren, with its sandy hues and jagged mountain silhouettes. The heart of the town was the bustling Casino Drive, a strip lined with grand resorts and casinos, all vying for attention with their unique architecture and dazzling lights. The hotels boasted a variety of themes, from the classic elegance of the Riverside Resort to the sleek, modern lines of the Golden Nugget.

Yet, Laughlin was more than just casinos. The Colorado River, a sapphire ribbon cutting through the arid landscape, offered a serene counterpoint to the town's lively atmosphere. With the river running right outside the doors of the ten-odd mega casinos, this tri-state area—California, Nevada, Arizona—proved a great year-round playground for kids young and old. Visitors enjoyed jet skiing, kayaking, and paddle boarding, adding splashes of brightness against the blue water with their colorful equipment. Riverwalks ran alongside the banks, dotted with palm trees.

Once the FBI located Magruder, they tailed him to the Phoenician resort in Scottsdale, Arizona, where he was spending a few days brushing up on his golf game. Shane didn't have him arrested on the spot. No sense giving him a lot of time to think before Shane and Kratz could get organized and ready to interrogate him. They needed to be on their game when they made the arrest. And they needed to make sure Magruder was off his. It would help if they could get him to come to them. While difficult, it was worth a try.

Shane's call surprised Magruder. Shane teased at evidence they had from Buffalo Thirty-Six and suggested Magruder could still help himself if he cooperated with the authorities. To Shane's relief, Magruder agreed to meet, likely to find out just what they had on him. With the Buffalo Thirty-Six action being low level, Magruder wasn't too worried. But he was unequivocal. He would meet with Shane and Shane alone. They humored him. He clearly didn't know the FBI had been tailing him for three days.

Shane arranged for the meeting to take place at the Edgewater Hotel and Casino. He tipped a cold longneck, beads of water running down its side, as he gazed at the river from behind the tinted windows of the bar. He watched the jet skis skim across the water, leaving wakes that created the criss-cross pattern of a barbecued steak.

Shane always marveled at the contrast between Nevada's gambling meccas, like Vegas—founded on the dual building blocks of greed and lust and transformed into a fantasyland cum Disneyland—and their surroundings, such as the Grand Canyon, one of the world's great natural wonders, just a few hours' drive away.

Laughlin seemed to compress the contrast between man's artificial world and the best nature offers. The tourists clutched their oversized marguerita tumblers and wandered amongst the one-armed bandits, with only the smoked glass separating their air-conditioned, plastic world from the intense heat and mighty Colorado.

Shane told Magruder he would be the Native wearing a black cowboy hat with a silver band, not a common sight in Laughlin. They set the meeting for 2:00 p.m. Shane's heart raced and his palms grew sweaty as two-fifteen approached.

At two-twenty, a big man wearing a Cubs hat sat down on the stool next to him. He turned to Shane. "Howdy, cowboy. Mr. Shane, I presume."

Even though he'd seen the pictures, the nasty scar startled him. This was one tough customer. "That's right, Mr. Magruder."

"Pleasure to meet you, man."

"Wish I could say the same."

"So, you said you had something for me—something I need to see. I hope this won't take long. I have a late afternoon tee time back in Scottsdale."

"I think not, Mr. Magruder. Your time is up."

Shane waved off the bartender. "I've got a room upstairs. We can talk there."

"Not a chance. I like public places. I guess you could say I'm a people person."

"Touching, I'm sure. But I meant it when I said your run was up." Shane signaled the agents to close in. Magruder reached for an inside gun, but the agents were on him before he could pull it free. During the ensuing struggle, two rounds went off. One shattered the big picture window behind the bar. The crowd stampeded for the exits. In the tumult, the agents manhandled Magruder to the ground. After securing him with handcuffs, they hustled him off to the elevators.

They made sure to tie Magruder securely to a chair across the table from them.

"Who the hell are you people, and what do you want?"

"My name is Ted Kratz. Senior agent, Washington bureau, FBI. You've met Mr. Shane, attorney for Wildcat Oil and Gas. You know what we want. A full and complete confession of your acts of sabotage against the oil industry, including the incidents at the Explorer Seven and Buffalo Thirty-Six well sites."

"You've got the wrong guy. If I'm not on my way out of here in one minute, you're going to be able to hire Mr. Shane to defend your sorry asses in a wrongful arrest action."

Kratz lit a cigarette, staring down at the river. "We've got physical evidence from Buffalo Thirty-Six. The evidence shows that the tank was blown. We've located the chopper pilot and have his statement. You're screwed, Magruder, plain and simple. It's time for you to be a little more cooperative."

"That pilot's full of shit. Anyone could have done that. There are a lot of crazies out there."

Kratz inhaled deeply and turned to face Magruder square in the face. "The kicker is we lifted your print at the Buffalo Thirty-Six lease site, on a pipe right next to the blown valve."

Magruder responded, calm as ever, "Fingerprint evidence? Seriously, man? You all know that's not enough to make a case. Big margin for error."

"How about DNA with a match probability of one in many million? Is that tight enough for you?"

Magruder couldn't hide his surprise. "How the hell did you get DNA?"

Kratz shrugged. "Same place as the print. You made a big mistake, Mr. Magruder."

Magruder regained his composure. "Well, that could put me at Buffalo Thirty-Six, but that was a small spill, no loss of life. What would I be looking at there, a few years, max? I had nothing to do with that other one, Explorer Seven. Isn't that the blowout in the Gulf? Now that is a tragedy."

Kratz waved at another agent, who turned on the projector. As the screen flickered to life, it revealed the gaunt face of Phil Desmond. He was answering questions asked by a person off camera. Desmond described how he took the trip out to the rig in the dead of the night, helped Magruder pack the C-4 in the bags, dropped him off at the designated time, and picked him up an hour and a half later once the charges were planted.

Kratz turned off the projector and walked away from Magruder, staring out the window . . . waiting.

Shane watched the change in Magruder's expression. After a long pause, Magruder's shoulders drooped. "What are you dealing?"

Kratz turned back to Magruder. "Now, that's more like it. We're dealing life. You give us everything we need to nail the bastards that hired you, and you live."

"What kind of fucking deal is that?"

"Best you're going to get. And more than you deserve. If I had my way, we'd blow scum like you off the face of the planet. Take you out in the middle of that,"—he waved out the window at the Mojave—"let you have an hour head start and then get some Air Force flyboys to take you out with a sidewinder.

"But you're lucky, Magruder. There are some other sons-a-bitches even more depraved than you. So, you're going to get the chance to live to ensure we get the snakes that hired you. I can tell you they won't be as lucky. They *will* die. Texas is a hanging state, or lethal injection, I guess, these days."

"All right, you made your point. What do you need from me?"

"Who's behind it all? You were obviously working for someone."

Magruder reached for a beer from the ice bucket on the table. "First things first. I need you guys to put it in writing that as an informant, you'll be doing for me what you can. That means no super max pen, medium at worst, and full privileges."

Kratz slid a document across the table. "Figured you'd need some love. Can't guarantee no super max, but we'll recommend against the death sentence. It's all here, just sign on the dotted line."

Magruder took his time reading the two-page agreement. "You guys have this all figured out, don't you?"

Kratz nodded. "We try. Sign it twice, one for you and one for us, and let's get on with it. We're on the clock."

Magruder took the pen he offered and scribbled his signature on both copies that were pre-signed by Kratz, keeping one.

"You guys ever hear of a guy named Kevin Flaig?"

Shane felt like an eighteen-wheeler had run over him. "Kevin Flaig from the Green Action Coalition?"

"The one and only." Magruder was enjoying Shane's reaction.

"Well, what about him?"

"It was all him. He ordered Explorer Seven and all the Buffalo Thirty-Six crap."

Shane felt dizzy.

Magruder continued. "Buffalo Thirty-Six

was just a side show. Explorer Seven was the real deal."

"And the GAC, are they involved?"

Magruder rolled his eyes. "What planet do you live on, man? The GAC is Flaig's front. It's nothing but a website and PR machine funded by Flaig. It was intended to give him cover and legitimacy, and it looks like it worked."

Shane gestured at an agent. "Keep an eye on him. Mr. Kratz and I are going to take a break. We'll be back."

They left the suite and took the elevator down to the lobby. Shane led the way to the riverwalk. He didn't say a word until they were outside.

"I needed some air. This is sick. The GAC is behind all this? It's hard to believe, but it makes sense in a twisted sort of way."

Kratz nodded, leaning on the railing overhanging the river. "Never underestimate man's capacity for depravity. It is hard to digest, but like you said, it fills in a lot of missing pieces. This GAC outfit came out of nowhere. Jenn told me what your friend at Greenpeace said."

"Yeah, still. We need to move fast. This guy Flaig can do a lot more damage."

"With you on that, Counselor. We need to use that bastard Magruder the best way we can." They spent the next half-hour mapping out a plan.

Magruder was finishing his second beer as they re-entered the suite. He asked simply, "What do you need me to do?"

Kratz was curt. "Carry a wire."

"Yeah, I figured. You guys are gonna be there, right? I mean, anything goes wrong and I could be tits up. Flaig will be desperate. He won't think twice about icing me if he suspects something."

Kratz stubbed out his cigarette, to Shane's relief. Kratz laid it out for Magruder.

"You'll have our protection. We don't want you blown away before you can deliver Flaig."

"How will I get his attention? I never deal directly with my clients. He's gonna be real suspicious if I just call up to chat."

"Yeah, we thought about that. We're going to release some of the evidence we found at the Explorer Seven site."

"What?" Magruder was incredulous. "You got fuckin' evidence on Explorer Seven? Give me a break!"

"Our divers checked out the sea floor. We found a detonator. From what you've told us, it could be yours. When we release this to the media, we'll indicate we carried out some sophisticated forensics on it and have a few leads. That should be enough for you to call Flaig and say you're spooked. Tell him you need to talk to him about Plan B—like what happens if we get to you. He'll understand that."

"Shit, yeah, he'll understand that. He'll want my head on a platter, man. He'll figure I'm a weak link that needs to be eliminated."

Kratz nodded. "Sure, there's some risk, but it's the only way to make it believable. Don't forget, we'll be there."

"Like that's a great comfort. OK, give me the details."

60

THE WOODLANDS, TEXAS

Sunday
August 5

The hard stream of water felt good as it pounded Shane's shoulders. Clouds of steam billowed from the shower. He felt his muscles relax under the massaging flow. His thoughts drifted, searching for something—something that had been in the back of his mind for a long time and left him with the nagging feeling it was important to the case.

"Hey, get outta here." He shoved the furry head out of the shower with his foot. Gus loved the water and often hopped into the shower with him if he wasn't spotted first. He tried once more, but this time Shane kicked his nose lightly.

BENDING THE ARC

With a snort, Gus threw him a disgusted backward glance and hobbled away.

Shane reviewed the case for the millionth time. The GAC sues Wildcat over frivolous claims. Their case is bolstered by incidents now revealed to be sabotage at the hand of Kevin Flaig, including the cold-blooded destruction of Wildcat-partner ARI's rig. Motive? To win the largest environmental lawsuit in Gulf history and establish the GAC at the forefront of the green movement. Was that enough to justify murder? Maybe, for a sick bastard like Flaig. But he was missing something.

How about Wildcat? A good company that made a strange target for an environmental lawsuit. There had to be better candidates. And why go against ARI just to catch Wildcat in the crossfire? It would be unnecessarily complicated to raise your profile in this manner. Then again, perhaps its brilliance lay in that very complexity. It was highly doubtful anyone would have traced things back to the GAC and Flaig if Desmond hadn't cracked or they hadn't been lucky enough to lift Magruder's print and blood at Buffalo 36.

Was he just over-thinking the whole thing? Lee would often tell him, "Steve, you think too much," after the fifth revision to a letter, with the last three revisions flipping back and forth between the same two narratives.

After fifteen minutes, the bathroom was a sauna. He shut off the water and grabbed a towel. Putting on some sweats and a T-shirt, he grabbed a cold one from the fridge and settled down at the loom.

He fell into the familiar rhythm of passing the boat back and forth. Shane loved the concentration required to ensure each new line followed the pattern he outlined before starting a new piece.

His movements were almost meditative, his fingers threading the shuttle back and forth, interlacing the weft with the warp. The loom creaked with each motion, a sound as soothing as a heartbeat. His eyes scanned the emerging pattern with meticulous care. The design was traditional, featuring bold geometric shapes and symbols: the zigzag of lightning, the stepped motifs representing mountains, and the sacred four directions.

As he worked, Shane chanted softly in Navajo, his voice rising and falling in a melody as ancient as the craft itself. The chants were prayers, invocations for harmony and balance, for the rug to embody hózhó, the concept of beauty, balance, and order in the universe. Each knot tied was a physical manifestation of this prayer, a tiny but significant part of the whole.

He paused for a moment, taking a sip from the longneck on the side table. Close to finish-

BENDING THE ARC

ing, he included a subtle spirit line with a strand of wool running from the interior pattern to the edge of the rug. His mother always warned him against trapping his spirit in a piece of work.

With Gus sleeping peacefully at his feet, he heard Val at the front door. Every second Sunday was girl's night out. She'd get together with her girlfriends for drinks, followed by dinner.

"Hey, babe, good time?"

"Yeah. But I'm so tired I had to cut it short. You ready for bed?"

"In a minute. Just finishing this piece. I've been thinking about the case."

"Any new leads?"

"No. But help me through this. He laid out his issues with the case. As he was concluding, it hit him like a thunderbolt. J*esus Christ. It couldn't be . . . could it? It made sense, in a very perverted way.* He grabbed the phone.

"Shane Law Offices, how can I help you?"

"Hey, Jenn, you're doing reception duty at ten at night?"

"Well, no one else is here to hold down the fort. My boss is a real slave driver, you know?"

"Yeah, I've heard. Listen, I need you to get up to Washington right away. We need to get the discovery team to find me a missing link. It's just a hunch at this stage, but a damn strong one." He laid out what he wanted her to look for.

61

HOUSTON, TEXAS

Tuesday - Wednesday
August 7 and 8

Shane called Val into the boardroom. Jenn was on the screen feed from the LawForce center in Washington. She was waving at a large room visible behind her.

"Hey, Val, I was just about to give Steve a video tour. How do you like our new data processing center? Not bad for such short notice, what?"

Shane could see they'd set up half the floor with ten-foot square cubicles. Jenn said there were thirty in all. Each cubicle had a table and a computer terminal.

"You've done a great job, Jenn. How do you have this thing organized, anyway?"

Jenn pointed to the cubicles. "We've distributed those hundred and fifty-odd boxes you sent up here amongst the students. We instructed them to review each file, each piece of paper, each letter. Any documentation relating to Explorer Seven is being input into the computer, along with a brief description. Our categorization for the papers includes internal memos, external correspondence, sender, recipient, and general subject area. I'm screening the summaries and short-listing them for you guys."

"Well, let's just hope it pays some dividends soon. We're getting squeezed big time in court. By the way, are you processing the drives too?"

"Sure. The paper's easy enough to handle. It's more a matter of manpower than anything else. With the hired labor from those Georgetown students on summer break, we should be able to get through everything in a few days. The ARI hard drives are more challenging."

"What do you mean?" Val asked, looking at a student scanning a drive at a workstation.

"Well, most people think that when they delete a file, it's wiped off the system forever. That's not the case. The system doesn't necessarily remove the files from memory. A simple software program from Office Depot can retrieve a good deal of that information and skilled hackers can get the rest—they can find virtually anything that was saved on the drive. Mike O'Day seconded a hotshot computer team from the Bureau to assist us in reviewing the hard drives. They're doing that off-site, at the FBI's cyber crime offices."

"Excellent." Shane pondered the possibilities. Jenn was sharp. He knew that if there was anything interesting in the deposition materials, it should surface in the computer's trashcan.

He saw Jenn turn as a group entered the room behind her. "Steve, Val, I was waiting for some folks, but I think I've got all the troops assembled now."

Jenn looked back at the screen. "You guys know Ollie, Mike, and Ted, but I don't believe you've met special agent Dave Bannion." She pointed to a man in a wheelchair at the side of the table whom Shane hadn't noticed before. "Dave is the explosives expert who's been helping us."

Shane nodded. "Nice to meet you. I heard about your dive, Mr. Bannion. I'm sorry about the outcome, but I want to thank you. We've had our suspicions all along that this case wasn't kosher, and we're grateful for your help. Hopefully, what you found will help us get to the bottom of this mess. Turns out that detonator means a lot more than we thought at first."

Bannion nodded. "Thanks. Lord knows I want to get these bastards as badly as the rest of you."

Shane led the discussion. "Well, I guess we knew the spill at Buffalo Thirty-Six was sabotage, but I for one never suspected the GAC. It is pretty radical to buttress a lawsuit like that. And Explorer Seven . . . unbelievable. ARI lost fifteen men in that blowout, not to mention the chopper crew that tried to put out the fire. And Cutter and Danny. This is murder. Ted, I suppose you guys are going to want to take Flaig into custody after the meeting with Magruder?"

"That's right, Steve. Magruder's testimony is enough to hold him while we build a case."

"I think we can help you with that. We want to protect Wildcat here and ARI as well, for that matter. What we'd like to do is get the goods on Flaig to exonerate Wildcat and ARI. You guys are going to need some hard evidence yourselves to supplement Magruder's testimony. That testimony might be shaky in court, considering it's coming from a guy that cut his own deal. So don't grab Flaig until we've had a chance to cross-examine him in court after the meeting, while he still thinks he's in the clear. We need that element of surprise. It gives us the chance to put a lid on it."

"In the meantime, he's at large?" Kratz shook his head. "Let's not forget this bastard isn't only responsible for all those deaths, he's also the reason we're fighting one of the Gulf's worst environmental disasters."

"There's more, Ted. I have a strong hunch this goes beyond Flaig." Shane decided he had no choice but to let Kratz in on his suspicions. He outlined his theory.

"Did Magruder tell you that?" Kratz's skepticism was apparent.

"No. I said it was a hunch. Magruder only took instructions from Flaig, but you have to agree, there are a lot of things here that don't add up."

Shane saw Kratz pace back and forth. It was clear he remained unconvinced.

Shane tried again. "Ted, you've already got him on twenty-four-hour surveillance until the meeting. We're just asking you to keep that going for another few days until we can get his court testimony. I'm sure I can get a court date for when I need it. If you pull him in after the meeting, you've got the tape, yes, if it's any good. But with a decent lawyer, Flaig's back on the street in no time and will clam up in court. Believe me, I know. An extra day or two can get us evidence we may never have a crack at again." Shane looked at Ollie.

"Ollie, what do you think? We can keep Flaig under tight surveillance. If it looks like he's going to skip the country we move in, but in the meantime, and again we're only talking a day or two, we have a real chance to get the evidence to put this bastard away for good, and maybe find out if it goes beyond him."

Ollie pulled Kratz aside for a brief huddle. "OK, Steve. We'll play it your way."

Shane slept over in the office, having stayed up into the morning hours helping Washington set up the Magruder-Flaig meeting. Kratz's agents worked up the details of the Bureau's special, nationwide, televised news conference. It ran the following morning and pumped up the fresh evidence they'd uncovered. Coming from Bannion in his wheelchair, the release of the information became that much more dramatic . The media ate it up. FBI agent on deep-sea dive below blazing inferno loses leg in fight to locate evidence that may point to sabotage! Now Shane could only wait to hear from Magruder and hope they had properly baited the hook.

The call came a few hours later. Bleary-eyed, Shane grabbed it on the third ring.

"Did he bite?"

Magruder's gravelly voice sounded amused. "Oh, yeah. Hook, line, and sinker, man. I called him after your news conference and told him I was spooked, like you said. He didn't seem surprised, but insisted we meet in Palm Springs. He was paranoid about meeting anywhere that risked a chance encounter with someone he knows. The meet's on for noon tomorrow, at the top of the aerial tramway."

"So, tell me again what you're going to tell Flaig."

Magruder sounded impatient. "We went over this forever a few days ago. I'm gonna tell him I think this goes beyond him and whoever is pulling the strings can sure as hell afford to send a little more my way."

"And what are you going to say when Flaig asks why you think that?

"I'll tell him I have my sources. A guy in my line of work is pretty well connected."

Shane nodded. He needed to make sure Magruder was fully motivated. "Remember, if you get us what we need, Kratz will *guarantee* you'll never do time in a super max." That sweetened the original deal considerably.

Magruder grunted. "Yeah, man, I get it. But I'm still hangin' my ass out there. Flaig isn't an idiot. Your fed buddies better have my back tomorrow."

62

WASHINGTON, D.C.

Thursday
August 9

Kimberly Bernhardt sat hunched over her laptop, the glow of the screen illuminating her tired eyes. Apart from the occasional rustle of papers and the muted murmur of a conversation in the distance, the war room was quiet. The clock on the wall ticked towards midnight. Kimberly was surrounded by stacks of legal documents, each demanding her attention. The gig was straightforward enough: review documents for Hendley Enterprises, flag anything unusual, and earn some much-needed extra cash to supplement her meagre student loans. She wondered what Hendley Enterprises was, but nobody was volunteering anything. They asked her to sign a confidentiality agreement before she entered the intriguing Washington premises. She could have sworn she'd seen the U.S. Attorney General in the office. They were obviously working on a high-profile case.

While they were using special computer search software, the human element was critical to assessing the importance of the many references the software detected. It was Friday afternoon, the middle of Kimberly's third full day of combing through the five boxes of files and assorted USB drives assigned to her. She'd gotten through the boxes, finding nothing of significance.

At first, the work excited her. She treated it like a treasure hunt. But following hour after grueling hour of finding nothing, she was getting discouraged. In the past half hour, her mind drifted. She scrolled up to the file she'd been reviewing for the previous few minutes to go through it again. She was working now on files the FBI's computer team recovered from the backup system drives—deleted files that were still accessible to a computer forensics expert with the right equipment.

Her fingers moved deftly over the keyboard, scrolling through pages of monotonous text. She adjusted her glasses, squinting at a dense paragraph. The work was tedious, but Kimberly was

BENDING THE ARC

methodical, driven by the promise of a paycheck and the hope this experience might someday translate into a full-time position. The scent of coffee from the nearby boardroom mingled in the air.

As she leaned back in her chair and stretched her arms above her head, she could feel the tension in her shoulders ease. She glanced at her watch and sighed, dreading the hours of work that lay ahead. She took a sip of lukewarm coffee, grimaced, and refocused on the document before her.

Then something caught her eye. A name she had seen before, buried within a sea of legal jargon. Her brow furrowed as she leaned closer, reading and re-reading the sentence. She recognized the name from the instructions they'd been given. A sharp, ex-FBI firebrand, red hair and all, had briefed them on the lawsuit. Jennifer Nelson told them of the urgent request from Steve Shane, lead attorney on the case, to review the files of the co-defendant, ARI, for any references to Wildcat Oil and Gas Ltd. Ms. Nelson described exactly what they were looking for.

What caused her heart to skip a beat was the name *Wildcat* staring out at her from a short memo covering the issues Ms. Nelson had mentioned. She didn't know the importance of what she'd found, but it had to mean something to them. Who knows, there could be a bonus for finding it. If she got a decent one, it might cover her third year at Georgetown.

The war room was silent now, the ticking clock the only sound. She closed her laptop, hands trembling. Gathering her notes, she slipped them into her backpack with deliberate care before rushing out of the cubicle to share her discovery.

63

PALM SPRINGS, CALIFORNIA

Saturday
August 11

Opened to the public in September 1963, the Palm Springs Aerial Tramway was an engineering marvel and gateway to another world, transporting visitors from the sun-drenched desert floor to the cool, pine-scented heights of Mount San Jacinto. As you approached the tramway, located a short drive from the heart of Palm Springs, the sight of the towering mountains against the clear blue sky set the stage for an unforgettable adventure.

Valley Station, the starting point of this journey, blended seamlessly into its rugged surroundings. Constructed of stone and glass, the building's design paid homage to the mid-century modern aesthetic that Palm Springs was known for, yet it exuded a contemporary elegance.

Five towers, ranging in height from fifty-five to two-hundred-and-fifteen feet, carried the two-inch thick cables far above the canyon floor. Two eighty-passenger, enclosed cable cars ran six thousand vertical feet from Valley Station to Mountain Station, whisking passengers from the scorching desert into an alpine environment. The cabins were retrofitted to revolve 360 degrees, one of only three revolving cabin tramways in the world.

Initially, the tram glided over sandy desert expanses dotted with hardy shrubs and cacti. As it gained altitude, the terrain shifted. The desert floor fell away, revealing the rugged cliffs and steep walls of Chino Canyon. The sheer scale of the rocky escarpments was humbling.

As the tram passed each of the five towers, riders felt a gentle sway, providing some added excitement. The air became cooler, a refreshing change from the desert heat below. Wildlife sightings were common—sharp-eyed passengers might spot bighorn sheep navigating the cliffs or hawks soaring on thermal currents.

After the ten-minute journey, that spanned two and a half miles, the tram arrived at Mountain Station, perched at an elevation of 8,516 feet. Stepping out, a different world greeted visitors. The crisp, pine-scented air was invigorating. Stretching before them was Mount San Jacinto Wilderness State Park, a 13,000-acre forest playground with miles of hiking trails, campgrounds, and a ranger station. In the winter, a Nordic ski center provided exceptional cross-country skiing. And the view year-round down on Palm Springs, the Salton Sea, and beyond was spectacular. At night, the twinkling lights resembled a cluster of jewels thrown across the desert floor by some immense, cosmic hand.

Down at Valley Station, the warm breeze from the late morning sun felt wonderful. Kevin Flaig adjusted his sunglasses, staring in awe at the tramway that stretched out before him and disappeared into the airy heights.

Flaig caught the eleven-thirty tram and ordered a beer in the bar at the top. Magruder joined him shortly before twelve. Flaig was surprised to see him so soon. "I thought I caught the last tram before noon?"

"You did. I watched you get off. Just wanted to know you came solo."

"Well, I did. Let's go for a walk. It's a little too crowded in here," he waved at the couple in the corner, the only other customers in the bar.

"Whatever you say, man."

They walked past the horse corral on a trail leading to a scenic valley overlook.

Flaig wanted to get it over with. He wasn't sure why Magruder wanted the meeting, but suspected it was all about money. It usually was. Magruder's recent angst with the operation was just a way to angle for a bigger cut. "What do you think they have on you?"

"I don't know, but if they have one of my detonators, who knows, man? These days, the things their forensics units can do are unreal."

"You're supposed to be the best. That's why I hired you. You charge like the best. So now you come running to me at the first hiccup. What kind of bullshit is that?"

"Hey, man, I didn't realize the kind of heat this stuff would bring down. You didn't level with me. You should have told me the stakes involved."

Flaig was having none of it. "You were told all you needed to know. And I thought there wasn't going to be any loss of life. Remember your lecture? Something about needless killing is for amateurs."

"I didn't know that thing would go up like Satan's lighter. Look, you got your fuckin' money's worth. The tank at Buffalo Thirty-Six blew with a full load. You know that wasn't easy."

Flaig admitted the timing was coincidental. "How did you manage that? Was the nest incident you too?"

BENDING THE ARC

"Damn straight. Work of art, man."

"Yeah." Flaig grudgingly admired the elegance of Magruder's work.

"And Explorer Seven," Magruder continued. "You told me you wanted it to look like an accident, right?"

"Yeah. An accident. But now they suspect it's more than that."

"Too much heat," Magruder muttered. "Too much heat, man. I didn't know this was gonna be such a high-profile play. I'm not saying they have anything on me. The detonators I used are standard issue. But they've got a full court press going here."

"So, what do you want?"

"I need more capital support to go under, deep, until this stuff blows over. Could be years."

Bingo. "That's what I thought," Flaig snorted. "Just another shitty little shakedown. Did I screw up when I hired you or what? How much?"

"Half a million."

Flaig wasn't happy, but in the scheme of things, the amount was trivial. "OK. I'll wire it to you once you're out of the country."

Magruder wasn't finished. "And by the way, you should have let me know you're only a middleman."

Flaig was stunned. *What the fuck?* "You were told all you needed to know, and how the hell did you find out about *Tame Wildcat?*"

"Is that what you guys called this op? Your boss has a flair for the dramatic, man. Anyway, you don't survive long in my business without connections. I have my sources. You don't think you're the first special ops guy your boss ever hired, do you?"

That son of a bitch! Magruder knew too much. He'd have to be dealt with permanently. But first, it was important to find out how bad things were. Flaig filled him in on the details of *Tame Wildcat*, probing to see how much Magruder knew and what his sources were. But Magruder didn't give up a thing. *No matter.* He would soon be history.

They boarded the same tram for the trip back down to the valley. While Magruder stood nearby, Flaig ignored him. Casually scanning the interior, he spotted a young couple kissing in the corner. Across the way, he nodded at Angelo and Vito Scarponi, two of his swarthy bodyguards.

He had to admit, the twins were impressive. Their muscles bulged under black T-shirts threatening to burst under the pressure. It wasn't odd to see such specimens in southern California, given its bodybuilding subculture. The two shared a common passion for the body beautiful. Flaig watched as his third bodyguard, Jesus Campano, engaged the twins in animated conversation. Slim and bearded, Jesus didn't look as lethal as the twins, but Flaig knew better. Jesus had been with him for over five years and throughout that time showed a chilling lack of emotion. *What the heck was he doing chatting with the twins? He should stake out another angle.* Flaig frowned at Jesus and discretely signaled him to move to the other side of the tram.

Minutes after leaving Mountain Station, Flaig wandered away from Magruder, pretending to enjoy the view out the back window. Magruder never saw it coming. Flaig watched Angelo deliver a massive blow to Magruder's neck and then place him in a crushing headlock. In the same instant, Vito shoved the tram operator out of the way and tore open the cabin door. The other hikers screamed. Flaig saw the young couple pull out handguns. *Jesus Christ! That bastard Magruder came with his own protection.*

The boyfriend fired at Vito, hitting him in the upper chest. He dropped at the feet of an old couple. In a panic, the girlfriend fired wildly at Angelo, striking him in the arm. He screamed in pain, but with animal-like strength, continued to push Magruder toward the open door. Flaig stood frozen, watching it unfold in slow motion.

As Magruder edged closer to the opening and the yawning chasm below, he fell to his knees, desperately jamming a leg against the door. The sheer might of Angelo's tree-trunk-sized leg pressed down on his chest, leaving him powerless. The girlfriend got another round off. This time her aim was true. Angelo fell backward, shot cleanly in the forehead.

Magruder tried to struggle to his feet but failed to hear the boyfriend's warning yell as Jesus charged him from behind, delivering a mighty drop kick. This time Magruder couldn't stop himself from catapulting across the remaining space to the open cabin door. Sliding out of the cabin, his fingers grabbed the door's edge for a split second, just long enough for a last murderous look at Flaig. As his grip failed and he plummeted to the jagged rocks below, his cry, "Flaaaaiiiiggg . . ." echoed off the canyon walls.

In the tram, Flaig remained in the corner. That last look from Magruder was satisfying. *That's what happens when you try to fuck Kevin Flaig.* The girlfriend dropped to one knee to steady her aim. She tried to line Jesus up in her sights, but he had the drop on her. Flaig saw her eyes narrow as she realized what was about to happen. Jesus's gun flashed, and she dropped to the floor, a crimson stain spreading through her tank top.

The boyfriend cried out and shot Jesus in the back of the head. Not stopping to watch Jesus fall, he spun around toward Angelo, who was already facing him, his good arm holding a handgun. For a second, they stared at each other in a classic Mexican standoff. Then both unloaded in the same instant, with the same lethal accuracy.

Flaig remained cool. At Valley Station, he disappeared in the confusion, failing to notice the two field agents step out of the station behind him.

64

TEXARKANA, TEXAS

Monday
August 13

The Todd Ives contingent was as confident as ever. Shane knew that calling Flaig as their last and star witness was Tillington's idea. He would want the jury to hear from the plaintiff directly, not just an army of hired consultants and experts. Todd Ives would have spent a lot of time briefing Flaig for his appearance. It was important that he project the right mix of credibility, sincerity, and even a touch of humility. He was good at that. He was the guy next door. And Tillington was an expert at setting the stage in his direct examination.

BENDING THE ARC

As Tillington rose to start his direct, Nabors waved for him to sit down. "Before we proceed with your witness, Mr. Tillington, I am going to ask Mr. Flaig to remove his sunglasses. I like to observe a witness's full reactions in court."

"Sorry, your Honor, no can do. I have a medical prescription for these glasses due to severe sensitivity to light in my left eye."

Shane grinned inwardly at the flippant response. Antagonizing the judge is not the fast-track to winning your case.

Nabors didn't hide her displeasure. "Very well, Mr. Flaig. I'll allow the glasses, but I would have appreciated a heads-up from your counsel."

Shane heard the pen clicking as Tillington stood back up to start his examination.

"Mr. Flaig, why did the GAC launch this lawsuit?"

Flaig leaned forward and faced the jury. "We didn't want to go to court despite what Mr. Shane may say. Our focus is on campaigns such as our international 'Save the Whales' initiative or, closer to home, the 'Take Back the Gulf' program. Litigation is only used when we feel all other options have been exhausted. We tried to talk reasonably with Wildcat. They ignored us at every turn. Their environmental record is abysmal. Quite simply, the law was our last recourse."

"Mr. Flaig, that sounds rather dramatic. Surely there were other avenues you could have pursued. What about reporting Wildcat to the public authorities?"

"We did that. We filed complaints with all relevant state and federal authorities. The simple fact is that these agencies are understaffed and overworked. The backlog of environmental enforcement actions is staggering. It's because of this backlog that legislatures have introduced the type of citizen enforcement actions under which we sued."

"And, sir, could you elaborate on this so-called citizen enforcement action?"

"Well, its policy is to allow citizens to step in and carry the prosecution of crimes against the environment. Citizens are empowered to assist the government in policing the public interest."

"That is interesting, Mr. Flaig. Are there any details of your particular enforcement action that are noteworthy?"

"Yes. We—the GAC, that is—have agreed that if we are successful in this action, we only recoup that portion of the damages required to reimburse our legal costs. The balance of any damages will flow to the EPA to support various environmental initiatives involving the Gulf. Initiatives such as artificial reef programs, beach cleanups, and so forth."

Shane could see the halo glowing brightly above Flaig's head. *Just shine it up, you son of a bitch.*

BENDING THE ARC

Tillington wound up his direct examination. "Thank you, Mr. Flaig. Your Honor, Mr. Flaig is available for cross-examination."

Shane sat still for a few seconds. The courtroom waited. He knew the dramatic pause was an effective way of focusing the jury's attention. He asked his first questions seated at the counsel table.

"So, Mr. Flaig, you were *forced* into suing my client?"

"Essentially, yes. We didn't want to take it so far."

"You mentioned you tried to talk reason with Wildcat. Could you tell me when and to whom you talked with at Wildcat?"

Flaig paused. "I cannot recollect specifically who in our organization made those contacts, but all our efforts at communication were rebuffed."

"Would it surprise you to know, Mr. Flaig, that no one at Wildcat ever received any calls, letters, or other form of communication from any party identifying their connection with the GAC?"

"Yes, it would. I find that hard to believe. I'm sure they simply can't remember."

Shane got up and strolled out from behind the counsel table.

"Mr. Flaig, the GAC is the plaintiff in this action. It is up to the GAC to prove its case. I've just told you that nobody at Wildcat ever heard from your organization. If you have evidence to the contrary, I suggest you enlighten us with it now."

"Well, I'm not sure if we spoke directly with your company, but we made our views known."

"By that, are you referring to your many press conferences?"

"Yes."

"So it's your position that negotiating in the media represents a sincere effort to seek some sort of common ground with my client?"

"Well, you make that sound so bad. We view our press conferences as an important part of being a publicly transparent organization."

"I'm sure you do, Mr. Flaig. Let's move on to the guts of this case, shall we? You've accused my client of several environmental infractions, all pointing allegedly to a pattern of negligence. In particular, you claim that the leaking oil tank at Wildcat's Buffalo Thirty-Six facility and, more significantly, the recent blowout of Wildcat's Explorer Seven well in the Gulf, are directly attributable to my client's negligence. Is that correct?"

"It is. We contend nothing short of negligence explains this string of environmental disasters."

"And if I were to suggest to you that the leaking tank at Buffalo Thirty-Six resulted from sabotage, not negligence, what would you say to that?"

BENDING THE ARC

"I'd say your client is grasping at straws."

"And if I were to suggest to you that explosives caused the blowout at Explorer Seven, what would you say to that?"

"Ridiculous."

"And that the fifteen Wildcat employees that died at Explorer Seven and the helicopter crew that perished in the capping effort were victims of a heinous terrorist act?"

"Again, ridiculous."

Shane's voice rose with the last few questions. But it dropped to a whisper for the next one.

"Mr. Flaig, a young man sacrificed himself in the successful effort to bring the Explorer Seven blowout under control. Danny Pearson was his name. Now that was a boy who believed in the environment. He wanted to bring that well under control. Wanted it so much he gave his life for it. And to save Danny, another man selflessly threw himself into the ocean and perished that night. His name was Cutter Davis. He had a young wife, Sarah, and two small children, Becky and Ben. What would you say, sir, if I were to call you a cold-blooded murderer? Responsible for all these lives and the ripple effect of pain felt by related family members and friends, myself included." At this, Shane's voice choked up, and he paused.

Tillington was on his feet. "Your Honor, Mr. Shane is engaging in the worst kind of innuendo and speculation. This is . . ." He stopped abruptly as the voices of Flaig and Magruder from atop Mount San Jacinto State Park flooded the courtroom.

The tape was playing from a boombox at Shane's counsel table. Tillington shouted to be heard over it.

"This is outrageous, your Honor. We had no notice of this evidence."

Shane stood up. "We were in no position to provide such notice, your Honor. This conversation took place Saturday. We only received the tape yesterday."

Tillington, who remained on his feet, was shouting again. "That's no excuse for ambushing us with it. I demand you order Mr. Shane to shut that damned thing off."

Nabors banged her gavel. "Shut up and sit down, Mr. Tillington."

The conversation played on for five minutes. In devastating detail, Magruder and Flaig went over Buffalo 36 and Explorer 7. The courtroom sat in stunned silence. The only sound was the clicking of Tillington's pen.

Shane got back on his feet. "Mr. Flaig, I am giving you an opportunity in open court to explain this evidence. Will you now, under oath and under peril of perjury, confirm for us you have no culpability for the Explorer Seven tragedy?"

Flaig shook his head.

Tillington rose. "You Honor, may I have a moment with my client?"

"Please, Mr. Tillington, I think that would be appropriate."

After a short huddle at the witness box, Tillington stepped back. "Thank you, your Honor."

Nabors nodded. "Mr. Shane, please continue."

"So, Mr. Flaig. Before your consultation with counsel, I asked you a question. I'll repeat it for the record. Will you now, under oath and under peril of perjury, confirm for us that you have no culpability for the Explorer Seven tragedy?"

"On counsel's advice, I invoke my right under the Fifth Amendment not to answer, on the grounds I may incriminate myself."

Nabors looked at Shane. "Counsel, I don't think we need to go further, do we?"

"No, your Honor."

She nodded. "Mr. Flaig, based on the evidence before me, I am asking the bailiffs to take you into custody pending further process. You will have access to an attorney of your choice."

She looked at Shane, then Tillington. "Is there anything left to this lawsuit? I assume Mr. Flaig is now facing criminal charges and the basis for the GAC's civil action has evaporated."

Tillington, still stunned by the rapid turn of events, spoke up tiredly. "Your Honor, I would like a chance to consult with my client."

"Very well. You have two days. Until Wednesday, nine a.m., gentlemen."

65

HOUSTON, TEXAS

Tuesday
August 14

Shane stared into his coffee, his mind spinning. Bringing down Flaig was bittersweet. It wouldn't undo the destruction to the Gulf, to the families of the Explorer 7 crew, to Danny, to Sarah, Becky, and Ben.

The ringing of the phone shook him back to the present. Lee's breezy voice came over the intercom. "Mr. Whitter is here, Steve. I took him to the boardroom."

"OK, I'll be out in a minute. Thanks." He grabbed the trial binder off the corner of his desk.

"What the hell is that?"

"It's called Down Dog, or some such goddamn thing." Shane grinned as the big man raised himself off the floor.

"Jenn's got me going on this yoga stuff. It's kinda fun. Getting me back some flexibility. You know, Steve, I seek to be lithe again."

"Well, BJ, lithe is good, but you're sure as hell the last person I would have put down for this. Jenn must be growing on you."

"She's a fine gal, Counselor." BJ dropped into a chair and looked up at Shane.

"Nice work on Flaig. Unbelievable, goddamn unbelievable. I hope he fries."

Shane nodded. He didn't share the discomfort of a lot his colleagues with the death penalty.

"Steve, I understand Leona will be joining us. That's good. We need to pull together and end this whole mess as cleanly as we can."

"You bet, BJ. Speak of the devil." They looked up as Anderson entered the boardroom with Hillerman in tow.

"That evil SOB Flaig got us, didn't he?" Anderson asked.

BJ grunted. "I would have killed that piece of shit if they hadn't taken him into custody on the spot."

Shane turned to Anderson and Hillerman. "Make yourselves comfortable. I need a few minutes with BJ." He gestured for BJ to follow him out of the boardroom and into his office.

After closing the door, Shane outlined the proposal he wanted to put to ARI. BJ nodded. "I told you, Steve, I want you to do whatever you can to help them out. Leona's always been a good friend."

"OK, let's get back in there."

Returning to the boardroom, Shane seated himself at the head of the table between Anderson and Hillerman on one side and BJ on the other. "I wanted to get us all together to talk about tomorrow. I got a call from Drew Tillington yesterday. The GAC will withdraw their lawsuit but our counterclaims live on. Leona, I'd like to call you to the stand for cross-examination."

Hillerman was the first to speak. "Whatever for?"

"We got a call from Kenton Engineering, the firm we hired for an independent engineering assessment of Explorer Seven. They discovered a serious error in the Seabright and Company report. The report concluded that ARI was negligent by missing its one-thousand-day major inspection. Kenton discovered that in counting days, Seabright and Company included transit days and port days. Explorer Seven had seventy-five travel days and was in port for a further one hundred and seventy-seven days before it was placed in service. These days shouldn't have been counted in calculating the time for the first inspection. Only actual drilling days count.

"So, Seabright and Company calculated the inspection to be due two hundred and fifty odd days before it was actually due. Bottom line, no missed inspection period. It would be good to get this on the official record before Wildcat withdraws its case against ARI. That would prevent anyone from trying to use the Seabright and Company report in the future. We might also have an action against Seabright and Company for negligence."

Anderson nodded. "Yes, I think that's reasonable. Even if we know Explorer Seven was blown up, I don't like the accusation of us having missed an inspection continuing to float around out there." She looked over at Hillerman, who, after a pause, nodded.

The lights in the Shane Law Offices burned through the night. Shane didn't like putting in an all-nighter before a day in court, but he had no choice. Val, Jenn, and Lee stayed with him throughout. By 6 a.m. they were ready.

66

TEXARKANA, TEXAS

Wednesday
August 15

People packed the courtroom. After the explosive adjournment two days before, the trial was the talk of the nation. *Dateline, 20/20, Primetime Live, Turbo News Now, Anderson Cooper 360*—they couldn't get enough. Footage from Cutter's funeral flooded the airwaves. The images of Becky and Ben tugged at heartstrings from Seattle to Miami, New York to San Diego.

Shane could see that the media frenzy did not amuse Nabors. Security was stepped up, with all parties having to pass through metal detectors before being cleared for the courtroom. Admission was restricted. A lottery system allocated the limited media seats. Nabors was adamant there be no television coverage. *The People versus Orenthal James Simpson* showed what a disaster that was.

Nabors pounded the gavel, and the assembled crowd gradually grew silent.

"Mr. Tillington, have you obtained instructions?"

"Indeed, your Honor. Thank you. The GAC wishes to withdraw all claims made against both Wildcat Oil and Gas Limited and, through third-party claim, against Anderson Resources Incorporated."

The crowd broke out in an excited babble. Nabors banged the gavel repeatedly. "Order! Order in this court. Messrs. Hillerman and Shane, any comments?"

Hillerman rose. "Thank you, your Honor. Anderson Resources Incorporated withdraws its cross-claim against Wildcat and suspends its counterclaim against the GAC, with prejudice. We will wait for the results of any criminal proceedings against Mr. Flaig and his association before deciding if we should pursue any further civil suits."

"Thank you, Mr. Hillerman. Mr. Shane?"

"Your Honor, we would like to call Ms. Anderson to the stand."

The crowd broke out in another round of loud whispering. Nabors pounded her gavel. "Order . . . *Order*! Mr. Shane, am I to believe that you wish to cross-examine Ms. Anderson prior to deciding on how to proceed with your cross-claim?"

"That's it, your Honor."

"Well, this is a first. Mr. Hillerman?"

"No objection, your Honor."

"Very well. Mr. Hillerman, I assume Ms. Anderson will testify on ARI's behalf. You may call her as your witness."

Anderson winked at Shane as she passed him on the way to the witness box. After Hillerman conducted his brief direct, Shane walked out from behind the counsel table toward the witness box.

"Ms. Anderson, would you agree that a failure to have a complex piece of machinery such as an offshore drilling rig inspected as per code would be convincing evidence of negligence, possibly gross negligence?"

"I don't know. I'm not a lawyer. Even you lawyers can't agree on what *negligence* is. I mean, isn't that what most civil litigation is all about?" The crowd tittered. Anderson was enjoying their little exchange.

"Would you agree that any such failure would be inconsistent with a prudent operating standard and good oilfield practice?"

"Well, I'd say you sure as heck aren't doing your job if you let your inspections slip."

"Thank you. Are you familiar with the report prepared by Seabright and Company and filed by the GAC as Exhibit Twenty-Seven in this proceeding?"

"Yes. I commissioned that report."

"And are you aware of the conclusions of that report—specifically, the conclusion that ARI did not have the Explorer Seven rig inspected at the required one-thousand-day inspection interval?"

"Yes, sir, I am painfully aware of that conclusion."

"Is that conclusion accurate?"

"Absolutely *not*. We have since discovered that Seabright and Company counted idle days in their calculations. By idle days, I am referring to days when the rig is not in active service, such as days when the rig is traveling and days when the rig is in port. The one-thousand-day inspection, which Seabright and Company allege was missed, should be based on one thousand *active* rig days. In actuality, Explorer Seven only had eight hundred and fifty-four active rig days at the time of the blowout. There was no missed inspection. If you want to talk about negligence, you should start with Seabright and Company."

"Thank you."

Anderson rose to exit the witness box.

"Just a minute, Ms. Anderson."

Anderson gave Shane a questioning look. Hillerman leaned over from his counsel table and whispered, "I think you've got the point on

BENDING THE ARC

the record, Steve. No sense prolonging things." Shane waved him off.

Anderson was still on her feet, looking over at Hillerman and Shane.

"Please, sit down, Ms. Anderson. I have just a few more questions," Shane said pleasantly, aware of Nabors' curious stare. Anderson sat down, visibly puzzled.

"Ms. Anderson, were you present on Monday for the testimony of Mr. Kevin Flaig, president of the GAC?"

"I was," Anderson answered cautiously.

"And did his testimony surprise you?"

"Yes, sir. I think it surprised every person in the courtroom except, perhaps, yourself."

"So you had no idea the GAC wasn't a legitimate environmental organization but a bunch of saboteurs?"

"I don't know what the heck the GAC is. I do know that Kevin Flaig is a very sick and twisted man."

"Ms. Anderson, if the GAC prevailed in its lawsuit against my client, Wildcat would have been liable for a significant sum of damages, in the order of one billion dollars or more. Isn't that correct?"

Hillerman was on his feet now. "Your Honor, I object to this line of questioning. I don't know where Mr. Shane is going with this, but I don't think it's relevant to his client's claim against ARI."

"Your Honor, I will make the relevance of this line clear in a few minutes."

"OK, Mr. Shane, I'm going to overrule the objection and allow you to continue. But I expect you to demonstrate relevance quickly."

"Thank you, your Honor."

BJ tugged on Shane's sleeve.

"One moment, please, your Honor."

Nabors rolled her eyes as if to say, *What now?*

Shane bent over as BJ whispered in his ear, "What's going on, son? Anderson's on our side."

Shane looked BJ in the eye. "Trust me, BJ. Remember, you promised to leave the legal stuff to me as long as I'm working in Wildcat's best interest. Believe me, I am."

BJ nodded. "OK. Do what you have to do."

Shane straightened and looked back at the bench. "I apologize, your Honor."

"Move on, Mr. Shane. I'm losing patience here."

"Yes, your Honor. Thank you. Ms. Anderson, I asked you whether Wildcat could have faced a one-billion-dollar plus liability if it lost the GAC lawsuit."

"I think the GAC was suing for one billion, so that would be the exposure, yes."

"Possibly even more if the jury were so inclined?"

"You tell me. You're the lawyer."

"Now if Wildcat lost based on the negligent operation of Explorer Seven, would you agree Wildcat would have been successful in recovering at least fifty percent of such losses from ARI?"

Hillerman was on his feet. "Objection!"

Nabors was equally swift. "Overruled."

"Ms. Anderson?" Shane watched Anderson fidget. She was no longer playing the ham, but deadly serious as she concentrated on her answers.

"Our Joint Operating Agreement with Wildcat splits liability for any losses because of negligence, simple or gross, based on our ownership, which would be fifty-fifty."

"Thank you. So if the GAC prevailed, each of Wildcat and ARI could have been on the hook for five hundred million dollars, or more, correct?"

"Yes, I suppose," Anderson replied.

"And, Ms. Anderson, how much of this exposure would have been covered by the insurance that ARI, as the operator of Explorer Seven, put in place on behalf of the partners?"

Hillerman was up again. "Your Honor?"

"Sit down, Mr. Hillerman. Mr. Shane will establish relevance very soon or this court will have something to say. Am I clear, Mr. Shane?"

"Crystal, your Honor. I'll tie all of this together in the next few minutes." Turning back to face Anderson, Shane noticed small beads of sweat breaking out on her brow.

"Ms. Anderson, I was asking you what insurance was in place to cover the liability of ARI and Wildcat in the GAC lawsuit."

"Our general liability policy does not cover the blowout. We have separate Environmental Impairment Liability—EIL—coverage for such events. The EIL policy pays a maximum of five hundred million dollars per occurrence."

"So, bottom line, insurance would have covered five hundred million dollars of any GAC award?"

"Yes, I think that's right."

"That would leave both ARI and Wildcat exposed to the tune of at least two hundred and fifty million dollars each, correct?"

"The math would seem to work out that way."

"Now, Ms. Anderson, what kind of separate insurance did ARI carry that would cover any excess exposure on the Explorer Seven disaster?"

"We have a general EIL policy. I believe the amount per claim is in the order of one hundred million dollars."

"Nothing else?"

"No."

"Ms. Anderson, you are not familiar with a new EIL policy ARI took out just three weeks before the Explorer Seven incident?"

BENDING THE ARC 457

A few outbursts echoed from the gallery. Nabors pounded away. Hillerman was shouting, "Your Honor, I object. This is a fishing expedition. It has no relevance to the case at bar."

"Actually, Mr. Hillerman, I'm starting to find this line of enquiry very interesting. Overruled."

"Ms. Anderson, I asked you about a new EIL policy ARI put in place weeks before the blowout."

"Yes, well, I don't recall. Maybe we put on some extra insurance. I may be the president of the company, but I can't keep tabs on everything that goes on."

"Well, Ms. Anderson, I have here a copy of that policy. I'd like it marked as an exhibit." Shane passed copies to the judge, Hillerman, and Anderson. "This reflects a new EIL policy in the amount of five hundred million dollars per occurrence, effective three weeks before the blowout."

Anderson was sweating visibly now.

"Ms. Anderson, if you look at the bottom of page twelve, you will see you signed this policy, as CEO of ARI, correct?

"Yes, but again, you can't expect me to remember every detail of running a billion-dollar company."

"So, Ms. Anderson, with knowledge of this new policy, would you agree with me that ARI would have more than enough coverage to withstand the GAC lawsuit?"

"Again, the math seems to work out that way."

"Thank you. So now it seems that ARI is covered, but Wildcat is exposed to at least two hundred and fifty million dollars, correct?"

"Well, I'm sure Wildcat has its own EIL policy."

"Would it surprise you to know that it does, but that the policy is in the order of fifty million dollars, reflecting the smaller size of Wildcat compared to ARI?"

"Yes, well, they do have extra coverage themselves."

"And, taking that into account, we still have a situation where Wildcat faces an exposure of at least two hundred million dollars, while ARI secured full coverage under a policy it placed just weeks before the blowout."

"I suppose so. We can't be faulted for protecting ourselves with proper risk management policies."

"Well, Ms. Anderson, we do question your timing in placing the policy that put you over the top here. Let me continue. Would you agree with me that two hundred million dollars of exposure would be significant for Wildcat?"

"It might."

"And if the lawsuit succeeded, Wildcat might be motivated to sell some assets to keep the company afloat."

BENDING THE ARC

"It might."

"And the only significant assets Wildcat owns, beyond the Explorer Seven lands, are interests in contiguous oil exploration blocks?"

"That could be. I am not familiar with all of Wildcat's assets."

"And if Wildcat wished to sell such interests, it would first have to offer a certain party a right of first refusal—that is, the opportunity to match any offer it might receive for such interests?"

"Could be."

"And is ARI the party to whom that right of first refusal is owed?" The room exploded. Nabors pounded away, to no avail. Several media people dashed for the doors, deciding to sacrifice the next few minutes' testimony for getting the story out. Tape recorders were left running in the courtroom.

After a few minutes, the crowd settled down sufficiently for Shane to continue. Anderson leaned on the edge of her seat. No longer concerned or wary, she was simply furious. The rapidly unfolding developments froze Hillerman.

Anderson was almost shouting. "So what if we hold ROFRs on Wildcat's lands? Nothing illegal about that."

"No, that is true, Ms. Anderson, but is it not also true that you have made several unsolicited offers to my client for those offshore interests?"

"Maybe."

"Oh, come on, Ms. Anderson—*maybe*? Is that the best you can do? We can file into evidence three separate written offers, signed by yourself, if we must. You want those lands and you want them bad, right?"

"So what?" Anderson stood up in the witness box, the veins bulging in her forehead. The bailiffs approached. Seeing them, Anderson sat back and seemed to find her second wind. She replied in a calmer voice.

"ARI was interested in those properties, that's true. But hardly surprising, considering our other interests in the area."

"Isn't it true, Ms. Anderson, that you engineered the Explorer Seven blowout to force Wildcat into finally selling you the properties you desire so badly?"

"Why, in God's name, would I blow up my own well?"

"I've just explained that to you. While you were insulated from the legal actions through insurance, you were aware that Wildcat wasn't. You ordered the deliberate destruction of life and property for your own gain. You, ma'am, are a murderer."

Hillerman was on his feet once more. "Objection!"

"Sustained. Mr. Shane, you'd better establish some foundation here fast, and by fast I mean *now*."

"Yes, your Honor." Everything Shane raised to this point was circumstantial. Time for a change. Shane was shaking as he asked his next question. He didn't know why. Likely a mixture of raw emotion and hate triggered by images of little Ben Davis staring at the lone jet peeling out of formation.

"Ms. Anderson, does 'Tame Wildcat' mean anything to you?"

Anderson's face drained of all color. She looked vacantly at Hillerman, the judge, the jury. "I . . . I don't know what you're talking about."

"That's strange, Ms. Anderson. It seems you coined that term. We have Mr. Kevin Flaig describing an operation sanctioned by you, nicknamed Tame Wildcat. It involves a diabolical plot to bring down Wildcat through a campaign of environmental sabotage. A plot whereby the GAC was founded and funded for the sole purpose of prosecuting the lawsuits against Wildcat. Have I refreshed your memory?"

Anderson stared at him with a look of pure hate. "No. All speculation and innuendo. None of it is true. You can't prove a thing."

"Well, perhaps I can. To refresh your memory, I'm going to play a bit more of that tape from Mr. Flaig's conversation with Mr. Magruder a few days ago."

Once again, the courtroom filled with the sound of the recording from Mount San Jacinto.

This time, with the conversation detailing Anderson's role as the mastermind.

Anderson collapsed in the witness box.

The dazed Todd Ives team, seated behind Hillerman, sat in utter confusion. The younger associates looked at Tillington. Where was the great Silver Fox? The litigator of the decade? Outmaneuvered by two kids six years out of law school. Each was at the moment rethinking their career at Todd Ives.

A man sitting behind Shane rose and stepped up to the counsel table.

"Your Honor, my name is Theodore Kratz, Federal Bureau of Investigation. We are taking Ms. Anderson into custody at this time on a multitude of felony charges."

"She's all yours, Mr. Kratz. Mr. Shane, you've got to rid yourself of this habit of having witnesses arrested following your cross-examinations. It doesn't leave much for this court to do. We stand adjourned."

67

WASHINGTON, D.C.

Tuesday
September 4

Shane looked around the room, happy to see Hendrix had assembled the core team—Val, Jenn, Lee, Hendrix, Ollie, and Kratz. They were in the LawForce Washington office. As for Kratz, Shane and Hendrix agreed the team needed a permanent Bureau liaison, and Shane had grown to like the taciturn, quietly efficient agent.

Hendrix got up to address the group. "People, we'll be digesting this case over the next number of months, but I wanted to start the debriefing with a face-to-face with all of you. First and foremost, I would like to express my appreciation for a job well done. LawForce was a dream up to this point, a concept with promise. Each of you has been instrumental in achieving that promise. This case did not go where we expected it would. Nevertheless, justice was served. I am sure you all concur.

"I believe it is important that we maintain a solid record of LawForce's cases as we move forward. We must document the effectiveness of this team and how it evolves over time. And evolve it will. As Churchill said, 'To improve is to change, so to be perfect is to change often.' At some point, we may go public, but for now we will continue to act behind the scenes in cases of fundamental importance to the nation. We will continue to bend the arc." Shane caught the wink Hendrix directed at Ollie.

The last reference drew puzzled looks from the group, but Shane had heard Hendrix wax on before about the famous quote. It felt good to be part of a team that would bend the arc. He realized that hollow feeling about his practice was gone. He had found his calling.

"I'm just so proud of all of you," Hendrix continued, his voice growing husky. And, damn, if he wasn't tearing up. The man had emotions.

Hendrix cleared his throat and looked at Shane. "You can kick off the discussion, Steven. Perhaps start by explaining why we chose this case."

Shane led them through the initial analysis of the GAC claims as classical harassment actions and the meetings that led to the formation of LawForce. Ollie followed by describing their efforts to establish the Washington office. He explained the hub concept of LawForce, with an inner core legal team and now an FBI liaison that would tap the services of a wider group whose expertise would depend on the case being tried. In the GAC action, for example, they'd used Mike for his environmental background and Bannion for help once the explosives angle developed.

Shane wrapped up by thanking his team and the AG's office for the foresight that created LawForce. As he finished, he looked around the room. "Questions on how the GAC action played out?"

Ollie was first in, waving his hand to get Shane's attention and sending his empty coffee cup sailing across the boardroom table. "Sorry." He smiled lamely. "I, for one, would like to know how the heck you made the connection to Anderson."

"It took me a while, Ollie. It started with something BJ mentioned to me way back when, before our first meeting with ARI. He said that Anderson was constantly bugging him about buying into Wildcat's offshore properties."

Jenn frowned. "People are always swapping lands and sniffing around other people's plays in the patch. That's the nature of the beast."

"Sure, but it's not just one thing, Jenn. It's everything together."

"So, what else?"

"Well, you remember Cutter telling BJ about some blasting caps they found floating around Explorer Seven."

"Yeah, so?"

"And you thought it was strange that Anderson played it down, saying it was no big deal, right?"

"Yeah, that's right." Jenn stood up. "I also thought it was strange that Anderson hired a small-time outfit like Seabright and Company for that report. I suspected ARI's enemies leaked it to the press. But few people, beyond Anderson, would have known about the report."

"Now you're getting the picture. And BJ told me it was Anderson that refused to hire outside experts to deal with the blowout. Instead, she ordered her own people to pursue that useless capping attempt."

Jenn nodded.

"Right." Shane looked around the room. "So, we have this string of environmental 'accidents'—the tanker spill, Buffalo Thirty-Six, and finally Explorer Seven. Explorer Seven was a shrewd twist, with the action targeted against an ARI-operated well. But the bottom line was still exposure for Wildcat. All this happened in less than six months. Up to that point, Wildcat had a

BENDING THE ARC 467

great environmental record. Hell, they were leaders in the industry.

"It was all too coincidental for me. When Bannion came back with proof that Buffalo Thirty-Six was sabotaged, the 'accident' theory went out the window. Then there was the leaked Seabright and Company report you had concerns with," Shane nodded at Jenn. "We put a full FBI team on investigating the package that showed up out of the blue at the *Tribune*. They traced it back to ARI's Dallas office."

Shane looked at Val. "I never told you, but Sarah said Cutter thought Anderson's initial response to Explorer 7 was incompetent. That, along with Anderson's nonchalance about Tillington acting against ARI, got me thinking. What if Anderson wasn't incompetent, but just wanted those lands so badly she was willing to sabotage her own well to force Wildcat to sell? It seemed a stretch, but I tend to play my hunches, especially when I haven't got much else to go on."

Val's voice was low. "So you made Magruder carry a wire to see if he could get Flaig to rat out Anderson? But how did you get the tape when Magruder's body was all mashed up at the bottom of Chino Canyon after that fall?"

"It wasn't a tape on a hard drive, Val. That's yesterday's technology. It was a live feed. Ted and his team were listening in the whole time."

Jenn nodded. "Still not clear how you figured out the insurance angle."

"Part of my hunch. I had Jenn and the Washington team comb through ARI's computer records, searching for any references to Wildcat and ARI insurance policies. The rest is now, as they say, history. Use the legal system to attract liability on yourself and your partner while ensuring you're insulated from your share."

Lee Chin still looked puzzled. "But why such a complicated scheme, that left ARI itself with all sorts of problems on the Explorer Seven lands? Outstanding lawsuits from employees, et cetera."

"Yeah, good question, Lee." Shane walked over to a map of the Gulf offshore hanging on the wall to the side of the table. He gestured at a large, half blue, half red area surrounded by many larger blue blocks. "Red is ARI, blue is Wildcat. The lands Explorer Seven was drilling on and which ARI and Wildcat held fifty-fifty"—he pointed at the larger red-blue block—"are in the middle of the balance of the properties owned one hundred percent by Wildcat. Anderson wanted it all. She wasn't just trying to buy into the Explorer 7 lands, she wanted to take Wildcat out completely.

"The plan was to force a sale of the company along with its associated liabilities—liabilities created by ARI. Encumbered by all that baggage,

Wildcat would be unattractive to outside buyers. But still very attractive to ARI, that would have to deal with those liabilities in any event, supported by its enhanced insurance policies. Wildcat would have to sell at a fire-sale price. You're right. It was a convoluted plan, but if she pulled it off, rather brilliant in a depraved sort of way."

"What would make someone go so far?" Val asked in a subdued voice.

Shane shrugged his shoulders. "I'm just a lawyer, and the law has its limits. Some questions belong before a higher authority."

68

BAR C RANCH, TEXAS

Saturday
December 15

Shane stared at the valley rolling out from the ranch house veranda. Gus lay quietly at his feet, exhausted from the last two hours of chasing cowboys on their evening ride. Sarah invited them to the Bar C for a barbecue three months after that dramatic day in court when Anderson was exposed. Val was in the back with Sarah, playing with the kids. Shane knew the approaching Christmas season, their first without Cutter, would be tough. He and Val vowed to spend as much time with them as Sarah was comfortable with.

BENDING THE ARC

As the sun dipped to the horizon, the sky transformed into a canvas of deep purples and soft oranges. A serene hush fell over the landscape, broken only by the occasional whisper of a breeze rustling through the needles of the tall pine trees surrounding the ranch house. The magic of Christmas came alive with the twinkling lights that adorned the pines. Strings of multicolored bulbs laced around each tree. The shimmering red, green, blue, and gold lights cast a warm and festive glow.

On the swinging loveseat next to Shane's rocking chair, BJ hooked his arm around Jenn. Shane was glad to see they'd gotten close over the last few months. BJ deserved some happiness, as did Jenn.

Shane watched BJ get up, wander to the front of the veranda and light a cigar. Tossing the match on the ground, he turned to Shane. "An engineer goes to hell. It's the first engineer they've ever had down there." Shane knew BJ was trying to keep things light. "The Devil puts him to work and is delighted to find him installing air-conditioning systems and building great works. The guy really reconstructs the place. One day the Devil is talking to God and mentions the fabulous new recruit in hell. 'Oh, yeah', says God, 'that was a mistake on our part. That engineer should never have gone to hell. We want him back.' 'No way,' says the Devil. 'He's the best damn thing that ever happened to us.' God gets mad and says, 'Listen, if you don't send him up pronto, we're going to sue.' 'Oh, yeah?', says the Devil, 'and just where are you going to find a lawyer?'" No laughter this time, just a slight, pained smile as he sat back down.

Shane watched Jenn massaging BJ's leg before the big man spoke again, still subdued.

"I don't know if we've told you, Steve, but we're damn glad we ran into you guys. Without your help, I think that son of a bitch Anderson might just have pulled it off. I'm still not sure how y'all did it, but we're grateful."

Shane gave BJ a nod. "Thanks, BJ, but we were just doing our job."

The cross-claim against ARI continued as an independent action, with modifications to include further causes of action. Shane was stunned when the jury returned a huge award, well above what he'd asked for. Numerous proceedings were still pending against ARI, including wrongful death actions on behalf of Sarah, Danny Pearson's family, and those of Herky Cantrell, Duane Follet, Rick Santos, and the others who'd died on Explorer 7.

"You know, BJ, when we started all this, I thought one of the fundamental flaws in our justice system was idiot juries. That juror who stepped down when she discovered she was a second cousin to one of the perished rig crew

BENDING THE ARC

impressed me. Now I understand that most juries consist of honest folk who struggle with the responsibility of delivering justice."

"They're just people, Steve, like the rest of us. Doing the best they can with what they've got," BJ agreed.

"That's just it. *With what they've got.* It's up to the lawyers to present the case properly. The lawyers serve up the ingredients the jury needs to deliver justice. If the lawyers screw it up, we can't put that on the jury." He mulled over the last thought. Somehow he suspected Hendrix knew from the start the problem was the lawyers and not the juries. He'd patiently listened to Shane rant on about bonehead juries, knowing that experience was the best teacher.

The sun shone its last fierce rays from above the hills at the end of the valley. Finally, he could come to grips with the old Green Badge case. It wasn't an idiot jury that screwed up the verdict. It was a young, green lawyer who failed to present a case that gave the jury a chance to serve up justice.

"Any plans for the future, BJ?"

"Yeah. I'm still worried about the fallout from all of this on Wildcat and in a broader sense on the industry. Now that everyone knows we were dealing with saboteurs, they shouldn't blame us for what happened out there in the Gulf. But people being people, I think those images of oil-doused dolphins and that spewing well will take some time to forget. I want to use a portion of the punitive damages to launch a PR campaign on behalf of the industry. We have to get better at communicating with the public."

"Sounds good." Shane took a long swallow from his longneck. "Sarah mentioned something about a memorial fund for Cutter. What's that all about?"

"Not a memorial fund. Everybody does that. Cutter deserves more. We're going to use the bulk of the punitive damages to establish a world-class research center dedicated to exploring the reasonable interaction between development and the environment in the Gulf. The 'Cutter Davis Center for Responsible Gulf Development.'"

Shane pondered the concept as he watched the sun melt into the horizon, giving way to the inky blanket of night.

They sat lost in thought, soaking up the silence of the valley. Sarah's soft voice floated out of the background. "Yes. I think Cutter would have liked that."

Milton Keynes UK
Ingram Content Group UK Ltd.
UKHW031118231024
450133UK00015B/734

9 781897 093146